Guy Fawkes: Demon Hunter

A Clangour of Bells

Benjamin Langley

Guy Fawkes Demon Hunter Book 1

First edition. June 5th 2022
Copyright © 2022 Benjamin Langley
Written by Benjamin Langley
Cover design © 2022 Mariah Norris
Editing done by Susan Floyd and Kaitlin Corvus
Formatting done by Mandy Russell

Published by Shadow Spark Publishing
www.shadowsparkpub.com

TABLE OF CONTENTS

FOR THE HISTORIANS: I'M SORRY

Prologue

A shock of white hair on the wrong side of the safety barrier catches Jamie Frost's eye. Panic races through his veins. That old man shouldn't be there. Jamie's expectations for his newspaper report on the Poppleton Centre Bonfire and Firework Spectacular had been low. He'd imagined a story detailing the crowds of smiling faces and the colourful display lighting up the night, the type of report the local paper loves. Instead, this intruder threatens to derail the show, or worse, turn it into a disaster.

From one side, a yellow-jacketed pyrotechnician approaches the mountain of felled branches, timber offcuts and smashed up pallets that make up the pyre, a flaming torch in his hand. From the other, the rake-thin, white-haired old man dashes towards the stacked wood. He points to the top of the pile, where an effigy of Guy Fawkes sits. "Stop!" he cries. "You can't burn him."

Over the sound of the loudspeaker, counting down to ignition, no one else hears him. Jamie scans the scene, looking for marshals or safety officers. No one else has seen the old man.

"He's a hero!" the old man cries.

"Stop!" Jamie shouts, but no one hears him over the sound of those joining the countdown. He raises his hand and points, but his actions mimic those around him waving their hands in excitement. The countdown is at seven. Still, no one else has noticed the interloper. At the cry of, "Six," Jamie clambers over the barrier. He sprints, glancing to the left, where the flame is but a few metres from the woodpile.

The countdown has reached three.

The old man is footsteps from the pyre.

Jamie knows he won't make it.

The crowd shouts, "Two." The flame is inches from the wood, ready to set it alight.

At "One," the old man crashes into the wood, reaching for the effigy. At the same time, the pyrotechnician touches the flame to the pyre and the wood, heavily doused in flammable liquid, ignites with a roar.

The old man is lost behind a constantly shifting wall of flame. Wood crackles and snaps beneath his weight. Still, Jamie runs towards it.

From the top, the straw-stuffed dummy shifts. A hand closes around its leg, and a half-second later, the effigy flies from the pile. It comes to rest in the grass to Jamie's right, flames licking at its clothing.

Jamie reaches the edge of the bonfire, but the extraordinary heat brings him to a halt. Every sense is embellished. His nostrils flare with the overpowering smell of burning. Every crackle of wood is a crack of thunder. A kaleidoscope of reds, yellows, and oranges dazzles Jamie, until, between the flickering flames, he spies one of the old man's legs.

Jamie reaches in without thought. The vicious lick of flame attacks his neck first, then one cheek, growing ever more painful, like a thousand simultaneous pin-pricks. He grabs the old man's leg and drags him from the pyre onto the grass.

Away from the fire, Jamie falls back and gulps at fresh air. Time slows as he ponders his actions and realises the consequences. His hands explode in agony. Pain flares in his neck and across his face. The sound of panic in the crowd pounds in his ears, and the brightness of the bonfire blinds him. He doesn't see the marshals until they're upon them. One man throws a fire blanket over the old man and beats the flames from his clothes. Another grabs the zip on the front of Jamie's jacket and yanks it down, then reaches for the shoulders and pulls the jacket off him. Before Jamie can question the action, he sees the glow in the fibres which are extinguished under the foot of the marshal.

Jamie looks again at the fire. Within, a branch breaks and the flames reach higher. He concentrates on his breathing, drawing in a deep breath, but as it hits his lungs, he coughs. All he can smell is burning–not only smoke but something else too, like burning hair. He puts a hand to the side of his head and brittle hairs break. When his hand drops to his cheek, agony explodes there again. Jamie falls to his knees as more men in fluorescent jackets arrive, two of them with a stretcher for the old man.

Another marshal crouches beside Jamie. She speaks, but Jamie doesn't take in any of her words. All he can hear is the roar of the fire and the noise from the crowd. The marshal places one hand on Jamie's shoulder. Jamie half-hears, half-lipreads the word, "Breathe." That's all he does for a moment, semi-conscious of movement around him.

Two marshals carry the old man away on the stretcher. Jamie looks from the fire to the old man several times, confusion racking his brain.

After a moment that could have been seconds or minutes, the marshal helps Jamie to his feet. She directs him towards the main hall of the Poppleton Centre where the volunteers of the St John's Ambulance wait.

Inside, several volunteers are already attending to the old man, cutting charred clothes away. Their actions are halted as he's overcome by a violent coughing fit. At least he's alive, Jamie thinks. The coughing stops and the volunteers put an oxygen mask over his face.

Another volunteer sees Jamie and winces before inviting him to sit. He's a middle-aged man, with cropped black hair, perhaps a few years younger than Jamie. He's dressed in the green of a St John's Ambulance volunteer. Partition walls separate the different temporary treatment areas, and while Jamie can no longer see the old man, he can hear those attending to him.

"Not again, Sidney," someone says.

Sidney? So that's the old man's name. Again, Sidney coughs.

The volunteer sits opposite Jamie. "I'm Michael," he says. "I'm going to wrap these wounds and assess whether we need to get you to hospital."

Jamie glances at his hands, the backs of which are red and swollen, the first signs of blistering present. He keeps them as still as possible, fearing any movement will bring a new explosion of agony.

"Would you like something for the pain?"

Jamie parts his lips to speak, but no words come. He nods, which alerts him once more to the pain in his neck and face. The tingling in his ear reminds him of the time someone who didn't want to be interviewed punched him in the side of the head.

Michael goes to the portable medical cabinet, returning with some paracetamol and a cup of water. "It'll take the edge off."

There's a pause as Michael realises Jamie is in no position to take hold of the pills and bring them to his mouth. "May I?" he says, indicating that he'll need to feed Jamie.

Jamie tips his head back a little and opens his mouth. Michael places the first tablet on Jamie's tongue, the latex of Michael's glove brushing against his lip leaving a lingering taste of rubber. Michael offers water, and with some difficulty, Jamie swallows. Michael feeds Jamie the second pill and sits once more, now armed with a bottle of ointment and a roll of cling film.

Michael delicately takes hold of Jamie's wrist to turn his left hand over. He examines it with care before applying the ointment and wrapping it.

"You saved that man's life," Michael says as he starts work on the second hand.

Jamie nods, words still too difficult to manage.

"These burns… second-degree, partial-thickness. It could have been much worse."

Jamie takes a relieved breath, but drawing in that much oxygen causes him to cough.

"You're suffering from smoke inhalation. That's why you're struggling to speak. Your nostril hairs are singed, too." Michael stares at the side of Jamie's head but says nothing about his impromptu new hair-do.

Understanding where the smell of charred hair is coming from is strangely comforting.

"I need to look at the burns on your face and neck." Michael stands and leans over Jamie, again applying the lotion to the affected areas. While it cools the area and brings relief, the nerve endings in every other damaged part of his body scream out for attention.

Michael sits once more. "Mostly first-degree... one spot could be partial thickness. One sec..." Michael gets up and walks out of sight.

Jamie wonders about the extent of the damage. Will there be a scar? How long is it going to hurt for? Someone calls from behind the partition., followed by lots of medical instructions. From the distance, the sound of an ambulance siren grows ever louder.

Michael returns. "You know what the situation is like with ambulances these days. We've got one coming for," Michael nods towards the partition, "so you might be in for a bit of a wait for another. Unless... I could take you?"

Jamie wants to protest. He only manages a hoarse, "No."

"It's no trouble. I'm working the night shift at the hospital tonight, anyway."

With that, Jamie accepts.

Michael drives to the hospital, taking it slow around corners and over speed-bumps. He parks in the staff carpark and guides Jamie towards the Accident and Emergency entrance. At the reception, Michael gives the necessary information about the injury but leaves Jamie to provide the personal details. Jamie delivers his full name and date of birth, in a voice no louder than a whisper, which Michael repeats for him.

It's busy in the waiting room, but there are a couple of spare seats next to a man and his son. The boy's hand is wrapped in cling film, like Jamie's. The man is watching a news report on his phone, the volume too high. Jamie's in no mood to listen to another story about the further cuts their Prime Minister, Alistair Barclay-Fitzwilliam has made to essential public services. As always, his rat-faced advisor, Kristian Byrne, stands beside him.

"So, you *are* Jamie Frost," Michael says, drawing Jamie away from the bleak national news. "I thought I recognised you."

A smile spreads across Jamie's face but quickly falters when it reignites his pain. There's something pleasant about being reminded of his time as the face of morning news on *Yorkshire Daily*, in the days before he decided it was nobler to seek out the news than to deliver it.

Glancing around the room, Jamie fears a long wait. He leans towards Michael. "You don't need to stay."

"I'll wait until you see the triage nurse. It will be easier if I explain the treatment I've already given."

Jamie is relieved he doesn't have to wait alone.

"You'd rather be writing the story, not be a part of it, I suppose?" Michael says.

Jamie smiles, then winces with the pain.

"Sorry. But plenty of people will be interested." Michael sits up straight and over-enounces his words, mimicking received pronunciation: "Local journalist heroically pulls man from fire."

Jamie stops another smile from spreading. "No, I don't want to be the story, but…"

"What?"

Jamie struggles to clear his throat. "Why do you think he did it?"

"Perhaps, when he's on the mend, you could interview him."

His journalistic brain tells him Sidney's story will sell, but he's not sure he wants to delve in further. Maybe he should put it all behind him.

Another hour passes. Jamie and Michael exchange numbers. Jamie learns that Michael is new to the area and doesn't have many friends. Jamie owes Michael a drink, at least, for all of his kindness and care.

Eventually, Jamie is called to see the triage nurse who confirms he'll have to be admitted. As they return to the waiting room, Michael checks his watch and apologises—his shift is about to start.

Without company, Jamie is left thinking only of his pain, with the memory of the old man running into the bonfire to save an effigy of Guy Fawkes. Why would someone do that?

Once Jamie is called from the waiting room, everything happens quickly. His burns are examined again and re-dressed. He's taken for a chest X-Ray to detect the level of damage from smoke inhalation. He's intubated to get oxygen into his lungs and put on a drip to help replace lost fluids. Strong painkillers make the rest of the night a blur.

The next day, a doctor removes his endotracheal tube but the intravenous drip remains until closer to his discharge. Pain killers barely touch the residual pain, but his ability to speak is much improved. A nurse talks to him about the lasting damage of smoke inhalation and tells him how to look after the burns, warning him to let the blisters naturally heal.

He gets a taxi home, and following the nurse's advice, takes himself to bed once more. Sleep doesn't come. His mind insists on playing the same memory over and over. He needs to know why Sidney ran into that bonfire. He needs to know why he didn't want to see an effigy of Guy Fawkes burn.

Jamie sends Michael a message, hoping his contacts at the hospital can get him some information about the old man. Maybe he can visit Sidney to find out more.

Three days later, Jamie's breathing is almost normal. The soreness has gone from his throat. Only the burns continue to pain him, particularly where blisters have formed. If he's careful, he can type a little and send out a few article pitches to some magazines he's worked for in the past.

Michael has been in touch with news on Sidney. His burns were severe. He's had to have a series of skin grafts, and he will be left with some hideous scarring. And, yes, Sidney is very interested in seeing the man who saved his life. Jamie has to go. It isn't just the pain that has kept him awake all night, the terror of the memory, or even the smell of burning that seems stuck in his nostrils. No, it's that old journalistic instinct again. That desire for the truth.

When Jamie arrives on the ward, he is shown to Sidney's bedside.

His arms, legs, and torso are heavily bandaged, as is the top of his head. There's a cannula in his hand attached to a drip, and other wires run from beneath his blankets to a vital-signs monitor. His face is not so badly damaged. It's red in places from first-degree burns, but that's it.

"I hope you don't mind me coming," Jamie says. He stands by a blue plastic chair, his hands resting on its back.

"I understand I owe you my thanks." Despite his recent trauma, his voice is clear. "Please, take a seat."

Jamie sits. "Mister…?"

"Call me Sidney."

"Sidney, I heard you call out about how burning effigies of Guy Fawkes is wrong… What made you put your life at risk like that?"

Sidney smacks his lips. "He's a hero, Guy Fawkes."

"What do you mean, a hero?"

Sidney groans. "You're not one of those awful local journalists, are you? Looking to ridicule me in your paper?"

Jamie's body tenses. "I am a journalist… but that's not why I'm here. When I saw you run into that bonfire, it was terrifying. You must truly believe in your cause."

"I do."

"Can you tell me?"

"It's a long story."

Jamie shrugged. "If you're comfortable telling it, I've nowhere to go."

"Well, settle in." Sidney clears his throat. "There's only one way to tell this right."

Chapter 1

IN WHICH OUR HERO IS BORN WHILE THE NEARBY BELLS OF A CHURCH AND CATHEDRAL RING

We'll start from the beginning. I know that's a little old fashioned, a touch Dickensian, but some stories need to start at birth, and aye, this is one of those stories. The history books will tell you Guy Fawkes was born on the thirteenth of April, 1570. That was a Monday. Those books are wrong. He was born on the twelfth, a Sunday, while the bells of Saint Michael le Belfrey rang in tandem with those of York Minster: the church and the cathedral calling their congregations for morning worship. Neither Edward nor Edith Fawkes would be in attendance, a thought that brought Edward more than a little anxiety as he paced his small study on the first floor of his Stonegate home. As an employee of the consistory court of York, non-attendance at church was frowned upon at best. At worst, it raised suspicions that one was not entirely devout, perhaps even a sign that one was Catholic.

While Edith Fawkes was pious, thoughts of the church could not have been further from her mind as she lay on her kitchen floor, panting. Alongside the pain of childbirth, came memories of last time and the tragedy that had befallen their family. She couldn't suffer this agony once more, only to be deprived of a family again. She stared at

Dorothy, her midwife, awaiting instruction, hoping to give the child the best chance of a healthy start in life.

"Now push!" Dorothy said. She was a skilled midwife, presiding over what may have been her one-thousandth birth. Dorothy, however, knew what it meant to be born during the ringing of church bells. Such a cacophony alerted the people of the parish and called angels too, and not only those in Heaven. Those that had taken the fall with Lucifer and dwelt in the pits of Hell also heard the herald, a painful reminder of the spiritual realm from which God had banished them. Given that the sound travelled above and below for angels good and evil to hear, children born during the holy peal were born with a talent; they could see and hear creatures from planes other than the earthly one on which they resided, restless spirits, angels and demons alike. Some called it a gift, others a curse.

How Dorothy wished the bells' cacophony would cease, but the health of the mother and child came first. She urged Edith to push once more, hoping it would not be the final push, that the child would resist for a little longer. Alas, with another agonised cry, the boy arrived into the world as the church and cathedral bells continued their battle for supremacy.

There was no time for lament. Dorothy cut the cord and swaddled the child before delivering it to the mother, whose wrinkled brow indicated concern.

Dorothy had delivered Edith's first child, a delicate girl who didn't make it to two months, so she knew those lines of worry were for this child, fear that he may live no longer than his departed sister. But this was a sturdy boy. Dorothy could have told Edith she need have no concern in that regard.

The life he would lead having been born at such a time, however, was sure to bring its share of worries.

After delivering the placenta and repairing the damage carefully with needle and thread by the light of the fire, Dorothy summoned Edward Fawkes.

The new father looked at his wife and the bundle in her arms.

"We have a beautiful baby boy," Edith said.

Edward knelt beside his wife and touched the thin ginger wisps of his son's hair. He gazed into the infant's dark eyes and then studied the hand that had escaped the swaddle, examining each tiny finger.

"Do you have a name in mind?" Dorothy asked as she washed her hands in the pre-prepared bowl of warmed water.

Edward turned to Edith, and she nodded. Having previously discussed the matter, he gazed upon his boy once more. "Guy."

"Guy Fawkes," Dorothy said, nodding. "A fine name." She hoped she had kept her concern for his fate from her voice. As the child opened its mouth and wailed, she wondered whether he was hungry, uncomfortable, or already troubled by voices from another realm.

If Edward and Edith Fawkes had had a natal chart created for the birth of their son, as many wealthy folks did, they may have had significant concerns about his future. It would have foretold hardship, strife, and periods of severe mental perturbation, it would have foretold of a life of injuries, pain, and torture, and yet it would have foretold acts of bravery, heroism and staring adversary in the face and not flinching. Had they those charts that tell of a person's personality and potential, they would have felt fear for their boy, but, unlike many of their middle-class peers, they eschewed astrology, believing God would put the boy on the right path if he remained pious, virtuous and true.

In that room, minutes after Guy Fawkes' birth, Dorothy alone suspected a bloody fate for the child. So instead of concern for Guy Fawkes on the day of his birth, his parents had only love and a touch of curiosity about from where the shock of red hair on the top of his head had come.

Twice more Dorothy visited the Fawkes' house: in 1572 for the birth of Anne and again in 1575 when Elizabeth was born. She could only be thankful that church bells accompanied neither sibling's birth. On both occasions, she witnessed the boy, and despite the smile on his youthful face, she knew what he had to come.

Chapter 2

IN WHICH GUY FAWKES HAS HIS FIRST ENCOUNTER WITH WITH THE DISEMBODIED HEAD OF THOMAS PERCY

While there may have been a few things seemingly from Hell in Guy Fawkes' nappy, I won't be dwelling on those horrors. The first years in that three-storey townhouse in Stonegate, York, were happy ones for the Fawkes family, but the same could not be said for the city in which they resided. Disease was rife: tuberculosis and typhoid took their share of passengers to the grave. Poor sanitation led to dysentery and cholera, which also thinned the city's herds. All mothers feared their children would fall foul of the sweating sickness, a particularly perilous strain of flu that few knew how to treat. Guy, fortunately, remained a fit and well child, barely suffering so much as a snotty nose. He was, however, a crier. Even when well fed, perfectly warm and dry, he would give out a most tremendous roar, so powerful his whole body shook. Edith had concerns about the intensity of expression on his face, but as quickly as the outbursts began, they disappeared, leaving Edith confused but glad her son had quietened. Had Dorothy, the midwife, been present, she may have told Edith what troubled her son: a passing spirit. Alas, Edith remained oblivious to the cause of Guy's trauma, and content that he remained free of the viruses that blighted so many.

But sickness wasn't the only thing that could cost a life in York. Thinking was a dangerous business, too. If someone happened to believe the wrong thing, or follow the wrong branch of a belief tree, and if they were daft enough to vocalise it before the wrong pair of ears, it wouldn't be long before there was an inevitable separation between their head and their neck.

One such man who thought the unthinkable and was foolish enough to act upon it was Thomas Percy, the 7th Earl of Northumberland, who decided to lead a rebellion in an age in which beheading was in vogue. Some called it the Rising of the North, and others the Revolt of the Northern Earls. Whatever name it went by, it failed, like most attempts to take on the powerhouse of the English monarchy. Her Majesty, Queen Elizabeth I didn't take kindly to attempts to remove her from power. In response, she took their heads. Once their puny rebellion was smote, with the aid of a chopping block, an axe, and a gentleman well practised in using both, heads rolled. They didn't roll for long. Guards took the heads and placed them where most visible. The Queen's subjects would not forget that rebellion was a terrible idea, destined for failure. This is how, in August 1572, Thomas Percy's head came to be upon a spike at Micklebar Gate, one of the four entrances to the city of York.

At two years of age, young Guy was not aware of this. Yes, he was a stocky lad, advanced for his age, but the concept of rebellion was not yet in his grasp (oh, but it would be). His parents were not the sort to take their two-year-old son to see a man beheaded, unlike a number of their peers who wouldn't eschew a morning's free entertainment.

So, while young Guy was oblivious to Thomas Percy's head in 1572, he became very aware of it in the summer of 1574.

Placing a head upon a spike, and putting it in a position for all to see within a prominent city is a grand statement, but at what point do you say *enough is enough? The people understand; let's remove the head?* The answer to that question, as it happens, is never. It remains there. It remains for the birds and the insects to feast upon. It remains until the flesh has rotted away or been consumed. Nothing eats the bone though, apart from time. Sometimes skulls fall from their position, and sometimes those sympathetic to rebels and villains who ended up with their heads on spikes recovered their remains. That's what eventually became of Percy's head–a sympathiser removed it, one who took a long time to realise he felt sympathy for the cause–but in 1574 it was still in place at Micklebar Gate and Guy saw it when travelling with his father out of the city to visit his uncle, Thomas Fawkes. Guy's journeys with his father were frequent. At that age, he didn't know how fortunate he was to have a father who liked to spend time with him. Whether they were visiting Thomas, or Guy's grandmother, or if they were only walking the streets of York, purchasing meat from The Great Flesh Shambles or fresh fish from Fossgate, Guy clung to his father's hand, firing question after question at him, such was his thirst for knowledge.

"What's that, father?" said the inquisitive youngster, pointing up at what remained of Thomas Percy's skull.

Edward Fawkes followed his son's finger. "That's… a skull."

And with some pointing and prodding at both his own and his son's head, Edward explained, to some level of understanding, what bones were, and in particular, the skull as the home to the thought centre for the human body, the brain.

This concept stuck with young Guy, as did the image of Percy's skull. He couldn't get his head out of his head. As such, he was un-surprised when the skull visited that night and conversed with him on matters of great importance.

Edith Fawkes had put Guy to bed a little before sunset. Guy had a bedroom on the second story of the Fawkes' Stonegate townhouse. His bedroom curtains were thin, and the last of the day's light had more than enough strength to illuminate all but the most difficult to reach parts of his room.

The skull materialised at the foot of his bed, floating at head height. The skull looked cleaner than it had upon Micklebar Gate, and brighter too. Its luminescence made it impossible to stare at for long.

When it spoke, the jaw moved up and down; however, the voice didn't come from the skull but materialised directly in young Guy's brain. The voice was deep and authoritative and initially spoke only his name.

Guy sat up and rubbed his eyes. He knew there was something unusual about the floating head at the end of his bed, but he did not feel alarmed. He had, after all, regularly seen things come and go, emerging from and disappearing back into the very air before him. Such was the fate of one born under a clangour of bells.

The head continued to speak. "Do you know who I am, boy?"

"The head from the gate?"

"Correct. In life, I was Thomas Percy, 7th Earl of Northumberland. Queen Elizabeth sentenced me to death for fighting for what is good and what is right."

Guy jutted out his lower lip as unease washed over him. He was not used to the beings that appeared before him speaking.

"Do you know what I was fighting?" asked Percy.

Guy shook his head.

"Demons."

While young Guy had no comprehension of what a demon was at that age, his whole body trembled.

"I am here, Guy Fawkes, for you have a gift. You can see those from the astral plane. As such, it is your duty to battle the forces of evil. It is a calling of great honour and a life of hardship and misery. But worry not, there are others on this path that will guide you, and I shall be with you, always."

The words of the floating skull of Thomas Percy etched themselves into Guy's mind, for while he did not understand the message, he recognised its importance. A time would come when he would gain a fuller understanding of those words, but that time would be when he no longer required a minimum of twelve hours of sleep a night. Guy closed his eyes and quickly settled into a deep and peaceful sleep.

Chapter 3

IN WHICH GUY FAWKES ATTENDS
SCHOOL FOR THE FIRST TIME

It's okay if you have some doubts about this. Guy Fawkes, too, convinced himself it wasn't real. For years, he dismissed the event as a dream. It had not recurred since, and there was no reason for a floating skull to have visited him. Yes, he continued to see other beings which he came to realise no one else could see, but none of those spirits spoke to him. He continued to grow at a good pace, his ginger hair requiring a regular trim to stop him looking unruly. Guy started to develop a sense of responsibility. He had two younger sisters, and his mother often told him it was his duty to watch out for them. Guy always felt pride when he returned a dropped toy to either Anne or Elizabeth. Horrific diseases he'd avoided, and he'd kept his head far away from the executioner's block. While today this may not sound like an impressive achievement, the plethora of heads on spikes at every gate throughout York suggested it was no mean feat. And the fact these heads were ever-present, and the stock frequently replenished, meant Guy could never forget about the head of Thomas Percy or the words he spoke, even if their meaning remained lost.

Having survived for over seven years, Edward and Edith rewarded Guy with a place at the highly reputable Free School of Saint

Peter, an establishment of education fourth oldest in the country. For centuries, those attending school in York would have gone to York Minster, but thanks to decisions made by Henry VIII (Queen Elizabeth's father) some decades earlier, school and religion had started to separate, and Master Fawkes' education would take place at a new building in the Horsefair, an area outside York's city walls.

On his first day, early on an overcast morning in late September 1577, Guy stepped out alongside his father. He couldn't help but note the way Edward Fawkes slowed as they passed York Minster. Guy's eyes were drawn to the horses tied outside the front entrance, powerful black stallions, with saddles and bridles decorated with jewels. Two men exited the cathedral, both wearing highly decorated doublets with golden thread, the ruffs at collar and wrist stiff and bright. Guy felt his father's grip tighten, and his legs had to work overtime to keep up with their renewed pace. Guy glanced back over his shoulder, but the men had mounted their horses and ridden away.

Soon, Guy and his father reached the walls and Bootham Bar, which would take them beyond the city. Leaving the confines of York always felt significant. The walls were there for a reason, ancient defences against invasion, and to be outside them was dangerous–even if seven hundred years had passed since Vikings invaded. Guy's only prior journeys outside had been to see Uncle Thomas or his grandmother, but to visit them, they always passed through Micklegate Bar. This was Guy's first foray through this exit, but it would be a route he would come to take hundreds of times throughout his school years. Guy stared at the narrow windows and the coat of arms hanging between them. A screech drew his attention to a writhing mass of black at the top of the gatehouse.

He didn't realise he'd stopped walking until his father tugged his hand. After a few reluctant steps, Guy distinguished individual shapes from within the mass above: wings and beaks. Something had drawn a murder of crows to the gate, something they scrabbled for and pecked at. Those without full beaks cawed until the bells of York Minster signalling the quarter-hour shocked them into flight.

On the gate were three new heads, fresh and bloody, the flesh lacerated by beaks. As a shadow fell on Guy, he glanced up, and at the same instant, a crow dropped its breakfast. With a plop, something warm and wet hit Guy's cheek. He reached up, plucked it off, and inspected it. His first thought was relief, for the bird had not defecated upon him, but then he realised what he held between his fingers: a red, pliable lump with a lighter colour on one side, a chunk of scavenged, human flesh. He flicked it to the ground and wiped his face, checking his fingers for any trace of blood.

Edward tugged on Guy's arm once more and they continued through Bootham Bar without so much as a word from the guards. Guy kept his eyes to the sky, wary of the crows until they were clear of the barbican. He turned back. The city's walls, he noted, looked so much grimier from the outside.

For a couple of minutes, they continued along Gillygate until his father slowed and pointed ahead. "Here we are."

Young Guy didn't have many expectations about school. Perhaps he expected it to be no larger than the shops on The Shambles, or the average family home in the wealthy parts of the city. He certainly wasn't expecting the grounds to dwarf half of the churches in the city, even if it looked insignificant next to York Minster. The school comprised several buildings and had a large, open courtyard.

"See the building on the left?" Edward pointed.

Guy nodded as he gazed from one window to the next.

"Some pupils here are residents. They live in the building and go to school here."

"They're at school all the time?" Guy turned his nose up.

"When they're in their rooms, they're not at school."

"What will the lessons be like?"

Edward bent down on one knee to his son's level. "We talked about this. They'll teach you to read, to write, and arithmetic. The skills you need to become a success."

"Do I have to go?"

Edward stood. "Yes. Education is important. This world consumes fools, and I won't raise you to be a fool. Now run along. You don't want to be the last one in."

Guy released his father's hand and turned towards Saint Peter's Free School. He took his first steps towards it and realised his father was no longer beside him. This, he had to do alone. The building seemed to grow larger with each step, the door at least five times taller than him.

As he entered the main building, a short, round gentleman with a full, dark beard, who he would later learn was called Lewisham, barked at him. "Name?"

"Fawkes, Sir. Guy." He looked at the man with mistrust, disliking the way his jowls quivered as he spoke. Guy also noted the top of a scar on his cheek, which disappeared beneath his facial hair. He was the sort of man Guy's father would have guided him away from when on Pavement (a street so named as it was the first part of York to be paved) perusing tradesmen's wares.

Lewisham loomed over him, looking down with a scowl. "What kind of name is Guy?"

"It's mine, Sir. The only one I have."

Lewisham dipped his quill in his inkpot and made a mark on his paper.

"Okay, *Guy*." He said the name in a condescending voice. "Enter the hall and sit on the floor with the other infants."

Guy gulped as he made his way through the double doors that led into the hall. Candles on wall sconces lit part of the room, and candelabrums hanging from the ceiling brought light to the centre.

Only in church had Guy seen so many people before, and he'd never seen so many children in the same place. There were some two-hundred pupils in attendance on the day of enrolment, a rare day in which the school had maximum occupancy.

Towards the front of the hall, children of a similar age to Guy sat cross-legged, facing a stage on which three gentlemen sitting on high-backed chairs all bore serious expressions. To the side, an older boy stood, his hair so blond it was almost white. He used his elevated position at the side of the stage to stare down upon the others as if he were better than the other children in the room. Guy immediately took umbrage at being looked down upon. What made him so special?

The gentleman in the centre turned to the boy, calling his name, "Oswald." As the boy approached, he issued a command too quiet for Guy to hear.

Oswald left the stage, and Guy wondered what his education would entail. His father had told him about reading and writing and arithmetic, but would there be more to it than that? If he had to pass through Bootham Bar every day to get to school, if he had to face those disembodied heads, would they learn how to avoid ending up alongside them? It seemed like an important life lesson. He thought about Thomas Percy's visit (which he was becoming increasingly sure was a dream rather than a genuine memory). What was it he'd warned him about? Demons? He'd surely learn more about them, too.

The man in the middle stood. He used a walking stick made from dark wood with a bird carved into its head as he took a couple of steps forward. He introduced himself as Pulleyn, the headmaster of the school. "But you may address me as Sir," he added. Pulleyn's most significant feature was his eyebrows, which gave him the appearance of an owl, not necessarily a wise owl either, but a predatory one, likely to swoop down from above and take any threats in his claws. Guy found himself watching Pulleyn's eyebrows as his facial expression changed. After a couple of minutes, Guy realised he'd not taken in a single word Pulleyn had said after his introduction. Maybe he'd missed something crucial, some important aspect of learning that would render all that followed utterly incomprehensible.

"Excuse me," Guy called, but Pulleyn continued to talk.

Guy stood.

Pulleyn's gaze fell upon Guy, and his eyes narrowed, the tips of the eyebrows lifting and quivering into an attack pose. "Sit down!"

"But I…" Guy plucked his hose from where they'd pinched between his bum cheeks while sitting on the cold, stone floor.

"Did you not hear what I said about discipline, boy?"

So, he *had* missed something crucial. He was so pleased he'd interrupted Pulleyn so he could start over.

"I'm sorry, Sir, but I wasn't listening. Could you tell me again?" Guy smiled.

"I'll do more than tell you, young man; I'll show you."

This education business was even better than he'd imagined. By speaking up at the right time, he was now getting a first-hand demonstration.

Alas, the lesson Guy was to learn was very different from the one he'd expected.

Pulleyn rested his stick against his chair and strode down the steps at the side of the stage, paced across the hall, and grabbed Guy by the arm. "Name?"

"I'm Guy Fawkes, Sir."

Pulleyn dragged Guy towards the opposite side of the hall.

"Oswald," he called. "Fetch the birch."

"Master Fawkes," Pulleyn said, his voice stern, the words dripping disdain. "So soon you have shown yourself to be disobedient. Disobedience will be introduced to the birch. Should disobedience remain, the birch will return. Do you understand?"

Guy did not understand. He did not know what a birch was, but the tone of the headmaster's voice gave him his answer: "Yes, Sir."

Unfortunately, Guy's ignorance of the birch did not last long, but first, he was introduced to another piece of apparatus. Pulleyn stopped beside a piece of wood, about a foot wide that curved up from the ground to a quarter circle, to above Guy's height, held up by two firm legs. Tiny indentations marked the sides, indentations that Guy would later realise came from the fingernails of those best acquainted with it.

Pulleyn gazed out, addressing the rest of the pupils. "This," he placed his hand on the curved wood, "is called the birching pony."

Oswald approached, carrying a bundle of twigs tightly wound together.

"And this is the birching rod." Pulleyn took hold of the bundle.

Guy's eyes met Oswald's, and he thought, for a second, they showed a hint of pleasure.

"Lean against the pony," Pulleyn said to Guy before addressing the crowd again. "Discipline is a foundation of this school and of your lives. Indiscipline will be punished, and punishment will be delivered by the birch."

Guy leant into the wood, pressing his cheek against it.

"I suggest you hold on," Oswald whispered.

Guy wrapped his hands around the birching pony. A second later, his backside erupted in agony as Pulleyn struck him with the birch.

He didn't hear the shocked gasps of the infants, or the air sucked between the teeth of those that knew what was coming. He didn't hear Pulleyn tell the pupils this was an example of what to expect if they broke the rules. No, Guy heard only the voice of Thomas Percy. The skull materialised in his head as the words came: "A life of hardship and misery."

So, this was school. As Pulleyn pulled Guy away from the birching pony, pointing to the position on the floor in which he wanted him to sit, he thought about Percy's other words. He thought about demons. And when Guy sat, reigniting the agony in his buttocks, he glared at Pulleyn, who had taken his place back on stage and wondered if he was one of the demons Percy had warned him about. If that were the case, he'd take pleasure in one day vanquishing him.

Chapter 4

IN WHICH GUY FAWKES MAKES A FRIEND AND FOLLOWS UP ON HIS DEMONIC SUSPICIONS

As I'm sure you'll understand, one ride on the birching pony was enough for Guy. The welts on his backside were a constant reminder in those first few weeks that he needed to pay attention. Guy soon figured out when to keep his mouth shut at school, which turned out to be every time they weren't chanting Latin phrases learnt by rote. But while he had avoided a further thwack of the birch, one of his peers had not. When summoned to the birching pony for the third occasion in a fortnight, this time for the crime of playing with stones when he should have been doing simple arithmetic, the young man prepared himself for the strike by digging his nails into the side of the wood. Those marks, Guy realised, were rarely made by first-timers, but by those with knowledge of pain; they'd cling on as if it were possible to divert the force of the blow back into the wood itself. The young man who had become so well affiliated with both rod and pony was a student by the name of Christopher Wright, better known as Kit. Alongside his brother, John, who liked to be called Jack, he was a resident at the school. Jack, two years his senior, had sufficient wisdom to avoid a rendezvous with the birching pony.

Immediately after his third birching experience, the school bell tolled morning break. Being one of the few with the knowledge of that pain, Guy approached Kit as he made his way to the courtyard. Tears welled in Kit's eyes, but he'd not yet let a single drop fall.

Guy was not in the practice of conversation and had little in the way of social skills. Instead, he leant on what he'd seen his father do when he met new people: he thrust out his hand. "Hello. I'm Guy Fawkes. A pleasure to make your acquaintance."

Kit stared at Guy's hand before grabbing it and giving it an awkward shake. "Aye, I remember your name. You got whacked on your first day."

Guy shrugged. Many people knew him, while he knew the names of relatively few. Infamy, even at such a young age, concerned him.

If only he knew how much worse it would get.

"I'm Kit."

Guy glanced at the pouch attached to Kit's belt. "Why do you do it?"

"Do what?"

"Fiddle with those pebbles when you know it'll get you in trouble?" Guy pointed to the leather pouch.

"I can't help it." Kit reached into the pouch and grabbed a pair of the flat, grey stones. Each had a carved marking, a combination of straight and curved lines, but not like any of the letters they'd learnt at school.

"Where'd you get them?"

Kit handed Guy a stone. The pebble itself was smooth. He traced the lines with one finger.

"My uncle, Francis, gave them to me. They're runes."

Guy turned the pebble over and rubbed his finger over the smooth back. "What's a rune?"

"Uncle Francis says they keep demonons away."

Such was the force of Guy's gasp, he almost toppled backwards. The word echoed around his head, repeating first in Kit's voice before morphing into the voice of Thomas Percy. This was it. This was the reason he was at school. Finally, he was going to get the answer to the question that had frustrated him for so long. But, wait, was that the word Percy had said? "Do you mean demonons or demons?"

Kit gazed up as if the answer was written in the sky. "No, definitely demonons."

"What's a demonon?" Guy struggled to remember Thomas Percy's words.

Kit shrugged. "Dunno."

Guy turned to make sure no one was listening. "Do you think Pulleyn might be a... a demonon?"

Kit reached to touch the heat radiating from his recently birched behind, stared into the corner for a second, then back at Guy. "You're right. Let's get 'im."

Guy lunged to grab Kit's arm, pulling him back. "Wait. We can't get him. He's bigger than us. He'll strap us both to the birching pony."

"What'll we do, then?"

"We watch him."

For the next two weeks, Kit and Guy observed, conferring over what they'd seen at every break. Admittedly, it wasn't much. Sometimes Pulleyn walked with his stick, sometimes without. Guy speculated that he needed it less when he was picking on children, so it must give him power. Kit noted that the bird carved at its head was a raven. Kit had the opportunity to observe it closely, for while Guy avoided the birch throughout the period, Kit had suffered it twice more. This was, however, a slight improvement on the previous fortnight's ratio. At the end of the week, an opportunity arose. After class, while Kit and Guy were loitering in the corridor, Pulleyn's office door opened. Oswald rushed out, a scroll in one hand and panic on his face. As he pulled the door closed, Pulleyn spoke: "And hurry."

Guy's dislike of Oswald had intensified since the first day. Older pupils such as him taught the younger pupils, Guy and Kit included. Rake thin and deathly white, Oswald led the chanting at high volume, his manner bordering on fervent. Oswald always picked on Guy during Latin-to-English translations, yelling if he took too long or made the slightest pronunciation error.

The opportunity to discover a terrible truth and destroy him for it could not be missed. Kit turned to Guy, and they nodded in unison. Whatever demonon business Oswald and Pulleyn were up to, they'd find out.

As it was the end of the school day, two young pupils leaving the grounds of Saint Peter's raised little suspicion, and the flood of student traffic meant Oswald was unlikely to realise they were close. However, once past the last of the school's residential buildings, Oswald turned not towards the city of York, but away from those walls.

"What do we do?" Guy asked. "Do we follow him?"

"We 'ave to!" Kit said, again lurching forward.

Guy dragged him back. "Stay back! If he turns around, he'll see us."

Guy and Kit crept beside the houses, dipping into every alcove, remaining a few doors behind Oswald until the thinning out of properties made that impossible. Stone paths gave way to muddy tracks as the first greenery on the outskirts of the city came into view, and the gradient shifted while Oswald headed downhill, towards a small wood.

Guy turned back toward the city, the walls now an indistinct blur on the horizon.

"Come on," called Kit, and this time, there was no stopping him.

Oswald ducked into the trees. At least there it would be easier to hide, Guy thought as he hurried to catch Kit.

The sun was already low in the sky on that late October day, and as soon as they were within the trees, the light could no longer reach them. The gloom made it impossible to see Oswald.

"We should go back," Guy said.

"A little farther," Kit urged, and once more Guy acquiesced.

The boggy ground underfoot sapped strength from their little legs, but soon a flicker of flame drew their attention. The trees thinned giving way to a wattle and daub building, two flaming torches marking the entrance. Wound-together branches that hung over the edge made up the roof. There was no sign of Oswald, but as they crept closer to the building, his high-pitched voice echoed inside.

"It is with great urgency that I bring you this request," he said.

Guy pictured Oswald handing over Pulleyn's scroll.

Kit reached up to the small window, pulled himself on tiptoes, and peered in before gasping and ducking away again.

"What d'you see?" Guy asked.

Kit held a finger to his lips to shush him and pointed to the window.

Guy rose onto his toes and peered into the dark room, barely lit by a candle on a table in the centre. A short woman dressed in dark rags bent down, her back hunched, and reached for a pot from a low shelf. Shelves lined with pots and jars covered the entire wall. As she rose as far as her crippled back would allow, Guy felt a hand pull at his arm and he gasped. He turned to see Kit and cupped his hand over his mouth.

From inside came Oswald's voice. "What was that?"

Kit fled, beckoning Guy with a swing of his arm. Within minutes, they were through the trees and back on the road. Kit continued to the other side before diving into a hedge. Guy leapt over it and ducked as Kit pushed through, leaves in his hair and a scratch on his face where a branch had scraped against it.

"What was that?" Guy asked.

Kit peered over the hedge and ducked once more, then scanned the horizon on the other side. "From what I've heard Uncle Francis talk about," he lowered his voice, "I think she might be a witch."

"What's a witch?" Guy asked.

Kit peered out once more. "They put spells on people. Or make them get sick."

"Why would Pulleyn send Oswald there?"

Kit's eyes grew. "Maybe he wants to put a spell on us. Maybe he wants us to get sick at school."

Guy gasped.

Kit dragged Guy down and pointed. Guy raised his head above the leaves as Oswald exited the cover of the trees, carrying one of the witch's pots. He looked both ways and took the path back towards the city.

Together, Guy and Kit rose from behind the hedge, waited until Oswald was a little distance away, and followed once more. He returned to the school, and as he crossed the courtyard, Kit stopped.

"What's wrong?" Guy watched as Oswald took a key from his pouch and unlocked a door.

"We can't go into school now. It's too late. There's no one else there, and he'll see us."

"So, what do we do?" Guy turned towards the heavy door as he heard it slam, with Oswald unfollowable on the other side.

"Pick up the trail tomorrow. Meet me 'ere an hour before first class?"

Guy agreed, and Kit headed for the school's residential building.

Guy looked up at the darkening sky. He'd not been out this late by himself before; he knew he'd be in trouble for not following the other boys back into the city and back home like he was supposed to.

Head down, trying to catch up with lost time, he took off at the quickest pace his little legs could manage. Guy glanced up as he approached Bootham Bar and dropped his gaze to the dirt again. He didn't want to lock eyes with any of those that resided on the spikes above. What powers might they have in darkness? He continued to run until his head collided with something spongy that gave out a winded, "Oof" noise, and he bounced off it and crashed onto his bum.

20

He'd aimed right for the middle of the gate, so he knew it wasn't the brickwork he'd run into, plus it was soft, and he'd yet to meet bricks that went "Oof." Looking up, he stared into two eyes, pupils blazing red. The man's flesh was tight and deathly white, his face extended by a grey beard and framed by a stiff, white ruff. His black cloak had disguised him well. Guy gazed into his eyes once more and realised his irises were not the colour of fire at all. It must have been the light from the torches burning at the side of the gate catching in his eyes.

From one side, the point of a pike veered towards Guy's neck. A soldier in armour, but with no helmet, pointed the weapon at him. "You'll apologise to the archbishop."

Guy stared at the soldier and then back at the other man.

"Sorry..." Guy muttered.

The soldier withdrew the pike, leant it against the wall next to a barrel, and offered a hand to help Guy up.

The archbishop continued to stare, and Guy was certain he could see the slightest glimmer of flame reflecting in those eyes once more. He glanced over his shoulder at the torch on the wall, then back at the man. Around and through the archbishop's legs, a black cat weaved. It turned to Guy and hissed. One of its eyes was missing, a scarred hollow in its place, the other a sick yellow colour.

"You should be more careful," the soldier said, drawing Guy's attention back to him, "Or you'll end up like this lot." He grinned as he reached into a barrel and plucked out a dismembered head. It was a middle-aged man, his face frozen in fear, a mask of terror, tendrils of sinew hanging from what remained of his neck.

The soldier stared at Guy as he shoved the head onto the pike, the tip rasping against bone before squelching into the brain.

The archbishop's gaze remained on Guy. His mouth twisted into a sick smile, showing yellow, pointed teeth, as he breathed in uneven wheezes.

"Guy!" came a shout.

He turned. Even in near darkness, he recognised the shape of his father.

Guy sprinted through to the other side of the gate.

"What's wrong?" Edward asked. Then he looked up at the men by the gate who had followed.

"You know this boy?" the older man said.

"Archbishop Sandys." Edward bowed. "He's my son."

The archbishop stared at Guy once more. "Make sure he takes more care when moving about the city."

"I will." Edward pulled Guy closer to him.

"Now he knows the consequences," he said and pointed up.

Guy followed his finger to the heads adorning the gate. These were less fresh, with bone showing through in places where the flesh had either rotted away or crows had consumed it.

"Thank you," Edward said before turning away, holding Guy close beside him.

Guy felt heat on the back of his neck as if the fire in the eyes of Archbishop Sandys burned into him. The sensation didn't pass until they turned a corner and were out of sight of Bootham Bar.

Chapter 5

IN WHICH GUY FAWKES ENCOUNTERS A 'DEMONON' FOR THE FIRST TIME

Friends and enemies: you make a few in your life. Guy had no idea how intertwined his life would become with that of Kit Wright as a friend, and that of Archbishop Sandys as an enemy. Yet, his young life nearly ended before any of those relationships had a chance to blossom.

The next morning, Guy left for school early. He'd had a telling off from his father the previous evening for not coming directly home from school, and his mother had wept, which was worse than the telling off.

Some of the weight of guilt lifted when he exited his home, but a terrible feeling remained that had physically manifested itself as a lump in the pit of his stomach, a lump that made him feel like he was going to vomit every time he thought about how bad he'd made his parents feel. The only way, he suspected, he'd be able to digest that lump was if he turned that disappointment into pride. His parents would be so proud if he revealed that Oswald and Pulleyn were demonons and if he stopped their nefarious plot against the rest of the school.

He leant against the wall opposite the school's residential building, waiting for Kit to emerge. Ten minutes passed, with no sign of him. A few minutes later, Kit's older brother Jack came out.

Guy waved his arms and called out until Jack, wearing a look of annoyance, trotted over. He was the more serious brother, never getting in trouble and often praised for his hard work. Jack had spent more time in the company of adults, which made him act more grown-up than his age. "What's up, Chummer?" he asked.

"Will Kit be out soon?"

"Kit? He left an age ago." Jack shook his head and walked off.

Before Guy had long to ponder Kit's whereabouts, a hiss drew his attention. A black cat, similar to the one he'd seen the previous evening, slinked away. Something compelled him to follow. He'd gone only one hundred yards from the school when the cat turned to face him. This wasn't the same cat from the previous night, for this one still had both eyes, and the colour wasn't a dull yellow, but a livid orange, like flame. Those eyes locked with Guy's before the cat turned and took off at a greater pace.

Guy broke into a run to keep up. Again, they passed where the houses thinned, but instead of following the road beyond the trees where Guy had gone previously, the cat darted along a path towards a farm.

Unlike his Uncle Thomas's farm, this one was silent. There was no sound of animals, no activity in the fields. What grew there was not crops like on Uncle Thomas's farm, but tall grass with patches of weeds and wildflowers doing exactly as they pleased. While Uncle Thomas took great pride in his cottage and his barn and stables, the buildings here were a ramshackle collection comprised of warped beams, weather-beaten walls, and thin and sagging thatch.

The cat paused in the middle of a barren yard, with the farm-house in front of him, the sables to the right, and the barn to the left. The only sign that this had once been a working farm was a dishevelled plough, long past its best days.

The cat darted to the left and under a rotten stable door. It looked as though there once would have been four doors in the stables, but three were gone, and the last hung on by a single hinge. Guy pulled open the door. Sunlight poured through the holes in the roof, illuminating a broken wicker basket, and a pile of rotting straw. Brown and flaking filth covered the rear wall. The cat was nowhere to be seen. The only way out again was back under the door unless it scaled the wall and left via the hole in the roof. It seemed too high, and surely Guy would have heard it. The pile of straw was insufficient for the cat to hide in, but where else could it be? The straw was black in places and reeked of rot. Guy prodded it with his foot, which only spread the stench of decay. Once certain the cat wasn't inside, he scooted the straw into a pile against the opposite wall. Drawn on the stone floor was a strange pattern: an eye with a wing on one side and a tear below it.

As Guy gazed at the symbol, he heard a grating meow. He exited the stable and spotted the cat halfway between the stable and the farmhouse where the door hung haphazardly open. Was it like that before? At the door, it stopped again, looking back, as if to make sure Guy followed.

He did.

But Guy wasn't about to go into the house unarmed. He scanned the ground and spotted a felled branch, twisted and crumbling to one side of the house. If Pulleyn had hurt his backside so badly with a bunch of twigs, imagine the damage an entire branch could do!

When Guy reached the door, he peered in: no sign of the cat. An empty dresser stood on the wall opposite, its shelves warped and bent. A small table, a film of dust on its surface sat next to the wall, beside the fireplace, still full of ashes. He stepped inside. A dusty and stained bedsheet covered another tall item of furniture, and a single cooking pot sat on the shelf to the side.

From somewhere inside, a door squeaked.

"Hello?" Guy called.

"Guy, don't come in!" Kit yelled from somewhere at the rear of the building. "There's a demonon."

As soon as Kit said it, the door slammed shut. Guy twisted round. What was once rotten now looked pristine. He scanned for a handle, but there was nothing. He pushed against the door, but it wouldn't budge.

25

In the fireplace, with a whoosh, flames appeared, followed by a booming laugh that echoed all around him, as if the entire house was laughing. He tightened his grip on his branch, ready to swing it at any adversary. From the fire, a jet of light shot out and hit Guy's weapon. As it erupted into flame, he dropped it. It fell to the stone floor, blackened and smouldering.

Flames flew at the dusty bedsheet, which caught alight in a flash, transforming it into a swirl of ashes. Beneath it was not a dresser, but a structure made of twisted branches, a cage large enough to hold a man prisoner. Windows transformed into solid stone, and every wall had a red glow from the fire.

"Kit," Guy called, "Where are you?"

"Get out," came Kit's cry once more.

There was only one door in sight. Kit had to be through there. Guy ran towards it, but not through it. Something solid blocked his path, an invisible barrier. He fell back, but not to the floor. Arms wrapped around him. He turned his head but could see no one. He scanned for the arms that held him, but there was nothing. All he could see was his clothing moving unnaturally. His doublet pressed tight against his body. That tightness grew and grew until the surrounding colours darkened.

When Guy awoke, he was on the other side of the thick, twisted willow branches, a wooden prison no more than a yard and a half square. Kit stood beside him, gripping the branches. Guy struggled to his feet and shuffled beside Kit, his face illuminated red and flickering as the fire before them burned, the flames reaching out from the fireplace towards them. There was always something about fire that suggested the idea of home. He could stare until he lost all track of time, all sense of meaning.

"Help me." Kit struck Guy on the arm. That's when he understood Kit was trying to force the branches apart. Together, they had a better chance.

The wood was hot from the proximity to the fire; nevertheless, Guy gripped it, but even with their combined force, pulling, pushing, twisting, the wood barely bent.

"He's awake," came a high-pitched, nasal voice from across the room. A man stepped in front of their prison wearing a robe, a dark hood covering most of his face. The bottom of the robe, which brushed the stone floor, rippled, and from within its folds, the cat emerged. The robed man crouched and stroked the cat's head. The cat purred in response. "And I have you to thank for bringing me two sacrifices. Mammon will reward me for this gift."

The man, their kidnapper, picked up a piece of chalk, turned to the boys, and smiled, revealing black and twisted teeth.

He turned away and dropped to his knees. With the view obscured by his kidnapper's body, Guy could not see what the man drew. When he started to chant, Guy remained confused. A few words were familiar from their Latin lessons, but nothing he could comprehend.

A log crackled in the fire, loud and sudden, like a clap of thunder, and the room brightened.

From the corner, the robed man grabbed a sack. The second he moved it, whatever was within writhed. He reached inside and pulled out a rat, clenching it in one hand. With his other hand, he grabbed a paring knife from the table, turning it so the blade glinted in the fire light. The rat squealed as the man gripped it tighter and plunged the knife into its belly. Blood ran over his fingers and onto his chalk pattern. Guy saw it in its entirety: a five-pointed star. Kit continued shaking and yanking at the twisted branches to no avail as Guy watched the blood drip from the rat and follow the chalk path along the floor. When the robed man had squeezed every drop of fluid from the rat, he tossed the carcass into the flames, which stilled as if time itself had frozen. Guy stared at the stationary orange tips of the fire. He'd seen fire burn so often, but never still. Thick, almost sentient black smoke billowed from the fireplace, swirling around the room before gathering in front of the fireplace as something near-human, illuminated by the still flames. The smoke-creature solidified, turning from smoke to ash to charred and leathery flesh. It was taller than the average man and topped with two goat-like horns. Its arms, legs, and truck were particularly thick, and twisting from the rear came a tail ending in a barbed tip.

The robed man fell onto his knees and bowed down. "Dark master, hear my plea!"

Fire burned inside the creature's eyes, intensifying as it opened its mouth, revealing a row of pointed teeth. "Filthy, pock-marked denizen of this foul swamp-stench land, why do you call me here?"

The robed man bowed again. "Demon master, I am all you allege and more. Great hardship has fallen upon me. My farm is in ruins. I offer you this feast in exchange for but a small fraction of the wealth of Hell."

The creature became smoke once more, darting across to the cage and reforming.

Guy watched, wonder trumping fear. So, this was a demonon, dragged up from the fiery pits of Hell. He couldn't take his eyes from the hideous beast despite his body turning against him, involuntarily trembling, the blood pumping through his veins so quickly he half expected it to fly from the ends of his fingers.

"Puny verminous pizzle-drops! This is a feast not for the lowest of demon spawn, let alone a lord of Hell." The creature turned to smoke once more before reappearing in front of the robed man. "What more canst thou offer?"

The robbed man bowed. "Anything you desire, my darkest master!"

"Then your soul! Your very soul shall be mine to do with as I please when your time ends on this plane."

"Yes, Mammon! Yes, Master! Anything you desire."

"First, I eat, then you sign your name in the black book." Mammon clicked his fingers. On the table, a weighty tome appeared, falling open to a blank page near its centre.

Mammon reappeared by the cage and placed one hand on a twisted branch. It crumbled to ash. He touched another, destroying it in the same way.

How Guy wished those branches he'd resented moments earlier remained.

As Mammon tested the gap to see if his arm could fit, the farm-house's door flew open.

With light pouring in from the door behind him, his pale skin and near-white hair made it obvious it was Oswald, dressed in a similar robe to the kidnapper, and no doubt there to join in the demonon celebration.

But then he spoke. "Back, back, foul servant of Satan."

Mammon swirled into smoke, reforming before Oswald, and flexed his fingers. From the ether, a handle solidified, several lengths of knotted cord hanging from one end. He flicked his wrist, bringing flame to the cords of the cat-o'-nine-tails.

"Master," the robbed man called, "rid us of this intruder so we can complete our pact."

Oswald drew his short sword.

Mammon grinned. "Your mediocre weapon has no chance here, you weedling boy, you coxcomb. Fall to your knees and pledge allegiance to me!"

On the table, the pages of the black book flickered.

Kit tugged on Guy's sleeve and pointed at the gap in the cage. While it was not wide enough for a hulking demonon's arm, two seven-year-olds with a desire to live squeezed through with ease.

Oswald held his weapon in front of his face, pointing it to the ceiling. Bright light consumed the blade. Guy and Kit had no choice but to look away. When they returned their gaze, the weapon had tripled in size, the blade glowing blue along its sharpest edge. All along the blade, golden symbols shone out.

Mammon flicked his whip, but it fell short of Oswald.

Guy and Kit edged farther along the wall, away from the cage, but then a pair of orange eyes fell on them. The cat hissed, drawing their kidnapper's attention.

"Master," he called. "Your feast is escaping!"

Mammon turned to face Guy and Kit. He ran the flaming cords of the whip over his open palm, then flicked it, the crack making the whole house shake.

Oswald took advantage, reaching once more into his robe. "Draw a circle with this and stay inside it." Oswald tossed a vial across the room.

Kit lunged. The glass hit the palm of his hand, but before he closed his fingers around it, the vial bounced out, spinning again into the air. If it shattered, they were finished. Guy dived to his left, reaching out with both hands. The vial struck his fingertips. With a grasping motion, he flicked the vial up once more before it fell into his open palm.

Mammon had disappeared.

The kidnapper had hold of the knife. He grinned at the boys.

Guy yanked the cork bung from the bottle. A sweet, floral scent hit him as he poured the milky liquid in a circle around both himself and Kit.

Oswald darted across the room, grabbed the man's robe and whipped him around. Blades flashed as the two commenced combat.

Smoke swirled around the perimeter of the circle. Mammon came to flesh once more. He gazed at the floor, looking for a breach in the protective line. He flicked the cat-o'-nine-tails. Kit arched back, trying to duck it, but it hit an invisible wall above the circle. Kit fell onto his bottom, outside the circle, and Mammon reached out to snatch him.

Kit whimpered as he tried to push himself up. Guy grabbed Kit's arm, dragging him back inside as Mammon's hand crashed into the invisible barrier.

Mammon grunted and then stood between the fire and the circle. "Come out! Come out and I shall reward you with such delights you have never before tasted!"

Mammon flicked his fingers. The whip disappeared, and in its place was a cake, still steaming as if straight from the oven.

As delicious as the cake looked, the smell did not penetrate the circle.

"Or maybe riches beyond imagination would appeal?"

The cake disappeared, replaced by a pile of gold coins. They fell from his clawed hand and clattered onto the floor, rolling to a stop at the circle's edge.

"Get thee back to Hell!"

The demon's actions had kept their attention from Oswald. The kidnapper lay on the floor, defeated. Oswald pulled another vial from his belt and threw it at the creature. Before it hit him, he dissolved into smoke. The liquid continued, penetrating the circle and drenching Kit and Guy.

"Let's go," Oswald cried, rushing towards the door.

The kidnapper's body flew up and crashed into the ceiling, exploding. Blood rained from the body, covering the three boys as they fled across the room.

Oswald reached the door and wrenched it open, holding it for the other two to run through as liquid and slop continued to drip from the floating corpse.

Guy was out first, with Kit close behind. They ran past the stables and slowed.

"Don't stop," Oswald cried. "Who knows what might follow."

Impulse took over. He craned his neck to look back, seeing Oswald's white hair stained red. Guy didn't see the rock in the path, and when his foot hit it, he flew forward and crashed to the ground.

Oswald and Kit stopped beside him. Kit held out a hand to help him up, but when he saw his friend dripping with blood, only the whites of his eyes showing, the whole world spun so quickly, blood rushed to his head, and everything went dark.

Chapter 6

IN WHICH A FAMILIAR FACE VISITS GUY FAWKES AND HE LEARNS PULLEY'S TRUE NATURE

Aye, it's a bit of a stretch to imagine a seven-year-old Guy Fawkes coming face-to-face with an unworldly creature like that and living to tell the tale, but he did. Otherwise, how could I pass it on to you?

But it was so, and Guy was flat on his back after passing out, and only a shout of "Hey," brought him round again. A haze hung over the world. He faced the farm, but all the buildings in that direction had disappeared, replaced by a misty plain. Where the house once stood, a great dark hole had taken its place, smoke swirling around its perimeter.

In the other direction, on the path heading towards the school, Kit walked beside Oswald who held a body in his arms, a body Guy recognised well. But how could he be watching Oswald carry him away from outside his own body?

Guy turned back to the farm. That great, dark hole, had grown only larger, impossible stars shining from its centre.

"Hey," came another shout.

A floating skull hovered before Guy; the head of Thomas Percy had returned.

"Look not to the darkness, boy. When you see the blackest void, run the other way." Once more, Percy's jaw moved, but the words materialised directly in Guy's head.

Guy gazed up at Percy. "What happened?"

"That was a demon."

Guy nodded. Wait, but did Percy mean a demonon? Or were they the same thing?

"Your first demon hunt was far from a glorious success, Master Fawkes. Very nearly was your flesh breakfast for a truly lowly servant of Hell."

Guy glanced one way, then the other for help, but no one and nothing else existed in his vision.

"Think before you act. Use your eyes. And for the love of all that is good and true, learn who you can trust and who you can't."

"Oswald?"

"You owe him your life. And to think you've been stalking him like an enemy."

"What do I need to do?"

"Learn, and quickly."

"But... how?"

"That is what school is for, young man."

Guy couldn't connect what he'd seen that morning with anything he'd done at school. The two seemed utterly alien to one another.

"But..." Guy started.

"Go," Percy's floating head rushed by Guy, turning his round and bringing Kit and Oswald back into his sight. Oswald continued to carry Guy's limp body away. "To be absent from one's body for too prolonged a period is a risk. You don't know what else can sneak in while your conscience is absent. Catch it!"

Percy's head disappeared.

The thickening mist of this hazy plain made all else obsolete. Again, Guy had lost sight of Oswald, Kit, and his own body. But where they had cut a path through the world, the mist swirled. "Hey!" Guy cried. "Wait!" but there was no reaction. He broke into a sprint, and as the school's main building came into sight, Guy was level with them.

He tried to grab Oswald's robe, but his hand passed through it. When he tried to touch Kit's shoulder, Kit shuddered, but he couldn't feel Guy's contact. He looked at himself, held in Oswald's arms, his body limp. He reached out, touched his own hand and experienced a sensation like his whole body was being run through a mangle until, once more, there was nothing.

Guy opened his eyes and gasped. His face felt cold, and his eyes stung. Moisture dripped from his forehead. Only when Pulleyn placed the pitcher back on the side table did Guy realise how Pulleyn had woken him.

Pulleyn glared at Guy, his face twisted in anger. From Guy's prone position, Pulleyn's eyebrows, which curled back on themselves like twisted horns, looked more menacing than ever and the lines on his face looked deeper, too.

Guy turned toward the fireplace as more water ran from his hair. He gazed up at the birching rod positioned above the mantelpiece. He'd missed his lessons. That was against the rules. Would he visit the birching pony immediately, or would he have to stew on his stupidity a little longer first?

"Can you sit up, boy?"

Guy nodded. He didn't wait for an invitation. He shuffled from Pulleyn's desk.

Pulleyn urged him to sit in the empty chair. Kit was already sitting upon its neighbour. Oswald stood by the door on one side, with Lewisham holding a pile of papers on the other side.

"It is imperative that you repeat none of what you saw today. Is that clear?" Pulleyn strode around the desk and sat opposite the boys; he leant forward as he spoke, his eyes boring into them.

"Yes, Sir." Guy and Kit spoke in tandem.

"What was it that drew you to that house? It is of the utmost importance that you are honest in your response."

Guy looked at Kit and they held each other's gaze. A brief conversation occurred between the frown lines on their normally smooth young foreheads.

"I followed a cat into the farmhouse," Kit said.

Pulleyn turned to Guy. "And you."

"I followed a cat, too," Guy said.

Pulleyn drew in an exasperated breath.

"We were looking for demonons." Kit added.

Oswald briefly turned from his sentry position at the door to look at the boys with confusion.

Pulleyn focused on Kit. "You were looking for demons?"

"Demonons," said Kit, correcting the headmaster with the confidence of one who had no recollection of how easy it was to fall foul of the birch.

"What's a… demonon?" Pulleyn asked.

Kit turned to Guy, passing him the metaphorical baton.

"Um… I'm not sure… but they're bad."

Pulleyn looked from one boy to the other with the air of a man charged with learning the art of translating the meows of cats. "Are you sure you don't mean demons?"

Guy opened his mouth to speak but had to pause while his brain caught up. "He might have said demons. Kit told me they were called demonons, though, Sir."

"Who might have said demons?"

Guy stared up at the corner of the room. If he concentrated hard, he could almost see the floating skull of Thomas Percy. He'd told him he needed to learn who to trust. Guy had suspected Oswald and Pulleyn were evil, but Oswald had proved otherwise. If Pulleyn and Oswald were so close, it stood to reason they had a similar cause.

Maybe Pulleyn was someone he could trust. Maybe this was how he would learn what he needed at school.

It would be so much easier if Thomas Percy's head materialised and explained everything to Pulleyn because Guy knew little, and the events at the farmhouse had only confused him further.

He turned back to Pulleyn and looked him in the eye. "Thomas Percy."

If Guy could read minds, he would have seen Pulleyn trying to calculate how old he was when Percy was beheaded. As he could not perform such a feat, he had to watch Pulleyn count on his fingers while sitting with his mouth open, much like one of the fish in Uncle Thomas's pond.

After what felt like an age in which his headmaster's eyebrows had completed a strenuous gymnastic routine, Pulleyn spoke: "When did Percy tell you this?"

Now it was Guy's turn to carry out complex mental mathematics, which was far more challenging, for he had a poor sense of time, and his ability to count was still in its infancy. It was time to confess his ignorance. "I don't know. It was after I saw his head on the gate. It came to visit me at night time."

Pulleyn linked his fingers together and relaxed in his chair. "What did Percy tell you?"

"He said he was killed because he had been fighting demon-ons…"

"Demons."

"And I would have to fight them, too."

Pulleyn stroked his chin. "Do you understand what that means?"

Guy shook his head.

"You can see and hear Thomas Percy. You understand that this is unusual?"

Guy's upper body tightened as if his body was held in a vice under inescapable scrutiny. "I do."

"Do you see other people that aren't really there or hear voices from those you cannot see?"

The vice tightened. Guy had spoken to anyone before about his strange experiences and only had a dawning realisation that others didn't see all that he did. "Sometimes… but only Thomas Percy speaks to me."

Pulleyn nodded. "Percy belongs to a group we could perhaps call the restless dead or the unquiet dead. Most people, when they pass on do so smoothly, but some retain a grip on the spiritual domain. It's from here the voices and visions come." Pulleyn took a deep breath. "Having awareness in the spiritual plane is what means you can sense demonic activity. It is onto this plane that familiars venture when they wish to summon something from beyond."

Puzzled, Guy turned to Kit who looked back blankly.

"Do you understand what you encountered today?"

Guy turned to Kit to see if he had an answer. They both shrugged.

"Let me see if I understand the situation." Pulleyn stood and paced back and forth behind his desk. "This morning, instead of attending class, you entered a nearby farmhouse, both lured there by a cat. You claim to have been hunting demons despite not knowing what they are."

Guy and Kit looked at each other and then nodded confidently.

"Can you comprehend what would have happened if my apprentice hadn't already been on the trail of demonic activity at that contaminated abode?"

Guy remembered the heat of the fire, the sound of the crackling logs, the brightness of the flames. He'd been warned plenty of times to stay away from fire. Worse was the sight of the demon, Mammon, its flaming cat-o'-nine-tails, its charred flesh and stinking breath.

"You'd be residing in a demon's gut now, but only after being roasted alive, and hell would have another pair of souls to fight against us in the eternal war."

In all honesty, Guy didn't understand this, but he understood the tone, and that was enough.

"Oswald, tell me more about this demon."

37

Oswald described the creature and their method of escape. "And the farmer referred to him as Mammon."

Lewisham stepped forward, shaking his head. "It seems unlikely one so low could have summoned a lord of Hell like Mammon. I suspect a lower demonic entity leapt upon the chance to answer the call in his stead."

"I suspect you're right. But these are troubling times, indeed, if a lowly farmer can summon anything at all with access to the black book. Lewisham, take two men and return to the farmhouse. See what evidence you can find and report back."

Lewisham shuffled his papers and left.

Once the door was closed behind him, Pulleyn turned back to Guy.

"Percy and I were associates. We spoke before his final offensive. He knew it was perilous. He knew he risked death. But he swore to me death would not be the end, that he would continue to recruit warriors in our fight against evil. If he came to you, he must have seen potential in you. It looks like you have been chosen, Master Fawkes."

Guy heard words like perilous, evil, and death, and he didn't like them. Was this what he was supposed to do with his life? Was he not going to follow in his father's footsteps? From what he knew of his dad's job as an ecclesiastical lawyer (which he could neither say nor explain), it seemed to involve a lot of reading and writing and meetings with very dull people. His Uncle Thomas kept sheep. Now, Guy liked sheep, but they weren't particularly exciting either. But when he was in the farmhouse trapped in that cage, the sense of excitement was unlike anything he'd ever experienced and he wanted more! Yes, it had its challenges; he had several new bruises, and nearly being roasted or eaten alive wasn't exactly his idea of fun, but it *was* exhilarating.

"Do you know what we do here, Master Fawkes?"

Mostly, so far, it had been chanting boring Latin phrases, but he couldn't say that. It remained likely Pulleyn would punish any cheekiness with the birching rod. He decided to play it safe. "Learn?"

Pulleyn smiled. "And the right pupils don't learn only Latin, mathematics, and composition. No, the right pupils here learn what it is to hunt demons! We send those pupils out on the most righteous of paths. How does that sound, Master Fawkes?"

Guy looked at his friend. "What about Kit?"

"Believe me, he wouldn't be here if he, too, wasn't under consideration. A relative of the great Francis Ingleby was always in line for this training. So, what's it to be?"

Guy and Kit nodded.

"Over the coming years, you will learn a great deal, but this is a secret association. You must not discuss this with anyone, or all of our lives may be forfeit. Before I dismiss you and you return to your lessons, do you have any questions?"

Guy looked towards the door, then at Oswald. "When do we get our big swords?"

Pulleyn smiled, a look alien on his face. "In good time, in good time! Now, we must speak about your punishment for sneaking out of school this morning."

Guy glanced at the birching rod.

"Detention! For the rest of the year, you will stay behind."

"Not the birch?"

Pulleyn turned to glace at the implement of punishment, then turned back, one eyebrow raised. "While you deserve it, your experience with so hungry a demon was punishment enough! No, dear boys, the detentions are merely a ruse, a cunning means to keep you in the school after hours when your training shall commence."

Guy and Kit looked at each other once more, their eyes wide.

"Oswald, have a letter drawn up for Mr Fawkes." He turned his attention back to Guy. "Try not to act too excited when you hand it to your father, boy."

Chapter 7

IN WHICH GUY FAWKES ATTENDS HIS FIRST DEMONOLOGY LESSON

If you've ever looked forward to anything in your life, you'll understand that anticipation is something with which you suffer. Guy Fawkes realised his life was soon to change forever, but the end of school the next day was *so* far away.

When Guy arrived home, excitement, alas, was the one emotion he couldn't hold back. He handed Pulleyn's letter to his father, practically dancing on the spot. Edward Fawkes skimmed the letter and glared at his son. "I don't know why you look so pleased with yourself. 'A poor attitude for a student at Saint Peter's.' How do you think I feel reading something like that?"

Suddenly Guy appreciated why Pulleyn had spared him the birch. The expression on his father's face hurt so much more. His mouth hung open, his eyes were wide, and even his cheeks sagged.

"I'm sorry, Father. I will work much harder, I swear."

"You will. This world is a dangerous place, and I can't have you walking around with your eyes closed like some fool ready to march blindly into the jaws of the beast."

Guy stared at the floor. "I'm sorry to have disappointed you."

Edward turned his head away. "Take yourself to bed. I cannot so much as look at you. You'll have no supper tonight."

With his head hung low, Guy headed for the stairs. At the bottom, he looked back. His father held the letter in his hands, reading the words once more. He shook his head. Guy could watch no longer. He hurried into his bedroom.

Sleep didn't come easy, but when he woke, he was sure of one thing: he would do all he could to make his father proud.

If Guy's school days had dragged before, he found himself in a new world of slow torture on the day of his first 'detention'. In arithmetic, the completion of every sum was met with the provision of two more, each one more taxing and time-consuming than the last. In composition, he felt like he'd written the same phrase a thousand times before they reached morning break, and he still didn't understand what it meant. His logic lesson spiralled into a discussion of a situation that made no sense. The only part of the day which passed with pace was when Oswald taught Latin. Instead of finding it dull to repeat the same phrases over and over, instead of finding Oswald's high-pitched and loud voice irritating, he tried to match that volume. His immature voice had no chance, but he almost had him for pitch. He now understood Oswald's passion for learning and his appetite for school because he was getting so much more from it, and Guy wanted that too–if only the standard school day would end!

And end, it eventually did. As usual, most pupils made for the exit in an orderly fashion, some heading back into the city, others to the residential building. Guy and Kit had no idea where they needed to go. First, they headed outside, but finding no one and nothing of relevance, they returned to the main school building. They tried Pulleyn's chamber, but he was not there.

"In there," Guy said, pointing to the library door as it crept closed. They hurried over and entered.

"What are *you* doing here?" Jack Wright looked down at his brother and Guy.

"We've got detention." Kit turned to Guy and winked in an over-elaborate gesture.

"They don't do detention here. Be off with you."

Kit took a step away, then stopped. "Wait a minute," he said, turning to face Jack once more. "What are *you* doing here?"

"Mind your own business. Now get lost. Scram."

Something moved in Guy's peripheral vision. He twisted around to face a bookcase against the wall, haphazardly stacked with books. Some were vertical, some horizontal, but the further left he looked, the more uniform the bookcase appeared.

A freestanding bookcase stood before the wall, and from behind this, Oswald stepped out. Guy was certain he had not been in the room when he entered.

"Welcome, young students," Oswald said, cradling his right fist in his left hand at chest height.

While Jack and Kit gave him their full attention, Guy continued to peer around him.

"Can any of you tell me where I came from?" Oswald asked.

"Easy," Kit said. "The classroom."

Oswald shook his head.

Guy stepped to one side and stared at the bookcase again. On the left, a line of books with black spines sat one above the next, creating a vertical line. The carpet before it was more worn.

"You came through there." Guy pointed at the wall.

Kit shook his head and Jack looked on, perplexed.

"Show me," Oswald said.

Guy still didn't fully understand, but he stepped forward, nonetheless. He felt it before he saw it, a slight draft whistling through the crack of the secret door. Guy studied the spines of the books and the front of the shelves until he could make out the top of the door. With his finger, he traced the outline of the hidden door.

Oswald raised his eyebrows. "Impressive, but can you open it?"

Guy knew which side the door was hinged on, and he could tell where the edge of the door was. This gave him a rough idea of where the handle should be. He plucked one book from the shelf, then replaced it. He tried the one next to it and found it would only come part way out. A chunk of the book was missing, allowing him to curl his fingers inside. He tugged at it. Yes, this was part of the door. He tugged again, but it wouldn't shift. He gazed up at Oswald.

"You've found one part of the mechanism needed to open the door. Alas, there are safeguards against anyone stumbling in accidentally, and some of those you're too short to reach." Oswald pushed in two books, one on the upper shelf, one at the bottom in line with where the door was hinged. He pulled out two books, one from below the handle, one from above it. "Try again."

Guy tugged at the book/handle, and the door, part of the bookshelf, swung forward. Inside, a dark passage led to steps heading down, at the bottom of which a candle flickered.

Oswald held out a hand, stilling Guy, Kit, and Jack's eagerness to venture into the hidden realm below. "You three are fortunate to be allowed access. You must give your word that you will speak nothing of what you see."

Only when all three boys had sworn secrecy did Oswald take the first step. Guy followed, running his fingers along the stone wall, imagining the hard work of those that had dug this secret passage out of the rock. Kit and Jack followed behind, with Kit babbling at Jack.

At the bottom, the passage widened to a small room lined with books, much like the library above, with a single table for study.

"More books?" Kit failed to hide his disappointment.

"These books contain the oldest knowledge we have about demons. There are Ancient Sumerian accounts, details of the dark arts of the Egyptians, instructions on how to create great Persian demon blades."

"Have you read them all?" Jack asked.

There had to be a couple of hundred books in the room.

Oswald shook his head. "Not nearly, but I hope to one day. During the Crusades, the Knights Templar scoured large parts of the world for these arcane texts."

Guy stood in wonder. He'd not had much time for books in his young life, but the people and the civilisations Oswald mentioned conjured such grand images that he longed to know more.

"So, it is just books down here?" Kit said.

Jack grabbed him by the shoulder, spun him around, and gave him a look, a subtle hint to shut him up.

"I think Jack was expecting more too," Kit said.

Jack sighed.

Oswald ignored them. "This way," he urged. There was no fancy mechanism for the second hidden door. Oswald reached for the edge of the bookshelf and shuffled it forward.

Guy followed Oswald into a large, circular room, stone pillars dotted around it to hold the roof up. All around the room, oil-burning lamps illuminated the chamber. On one side, a group of boys and young men held glowing weapons, practising strikes as indicated by Lewisham, who stood at the front, marking a piece of parchment as he observed his students. Beside him stood another tall man.

Kit's neck jutted forward as he stared at the man.

"Uncle Francis!" Jack cried.

Oswald stretched his arm out across Jack's chest, stopping him from approaching. "It's time for your first lesson."

Oswald led them away from the training area, but as they passed the weapons rack, Guy and Kit stopped. On it were swords with blades of all different shapes and lengths, axes, flails, and a mace. Kit reached out and grabbed the handle of an axe.

"Put that down," a voice boomed from the darkness. Pulleyn stepped into the light, his face stormy.

Still, Kit clung on to the axe handle, a weapon that was far too heavy for him to lift.

"Let go," Guy urged.

Jack stepped between Guy and Kit. He glanced in turn at Pulleyn, Oswald, and then Guy. "When he panics, he forgets, sometimes."

Jack put one hand on Kit's shoulder and spoke in a soft voice. "Kit, come on. Relax your fingers."

Kit let go of the axe and gasped as if he'd suddenly remembered he needed to breathe.

Jack guided him from the rack, towards Pulleyn, who leant on his stick, awaiting the pupils.

Guy took a last glance at the weapons. Surely it would only be a matter of time before he got his hands on them. But if they weren't going to learn to use them, what would they be doing? Learning how to fight demons without weapons? Creating great potions to ward them off?

Oswald indicated the group of six desks and asked the boys to sit.

These were just like the desks in the classrooms upstairs!

Pulleyn, now looking much calmer, waited for the boys' attention, then spoke. "Welcome to lesson one in demonology and witchcraft."

Guy couldn't help but sigh. Another lesson? That was the last thing he wanted.

"The first thing you must understand is that what little you think you know about witchcraft, about black magic, about demons, is wrong."

Guy pondered for a moment. Despite his encounter, he didn't know much about demons at all. That didn't make him quite as wrong as Pulleyn suggested. For young Guy, this was a victory.

Pulleyn turned to Kit. "Oswald tells me you followed him into the wood. Tell me what you saw."

Kit glared at Oswald. "You knew?"

"Please! Your footsteps were so heavy, I suspected your boots had been soled with lead."

Kit looked down at one boot and then tapped the leather sole.

"We followed Oswald," Guy said, "and found a sort of building…"

"With a witch inside!" Kit added

"And that's where you'd be wrong." Pulleyn shook his head and pointed at Guy with the head of his walking stick. "What did you see? Fawkes, you tell me. Young Wright, keep your mouth closed for a moment."

"The woman inside, she was old and bent, and her room was full of jars and pots."

"And what do you think she does with the contents of those pots?"

Guy screwed his face up. What was it Kit had said? "Does she make spells?"

"And there's the misconception." Pulleyn held his index finger aloft. "What is a witch? That is our first lesson. Soon you will learn it is not the old lady who isolates herself from the townsfolk and has expert knowledge of the healing properties of plants and other compounds.

"A witch practices the dark arts intending to do harm. A witch opposes the Kingdom of God Almighty. A witch draws power from the darkness that resides below, not caring that they wish to draw our world into chaos, for chaos is the very thing a witch craves!" As Pulleyn spoke, the lines on his forehead grew deeper, the tips of his eyebrows arched ever higher.

Such was the power of Pulleyn's voice, the very room seemed to close on Guy.

Kit, unperturbed, spoke: "So if she wasn't a witch… what was she?"

Pulleyn glared at Kit. The nearest oil lamp seemed to burn brighter. "She is a healer, one of the best in the region. Alas, she is the very type of woman labelled a witch and persecuted by the agents of evil. Those that have the highest power in the land, those in parliament and dwelling even in the houses of God, claim to be opposed to evil, claim to be on a quest to end the scourge of witchcraft. They scapegoat the healers, the outsiders, and people cheer their execution, ignorant of the wisdom they have lost."

Jack put up his hand and waited for Pulleyn to invite him to speak. "What do witches look like, then?"

Pulleyn cleared his throat. "'Witch' is a term that covers all that practice the dark arts, whether they be man or woman, rich or poor. As such, a witch can appear in many guises. A witch communes with the dead for evil purposes or with the denizens of the underworld. They take many forms and practise many arts, all of which you shall learn in your time at this school, not in its grand halls above, but in these passages hidden beneath the earth, for we that oppose witches are the hunted. We are the enemies of the current world order."

Guy thought back to the times in which Thomas Percy had visited. As far as he understood, he was dead. Was it wrong of Guy to have spoken with him? Did that make *him* a witch? He considered asking, but fear of the answer kept his fingers linked on his lap.

Pulleyn continued. "Fawkes, young Wright, your encounter yesterday has brought you here earlier than intended, for you both are still young. Yesterday, you almost walked into a trap, and that is why, today, I give you this warning. Demon hunters see what others cannot see, feel what others cannot feel. What took you to that farmhouse?"

"The cat!" Guy and Kit called out in tandem.

"It wanted me to follow it!" Guy added.

"Oswald, would you like to explain?"

"Yes, Sir." Pulleyn stepped back and Oswald took the position before the desks of this strange underground classroom. "Thank you, Sir." Oswald took a deep breath. "The creature you followed, while it looked much like a cat, was not a cat at all."

Guy and Kit stared at one another, puzzled. Guy was certain it was a cat. He had heard it meow.

"Those that commune with the devil's legions," Oswald continued, "witches, as some call them, are trusted with a 'familiar'. These creatures are the spawn of hell itself. They act as a go-between from our sacred Earth to the cursed underworld." Oswald looked to Pulleyn and only continued when a nod indicated he was on the right track. "A familiar can shift forms, often appearing as an animal. When they wish to communicate with their human master, they shift into a humanoid form."

"Thank you, Oswald, very good." Pulleyn reassumed the position at the front of the makeshift classroom. "Of this, above all, you must remain mindful. The forces of darkness could use a similar ruse again to draw you to them. Next time, you might not be so lucky. So, what have you learnt today?"

"Don't follow cats!" Kit cried out.

Pulleyn stared and continued to stare until the smile dropped from Kit's face and he squirmed in his seat.

"Master Fawkes, can you do better?"

"We must keep our eyes open. We see things others can't, so we must be on the lookout at all times. We must recognise the signs of witchcraft."

"And do you know what these are, boy?"

Guy opened his mouth and stopped before answering in the affirmative. It had been usual in school to issue a 'yes, Sir' regardless of comprehension, but something told him this was not one of those times. This was a time for honesty. "No, Sir. I will be wary. I will keep my eyes out for creatures that can be familiars, but it would be a lie to say I knew all signs of witchcraft."

Pulleyn's face changed. It shifted, almost bearing a smile. Not quite a smile, but it was rare indeed when he wasn't wearing a frown.

"Dismissed. Oswald will lead you out by the emergency exit, for it may in time serve you well to know how to escape here, and indeed, how one day you may sneak in."

Pulleyn left via the route Guy and the others had entered. Oswald urged the small class of junior demon hunters to stand, before leading them deeper into the caves carved beneath the school. The large chamber comprising the classroom and combat practice arena was by far the largest open space. While it had been busy when they first entered, the students had subsequently left. At the end, a corridor curled around into the darkness. Oswald grabbed a lamp to light the way. A little way down, on either side, were several openings. Guy glanced in to see little more than a basic straw bed in each. He hoped the residential building above in which Kit and Jack lived had better facilities. Once past the last of these chambers, the passage snaked again one way, then the other. The ceiling became lower, making Oswald stoop as he continued through the passage. The ground became wet, with Guy having to wade through several puddles that left his shoes wet, the cold water seeping through to his feet. After several minutes, the gradient increased. A great number of wooden beams and struts supported the tunnel, and in odd places here and there, roots stuck out of the ceiling, escaping through cracks in the rock.

Oswald stopped and placed the lantern into a recess carved into the wall. When he stepped away, he revealed a rope ladder.

"Climb up and out to freedom, and prepare for your next lesson," Oswald said.

As the oldest, Jack went first. He tested the reliability of the ladder by placing his weight on the bottom rope. Sensing it was secure, he started to climb.

Inquisitive as ever, Kit scrambled beneath his brother and gazed up as a cascade of soil and sawdust fell from above. Kit coughed and wiped as much debris from his face as he could.

"I'm out," called Jack, and Kit followed, darting up the ladder in a blur.

Guy stood back, waiting for another fall of earth. Once there was no sign of Kit's feet, he too climbed. The rock the ladder faced gave way to earth, which gave way to wood, and soon, Guy tasted the evening air again, emerging from the centre of what remained of a rotten oak. He climbed the rest of the way through and fell onto the damp earth, trees all around.

"I'll see you back at the school tomorrow as long as you're successful in the next test," Oswald called from below, and then, as he moved away from the ladder, any light given by his lantern disappeared.

"Give us a hand," Jack said. He shuffled a rotten lump of wood towards the trunk from where they emerged. "We need to make this appear natural."

Between the three of them, they shifted leaves and fallen branches to disguise the exit as best they could.

As the three of them looked around to figure out the best way home, a cackle echoed through the trees. "Who dares enter my domain?"

Chapter 8

IN WHICH GUY FAWKES UNDERSTANDS THAT EXTRA-CURRICULAR DEMON STUDY IS NOT WITHOUT EXAMS

There are times in life when you have to think fast. Not everyone has that instinct. I guess you must have, considering how you dragged me from the flames. When that voice cackled, the three boys proved their survival instincts.

Little light crept through the canopy of trees on that early evening in October, and as the voice resonated around them, the trees seemed to close in.

"This way!" cried Kit, pointing towards a glimmer of yellow light and taking off before either Jack or Guy could consult him on the wisdom of his choice. They had no choice but to follow.

Jack's longer stride, at two years older than Kit, meant he quickly caught up with his younger brother. Alas, that did not make him slow in the slightest. If anything, he increased in speed, grabbing hold of Kit's arm and dragging him along, still heading for the flickering light, the location of which shifted time and again, first further into the distance, then off to the left, then closer, but on the right. This, however, was not the cause of Jack's haste. The impetus for his increased vigour was another sound, worse than a mysterious cackle or challenging words: a wolf's howl.

As much as Guy wanted to keep up with Jack, his little legs couldn't manage it, the terrain difficult to navigate at speed. Fallen branches, hidden by the first layer of autumn leaves, caused stumbles every dozen or so strides. It was all he could do to keep Jack and Kit in his sights until they came to a sudden stop.

When Guy arrived beside them, he realised what had brought them to a halt. The hidden abode within the trees with the roof constructed from living branches, the place Kit and Guy had followed Oswald to a few days earlier, stood in front of them.

"Enter," bade a voice from within.

A low mist ebbed out of the door, and as the three boys approached, the vapour drifted around their feet. From inside, the smell of a delicious vegetable stock spread.

The boys looked at one another, questions flooding their heads but none reaching their lips. Compelled, they continued forward.

As they reached the doorway, the old woman Guy and Kit had seen Oswald meet stepped out. Her clothes were little more than grey rags. She needed a stick to keep herself upright with her back badly bent. Her skin was wrinkled and hung loose. Thin, white hair escaped the perimeter of her ragged hood.

"I have but one question," she said in a frail voice. "What am I?"

Guy turned to Kit, who opened his mouth ready to shout his answer. He'd not known Kit long, but even that was long enough to know his mouth acted much faster than his brain. Guy leapt at his friend, cupping his hand across his mouth before his word could escape. His momentum crashed the pair of them into Jack, who had seen them coming, giving him enough time to brace himself and keep the trio on their feet. "You're a healer, Madam," Jack said, pushing Guy and Kit away from him.

The woman bowed her head and stepped aside to allow entry into her abode.

Guy released his grip on Kit's mouth.

"Hey, that's what I was gonna say!" he said, looking accusingly at Guy and Jack.

The old woman smiled, and as Kit and Guy passed her, Kit leaned over and whispered in Guy's ear. "To be honest, I would've gone wi' witch…"

Guy glanced over his shoulder at the old woman, but she showed no reaction to Kit's awful attempt at whispering.

Once all were inside, the old woman urged the three boys to sit around the large cooking pot in the centre of the room that sat over an open fire. While it was the very definition of a cauldron, Guy refused to acknowledge it as one, and when he gazed in at the boiling liquid, it was out of curiosity about the vegetables that were cooking. If asked if he was checking for anything unsavoury, he would have denied it vehemently. The seats were little more than sacks stuffed with straw, but Guy had sat on worse.

The old woman sat opposite the three boys, forcing them to peer through the rising steam at her, constantly distorting her image. "My name," she said, "is Gretchen Pake. For many long years, I have lived within reach of the city, but I know my kind aren't wanted within the walls."

Kit glanced at Guy and mouthed 'witches' again. Guy turned away, trying both not to encourage Kit and to show Gretchen that he was listening to her, that he wasn't in acquiesce with his friend.

Gretchen pointed to Jack. "You identified me as a healer. You are correct. But why am I not wanted in the city? Ignorance. Nothing more. They have not the facility to understand what I do, what I create, so I am cast out. But not by your school." Gretchen stood and stirred the soup. She moved to her shelves and grabbed four clay bowls and a ladle. With a steady hand, she served the soup. Once more, they looked at each other before they took action.

As Guy was about to raise the spoon to his lips, he heard a low growl. His chest tightened as he recalled the sound of the wolf in the wood. He turned to the source of the sound and found a young hunting dog, little older than a pup.

Gretchen pointed at Guy with the ladle. "You! Why do you pause? What do you fear?"

"The dog," Guy said. He glanced at the thin broth on his spoon.

"And what was your first thought?"

"First, I thought of the wolf," Guy said.

"And then?"

"A familiar." He paused. He'd spoken without thinking whether that could have offended her.

"And is it?"

Guy bent down, craning his neck to get a better look at the creature. "No."

"Are you sure?"

In his head, Guy knew the answer, but putting it into words was more difficult. The cat he'd followed had been different. There was something about the look in its eyes. It had simultaneously looked both at him and beyond him into another place. Its movement, too, had suggested it physically existed on another plane altogether.

"This dog…" Guy said, "I can see it's really here. It belongs only in this world."

Gretchen nodded. "But you had to think. You are wary of me still, no?"

This time, Guy did ponder before giving his answer. "It's what Pulleyn said. We have to be wary."

"But are you wary still, I wonder?"

Guy looked at his spoon. He raised it to his mouth and took a sip of the broth. While thin, it was full of flavour, infused with herbs to give it a refreshing taste.

After seeing Guy eat, Jack did likewise, and only after some not-so-subtle gestures from his brother did Kit try the broth.

The boys sat in silence, enjoying the broth, not quite understanding their purpose in Gretchen's home. Only after she had finished her bowl did she speak again.

"Two of you have shown you have the forethought, the wisdom to take the path of a demon hunter. *You*," she pointed at Kit, "have yet to demonstrate your knowledge. Tell me, here I made potions and powders with the power to heal… but what else?"

Kit gazed around the room. "You blessed the water… you must be a holy woman."

Guy and Jack both glared at Kit, shocked.

"Explain," said Gretchen.

Kit pointed to a row of bottles on a low shelf. "Oswald had one of those bottles. He made a circle, and the demon couldn't cross it."

"Go on."

"That suggests the liquid is holy or blessed… and as Oswald got it from you, you must be holy."

"But women can't be…" Jack trailed off.

"In the limited churches inside your walls, they tell you what you can and can't be. They summon you with the clangour of bells, fill your heads with their version of the Lord's word, and let you go again. But there is a whole world more to learn."

"So, who trained you?" Jack asked.

"An ancient order. You will learn of them in good time. For now, I am pleased to say you have shown the qualities needed to continue on this path. Now go–follow the path back through the woods. You know the way."

Gretchen smiled, staring at Guy and then Kit.

"You knew we were outside?" Kit asked.

Gretchen nodded. "Rest well, for there is much for you to learn."

The three boys exited Gretchen's home, only to be confronted by another figure familiar to the Wright brothers.

"Uncle Francis!" Jack and Kit cried together. Francis Ingleby was a tall man, with thin, pursed lips on a rugged and serious face with a firm jaw. His hair was a sandy colour, wild and uncombed.

"Dad said you were in Oxford, but I knew I saw you!"

Ingleby knelt. "It's so good to see you. It fills my heart with joy to see your faces and to know you are joining our noble cause. But when you write home, you cannot mention any of this. You can't tell them I'm here."

"Is it a secret?" Kit asked.

"Everything we do is a secret."

Guy saw his opportunity to butt in. "Are you going to be the one to teach us how to use those swords?"

Ingleby chuckled. "This must be the Master Fawkes I've heard so much about. Your time will come with the sword, but not yet."

"So, what are you doing here?" Jack asked.

"Checking whether you passed the test and making sure you get back safely."

As they made their way through the trees and back towards the city, Kit and Jack peppered Ingleby with questions, most of which he swerved. Guy was only half listening. He had a sense he'd achieved something, a feeling quite alien to any of the other days he'd spent in school.

Once they reached the point where they had to part ways, the Wrights returning to the school accommodation, and Guy back to his home in York, Ingleby waved goodbye to his nephews, promising to deliver Guy home. As they passed through the Bootham Gate, Ingleby gazed up at the fresh heads and made the sign of the cross. No sooner were they inside the city walls than the bells of York Minster clanged. Ingleby glared up at the building and moved closer to the wall, deeper into the growing darkness of the evening. "The bells carry strange whispers," he said. "Listen carefully." But the whole time the bells rang out, Guy heard nothing. They moved along the street at a good pace, something Guy was thankful for. The last thing he wanted when he arrived home was a further scolding. Ingleby stopped on the street and scanned his surroundings. Guy gave him a final nod before hurrying inside. His mother rushed to greet him and inquired about his day. His father had yet to return from work. If only he could tell his parents what he'd really been up to. If only they could feel as proud of him as he felt of himself.

Chapter 9

IN WHICH GUY FAWKES EXPERIENCES DEATH

Guy had a lot to learn. If you want to understand his story, you too need to know a few things about the different demons he faced. I'm not saying you need to take notes, not with that journalistic brain of yours, but listen carefully. It'll set you in good stead.

Weeks passed, and Guy got no nearer to wielding a sword. He could, however, explain the difference between a necromancer, a pyromancer and a hydromancer. He could demonstrate three symbols that, when drawn in holy water, offered spiritual protection. Several items of *instrumenta maleficialia*–the paraphernalia of demonic spellcasting–he could identify and knew how to destroy. Moreso, Guy understood *why* he wasn't ready to pick up a weapon. His opinion of Pulleyn underwent a drastic change too. No longer did he find the headmaster intimidating but inspirational. His attitude toward education had transformed since his first day and his unfortunate experience with the birching pony.

The end of the year neared, and Pulleyn was in the midst of teaching about the different ranks of demons, waving his stick and gesticulating wildly as he progressed from step to terrifying step. "The lowest level of demons, those at the ninth tier, are tempters and ensnares. These earth-dwellers seek the seed of evil that dwells within us all. Should they sense that seed has sprouted, they lure their quarry in deeper. Ever-present, they seek the opportunity to corrupt.

"Next, the whisperers lie at the eighth tier. Again, they are part of our world. Their hearts are dark and they desire only chaos, like those at all levels of devilry. They disseminate false accusations, making good folk think ill of their fellow men, the propagators of bitter envy. They take the form of men or live on the lips of those corrupted by the ninth tier."

Guy thought about the shady characters he'd seen at Pavement, loitering beside certain stalls and whispering into men's ears. Were these people demons?

Pulleyn continued, shaking his head to show his disgust. "The Furies come next, truly demonic in form. These demon-spawn are crude deformities aping humanity but soulless, utterly soulless. While weak, they are legion, and demons at the upper end of the hierarchy control them in their multitudes. Demon lords send Furies as a great army bent on destruction.

"At the next level, the demons number few, but they are devastating. Aerial powers defy God himself and fly to the clouds to mock him at heaven's edge. They do all they can to hurt earth, sea, and sky. It is they that bring great fogs of sickness, they that open the earth to consume entire cities, they that destroy crops, that bring storms, rain fire from the sky and make the seas boil. While their strength is beyond comprehension, they lack stamina, so, while we cannot defeat them, our struggle is to endure their bleak duration."

Kit put up his hand and shuffled awkwardly in his seat.

"Yes, Master Wright?" Pulleyn leant on his stick as he awaited Kit's question.

"Are all bad winds demons?"

"Fortunately, no. You must learn to detect the difference between the purely natural and the malevolent before it has time to unleash its foul purpose."

Kit settled back in his seat and Pulleyn continued. "The fifth are those most commonly summoned by man, those that will issue familiars to do their bidding on Earth and convey their evil. They delude our fellow men, convince them great riches or great powers will be theirs in exchange for a few favours, and a contract for their very soul. These demons are myriad, and ridding the world of as many of these is the bulk of our purpose.

"Next come the vengeful spirits. These wraiths, consumed by hatred so bleak, so intense, so utterly absorbing, seek others who have been wronged, and, together, their loathing magnifies. They feed the sense of injustice in our fellow men, stir their spirit into violent misdeeds until we see a red reckoning. When their bloodlust has been satiated by the human kindred spirit, they feel success, but it is not long before they need to spread their hate and their vengeful spirit returns."

Pulleyn stopped to clear his throat. He took out a handkerchief and mopped his brow. "While those at the fourth tier have reasons for their hate, those at the third are so much worse, for they do not. They are hollow, senseless rage, causing destruction for the sake of it. Their power is near limitless and they control legion after legion of Furies. It is only their apathy that stops them from consuming all.

"Next come the Spirits of Lies. Malevolent mistruths and misinformation can cause more harm than empty anger ever can. These are the spirits called to séances to whisper false promises. They are the upper tier of familiars whispering untruths into their masters' ears, working to turn man against man. They use man's ignorance against them, convincing them that those who are different are bent on their destruction. When they see a rift, they dig in and tear it wide open. Their work brings war. It is they that God despairs over most, for He hates to see those formed in His image corrupted and convinced to do ill to his fellow man."

When Pulleyn paused, Guy glanced across at Jack. His brow was wrinkled in concern.

Pulleyn once more mopped his brow and took a deep breath. "And at the upper echelon, we have the false gods, the named demons. Those worshipped by men turned rotten, though they rarely answer their calls. Deceivers, they are known by myriad names and their numbers remain unknown. Even Satan, their king, answers to Lucifer, to Beelzebub and any bastardisation of these titles. At this tier too are his princes, including Leviathan, Belial, Mephistopheles, Pazuzu, Mammon."

"Ooh! We fought him!" Kit chimed in, forgetting he'd not so much fought a demon that day but been near consumed by one.

Pulleyn shook his head. "Demons are great deceivers, always. While that poor corrupted soul may have summoned Mammon, Mammon did not answer his piteous call. No, it was a mere deluder, and one which Oswald kept back with aplomb."

Jack raised his hand. "Why do they lie?"

"Lying is a sin, and sin comes as easily to them as breathing. It is through lies they win the hearts of weak men. Demons endeavour to win souls to bolster the ranks of Hell. Demons claim to witness all, but they do not see as God sees. They are Ministers of Terrors only. They move at the speed of light, so can know of events far away in an instant, claiming to have knowledge of things to be. This they use to trick others into having faith in their prophecies. Alas, they are false. God and God alone is omniscient, knowing all things past, all things present, all things yet to be."

Guy raised his hand. "So, God knows everything, right?"

"That is correct," Pulleyn replied.

Guy raised his hand once more, and Pulleyn nodded, indicating that he should speak. "And God is all-powerful too, right?"

"Also correct."

"So, he's stronger than all demons? He's stronger than the devil?"

"Infinitely so."

Guy's brow furrowed. "So why doesn't he kill all demons?"

Pulleyn raised his index finger. "For this is the very thing that the Dark Lord desires. If God shows his wrath, if God defeats his enemy, then has God not become every bit as dark as they are? If our God smites like this, using his superior and infinite power, it would not be a fair fight. Morality is dead. Heavenliness dies. In effect, God becomes the devil."

"But we can fight them?"

"Yes, for compared to the myriad legions of Hell, we are weak. God, however, can lend us a portion of his strength to allow us to succeed. Only in this manner can the weak overcome the strong. Only like this can goodness prevail."

"But can we win?"

"It is a hard fight. It is a long fight. If we don't let our noble purpose waiver, if we cling to that eternal light, if we make the right decision when faced with a thousand ill choices, then yes, we can win."

Guy glanced over to the senior pupils who were practising with their weapons, overseen by Lewisham and Ingleby. Once more, the words wouldn't come, but he appreciated all he had to know before he was ready to hold a blade and face evil, to make sure that evil didn't twist and corrupt him, didn't use the blade in his hand and turn it against those he loved. Still, it would have been nice to at least hold a sword, get a feel for its weight and release a little of that frustration about them being so near, and yet so far away.

With the winter solstice approaching, darkness descended early. By the time Guy finished his after-school demon-hunting lesson, there was little light left in the day. He knew the way home by heart now, and the lanterns at Bootham Bar made sure he didn't miss the entrance. He usually arrived home before his father and had become trusted to chop some of the smaller pieces of firewood to make them last better on the fire. However, as he approached home, he saw, to his surprise, a horse tied up outside. Even stranger, his father awaited him, pacing back and forth in front of the fire.

"Ah, Guy, you are home. Good. You must accompany me. I have received news of your grandmother."

Even though Guy had accompanied his father on visits to see his grandmother on several occasions over the last few years, he'd yet to see her out of bed. She lived with a cold woman named Helen who didn't let him have any fun. He only had to breathe too loudly, and he'd get a firm shush. Never, though, had they rushed there in the evening. It had only been a journey undertaken on Saturday afternoons. Still, this chance to go on a journey with his father was a welcome change from the usual routine.

Within minutes Guy had packed a change of clothes, grabbed provisions from his mother, and given his sisters a brief hug. Then they were on their way, Edward Fawkes riding on horseback with his son clinging behind him. They rode for an hour beyond the city walls, deep into the countryside. On their journey, Edward quizzed Guy on his numbers and his knowledge of important passages from the Bible. While Guy felt he held his own in this round of questioning, he longed to share more about what he did in 'detention' and what he'd learned of his true purpose.

Distant lights grew ever nearer until Edward passed a small farm building. He rode around the back, into the stable, climbed off the horse and tied it up before helping Guy down. They hurried into the small house. Helen, his grandmother's companion, answered the door and ushered them in with pursed lips. Inside, Guy's uncle Thomas greeted them.

"How is she doing?" Edward asked.

"She's fading in and out." Thomas stepped aside to allow his brother to enter the bedroom.

"And how are you doing, young man?" Thomas asked, mussing Guy's ginger hair. "Your father told me you'd started school. How's that going?"

Again, Guy constrained his response. "It's going well."

Before Thomas could probe further, Edward emerged from the bedroom and summoned Guy in.

The bedroom was too hot. A fire raged, but over the smell of smoke was something else, a sick smell of decay and waste. In the bed lay the old woman, who no longer resembled his grandmother, her skin so thin on her cheeks he could almost see through to the bone. It couldn't have been over two months since he'd seen her last. While bedridden in those prior visits, she still sat upright and asked so many questions. She used to ask about York, where she'd lived for most of her life. She spoke of her father, once Lord Mayor, and of her husband, who the people spoke of as the most honest man in the city. Now she barely had a voice at all.

"Sit down." Edward pointed to the armchair next to the bed.

Guy didn't realise he'd been loitering in the doorway, lost in his recollections. He sat. His grandmother tilted her head towards him and wheezed. A white haze masked the blue of her irises. She took several deep breaths, then struggled to say two words: "For you."

His father knelt before him, proffering a small wooden box. Guy turned to his grandmother and then took the gift. It was small and shaped like a chest, hinged on one side. Guy lifted the lid and tipped it back. Inside was a small figurine of an angel. He lifted it out, admiring the way the gold glimmered in the fire's light. Also in the box was a whistle carved from bone. Guy placed the angel in the box and lifted out the whistle. He turned it over in his hand and pondered putting it to his lips.

"Not here, son," his father said.

Guy placed the bone whistle back in the box next to the golden angel. "Thank you."

His grandmother reached out, and he allowed her to place her cold and bony fingers on top of his hand, which looked podgy by comparison.

A sudden sharp intake of breath from his grandmother shocked Guy. Helen sped to the other side of the bed to check on her.

"Okay, Guy," his father placed his hand on his shoulder, "return to the kitchen."

As soon as he left the bedroom, Thomas went in, leaving Guy alone to sit in the armchair next to the dwindling fire. He opened the box once more. He took out the angel and studied it, first admiring the facial features and the look of peace the artist had created. Then he turned it over to study the exquisite detail of the wings, each feather carved into the gold. He placed it back in the box and took out the whistle. He felt the smooth texture of the surface. It was about the length of his hand, and hollow, with holes at either end. About a third of the way down, there was a hole in the top, and when he tipped it up, something moved within. He turned towards the bedroom door. His father and uncle were busy. They wouldn't mind if he tried it? He put the end of the whistle in his mouth and blew gently. Nothing happened. He tried blowing into the other end, achieving the same result. Blowing harder had no effect. No, the whistle didn't work. He put it back in the box, curled up in the armchair and drifted off to sleep.

When Guy woke, day had broken. A shaft of light shone through a gap in the curtains and fell upon his face. His father and his uncle sat at the table, deep in conversation. From his position he could see his father, his head propped on his hands, his eyes ringed red. Guy shifted from his slumped sleeping position to sit upright.

His father wiped his eyes with the back of his hand before standing and approaching Guy's chair. "Your grandmother has passed on," he said.

Helen remained in the bedroom, sitting beside the dead woman, and there she would stay, keeping vigil until her companion's burial.

Death, common in the city of York because of disease and violence, lingered, for the first time, in the presence of Guy Fawkes. When he thought about his grandmother in the room next door and the fact that he'd only spoken to her the previous day, it didn't matter that he had few memories of her, it didn't matter that they weren't close, for he could not stop his tears from falling. His father pulled him close and held him until the sobbing stopped.

The ride back to York was a quiet one. Guy couldn't get the image of the golden angel out of his head, and it didn't matter that the whistle didn't work. It was a parting gift, something she desperately wanted him to have. He didn't yet know how special it was.

Chapter 10

IN WHICH GUY FAWKES WITNESSES
GRIEF SPIRAL INTO OBSESSION

Now we've got the first death out of the way, I must warn you, there's plenty more to come. Death and Guy were never long parted after that. While other deaths would hit the Fawkes household further, they had to struggle through this one, oblivious to future heartbreak.

    In the days that followed, Guy learned a great deal about grief. He held his artefacts close and watched his father closer as he passed through the stages of mourning. First, he watched him descend into a deep sadness, frequently watching him weep when he thought he was alone. Next, followed a period in which he clung to his family. Edward excused Guy of wood-chopping duty, choosing to do it himself while seeming to enjoy splintering wood to pieces in their backyard. As the days passed, he spent more time with Edith, helping around the house when before he had always kept out of the way. Edward became more caring towards his daughters, beckoning them to his lap. He'd carry two-year-old Elizabeth around, hugging her tightly, sometimes calling her Little Ellen rather than by her name. Edith had to explain to Guy and Anne that Ellen had been their grandmother's name. Regular family walks occupied the Fawkes family in the evenings and on Sundays, after church, in which they'd wrap up warm against the icy temperatures. When their route took them past York Minster, Edward would speed by, keeping his head low.

After that period of affection came discipline. Elizabeth's constant crying no longer led to her being held and comforted but to being yelled at. Edward's raised voice only made the crying louder. Guy's detentions became a source of annoyance, for more time out of the house meant less time for the chores a boy nearing eight should do. So, when the school reopened after the brief winter break, Guy had told his father not so much the truth, but a smaller lie: he was no longer required to stay behind at school for detention, but because he chose to undertake an extra hour of study. Guy hoped his father would assume this was because he wanted to follow him into the profession of an ecclesiastical lawyer. Before the winter break, he had enjoyed spending extra time at school learning about the dangers of the dark arts. Now it had an additional benefit: it kept him out of the house longer, away from the ever-growing tension.

His father had changed so much, he even asked Pulleyn if he might be turning into a demon.

"Grief is like a demon," his headmaster had said, "one that digs into the brain and infects every other thought but not one that blades can defeat. Grief is a demon that dissipates, slowly. Though perhaps kindness can quicken its passing."

Guy tried to show his father how hard he was working, but when Guy ventured out with his father to the market at weekends, he was notably anxious. While they used to take time and have a stroll around York, Edward conducted their business as quickly as possible. Each time they ventured out of the house, Edward took a new route, the only certainty that they'd avoid York Minster.

Edward had pleaded with Edith not to take the boy with him. "I don't want to put him in danger." Guy had heard his father say. But Guy sensed no danger in the streets. He used his training, but he had seen none with yellow eyes. There were more subtle signs to look out for–those who eschewed the fashion of the age would arouse suspicion. A man without hose or stockings was one to be wary of, particularly if his legs were bare. Long cloaks were everywhere, so a demon could hide its clawed hands, or a familiar could accompany its master without detection. But Guy feared that the servants of demons were indistinguishable from other humans. He knew demon worshippers had a penchant for puffed sleeves, frayed edges and decorative lace frills or elaborate ruffs, but this was also the fashion choice of the wealthy, and Guy knew not how to distinguish each from each.

During their walks, they would take a route down the Great Flesh Shambles, often referred to as The Shambles, a narrow street in which the upper storeys of the buildings loomed over the street below, leaning forward as if trying to kiss their opposite neighbours. This structure offered those that kept shop larger living quarters, and the upper storey gave shelter to the shop front below, where shopkeepers placed tables to display their wares. The most abundant business was butchery, so a channel in the centre of the street often streamed with blood and offal as the butchers washed away their waste. Butchers often drove livestock down the street and through narrow passages to where they operated their slaughterhouses.

One afternoon, Edward stopped outside his usual butchers, placing a hand on Guy's shoulder to stop him from wandering away. The butchered meat hanging from hooks outside the stores often drew Guy's attention, and Edward had to keep a close eye to make sure he didn't lose him. The butcher displayed no meat on the table, and while the window had the usual layer of grime covering it, it was empty inside.

"You won't get no meat from Clitherow's today," said an elderly man as he passed. "Soldier carted Mrs Clitherow off to the castle this morning."

And while the butchers reopened a few days later, The Fawkes family found somewhere else to buy their meat, and when next they passed Clitherow's, Edward steered Guy onto the other side of the street.

It was after this their walks became even shorter, with Guy struggling to keep up with his father's pace as he sped to complete any urgent business, desperate to return to the comfort of his own home, rarely bothering to choose the best of the fresh fish from Fossgate or taking time to haggle for a better price with the traders on Pavement.

Without bringing his father any comfort by joining him out in the city, Guy tried another approach. One day in mid-January, after his father arrived home from his work, Guy jumped in with both feet and mocked a keenness to follow in his father's footsteps. To Guy, there was little more boring than a life spent poring over documents and checking clauses. He wanted to hunt demons, not loopholes! When his father had tried to explain his job in the past, it had been in such dry terms—no wonder young Guy had been turned off by the idea, especially as he was only five. Aged seven and with some schooling in him, he could try once more to understand. Telling his father he was eager to learn of his occupation raised the first smile he'd seen on his face for days. For an hour, Edward explained to his son the role of an ecclesiastical lawyer. He explained how he helped the public in matters of the law. He explained his responsibility for carrying out business on behalf of the church, including managing their growing number of properties.

The following day, Edward spoke about his work with increased zeal, explaining his exciting discovery to his son, pointing at various underlined words on documents. Even though Guy struggled to follow his father's logic, there was something infectious about his exhilaration. He kept talking about two gentlemen, Hastings and Sandys, claiming that his discovery would lead to their downfall.

"The man we saw at Bootham Bar that one time?" Guy asked.

The event had had a more lasting effect on the younger Fawkes than on the older, who looked at his son with some confusion and then nodded in agreement.

The names were also familiar from Guy's demonology lessons, for Pulleyn often mentioned the two in connection with several unsavoury practices in York that he suspected they were involved in. When Pulleyn spoke of the duo, it was with an equal amount of enthusiasm, and it was apparent these two men engaged in demonic activity. If his father was doing something that could get rid of them, that was worth celebrating.

"Can you explain what they did again?" Guy asked.

Edward looked at him with wide eyes, perhaps because it was the first time his son had shown any interest in his occupation.

Edward shuffled his papers and pointed at several underlined passages. "These show properties of which Hastings, head of the Council of the North, and Sandys, the Archbishop of York, have come into possession." Edward again shuffled through the papers and pointed at an underlined passage. "And this shows that those acts were not lawful."

Guy frowned. His father was back to talking about things he did not understand. Maybe he could turn the conversation to something he understood. "Are they evil men, father?"

"They are cruel and callous. They claim to be men of God, but their actions indicate the opposite."

"Can you do anything to stop them?"

"I must inform Sir Francis Walsingham. He reports to the Queen herself. He will remove them from power. We can't be as unfortunate as to have men with worse temperaments replace them."

"Can the Queen stop them?"

"The Queen can do anything she likes. Now excuse me, my boy. I must pen this letter in great haste."

If Edward Fawkes had known he was as good as signing his death warrant, he may have written a little slower.

Several weeks passed, and over that time, a further change came over Edward Fawkes. This new complication with his work seemed to ease his grief-stricken mind, but a whole host of new worries had arisen. He spent even longer hunched over his desk in the evenings, scrawling notes on papers and copying out long sections. Despite being in the safety of his own home, he constantly looked over his shoulder. His clandestine behaviour drew Guy ever closer to his father. He stood in the doorway, watching as his father sat in his study, scrawling notes. Once, he even saw him remove a brick from within reach of his desk and slide a pile of documents onto a small stack forming inside.

One Saturday morning, as he rose to ready himself for school, he heard voices in his father's study. He noticed the door was open, his father again hunched over his desk, his pile of papers larger than ever. His hand shook so badly, he could hardly hold the quill. "I won't do it," Edward said.

There was a pause as if he awaited a response, and then he spoke again. "I won't falsify the documents. The evidence is all here."

Guy entered the study, curious about whom his father conversed with. Alas, no one but his father was present.

Hearing movement, Edward spun around to spy his son looking at him. "What, my boy? Up so late?"

"Late, father? It is morning. I am shortly away to school."

As Edward stared at his son, taking an age to process the information, Guy noticed the heavy bags under his father's red eyes and the extra grey hairs at his temples and in his unkempt beard. His face had thinned too, cheekbones protruding in a way that made Guy recall his grandmother's face on the day she died.

Edward beckoned his son over. Guy approached and let his father grasp his hand. "Your schooling is important, son. I've said before, wisdom is more valuable than ever in this day and age. Do you agree?"

"I do."

"Then know this. York is in the thrall of evil men. I'm trying to do what I can to rid this city of them. It's hard work, but it's important. Do you understand?"

Guy nodded.

"I want you to follow in my footsteps, Guy. I want you to fight for the good of the common man, to know when someone has been wronged and to do what you can to right it. Does that sound like a noble life to you, Guy?"

"It does."

Edward released his son's hand. "Then do your best at school today, son."

"I will," Guy said, but his father had already turned back to the documents, muttering to himself once more.

Guy raced to school. His mind swirled with fears as the image of his father in such a state refused to shift. He entered Pulleyn's chamber, finding him poring over an ancient text. While Guy, alongside Jack and Kit, had been brought into the circle of demon hunters trained within the school, they were very much part of the lower echelon. Pulleyn had spent a significant amount of time with them going over the fundamentals, but he still had to carry out his studies and investigations alongside maintaining the pretence that they were very much an ordinary school. Guy had been told to address any queries initially to Oswald, and then to Lewisham, only approaching Pulleyn in times of dire need. His father's face indicated dire need. As much as Guy knew he was foregoing protocol, he trusted Pulleyn most, and he sensed Pulleyn had at least the tiniest bit of fondness for him. Guy assumed this warmth came from having the stamp of approval of the floating skull of Thomas Percy.

Pulleyn glared at Guy, who could feel the weight of those eyes upon him.

"You have a message for me?" asked Pulleyn. It was normal for teachers to send pupils as messengers within the school, but Guy could not help but feel a pang of sadness for being thought of as little more than a message boy.

"No, I… I need to talk to you about something."

Pulleyn's gaze returned to the documents on his desk. "And no one else can resolve this?"

"I don't think so."

Pulleyn sighed. "Do we need to do this in the library?"

Guy nodded.

Together, they walked through the corridors and into the library. Checking to ensure they were alone, Pulleyn turned around, and only when he was certain of privacy did he open the secret passage that led below. They descended the stairs and stopped in the small room with the occult books.

"So, what is this business?" Pulleyn said.

Guy looked at the further bookcase and studied the titles for a moment as he waited for the words to come. When they did, he didn't know where to stop. He reminded Pulleyn of his grandmother's death, and the change in his father's behaviour, to which Pulleyn seemed nonplussed until Guy mentioned the names of Hastings and Sandys.

Suddenly Pulleyn was hungry for more information, leaving Guy struggling to pull details he felt were inconsequential from the very depths of his memory.

"Your father is right to be concerned," said Pulleyn. "Hastings and Sandys are dangerous men. That pair have seeded much of the root of demon worship we have dug out here in York. If your father wrote to Walsingham, he could be in great peril."

The word 'peril' echoed around the chamber until it sunk back into Guy's gut and sat there as heavy as a lump of lead. He swallowed hard. "I heard him this morning talking to himself. He was refusing to…" Guy struggled to remember the words, but they wouldn't come. "Something to do with his documents."

Pulleyn grimaced. "He was talking to himself, you say? It may be one of the lower echelons of demons has his ear. More likely to be one of the tempters of the ninth domain rather than a deluder if there was no physical presence. Given your keen eye, I'd expect you to have seen something of a higher level. I'm sorry to say this is troubling news indeed."

"What can we do?"

Pulleyn placed an arm on Guy's shoulder which went some way to dissipating the heavy feeling in his gut. "You are still too green to take on what threatens your father. We may need to get him out of York, get you all out of York, for his actions may have put you in great danger."

"Will they try to hurt him?"

"Undoubtedly."

Bilious panic sped thickly up from Guy's gut, racing to his oesophagus and into his throat before he swallowed it back down, leaving the taste of bitter fear in his mouth.

Pulleyn took a step back then hurriedly continued: "We will do what we can to mitigate the danger until we can get you all safe."

Guy took a deep breath and swallowed several times, trying to rid his mouth of the disgusting taste. "Did I do the right thing in coming to you?"

"Yes, you did, young Fawkes. It is becoming ever clearer why Thomas Percy has singled you out."

Once released by Pulleyn, Guy returned to class feeling much more comfortable and less nauseous. A sense of pride swelled within him, knowing his actions may well have saved his father's life.

Chapter 11

IN WHICH DEATH REPRISES HIS ROLE IN GUY FAWKES' YOUNG LIFE

Alas, it was not long before Guy and Death came face to face once more. Guy thought he'd done enough in informing Pulleyn of his father's woes, for Pulleyn had actioned a plan that very same day. A sentry watched over his house from the streets, and members of the school spied upon Sandys and Hastings, tracking all that left their sides. And yet, for all their endeavours, they could do nothing to stop the attack, for it came in a form none had ever encountered before.

As much comfort as Pulleyn's plan brought him, Guy did not sleep well. He crept out of bed in the small hours to spy on his father. He found him, once again, sitting at his desk, slumped over a stack of papers, lit by the flicker of a single candle. Guy dared not disturb him and instead returned to his bedroom. He checked the window once more. In the dark, it was impossible to tell who, but someone loitered outside. Without this presence, Guy doubted sleep would have returned at all. As it was, he drifted off while thinking about how the organisation he was part of had arranged and resourced an around-the-clock watch in a mere few hours.

When daylight came, Guy saw another member of their community of demon hunters arrive, one he could name this time. Francis Ingleby busied himself on the street outside, looking inconspicuous.

At breakfast, his father had joined the family, but said little, leaving Edith to drive the conversation to Guy about his school days while trying to direct food into two-year-old Elizabeth's mouth. Guy answered the questions, but one eye remained on his father, whose hands shook as he tried to manipulate his knife and put a little spread on his bread.

Edward stood after eating the smallest portion of breakfast.

"You'll be readying yourself for church now?" Edith asked. It was the kind of question familiar to Guy, an implied command, but he was not used to his mother issuing them to his father.

"Soon, my love. I must finish transcribing this document."

Edith sighed and cleared away the breakfast plates.

"Ready yourselves, and I shall be by your side when the time comes." Edward hurried up the stairs back to his study.

"Guy, put on your Sunday best. Anne, come with me." Edith picked up Elizabeth and headed upstairs towards the girls' bedroom, Anne following.

En route to his room, Guy looked in on his father. Once more, he was at his desk with the quill in his hand, which he had to support with his other hand to stop it from shaking.

Guy changed into his usual church attire, a scratchy woollen doublet which grew snugger each week, and his best hose which were a little thicker than the pairs he wore to school. He looked down at himself, adjusted the hose at the knees and then returned to the kitchen, once more peering at his father as he passed the study. He wrote furiously. When Edward reached for that removable brick, Guy hurried away, a guilty feeling washing over him at witnessing something clandestine, not meant for his eyes.

Moments later, Edith returned with the girls in their grey satin church dresses. "Guy, watch your sisters. Make sure they stay away from the fireplace."

Guy glanced out of the window to check Ingleby remained outside, then turned his attention to Anne and Elizabeth. When his mother returned, she wore her brown church dress.

A call came from the bedroom. "Go ahead with the girls. Guy and I will follow right behind you."

Edith glanced back towards the stairs as the church bells started their clangour. She took her girls by the hand and bend down to address Guy. "Go up to your father in two minutes and remind him how improper it will be for us to arrive at church without him."

Guy nodded, and his mother left with his sisters.

With the door open, the church bells sounded louder than ever.

Elsewhere in York, Dorothy, the midwife, attended to a patient. She hoped the expectant mother would not feel the need to push until the uproar of the churches and the cathedral had ceased. She knew what lay in the path of those born under the sound of such bells.

While Dorothy had these thoughts, Guy's mind swirled with concern, which only grew when he heard hooves clattering on cobblestones. He gazed out of the window to see a horse come to a stop and a gentleman dismount almost immediately outside their door.

From across the road, Ingleby sprang into action, stepping between the gentleman and the Fawkes' door.

"Can I help you, my good Sir?" Ingleby spoke in a voice different to his own.

The gentleman responded in a sneering, lordly voice. "Not unless you are a Mr Edwards Fawkes. I believe this is his abode."

"He is an associate of mine," said Ingleby.

"I must insist I see this letter delivered."

"Then you may watch me deliver it to the master of the house."

"Come on, son." Guy turned to see his father at the bottom of the stairs, now in his finest doublet, and while his face was pale and his eyes red-ringed, he looked fresher than he had in many days. "We cannot keep your mother waiting."

At that moment, Ingleby knocked.

Guy raced for the door, but his father was closer. As he opened the door, all Guy could see was the frame of Ingleby. He'd placed himself as a barrier between the man and the house.

"A letter for you, Sir," said Ingleby. He turned, took the letter from the gentleman, and handed it to Edward before stepping inside and pulling the door closed.

"Excuse me?" said Edward, no doubt perplexed about the messenger's ingress into his house.

"I am a friend, Mr Fawkes. I am known to your son, and he has made us aware of the great danger you may be in."

"Yes, but all of my worries are soon to come to an end, for this is the communication I was expecting from Walsingham."

"He may not be able to protect you from what is already set in motion." Ingleby grabbed Edward by the shoulders. "Did you know the sign of the evil eye marks your door in chalk?" Ingleby released Edward and hurried to the window, glancing to check if the messenger had left.

Edward, however, was more interested in the contents of his letter. He cracked the seal and folded back the paper, revealing the contents.

"Wait," called Ingleby, a futile word coming too late.

Guy watched the inky letters on the paper shift, coming together to form the shape of a bat, which rose from the page. With a couple of flaps of its wings, it was at his father's face.

Had Edward Fawkes been getting a reasonable amount of sleep, he may have dodged it or swiped it away. In his near-comatose state, however, he barely twitched as the inky creature disintegrated into dust and flew up his nose.

"No!" cried Ingleby, diving into Edward and knocking him to the ground.

From the floor, Edward's face contorted. His nose curled, and his nostrils flared as his eyes widened and became more bloodshot. He continued to sniff, his face twitching. The cords in his neck became prominent, and the veins on his neck and face darkened.

77

Ingleby sat astride him, trying to pin his arms to the ground.

Edward bucked his body, almost throwing Ingleby off, moving in rhythm to the incessant church bells.

For a moment, Guy could only watch as his father writhed on the ground.

Edward became tense and his head tipped back. At first, only the whites of his eyes were showing, but these soon faded to a sick and dirty grey.

"What's going on?" said Guy.

Ingleby's voice was strained as he tried to keep Edward down. "Whatever was in that letter, whatever he breathed in, it's infected him."

Edward twisted his head, making eye contact with Guy. He spoke with a deep and distorted voice. "I'll kill you. I'll kill you and your sisters, and I'll strangle your mother with your gut strings."

"You have to save him." Guy's hands came together as if in prayer.

Again, Edward bucked, almost throwing Ingleby off.

"There is no saving him. He's growing in strength. He must be vanquished."

Guy looked from his father to Ingleby and back again. A sick smile spread across his father's face as fear consumed Ingleby's.

"Is he… a demon?"

"One has taken hold of his body, a cruel and powerful one."

Guy looked at the figure on the floor. While he resembled his father, inside, he was no longer there. No love resided in those eyes, no colour in those cheeks. Even the beard looked like dried thatch. A hideous demon had taken over.

Edward's body bucked again. "You can't hold me, you feeble-armed pizzle rag. I'll dine on your soul, whoreson."

Guy backed away, leaning against the dresser as Ingleby gritted his teeth and glanced at the scabbard on his side.

Edward laughed. "Go on. Reach for your sword, see what happens! I'll consume you both. I've picked better breakfasts from my teeth." He grimaced, showing teeth no longer those of Edward Fawkes but a series of chipped and greying points, like a poorly maintained saw. From between the gaps, a black worm writhed out, fell to the floor, and disintegrated.

Guy stared at what was once his father and at Ingleby struggling to hold him down. There had to be something he could do. He looked at the candlestick on the dresser and the hymn book beside it, a bookmark on his mother's favourite page. Neither could help him.

Francis released one of Edward's hands and reached for his sword, but before his hand closed around the hilt, Edward jabbed his thumb into Ingleby's side and bucked, throwing Ingleby off to the side.

Edward and Ingleby scrambled to their feet and faced one another.

Edward laughed. "You cannot stop us, smellfungus stampcrab! A fire burns for you in Hell!" He lunged at Ingleby, who leapt back.

Still, Guy looked on. How he'd longed to take on a demon. Suddenly, Guy understood what people meant when they told him to be careful what he wished for. But he couldn't stand there and do nothing. He grabbed the hymn book and hurled it at the back of his father's head.

Edward turned and snorted, smoke billowing from his nostrils. He pointed at Guy. "Poxy half-pint nincompoop!"

From behind him, Ingleby chanted in Latin, and with a woosh, his sword blade came alive with flame.

Edward turned back to Ingleby. "Your sword is useless. Puny weapon. You'd be better to strike me with your meat stick."

Ingleby slashed at the parasitic demon. It leant back out of the way, controlling Edward's body with precision to avoid every attack.

Ingleby drew in a deep breath and the demon lunged forward, slashing down at Ingleby's sword arm. He released the blade and it clattered to the floor. Now it was his turn to dodge the demon's slashes, leaning to the left to avoid one, and ducking another. As the demon came again, slashing with one hand then the other, Ingleby twisted, avoiding one swipe, but the second caught his hip, knocking him off-balance. Edward kicked the side of Ingleby's knee, and he collapsed onto the floor.

As the demon leered over Ingleby, Guy grabbed the candlestick and tested the weight in his hand. He could crash it down on his father's head. He took a step towards what was once his father and lifted the candlestick high.

Guy knew if he left it any longer, it would be too late. He didn't want to strike his father, but he didn't want his sisters dead either. He didn't want his mother to see this, or to suffer at the hands of a demon. Besides, this wasn't his father. Those evil men, Sandys and Hastings, had got to him.

The demon turned its head a full one hundred and eighty degrees. "Guy." This time, it sounded like his father. The red had receded from his eyes. His teeth returned to their normal shape. "You'd not hurt your father, would you, my boy?"

He could see the wateriness of his eyes, the way his father looked at him when disappointed. Guy only ever wanted to please his father.

But one thing his father had taught him was not to be foolish, to listen to the lessons he had learned in school and make use of that knowledge every day. He thought of all Pulleyn had taught him. Demons are ever deceivers and tricksters, drawing in victims through false hope.

Guy broke eye contact with the demon and swung the candlestick. His weapon bounced off the demon as if it were made of cloth, not pewter. Edward grinned and shoved him, knocking him back into the dresser. The demon turned back to Ingleby who had risen to one knee and shoved him down once more. "Eternal suffering awaits." He laughed and placed one foot on Ingleby's neck.

A horrible choking noise struggled from Ingleby. He pushed at Edward's foot, but the demon's weight was greater than his strength. He cycled his legs, kicking out for anything which could give him some leverage, but there was nothing.

Ingleby's face had reddened. He let go of the foot giving up the struggle to stretch his fingers for the sword. The demon chuckled, knowing it was out of his reach.

It wasn't out of Guy's reach, though. *This is not my father,* he told himself as he cried out, and plucked the sword from the ground.

Guy leapt towards his father and swung the sword.

The demon turned, Edward Fawkes staring at Guy as the blade sliced through its neck. Head and body were twain, and both tumbled to the floor.

Guy had defeated his first demon. He'd severed his father's head.

Outside, the bells continued to toll.

Chapter 12

IN WHICH GUY FAWKES IS VISITED ONCE MORE BY THE FLOATING HEAD

Everything happened quickly after the death of Edward Fawkes and the vanquishing of the demon that had ransacked his body.

Ingleby struggled to his feet, his hands going to his throat as he made for the door. He signalled the pupils waiting nearby and issued orders. Guy, however, remained motionless. He couldn't take it all in; he knew only that action occurred all around him. His ears felt blocked. The sound of the sword cutting through the air still resonated in his head. The lack of resistance as the bladed seared through flesh and sinew remained as a memory in his muscles. The subsequent thump as his father's head hit the stone floor pounded over and over. The sword had fallen from his hand, but he neither heard it clatter, nor saw it lose its gleam and return to its original size. Guy's eyes fixed on the head of his father. His eyes remained open. Guy realised the last thing his father saw was his son wielding a giant blue-flaming sword against him. The monstrousness that overcame Edward Fawkes departed at his death. Could they have removed it without ending his life? Had they acted hastily?

Time passed, and still, Guy stood, exposed to the maelstrom of blame he'd created. Ingleby crouched beside him, and while Guy recognised the softness in his voice that tried to show compassion, the words did not hit home.

He was aware of movement in the streets, and of others coming and going, but he was unready to move on, not until a hand rested on his shoulder. When Guy looked around, he saw the face of his father.

All of Guy's senses returned to full functionality as he looked at the familiar face and realised that while it resembled his father's, it was not. The hair was longer and shaggier, the skin weather-beaten. No, this was not his father, but his uncle, Thomas, dressed in his Sunday best as a messenger dragged him from church.

"Guy, we must leave."

What Guy needed at that moment was absolute dependence, and his Uncle Thomas had always been someone he could depend upon. Thomas had taught him to ride a horse, and how to best sharpen a stake for driving into the ground when mending fences. Whenever Guy had faced doubt, Thomas had known what to say.

"No one should have to do what you did, but if you stand here, if Hasting sends his men and they find you, they'll cart you off to the castle and hang you for murder."

Those words melted Guy. His knees buckled, but before he fell, his uncle grabbed him. He allowed himself to be led to a horse-drawn carriage, and when he stepped inside, a flood of emotion hit him, for his mother and his sisters were there. No doubt someone had fetched them from church, too. His mother's eyes were wet, and she held Elizabeth close. Anne rested beside her, tucked under one of her mother's arms. There was room on that side of the carriage for Guy to nestle into, but he knew his grief and their grief was not the same; unworthy of their love, of their comfort, he sat opposite. They had not entered the house, though. That thought lifted him. Ingleby and Uncle Thomas had spared them the sight of the horrific combination of the headless body and bodiless head of a man they loved so dearly.

83

Thomas Fawkes had insufficient space in his farmhouse for four extra bodies, but his farmstead had other buildings which would offer shelter, and, over time, could be converted into something homely. Until then, the barn would have to suffice. Not that Guy would have cared where he got his head down that night. An emptiness inside ached, and somehow that hollow had pain like nothing he'd experienced before. Each breath was weighted with sobs and his face was thick with snot. Even drawing in breath was an effort. The sight of his father's head separating from his neck held a prominent place in his memory. The swish of the sword and the thump against the floor played on a continuous, punishing loop. He dared not look at or speak to his mother or his sisters. After all, he was the one who had deprived the two young girls of a father, his mother of her husband. Relief washed over him when he was invited to sleep in the stable's hayloft.

When Thomas made the offer, it didn't feel like a reprisal for his actions. No, there was something in Thomas's eyes that suggested he knew what Guy needed, that solitude would benefit more than hurting himself by spending time with those he'd hurt. Thomas put the ladder in place and watched Guy climb, then lifted the ladder, allowing Guy to pull it up with him, giving Guy control over the access to his space.

Darkness came and sleep too but fleeting and insufficient. On one of those many occasions in which he opened his eyes, it wasn't the wooden beams above that he saw, but the white of bone.

The skull of Thomas Percy hovered before him.

Even in the hayloft's darkness, it was visible, for the skull had its own luminosity.

"Guy Fawkes," Percy said.

Guy had quite forgotten the sensation of the skull speaking to him, the voice materialising inside his head rather than being heard. Despite this, its jaw moved in time to mimic speech.

"Guy Fawkes, you have experienced a terrible loss."

Guy stared at the skull. He had no suitable words available to respond to that statement.

"It will not be the last loss you suffer as you continue on this path."

Guy pondered the words: *as* you continue, not *if* you continue. Surely, he had a choice? Surely, he could walk his own route? Guy drew air between his teeth and shuffled back on his makeshift bed. "I don't want this. I don't want to be on your stupid path."

"Alas, Master Fawkes, you have already taken the first steps."

Guy shook his head. "I'm turning back."

"That's impossible. I can see your path stretching out before you."

Guy reached down beside his bed and scrunched straw between his fingers. "If it's all mapped out, what's the point in even trying?"

The head swooped in closer. "The fates define the path, not how you take it. If you falter now, that road can end, and you alongside it. But your strength will determine for how long you endure, for how long you persist."

"Why did my father have to die?"

"Your father was a good man trying to do the right thing. Such men are few. Such men live a life of peril. He stood against what he saw as wrong, and it cost him his life."

Guy launched himself from his straw bed and swung a fist at the hovering skull. He expected his fist to connect with bone, not to pass through it. His momentum carried him forward. He fell onto his knees and with a crack, the wooden slat which held his weight broke. Guy grabbed the next slat as the wood beneath him fell away, leaving his feet dangling below.

Thomas Percy floated down and then returned. "Guy, pull yourself up! There's a pitchfork sticking out of the hay. If you fall upon it, surely you will die."

Guy gripped the slat, cycling his legs to gain purchase on something, anything, but there was nothing. He reached out his hand, trying to grab hold of something with which he could pull his bodyweight up. "Help," he gasped.

"I cannot," said Percy. "I have no physical form. It's all on you."

Guy forced all of his strength into his arms and tried to pull himself up. Nothing. He considered letting go. It would be so much easier if he fell to his death.

"Guy, your father may be dead, but he did important work," Percy said, floating nearer once more. "What he discovered could bring down those evil men."

Guy struggled to drag himself to safety once more, but his legs felt heavier than ever, and their involuntary cycling sapped his strength.

"You're the only one who saw where your father hid his papers. If you die, your father's work dies with you."

Guy roared. He stretched out his arm, feeling his shoulder push almost to the point of dislocation. His fingers fell into a knothole on the next slat along. Holding onto that, with his other hand, he dragged his torso up and wriggled back to safety. At last, he lay on the secure wooden slats, panting.

"So, you do have the strength to carry on the fight." Percy hovered down close to Guy.

Guy continued to gasp, drawing as much oxygen into his lungs as possible. As much as he resented that skull floating in front of him, he knew it was right. He wasn't ready to give up. He wanted those men who had killed his father crushed.

"What do I need to do?"

"First, don't let your father's endeavours die. Collect his papers."

Guy had watched his father many evenings, slaving over the desk, finishing copying one document and hiding it within the hollow in the wall.

"And then what?"

"I know you have few memories of your grandmother, but when she passed, she left you with some trinkets."

Guy remembered the small, wooden box. "The whistle and the angel."

"A golden angel and her best whistle."

Guy wrinkled his brow. While the angel had amazed him with its level of detail, it was a trinket, and nothing more. He'd blown into the whistle to no avail.

"You'll need them," Percy said.

"But why?"

"Have faith that your grandmother passed those things onto you for a reason. When you return to your house, you must retrieve them, too."

"Will it be safe?"

Percy laughed. "Quite the opposite, young Fawkes. This may be your greatest test. Do not go alone."

Guy had nothing more to ask, and Percy nothing else to say. The skull floated up towards the beams, and when its light extinguished, Guy knew it was gone.

Guy didn't want any of this. He wanted to remain on his bed and never get out again, no matter how much straw was sticking into his back. But he couldn't stay there forever. It would only be a matter of time before his old house was ransacked or repaired. What was hidden would remain forever lost. Worse, those with ill intentions might discover it. He had to go back, and if Thomas Percy said he wasn't to go alone, he knew who he needed to take with him.

Chapter 13

IN WHICH GUY FAWKES MAKES A DARING
ESCAPE FROM HIS FORMER HOME

The visit from Thomas Percy brought little comfort. The warning of more death to come, the fear of losing more people he loved, threatened to alter Guy's relationship with his sisters forever. Guy felt heaviest while inactive and closed in with the rest of his family. It wasn't that he didn't love Anne and Elizabeth, but the fear that his love for them could be used against him made him realise he needed to keep a distance between them. Anne, however, made that difficult. With the death of his father, he had the responsibility to ensure the safety of his family. If acting like he didn't care would protect them, then so be it. So, when Anne started following him around Uncle Thomas's farm, wanting to copy everything he did, whether that be feeding the sheep or milking the cows, mending the fences or chopping the firewood, he always told her to ask her uncle.

"He said you'd show me," she'd say.

With that, Guy would hurry the chore, interacting with Anne as little as possible. She was a persistent and resilient little thing. Like Guy, her hair was also ginger, though her mother tidied it into a ponytail, which would whip back and forth whenever she shook her head in defiance. And it was her defiant streak that Guy admired. He couldn't help but smile at her when she insisted on doing things her way, and those smiles only made her stick to her brother more.

He wanted to go to Uncle Thomas for advice, but he too suffered the pain of the loss of his brother. His brother's family was a burden Uncle Thomas never desired. Thomas did so much to offer Edith Fawkes and the children support, and while Percy had suggested he might find an ally there, Guy sensed it was not the time to seek assistance.

Understanding the urgent need to visit his former home, Guy suggested he was ready to return to school only days after the horrific incident. His mother and his uncle both agreed this was a wise course of action, even daring to suggest it may help to take his mind off the terrible event. Alas, that's all Guy thought of. Indeed, his true motive to return to school was to enlist help. For if he secured his father's secret papers, then his work would not have been wasted. Maybe those papers would help gain revenge. But every moment that passed was an opportunity for someone to swoop in before him and steal those papers.

When Guy arrived at school the next morning, somewhat later than his usual arrival time as the journey from Uncle Thomas's farm was further than from his old home, he found Kit standing outside the school, his brother Jack beside him.

Jack had bulked out in the few months Guy had known him. While Kit was slender and speedy and could climb anything in an instant, Jack was more like a barrel, but sometimes a barrel was useful. They had similar faces, with round, brown eyes that suggested trustworthiness, and flat noses capable of taking a solid punch. They had jet black hair, cut much shorter than their peers, which gave them the look of outsiders.

Guy increased his speed when he saw them, even though his legs ached from the walk.

"Hey, Chum," called Jack.

Kit raced to meet him, thrusting out his hand to be shaken, mimicking their first meeting so many months before.

"How did you know I was coming back today?" Guy asked.

"Well…" Kit looked at the ground.

"He didn't," Jack added. "He's been waiting for you every day. Ever since he found out."

Kit looked up and met Guy's eyes. "I asked Francis if he could take us to see you, but he said you might need a bit more time."

"Listen," Guy said, beckoning them closer to speak in a whisper. "There's something I must do this evening. I need the help of a friend, two if possible."

Guy, Kit and Jack met at the entrance to The Shambles, having left school and taken different routes through the city. They planned to liaise at the same spot upon completion if they became separated. While much of the city was in darkness, the shops of The Shambles remained lit by lanterns and oil lamps. By late evening, the squeals of pigs had long since passed, with the slaughter completed in the mornings. The Shambles remained busy with those returning from work, either making their way back home or looking to pick up bargains from traders eager to sell the last of their day's slaughtered and butchered products.

Arriving from the south would mean they'd have a clear view of the house before they got too close. Regardless, with each footstep, Guy's anxiety grew. He knew not what to expect when he arrived at his old home. He heard Uncle Thomas talk about reclaiming the body, so he didn't expect that to be there, and he'd collected their essential possessions, but the furniture should still be present and the trinkets and decorations, but how would it feel to be back where something so awful had happened? What crude sign of their struggle might be left behind? What if someone had beaten them to his prize?

Once they reached Stonegate, Guy urged Jack and Kit to stop.

"What is it? Demons?" Kit said.

"No," said Guy. "We should be careful in case anyone is watching the house."

Jack looked up and down the street for the telltale signs of demon worshippers or their familiars. He scrutinised the gutters for black cats, rats, or other demonic spies. Once satisfied, he gave Guy a nod, and they continued.

The front of the house was clear. Part of him, perhaps, had wanted to see someone standing guard, something that would stop him from entering, for if there was a threat, they would have to postpone their mission; with no weapons and little expertise, they were ill-prepared to enter a dangerous situation.

Guy approached his old home. So many times, he'd walked along Stonegate with his father by his side. Never again would he do that. Never again would he have that sensation of absolute security that came when his father took hold of his hand. He had to stop those responsible. He had to avenge his father's death.

Despite what his uncle had said, he expected to see his father's body on the floor when he pushed the door open. However, it was so dark, they saw nothing. They had a supply of candles which Kit had secured during the school day. What Guy saw when he lit a candle was worse than his father's body would have been. A blood shadow on the stone slabs outlined the story of the room's gruesome recent history.

As Guy stared at the stain, Kit's hand rested on his shoulder. Even at that early age, he hoped he had a friend to depend on no matter how horrendous the circumstances. Guy scanned the rest of the room. Yes, they'd had visitors. The drawers in the dresser hung open, and someone had displaced the trinkets on the shelves. He had to hope they'd not found his father's secret hiding place.

Before leaving the front room, Guy drew in a deep breath. With it came the odours that had defined his young life: the charred remains in the fireplace, the residue of the last meal cooked on the flames, and freshly laundered sheets. Present smells, however, overpowered those of the past, the metallic tang of blood coupled with an earthy corruption. That smell stirred Guy's desire for revenge. It was the corruption that had taken his father, and his father's notes could bring that corruption to an end. He climbed the stairs and entered the small room that had recently been his father's study. The remains of the desk lay in ruins. Papers littered the floor. A black stain on the wall running towards the ground showed where someone had hurled the inkwell in anger. Someone had already come looking for his father's secret.

When watching his father, the hidden brick's location was obvious. Without the desk as a guide for height and with only candlelight to help, Guy had no choice but to trace each brick and test for movement.

"What're you after?" asked Jack.

Guy poked and prodded at the brickwork. "There's a loose brick."

"Can we help?"

"Keep an eye out."

Kit approached the window while Jack stood close to Guy, providing light with a candle.

Moments later, Guy squealed in triumph. He'd found the brick and was working it out.

"I hear horses," Kit said.

"I've got to get something from my room. Jack, can you pull this brick out and grab what's behind it?"

Guy left the brick half out and dashed up the stairs to his room. Uncle Thomas had collected his clothes, so his wardrobe was empty. Only a few decorative items remained in the room. Guy had shoved the heirlooms left to him by his grandmother under his bed only weeks earlier, weeks that now seemed like many years in the past.

As he got down onto his belly, Kit called again: "They're coming in!"

Guy dragged the box out from under the bed and sat up. He opened the box and grabbed the whistle, which he slipped into the pouch attached to his belt. The golden angel, however, was too bulky, so he held onto it.

"Have we got time to get out?" called Guy.

He heard footsteps on the stairs before Kit appeared in the doorway. "No, they're huddled around the door."

Thomas Percy had warned this would be dangerous. What would those men do if they found them? He considered the layout of the house and what the men were after. Surely, they'd not concern themselves with a child's bedroom.

"Quick," he said, beckoning Kit with his arm. "Hide in here."

Jack appeared behind Kit, a pile of papers in one hand, the brick in the other.

"Did you get everything?" Guy asked.

Jack nodded.

Guy grabbed the papers and tucked them inside his hose. He placed the angel down to tighten his belt to make sure those precious papers couldn't escape. As he grabbed the angel once more, a gush of wind flew in, extinguishing their candles. The invaders battered the door open and it collided with the wall.

The sound of heavy feet on stone sounded from below. Stern but frantic voices followed. "You sure this is the place?" The voice was deep and menacing.

Someone else cleared their throat. "This is the address Hastings gave us."

"Didn't he already send a crew?"

"Aye, but they didn't find anything."

"What we gonna do?"

"Ransack the place. If we find it before Hastings arrives, he might reward us."

Jack gasped, then immediately cupped his mouth as if he could put the sound back.

"Get in the wardrobe." Guy pointed at Jack. "Kit, under the bed."

Jack stepped inside the cabinet and pulled the door closed behind him.

Kit and Guy dropped onto their bellies and shimmied backwards under the bed, facing the door. Moments later, feet stomped up the stairs. Guy's room wasn't the first they entered, but a pair of boots appeared at the door a few minutes later.

"This looks like the boy's room," said the man with the deep voice. He took a couple of steps further in, so he was standing beside the wardrobe. "Is there any point looking in here?"

A grating sound came from below as one of the men cleared his throat again before speaking. "No, come back downstairs. Hastings is here."

The intruders plodded back down the stairs.

A third voice spoke, sneering, lordly, and surely that of Hastings. "Did you find anything?"

"Nothing, Sir."

"And what say the reports?"

"A body was taken from the premises. Then a head. The witness, a neighbour, confirmed it belonged to Fawkes."

"Someone must have beheaded Fawkes after his demonic turn."

"Will you hunt them down, Sir?"

"No need. It was Fawkes who wrote to Walsingham, Fawkes who held the evidence. With him gone, he cannot share it."

"Might the evidence still be here?"

"Perhaps. Burn it to the ground. Let fire feast on any remaining evidence."

"We've got to get out," Kit whispered.

Guy grabbed Kit's arm to stop his squirming free. "If we go down now, they'll kill us."

"If we stay, they'll burn us alive."

"We'll have to run out after. They won't stick around to watch it burn."

"Are you sure that's safe?"

94

"What other choice have we got?"

Guy listened to the noise below. Something smashed, followed by a crash. He visualised toppling furniture. Only when it again became silent did Guy worry.

He shuffled out from under the bed. "Get ready."

What surprised Guy was how quickly the heat from the fire reached him. No sooner had it been ignited than a whoosh of hot air tore through the house.

Kit slithered out and Guy opened the wardrobe door.

Jack looked back at him, his face white with surprise. He still held the brick in one hand. "What's going on?"

"They've set fire to the house. Let's go."

Guy turned towards the stairs.

"Have they gone?" asked Jack.

"Of course they've gone," said Guy. "What kind of fools would remain in a burning building?"

Guy and Kit stared at each other.

"Come on!" cried Jack, pushing Guy towards the door, and dragging Kit alongside him.

Guy ran down one flight of stairs, but when he turned to take the second flight, he stopped, mesmerised. Flames flickered on the walls of the ground floor. The magnificent heat drew moisture from his skin. His exposed flesh first felt the intense heat before extreme warmth spread to all parts of his body. In the thrall of fire, he watched the flames dance on the furniture, he watched the flames lick at the walls, he watched the flames creep onto each floorboard. The fire grew like a living force more powerful than anything he'd ever known, an ancient god worthy of great reverence. Each creeping lick of flame lured him to become part of something eternal.

"Don't just stand there," Kit said with a nudge, "move!"

Guy woke to the great roar of the fire, snapping him from his reverie. Great peril trumped the wonder of the flames. He drew in a sudden breath, coughed the smoke immediately back out again and stumbled down the next step.

Shocked by how far the fire had advanced, Guy stopped on the stairs again. Between them and the exit was a maze of flame. Hasting's men had pulled the dresser from the wall and thrown the chairs around the room to help the fire spread.

Every second he spent considering the route out, the flames grew stronger and the air thicker with smoke. He coughed and realised there was little time to waste. He ran to the bottom of the steps. A chair blocked the path, but the fire had not caught the front legs yet. He kicked at it, clearing the path a little further. The door was aflame, and the dresser beside it consumed by fire.

"What do we do?" asked Guy, looking back at his friends.

"Window," said Kit, pointing at the clear path towards it.

"How're we gonna get through?"

"I still have this." Jack lifted the brick.

That was all the encouragement he needed. They headed for the window, and, when close, Jack hurled the brick. Glass tinkled to the ground, but flames swelled as the oxygen from outside fed the fire. It pulled all around, licking at their backs and singeing their hair. Smoke billowed around them, stinging their eyes and sticking to the inside of their lungs, drawing out racking coughs.

"Get low," Jack said. "Uncle Francis says in fire, you always keep low."

The three crouched and started for the window. Shallow breaths came slightly easier down there.

From above, flaming chunks fell as the beams lost their battle against the fire. With it came an awful creak. Above, another beam cracked. Guy yanked Kit by the back of his neck and shoved him toward the window. With his elbow, he knocked out the remaining glass in the frame and scrambled out.

As the beam fell, a chunk of splintered wood bounced back from the floor, striking Guy on the side of the head. He felt himself toppling, but then he was suddenly righted. Jack's grip on his arm held him firm. He pointed toward the window, urging him to get out, but Guy heard nothing but ringing in his ears. It was like hearing those church bells once more, the ones that resounded so loudly the moment he'd ended his father's life, a moment that happened only days ago but would last for an eternity in his mind. He looked once more at the flames above, the flames swallowing the furniture, and the flames crawling the walls. It felt like destiny to be consumed by them, too, but Jack wouldn't release his grip. Jack turned him round and practically threw him through the window.

Guy landed on the glass on the road which crunched beneath him, and a jab of pain hit his hand as he rolled over. He dropped the angel and studied the source of pain. A shard of glass stuck out of the palm. He winced as he yanked it out, then covered the wound with his other hand. Outside the air was cool, but when he breathed his lungs burnt and he coughed it back out again. He felt the wetness of the ground seeping into his clothes and stood beside Kit, facing the house, waiting. Jack stood at the window. His foot touched the frame, then something clawed him back in. He came again, his knee on the window ledge, but when he placed his hands on the frame to pull himself through, flames ripped them away, and again he fell back.

"Head first," Kit cried.

Jack came once more, drawing breath into rasping lungs as he reached the window. Guy grabbed one arm, and Kit the other, and they pulled him the rest of the way out, falling back onto the street. Jack's hose were aflame. He lay in a nearby puddle to extinguish the fire. Likewise, Kit and Guy rolled on the ground, extinguishing the last of the embers on their clothing. They sat in the street thankful for every breath, even if their lungs coughed it back out. Soot covered their face, and their clothes were full of holes, eaten away by the flames.

Another crash from inside sent a plume of dust and smoke belching out of the window. Guy glanced up to see part of the roof give way. He checked the bundle of papers tucked into his belt. Nothing seemed to have come loose, but they may have become a little wet from the damp ground. He'd recovered what he needed and escaped to tell the tale.

The collapse of the roof and the spread of flame to neighbouring properties had drawn attention, with some hurrying to the nearest well, others pointing at the chaos and discussing with neighbours, sharing interested coos.

"Oi, you!" came a shout from further up the street. It was the man with the deeper voice who had been in the house.

"Run!" called Kit.

Guy stopped only to grab the gold angel and they took off back the way they came, back through the same streets and then among the crowds in The Shambles.

A woman stood in the street. "In here!" came a shout. A low door opened in one of the butchers. Kit ducked inside, and the others followed. The smell of pigs and butchery struck them, and as the door slammed closed, they found themselves in darkness. They had to crouch, as the small passage was low. A stone wall penned them in on one side, and a wooden one on the other. From his visits to the butchers on The Shambles, Guy realised it was a pig door they'd gone through which would lead to the rear of the property where the butchery was done, but the sound of movement in the dark indicated they weren't alone: a snuffling sound came first followed a grunt.

Moments later, light poured into the room from a hatch above. Two pairs of eyes peered at them, one from above, one to the side. The pig beside them oinked and shuffled past Guy, bristling him with its rough hide.

"What have we got here?" said the woman, peering through the hatch with a bloody knife in her hand and a look of menace on her face.

Chapter 14

IN WHICH GUY FAWKES FEARS JUMPING FROM THE FIRE INTO THE FRYING PAN

Before we move on, you need to understand in York at that time, there were a great many people who would have turned Guy and his friends over to the authorities without so much as a moment's hesitation, especially if there was a promise of a golden reward. As Guy looked into the eyes of the woman above, he wondered if they'd be safer with the men who'd given chase. But there was more than menace in the eyes of that woman, Guy knew it. He thought he recognised her too. There was something familiar about those thick, dark curls in her hair and her broad face. Before he could make the connection, she pulled the hatch shut and they were in darkness once more, save for the meagre light that poured through the knotholes in the wooden wall.

Outside, footsteps clattered first on the other side of the half-door, then within the shop.

"Did you see three boys pass by?" It was the deep, booming voice of their chaser.

"What if I have?" came the voice of the woman. Again, Guy struggled with a memory.

"I would have thought your stay in the castle would have loosened your lips. Hastings can have you locked up again in a heartbeat."

"Be off with you. I saw no boys pass."

Guy heard a scramble of movement and a gasp. He shuffled onto his side to peer through a knothole. The woman faced him, their chaser behind, one arm around her waist, the other holding a dagger close to her throat. "Maybe the feel of steel will jog your memory."

The woman gritted her teeth. "No boys came through the door and I saw none pass either."

The man withdrew the knife and released the woman, shoving her away. "No, harbouring thieves isn't your trade. If it were heretics, we'd turn this place over."

Still carrying the remnants of smoke in his lungs, Guy felt the overwhelming urge to cough. He gulped in air and tried to swallow away the persistent tickle as the conversation continued.

"Be my guest. You'll find nothing but pig blood and bones. I might have a bit of offal for you."

"Tush! You'll be back in the depths of the castle before long, mark me."

With the conversation over, Guy listened for the sound of exiting steps before he coughed and spluttered into his hand. As he was doing so, once more, light returned as the hatch slid open.

This time Guy recognised their saviour. Until recently, he and his father had been regular visitors to the shop. Of course, this was before his father had forbidden him to return, and yet, here he was once more in Clitherow's Butchers, with Margaret Clitherow looking down on him.

"So, thieves, are you?" Margaret said.

"It's not thieving if you're taking from your own home." Guy touched the pile of papers through his clothes.

"That looks valuable." Margaret nodded towards the golden angel Guy gripped in one hand.

Guy pulled it closer to his body.

"Relax. I've no interest in taking from you." Margaret sniffed at the air. "You smell like you've been smoked."

"Nearly burned alive, more like." Kit reached for the hatch, ready to climb out.

"No, you don't." Margaret slid it closed again, and there was a sound of a bolt sliding into place.

Kit pushed, but the hatch wouldn't budge. "Help," he called, but before the others could join him, a small door opened on the other side, leading into the back room.

"What do you think I'm doing?" Margaret said. "But if you don't keep that racket down, you'll be beyond help."

The pig passed through the hatch first, and Jack followed on hands and knees.

Kit grabbed Guy's leg before he could do likewise. "If we go through there, she'll carve us up and sell us with that pig."

"No…" Guy started.

"Didn't you hear her say we're already smoked? She'll slice us and fry us and serve us with eggs for breakfast."

"Come on," Jack called.

"I know her," Guy said. "I used to come in here with Father." A pang of sadness hit him. "It'll be all right."

Guy crawled through into a room lit by a single window and a candle in the corner. An overpowering stench of blood brought water into his mouth that he had to choke back down. They were in another pen, but Margaret held open the gate through which they could leave. Margaret had corralled the pig to the opposite end, for he wasn't to be so lucky.

"You must be Edward's boy." Margaret placed her hand on Guy's shoulder.

"You remember my father coming here?"

"I knew him better than a customer, my boy. But when the dark eyes turned on me, I told him to keep his distance." Margaret sighed. "So, what did you need to go back to your house for?"

Those papers seemed to dig into Guy's side and for a moment he wondered if it were a sign that he should surrender them to Margaret Clitherow and be done with it. Instead, he held up the gold angel.

"A worthy treasure indeed." Margaret's eyes dropped to his side. "If there was anything else of import, I'm sure you'll see it's looked after."

Kit stepped forward. "Can we go now, Miss?" He pinched his nose. "It stinks in here." Kit stared past Margaret at the knives on the table opposite.

"Not a fan of butchery?"

Kit looked from the table to the exit.

"You'd best stay a little longer. They'll still be searching for you, but it's good you don't trust me, good that you keep looking for the best way out."

Jack looked nervously around, and Kit stepped forward. "Why? What are you going to do?"

Margaret smiled "Me? Nothing. But prepare for every eventuality. You boys go to Saint Peter's?"

The three boys looked from one to the other.

"You don't have to say anything. You look like the sort that might end up having to stay behind."

Again, the three boys shared nervous glances.

"Yellow eyes hath the beast, and coarse hair on his clawed hands."

Kit gasped. Guy recognised the lines as quoted by Pulleyn.

"You're right to stay tight-lipped, but you give yourselves away when you don't say nothing either. You've got to learn to keep control of your faces or that look'll get you killed."

The three of them stared at the floor.

"We move in similar circles, you and I," said Margaret. "We have our concerns about Hastings and Sandys, too."

"Hastings had my house burnt down," Guy said.

"And almost with you in it. I hope going back was worth it."

Again, Guy pondered giving up his papers.

"I know what you boys do, and I know it has its limits. How'd you like to work for me? I'll show you how to do more than butcher a pig with those knives, and there's plenty more I could teach."

None of them answered immediately, so Margaret left the boys to ponder the offer while she exited through the door at the back that led upstairs, no doubt to the living quarters. She returned with her husband, John Clitherow, the master butcher, and they came to an arrangement. Working simultaneously would be impossible. There wasn't enough work and having more people in the shop than necessary would arouse suspicion. But they could come on different evenings after school to help with the cleaning; during this time, Margaret would train them.

Once they'd reached an accord, night had fallen. John sent one of his servants, a young man by the name of Peter, to accompany the boys home, first to the school to drop off Kit and Jack, and then to Uncle Thomas's farm.

Upon reaching the farm, Uncle Thomas welcomed them into his small farmhouse. Guy's mother and sisters sat by the fire.

"We were worried about you, Guy," Edith said.

"My master offers his apologies," Peter said, before explaining the offer of an apprenticeship to Thomas.

"Is that what you want to do, Guy?" Edith asked.

Guy picked up the distinct impression that his mother would be happy if she saw less of him. "I am keen to learn, Mother."

Thomas gave Peter a nod. "It will be good for the boy to do some work. At his age, there is plenty of time to choose a profession, and learning the skills of butchery will put him in good stead. I can make use of those skills here, too."

With that, Peter left.

"Your uncle has been busy while you've been out," Edith said. She beckoned Guy to follow and led him to the barn. Thomas had constructed new walls to make the space cosier, almost resembling a home. It was notable there was insufficient space for him, but at least Uncle Thomas had repaired the hayloft and placed the bed in a much safer position. Guy climbed up, and once alone, he pulled the papers from where he'd secured them. He flicked through the bundle. In the darkness, he had no idea what was written on them, and even if he had the light to see, he doubted whether the words would mean much to him. He knew what he had to do, though. As he'd seen his father spend night after night making copies of these documents, he would do likewise. Even if he did not understand what the words meant, he'd make his own set, and only then would he hand what he had to Pulleyn. He would not let go of what his father had died for without making sure he kept hold of that knowledge, too.

Chapter 15

IN WHICH THE YEARS ROLL EVER
ONWARDS

Not every year of Guy Fawkes' life was significant, so I'll give you a bit of a potted history, a flavour of what was going on in young Guy's life at those times. After he rescued those papers and after he met Margaret, his life settled, and as such, we can hurry through a little. Time moved on. As Guy spent his evenings duplicating the documents, the winter gave way to spring, and Guy turned eight. As summer approached, he passed his duplicated bundle to Pulleyn. The numbers being trained in the caverns beneath Saint Peters blossomed. Guy continued his book-learning alongside Kit and Jack. Pulleyn had them work on a translation of *A Tabernacle of Fleshmongering Spirits* which had described terrible demon kings, such as Vercan, Arcan, and Sarabotres Rex. As fascinating as this was, Guy thirsted for more. The older students whispered of nightly battles with the forces of the underworld. When those whispers reached Guy, he longed to join the action. Oswald bulked out from the once rakish figure he had been. A deep scar, an angry purple smear, ran down one cheek, one of many souvenirs from his myriad encounters. Lewisham disappeared from the school altogether, with Pulleyn refusing to share details of the "unfortunate incident" with the younger members of the school community. As much as Guy longed to take on the demonic threat, his time at Clitherow's Butchers eased his agony over his lack of combat training at school. Guy put his time with Margaret to good use, not only learning how to cut and slice with a knife, but how to wield a short blade as a weapon, too. He also learnt how best to maintain a blade. He took this skill home, becoming responsible for looking after Uncle Thomas's knives and butchering his livestock when the time came. Margaret also taught the boys how to imbue their weapons with a touch of the demon-defying power Guy had witnessed with Ingleby's sword, showing them how to bathe it in holy water to make it accursed to demons.

Ingleby made York his permanent home as summer gave way to autumn, taking over some teachings of lore in the school and some of Lewisham's former duties. Soon it was winter once more.

Similarly, 1578 became 1579, became 1580, became 1581. Working with Pulleyn and Oswald, Guy gained a better understanding of the spiritual plane and learned how to tune out the everyday voices of the restless dead that spoke to him. He could cleanse his mind of all of the aggravation and leave the channel open to listen for signs of demonic activity, or for other unquiet spirits, such as Percy speak to him.

Life on Uncle Thomas's farm was peaceful. Guy enjoyed it more than he ever had living within York's walls, even if that walk to school was time-consuming. Uncle Thomas had constructed a second home for Edith, Anne, and Elizabeth. While Guy had a room there, he preferred the hayloft. Raising the bed off the beams a foot decreased the chance of spending the night with vermin. Guy had also learnt carpentry skills from his uncle with which he'd made his own set of drawers where he kept his clothes and his scant other possessions, including one gold angel and one whistle made from bone.

Guy felt more comfortable in the home of his uncle than that of his mother. While together they talked from time to time, Guy's guilt over his father's death had built a wall between them. He told himself this was for the best: living the life of a demon hunter could put them at risk. Alas, as aloof as he tried to be around his family, Anne remained difficult to shrug off. Guy had reached the grand old age of ten, fast approaching eleven, and Anne was eight. She was almost as tall as he and every bit as eager to learn the skills needed to run a farm. She even took an interest in carpentry, stealing a small paring knife to whittle small toys for Elizabeth out of wood. Anne often sought Guy in the evenings and liked to sit and talk to him, and while Guy could have pulled up his ladder to maintain privacy, he never did. He enjoyed seeing her mop of ginger hair bob into view as she reached the upper rungs.

And while much had remained the same, one day in April as Guy's eleventh birthday approached, he received news of a forthcoming change, one of huge significance, one that left him shocked, but more than that, disappointed.

After school, which had moved on from the days of learning Latin phrases by rote to carrying out mathematical equations and more detailed composition, Guy and Kit were with Francis Ingleby. Jack, at twelve, had progressed to the early stages of combat training, much to his glee and Kit's disdain.

Ingleby was approaching the end of a lesson on the summoning of demons: "It is common for those wishing to summon a demon to give a sacred offering." Ingleby had explained in the past about feeding familiars, and how the tempters and ensnarers would often appear as hungry animals looking for those of like mind to draw into their cabals. "Therefore, at church services, during the Eucharist, you must be vigilant. Ensure that not so much as a crumb of God's bread leaves the holy place palmed by a would-be deserter from the faith. Sacrilegious acts tempt demons, and what could be more debase than tainting the body of Christ by feeding it to one in league with his enemies?"

Guy and Kit nodded at one another, a silent agreement to have their eyes open to such corruption even during religious worship.

Ingleby had not finished, "There is an account," he said, picking up another ancient book, the cover torn and the pages thin, "of one here in this very county who fed to a black and warty toad the sacramental bread of our Lord week after week until it grew fat. After every church service, he found this corrupt creature waiting for him and with each feast, it grew larger, more deformed, until two additional legs sprouted from its side. It was at this point that the feeder called upon the lords of darkness, and so pleased they were with his offering, that they rewarded him with the services of the aerial powers. With these, he drew the water from all wells but his own, forcing the rest of the community to beg him to allow them to take water from his spring, which continued to flow with life. This power he used to extort coin from his poorest neighbours, and those that couldn't pay, he took into his home, carrying out acts of extraordinary wickedness."

Ingleby had a habit of leaving key details of the stories to his pupil's imagination. When he paused, Pulleyn arrived to fill the gap, Oswald by his side.

"I trust you were about finished?" Pulleyn said.

Ingleby stepped back and allowed Pulleyn to take the floor. It was strange seeing Oswald beside him in this manner. It was as it used to be in the early years of Guy and Kit's teaching; since Oswald's transformation had been severe. His hair colour had changed from that almost white shade of blond to a mousy brown. The scar on his cheek, which had remained that livid shade of purple for so long, was now a raised ridge, partially hidden by the beard he had grown. His eyes were sunken as if, in his youth, Oswald had witnessed one too many horrors. He'd developed a nervous twitch, his head jerking from one dark corner to another.

"Oswald wanted to tell you his news himself." Pulleyn opened his palm, inviting Oswald to speak.

Oswald stepped forward. "I will soon leave here to travel across the sea to continue my studies in Rome."

"No!" Guy called, then cupped his hand over his mouth. Oswald had been Guy's window into the upper tier of demon activity at the school, for in those quiet times when the library was otherwise unoccupied, Oswald had kept Guy abreast of the developing situation with Sandys and Hastings. It was Oswald who revealed what Edward Fawkes' documents had allowed them to discover. All over York, under the guise of church business, Sandys and Hastings had purchased properties that aligned with the rumoured locations of ancient long-buried artefacts, of places where the connection to the underworld was strongest, of places where they could tap into dark powers. Over the last three years, through countless battles, the school had discovered many witches, true witches, those that use their connection with the dark side for their own gain and to bring chaos. They'd sent countless demons to Hell, places of power were once again shut off, and they'd recovered forbidden artefacts before they fell into the hands of witches with dark intentions.

Oswald crouched beside Guy. "This will not be the last we see of each other, of that I am sure." Alas, maintaining eye contact for that short duration proved a challenge for Oswald, and Guy doubted the honesty of his statement.

Kit leaned forward. "Are there loads of demons to kill in Rome?"

Oswald stood and shook his head. "My path now lies in another direction. Much wisdom there is in Italy. I hear God's call and know he will take me into his arms there."

Guy pointed toward the hidden library, and then above to the school's main library. "But you've got all the books in the world here. What do you need to know that you can't find here?"

Oswald smiled, and the darkness lifted from his face a little. "Why."

"I need to understand why you're leaving us, that's why."

"I wasn't asking a question; I was answering yours. What I need to know is *why*. *Why* are we embroiled in this eternal fight? *Why* did it start? If we win, what comes after?"

"And all the books in the school won't answer that?"

Oswald sighed. "I've looked." He stepped back, urging Pulleyn to once more take the lead.

"Oswald is not leaving us right away. He will remain in York until Walsingham's visit has passed. He may even follow that party down to the capital before heading to the coast to seek transportation across the sea.

Walsingham! The very name still brought the hot blood rushing to Guy's face, for it was he that his father had written to for support. Instead, a poisoned letter had arrived. Guy had learnt much of Walsingham in the intervening years. It was his name on a thousand death warrants, he that hunted healers and called them witches, he with his

109

insidious network of spies that listened at every door and whispered their secrets into his eager ears. As much as it was his role to protect Queen Elizabeth from those that worked against her, Walsingham also poisoned her mind with lies, inventing tales of smote witches, when the whole time he was in league with the dark forces. Once, in the library, Oswald had whispered to Guy that he believed Walsingham himself would one day be unfaithful to his queen. Rumours claimed he sought a route to place a dark prince on the throne. By 1581, the most desired path—by seeding the queen—was impossible, for she remained adamant she would rule alone, needing no man at her side. Oswald revealed that Queen Elizabeth was a woman of strong mind and indefatigable spirit, for many times Walsingham had tempted her with incubi, but each she saw through as if their very horns showed, as if their very charm dripped away in her presence and rendered them gibbering meat-sacks.

If these tales of the Queen's strength were supposed to inspire Guy, they failed, for they brought him great fear. If Walsingham could get close enough to the Queen to tempt her, then he was powerful indeed.

But for the first time, Guy had foreknowledge of Walsingham's visit to York. He would not pass up the opportunity to look upon the man who had written his father's death warrant.

Chapter 16

IN WHICH GUY FAWKES CONSIDERS THE EVIL TRIO

While Guy had never come face-to-face with Walsingham, he had crossed paths with both Sandys and Hastings many times. He always feared Sandys would recognise him as the son of Edward Fawkes, remembering that he'd bumped into him at Bootham Bar all those years ago. The Archbishop of York, however, never gave him so much as a second glance that suggested recognition.

With both his school and his home outside the city's walls, Guy didn't spend as much time inside the city as in his infant years, but his apprenticeship continued at Clitherow's Butchers, even at those times in which Margaret found herself detained at the castle. The paperwork stated it was for hiding Catholic priests in secret places in her abode, but in truth, it was because those demon-loving lords that ran the city suspected she was part of the underground plot to oust them. Had they so much as a shred of evidence, Margaret, too, would have found her head adorning one of the city's gates. Whenever the men came looking, there was never sufficient evidence to find her guilty.

While Margaret was detained, John offered training, focusing on the skills of a butcher, with a significant increase in cleaning duties.

The former assistant, Peter, had left to open his own butcher's shop, leaving more work for Guy.

Working at Clitherow's and attending church were the primary reasons Guy visited York, and it was in his journeys in and out of the city that he saw Sandys most. Whenever soldiers placed new heads on the gates, Sandys was there. If anyone was brave enough to question Sandys' presence at such barbaric events, he would claim his purpose was to grant sinners forgiveness so their souls could pass on. He would state that their physical remains would now do God's work and stop ill-thinking men from taking the same dark path.

Guy suspected Sandys' motives were more sinister. Whenever Sandys looked up at a freshly placed head, a crooked smile spread across his face, and that one-eyed cat would weave its way around his legs, disappearing and reappearing from within the folds of his robes.

It took six or seven spying attempts for Guy to realise his purpose there; when that first morsel of flesh dropped from a fresh skull, the cat, Sandys' familiar, hopped over to it and lapped it up. Shortly after, Sandys would make his excuses and leave. What better treat could there be for a familiar, for one so close to the demonic powers, than the taste of the flesh of their enemies? No wonder the dark lords were so inclined to lend Sandys such power.

Hastings, too, was often in York. The 3rd Earl of Huntingdon, to give Henry Hastings his proper title, used the city as a base for much of his time as president of the Council of the North, that administrative body set up to uphold the law of the land in areas far from London, extending the reach of the monarch and quashing any hints of insurrection. For every death warrant that Walsingham had signed for residents of York, Hastings had signed three. It was some of the men that he damned to death that Sandys' familiar feasted upon. Based at King's Manor within the city, it was Hastings' habit to spend much of his time on horseback on the streets, dressed in his customary robe bearing the insignia of a Knight of the Garter, and his comically large and stiff ruff. With him always was a small army of soldiers, also on horseback, wearing battle-ready armour. Many in the city mocked his officious manner and his heavy-handed entourage, but not openly, for they feared a public beating. Closer still to Hastings than his guards was another who accompanied him always, a sick-skinned and skeletal man whose attire remained minimal regardless of the weather, both hose and doublet the same shade of scarlet. A thick gold thread ran through his outfit. His feet appeared small, almost ridiculously so. His shoes tapered to a point, suggesting he either lacked toes or the end of his shoes was for show. On his head, he wore a coif of the same whiteness as his flesh to cover his balding skull, a sight which had brought tears to many a child. While no one heard him speak, he rode close enough to Hastings to whisper in his ear.

Oswald had described this man long before Guy saw him, and he made one thing very clear: this was not a man at all, but a familiar. Hastings demanded demonic counsel at all times, and this creature remained in human form, acting as a constant conduit between Hastings and the underworld.

Guy knew the premises Hastings visited most on his travels well. The addresses were all listed on his father's documents–properties purchased for myriad evil purposes. Indeed, when Guy wanted to watch Hastings, he'd loiter at those addresses. Guy liked to look upon his enemies. He needed to know who he was preparing to battle, whose destruction he sought.

This opportunity to see Walsingham for the first time would allow him to decide if he was truly an enemy. Guy's father had spoken of cleansing York. Guy now considered this his duty. Sandys and Hastings caused most of the city's terrors. But if Walsingham combined with them to create a demonic trio, then he, too, would have to face vengeance.

At his level in the grand scheme of demon hunters, Guy was still a long way from being informed of plans. Oswald only gave him details of what happened later, but this time, Guy believed he would clue him in as a last act of kindness. Maybe, if all three were together, Pulleyn would orchestrate a strike to lift York from the scourge of demon-worshipping witches for good. The news would get back to Queen Elizabeth, and she would make them all knights. They'd be heroes.

As the day of Oswald's departure neared, Guy found him in the library.

"Can you tell me again why you're leaving?" Guy asked. It wasn't that he didn't remember, but he needed a way into the conversation.

Oswald explained once more his desire to study philosophy.

"And when are you leaving?" Guy asked.

"Once Walsingham's visit is over."

"And what are we doing while he's here?"

Oswald opened his mouth, and Guy thought, for a second, he had a chance of getting some information.

Then Oswald smiled. "You know I can't tell you." He moved away from the shelf he had been perusing.

Guy followed. "But you tell me so much."

"Yes, after the event. I can't give you our plans."

Guy moved around into Oswald's eye-line. "So, you're telling me there's a plan?"

Oswald sighed. "If I confirm there's a plan, will you leave me alone?"

"Of course." Guy smiled.

"Then there's a plan. I might have time to give you some details once it's over."

He might not witness the events as they unfolded, but knowing they planned to act against his enemies was something. If Walsingham was certain to be in the city over the next couple of weeks, he would visit the Council of the North. All he had to do was keep his eyes on King's Manor, or Hastings' route around the city, and he'd finally look upon the face of his potential enemy.

Chapter 17

IN WHICH HASTINGS OVERSHADOWS WALSHINGHAM'S ARRIVAL IN YORK

While the opportunity to set eyes on Walsingham brought him some satisfaction, Guy couldn't help but feel a pang of disappointment about not doing more. Once again, he'd find out about the key events in York long after they occurred. He trudged away from the school, toeing a stone along the path.

"Guy, wait," came a shout.

He turned to see Kit racing towards him.

"Will you be in York on Sunday?" Kit asked. He drew in several deep breaths in recovery from his sprint.

"Sunday?" Guy wrinkled his brow. "What for?"

Kit held up a finger and took in several more deep breaths. "Weren't you talking to Oswald?"

"I was."

"Didn't he tell you anything?"

Guy's mouth dropped, and he gave Kit a playful shove on the shoulder. "No! What did he tell you?" As much as Guy's face tried to show mocking ire, a needle of hurt pained his gut. How could Oswald tell Kit what he'd refused Guy?

"Oh no, Oswald didn't tell me anything."

And with relief, the pain disappeared.

"But Jack did. He's going to be a sentry, watching for Walsingham at one of the city gates."

"This Sunday?"

Kit nodded. "Aye. Uncle Francis intercepted a messenger. He's coming on Sunday and will be in York to conduct business for a few days."

An image of his father's face as the poison demon entered his body struck him. Guy sunk into a crouching position.

Kit rested one hand on Guy's shoulder.

Guy glanced up at Kit. "Do you know the plan? Are they going to capture him? Quiz him? Find out if he's in league with demons?"

Kit shrugged. "I only know what Jack told me. He'll be keeping watch at Micklegate Bar, and will give the shout to the horseback rider who'll spread the word. What happens next is a mystery."

"So, are *you* going into the city on Sunday?" Guy asked.

"Uncle Francis said I'm not to, but Jack said as long as I keep out of the way, I wouldn't get in any trouble. You?"

"You can count on it."

Sunday seemed a month away instead of only three days. Guy slept poorly, focused badly at school, and Uncle Thomas twice had to give him a shout when chopping wood for the fire to avoid a tragic accident.

And when Sunday arrived, Guy woke before sunrise, hours before necessary. He started his chores early, hoping that keeping himself occupied would speed the hours away, only to find that he'd exhausted all necessary business before his mother had begun breakfast.

After a walk to clear his head, Guy returned, consumed a breakfast gone cold, and then changed into his church attire, for it was still his family's practice to travel the short distance into the city in their wagon to visit Saint Michael le Belfrey. Only after the service would he have time to roam the city, meet with Kit, and spy upon Walsingham.

But Guy put that out of his mind during the service. Instead, he observed members of the congregation, seeking acts of sacrilege. Towards the end of the service, during the Eucharist, Guy watched each person as they took the offering of Holy Communion, to detect whether they swallowed the bread or palmed it. The last of those in line took the offering, placed his hand to his mouth, and drew his hand to the side. Guy saw no chewing and suspected he had ill intent for that piece of God's bread.

Guy kept his eyes on the man. He looked so plain, not like those he'd been warned about with all of their finery. His grey and ragged clothing and his hair brown meant he resembled so many of the church's patrons. Guy watched as he returned to his pew towards the back of the church, intending to leave before the crowds.

When the service was over, Guy stood.

"Will you be returning with us?" Edith asked.

"We'll be heading back in about an hour," Uncle Thomas added.

"No… I'm meeting Kit this afternoon."

Guy watched the bread thief leave. He touched his mother's hand, smiled, and hurried from the church.

Outside, Guy's eyes fell upon the man. He was already outside the church grounds and moving down Petergate. Dressed so inconspicuously, he merged with the crowds leaving the church and going about their daily business. Guy followed, and almost lost him when he turned down Stonegate, but he caught a glimpse of him as he detoured around a couple of slow walking churchgoers.

Guy continued to follow, glancing at the wreck of his old house as he passed it. Soon, he reached the corner. His quarry had slowed, and then another man joined him, this one wearing a long robe. The two of them approached the abandoned Saint Helen's Church, which the authorities had declared redundant some thirty years prior.

Saint Helen's was on the road with no grounds around it. The two men stood with their back to the door. First, one slipped in, then, seconds later, the other did likewise.

Guy knew he couldn't follow them inside–they'd see him the second he opened the door. Instead, he went to the window and peered in. Encrusted with filth, it was impossible to see anything but shapes. Guy glanced at the sleeve of his doublet. It was the finest item of clothing he had, but what choice did he have? He wiped the window with his sleeve, clearing a square through which he could make out the activity inside. The two men crouched by the font. Each reached into the folds of their clothes, and while he couldn't tell what they held, the crumbling motion of their hands suggested they were breaking the sacramental bread into crumbs. Even from that distance, the clear shape of a rat crept out of the shadows and fed upon the offering. After consuming the final crumbs, it twisted and bent, first doubling in size, and then trebling from that new mass. Limbs unfolded, and it stood in the form of a child. The robed man bent down to it, and the creature cupped its hand to whisper in his new master's ear.

Guy closed his eyes and focused his mind in the way Oswald had taught him. Aye, he could hear their whispers. As the creature communicated its dark intent, Guy heard every word. Alas, every word was in a tongue Guy didn't understand, but it didn't take comprehension to understand its malevolence.

After the creature had communicated its message, the man swept it up as if it was an infant child and placed it within the folds of his robe. Together, they moved for the exit. Guy stepped away from the church, into an archway opposite and pretended to adjust his leather shoes.

The men and their swaddled creature left the church and continued along the road, heading for the river.

Guy's planned meeting time with Kit fast approached, but he couldn't abandon his pursuit. Clearly, the men had fed the familiar, and it had changed form before them to issue a message. Their instruction came from Hell itself.

A crowd had gathered before the Ouse bridge, and the two men joined it. Guy loitered nearby. The one carrying the creature shifted his clothing. He plucked the infant from his body and set it upon its frail legs. For the first time, Guy saw its face. Though the size of a child, it had the whiskers of a young man growing his first moustache. Its two incisors stuck out and much of the face was smeared red, no doubt from suckling the man's blood, explaining the carrier's sickly white complexion. The familiar tugged on the man's robe. The man crouched beside the creature, and once more it whispered dark secrets. He stood, and the familiar slipped between the folds of the man's robe, as a shy child is wont to do, but from it, he never emerged. Back in rat form, it scurried out, onto the bridge, and off the side, plopping into the river.

A moment later, a great roar resounded as a party on horseback appeared on the other side of the bridge.

A sudden feeling of dread struck Guy as if a hook had been attached to his insides and dragged down. At speed, the party raced across the bridge. At its head was Hastings. The two men Guy had followed from the church raised their arms in triumph and ran to meet the rapidly approaching group. Hastings swerved, but not away from the men, pulling on the reins and forcing his horse to knock them down. One fell to the side, but the other fell beneath the feet of the horse, which trampled him and continued on its way. The other riders leapt over the fallen men and sped into the distance to the cheers of the crowd.

Guy watched the less severely injured man pick himself up. He approached his associate, and dragged him to his feet, and then across to the edge of the bridge for support.

Others crossed the bridge, some ordinary members of the public, some that had followed the party as they entered the city. Among them was Jack, his face red as he sprinted.

"Jack," called Guy, stepping away from the side of the bridge to meet him.

"He's here," Jack said. "Walsingham's here."

Guy glanced back to where the riders had disappeared. "But that was Hastings…"

"Aye, he came through Walmgate Bar."

"Do you know where they were going?"

Jack took a deep breath. "Rumour says York Minster. I've been told to spread the word."

"Do you need me to tell anyone?"

"No, I can't let them know I told you." Jack nodded at Guy, gulped at the air again and ran off.

Guy took off at pace, returning whence he'd come, back past the abandoned church, back down Stonegate, but past Saint Michael's and to York Minster. There, too, a crowd had gathered. Guy pushed through to see those that had passed him on the bridge. Many of the party had dismounted, but not Hastings, and not his familiar.

Only one other man remained on horseback, the only man to wear a ruff more outrageous than Hastings. And only when one of his men came to his side to assist him did he dismount. As he turned to look upon the crowd, Guy was certain that he looked upon the face of Sir Francis Walsingham. The way his beard narrowed to a point gave the impression that his head was triangular, a wide forehead giving way to a widow's peak hairline of jet-black hair. His cheekbones were prominent above hollow cheeks, further contributing to his angular appearance. In the light of that winter morning, his eyes appeared at first green, but then a hint of yellow shone through. His face shifted into a sneer, revealing pointed teeth.

With his advisor by his side, he walked towards the entrance to York Minster. The advisor kept his hood up. Guy suspected this too was a familiar, whispering secrets from his demon guides to him.

Walsingham's party had joined Hasting's group following their race through the city. Walsingham and Hastings were deep in conversation when they were joined by another of Guy's mortal enemies, Edwin Sandys, emerging from York Minster. The faces of Sandys, Hastings and Walsingham shared that look of corruption, that cold sneer that indicated the pure hatred that consumed them. Around Sandys' legs, his one-eyed cat wound, disappearing between the folds in his robe only to emerge again later. Over the years, its limbs had grown while its body had remained lean, the ribs showing through its short hair. Sandys reached down and stroked the cat as it nuzzled its head into his palm.

"Hello, Guy," came a voice from his side, followed by a tug on his sleeve.

He looked down to see Anne, and further behind her was Elizabeth, his mother, and his uncle.

"Why are you looking at those men like that?"

Guy felt his frown stiffen. His face ached and his throat was dry. He knew he shouldn't say anything, but the pain of repressing the words was too much to bear. He pulled Anne to him, forcing her head away from the sight of such evil men as the party entered York Minster. "Those men killed our father, and one day, they'll pay."

Chapter 18

IN WHICH GUY FAWKES' FRUSTRATIONS GROW

What is it they say, a problem shared is a problem halved? Guy didn't get that weight lifted from his shoulders. No sooner had he said those words than pressure came upon him instead. Uncle Thomas stood over him, blocking out the light, one hand on his shoulder, anchoring Guy to the spot.

"I'll need you back at the farm, Guy," Thomas said, his face white, his expression stony.

Guy shrugged off his uncle's hand and stared up at York Minster, drawing air into his lungs in uneven gasps. Inside there were murderers, and they'd drawn a crowd to cheer them.

Again, Uncle Thomas placed his hand on his shoulder, but this time with a resolute firmness. He pulled Guy round and stared into his eyes. "What did you say to your sister?"

Guy glanced at Anne. Her face was wet with tears, and a thin trail of watery snot glistened on her upper lip. It was only at this point Guy realised his face too was wet. He ground the meat of his hands into his eye sockets to wipe them clear. "She deserves to know."

Thomas spoke through gritted teeth in a seething whisper. "Does she? How exactly is knowing going to benefit her? How is knowing what became of her father going to help her sleep at night?"

Guy opened his mouth, but Thomas widened his eyes, silencing him. "You've got to live with that burden of knowledge. It's a lot to bear. I get that. Don't lighten the load by putting it on your sister."

Guy felt Anne reach for his hand. He squeezed it and then released her. "How can they live with themselves?"

"That's dangerous talk."

"You say I've got to carry this alone." Guy gave his uncle a shove to put a little distance between them. "Then I'm doing something about it."

Guy had taken no more than five steps towards York Minster when the hand of Thomas Fawkes came once more, stronger still, the fingers digging into the tender spot beneath the collarbone.

Guy whipped around. "You can't stop me."

"You want an arrow through your neck? There are at least a dozen bowmen who have taken a sudden interest in your movements."

Guy turned to gaze up at the buildings, but Thomas grabbed his face, his thumb under the chin, and pulled Guy back to him. "I thought they would have taught you better at that school of yours."

Guy froze. Uncle Thomas knew? Then why had he let his father's death pass without action? Why had he let him struggle alone for so long?

After what felt like an eternity of inner struggle, Guy looked his uncle in the eye. "We can't let them get away with this."

"I'll say it again, as you weren't listening. That's dangerous talk, Master Fawkes. There aren't just arrows on you. Ears too. Always. Talk like that will see you on the scaffold. Talk like that will see your head on parade. You want that? Bootham Bar take your fancy?"

Guy shook his head.

"You think Anne will sleep better at night seeing that? And little Elizabeth? And your mother?"

Guy turned to gaze at York Minster once more, but the fight had been talked out of him, and, subservient, he followed his uncle to join his mother and Elizabeth. Only when Anne offered her hand once more did any warmth return. That's when he knew he had to be honest with his uncle. Once they reached the farm, he told him everything, his visits from Thomas Percy, what he did after school, and the real purpose of his apprenticeship at Clitherow's Butchers.

Monday came, and inside, Guy's anger still boiled. Not only was he no closer to avenging his father, but his uncle had dismissed everything he told him, telling him to focus on his schoolwork and learn a trade with which he could make something of his life. Guy spent most of the long walk to school staring at the ground and kicking stones along the pathway. He didn't even see Kit until after he heard him shout.

"Where were you yesterday?" Kit asked. He pushed himself away from the wall of the school's residential building and limped alongside Guy.

After a few steps, Guy stopped and looked at his friend. He also had a significant bruise on his cheek. Had something gone down after Thomas had dragged him from the city? Had Kit been involved in the action? Were Sandys, Hastings and Walsingham dead? Guy had so many questions, he didn't know where to start. Instead, he blurted out an incomprehensible jumble of sounds.

"What's up with you?" Kit asked.

Guy took a second to compose himself. "What happened?"

Kit glanced at his leg, then touched the bruise on his face. "This?" he asked. "Oh, I fell out of a tree."

"What were you doing in a tree?"

"Climbing."

"I mean, who sent you up there? Where you a look-out?"

"A look-out? No."

"So, why did you climb the tree?"

Kit stared at Guy. "Because it was there."

"It had nothing to do with the operation in York?"

"Oh, I haven't seen you since, have I?"

"Since what?" Guy grabbed Kit's arm.

"So, I haven't told you?"

"Told me what?"

"About what happened on Sunday."

"No, go on." Guy's grip on Kit's arm tightened.

"Go on, what?"

"Go on, tell me!"

"Jack had to run across half of York shouting the word that Walsingham arrived."

Guy rolled his eyes and released Kit's arm. "I know that. I saw Jack."

"Oh, okay."

"What else?"

"What else what?"

"What else happened?"

"Nothing. I was waiting for you half the afternoon. You didn't show up. On the way home, I climbed a tree."

"And?"

"And I fell out of it."

Guy felt his heart sink once more. Kit knew no more than he did.

But inside the school, something *had* changed. The few members of staff on duty issued brief commands to the pupils, and all day, Guy and Kit had their lessons covered not by their usual teachers, but by older pupils. There was no sign of Oswald, which was to be expected, with his planned departure. Pulleyn's absence, however, was of great concern.

At the end of the teaching day, when Kit and Guy went into the library, the secret door release mechanism didn't work. Jack and the other older boys waiting for their clandestine lessons had no idea why.

"Something's going on," Guy said.

Kit shook his head. "It looks like nothing's happening to me."

"Not here. In York. With Walsingham," Guy said.

"Should we go?" Kit asked.

Guy and Jack agreed. Jack's enthusiasm surprised Guy. Since he'd joined the big kids, training with weapons instead of a diet of only book lore, Jack had rarely joined Kit and Guy on their jaunts, even suggesting they were a futile waste of time. However, the locked door in the library troubled him, and while he may not have believed he was going to find anything useful within the city walls, it would give him something other than pondering to do. Given his uncle Francis was among the school absentees, his concern was understandable.

"Where should we head?" Jack asked as they passed under Bootham Bar. Even at dusk, when there were plenty of shadowy corners in which to hide, they preferred to keep moving. The influence of Sandys and Hastings had made York a worse place in recent years. Hastings' brutal soldier broke up gatherings of over three people under the guise of protecting the law of the land and the law of the church. They turned neighbour on neighbour with their quiet army of whisperers, suggesting that unholy practices were being conducted in darkness, as if they weren't the masters of the unholy. If Uncle Thomas was to be believed, half of the town was whispering, through a network of conduits, into the ears of Hastings and Sandys, so no secret was safe for them.

"They'll either be at York Minster or King's Manor."

However, they'd gone no more than a couple of hundred yards when the sound of hooves on cobblestone caused them to turn.

Soldiers on horseback rode towards them. Guy darted to one side to let them by, pressing his back against the wall as his friends did the same.

Hastings passed at the rear of the group, his familiar in human form once again riding alongside him.

Guy glanced at Kit and then Jack and they followed at a quick walking pace–any faster would make their pursuit obvious. The riders turned down Friargate.

Once the horses were out of sight, the boys broke into a sprint to close the gap, but as they reached Friargate, they had to come to a sudden stop, for Hastings and his party too had stopped only a few doors along the street.

They didn't have to get close to hear the familiar crackle of fire, of beams creaking, breaking and smashing to the ground, the plume of smoke that puffed through the window visible in the torchlight of Hastings' henchmen.

Hastings pointed at one of his men, then at the burning building. After a second of hesitation, the crony ducked under the door. Where a small crowd had gathered, Hastings urged his men to scatter them, and moments later, he understood why. Hastings had sent them to gather buckets of water from the well.

"Come on," called Guy. "Let's help."

"Why would we want to help Hastings?" Jack asked.

"We're not. We're stopping the other buildings from catching fire… and it'll get us closer."

The first of the men had arrived with a bucket of water from the well. He tossed it onto the outside of the building to little effect. He sighed, turned, and ran off.

"Form a chain!" came a shout as others arrived carrying buckets. Guy, Kit and Jack positioned themselves a couple of doors from the burning building, as two lines formed, one to pass full buckets towards the fire, the other to speed empty buckets back to the well.

Guy was close enough to the front of the line to see flames escape the door, licking out towards the street, but the door frame was too wet for it to take hold. Still, Guy was mesmerised by the orange tongue of fire, and felt it calling to him… but before he could move, Kit yelled his name and thrust a full bucket into his chest. Guy passed it forward and told himself to avoid staring into the doorway. Something about those flames was so tempting.

The sound of collapsing beams came again from the building. The properties on either side were unaffected by flame, but it would only be a matter of time. Or if the roof of this building collapsed it might drag its neighbours with it. The thought of people losing their properties and their possessions filled Guy with a familiar dread.

The ceiling gave way as Guy threw his seventh bucket of water on the building, and a bulky man stepped from the hungry flames and collapsed in the doorway.

At first, Guy thought it was a piece of furniture until it moved. A limb crept out and slapped the cobblestones. It was the man Hastings had sent inside.

Another of Hasting's men snatched the bucket that neared the front of the line and tossed it over his colleague, extinguishing most of the flames. With one foot, he rolled him over to put out the last of the flames that assaulted his back.

Guy continued to work the line, waiting for a bucket from Kit and passing it along. Hastings bent down in front of his prone henchman. He had to raise his voice over the sound of the fire. "Is it intact?"

The man on the ground weakly shook his head.

Hastings approached his familiar, that feeble slave that always rode by his side. He had remained stationary on horseback while others attended to the fire. After a brief conference, Hastings called, "Away!" He and the rest of his men mounted their horses and rode off, leaving one of their number dying on the street.

"Shall we follow?" Kit asked as he passed yet another bucket forward.

"No," Guy yelled. "We can't break the line. We have to stop the fire."

Half an hour later, the last of the fire's glow had dulled to nothing. Darkness had fallen, with only the lanterns of a few loitering neighbours illuminating them. Most of the building's front was gone, and half of the roof had caved in, but the properties next door seemed to be okay. No doubt there was some dependence on their neighbour for stability in a terraced row, but they'd be able to brace it until they could rebuild.

Guy didn't need to check his location, but he glanced at the neighbouring door, regardless. Yes, this was 16, Friargate. One of the many buildings burned into his memory, one of the buildings recorded in the list of illegal purchases his father had died for taking an interest in.

Guy looked at the still body of Hastings' guard. How many more lives would be lost as a result of the nefarious business of those that held York in their grip?

Chapter 19

IN WHICH GUY FAWKES LEARNS MORE FROM MARGARET AND THE DEMON HUNTERS RETURN TO SCHOOL

Nobody likes to feel powerless, but when you're young, there's so much out of your hands. As I'm sure you understand, Guy found this a frustrating period of his life. All around York, he could see the ill effects caused by the actions of those in power. There was evidence of ongoing activity at school that he longed to be part of. But blank stares met every question Guy asked. Tuesday at school was much like Monday, with a dearth of senior figures and the underground areas inaccessible. After school, it was Guy's day at Clitherow's Butchers. Margaret differed from other adults. She told him what she knew and admitted when she knew nothing. He never got the impression she hid anything from him. He'd learned how to cut a decent joint of meat, too. His time at Clitherow's Butchers meant he felt not only capable with a knife but adept. He carried his weapon at all times. Moreover, he'd learned secrets of the city that the school would never reveal such as the places where the practice of captromancy or scrying was performed and of the secret tunnels that contained wax images of all past monarchs for reasons unknown. He even came to understand some of the significance of his father's discoveries, and there was so much more than Oswald had told him: the properties Sandys and

Hastings had taken possession of, often through illegal means, were at points where they could access the netherworld. Hidden in the cellars of these buildings were foul, spiritual doors through which witches could summon the souls of demons and then implant them in human hosts, some willing, some less so. Hell's evil overlords granted witches in good standing the power to enlist foul demonic creatures to do their bidding.

Guy swept the slaughterhouse floor, while Margaret sharpened her knives.

"The house of Friargate that burnt down," Guy said.

"What about it?"

"That was on my father's list."

"Aye, so it was." Margaret smiled.

"Do you know what happened?"

"Do you?"

Guy stopped sweeping. "I'm guessing, with Walsingham in York, he was going to summon something from that dark passage."

"Do you think?" Margaret asked, widening her eyes.

"I think someone got wind of those plans and made sure that gate was closed."

"A fine plan."

Guy sighed.

"What is it, young man?"

"Can't you just tell me?"

"Master Fawkes, you already know a damn sight more than I do about what happened at Friargate."

"You had nothing to do with it?"

"Not that one."

Guy leant forward on the broom. "Then what?"

"A house at Ladygate had a similar unfortunate fire."

"Can you tell me more?"

"The reason you gave to destroy the house at Friargate stands true for Ladygate. What happened after that? I'm as in the dark as you are."

"You're not keeping anything from me?"

"No. Speak to your schoolmaster. He'll know more about it."

"But he hasn't even been there the last two days."

"He'll soon be back."

"Do you know, or are you just saying to make me feel better?"

Margaret smiled. "You're a smart lad. Let's call it an educated guess and be done with it, hey?"

"Okay," Guy resumed his work with the broom, reaching into the corners to sweep up the flakes of dried blood that had escaped previous attention. Another question entered his head.

"I saw people throw themselves in front of Hastings' horse on the day Walsingham arrived. Why would they do that?"

"Now that, my boy, is a question. Finish sweeping the floor, then head upstairs. I've got some reading for you."

While Guy rushed his sweeping, not a corner of the room was untouched by the broom. Upstairs, Margaret had already lit the candle in the small back room where he sometimes studied texts. These differed wildly from those studied at school.

Margaret handed Guy a yellowing piece of paper, stiff with age. "Now I don't know how much they teach you at that fancy school of yours about the trustworthiness of texts? About first-hand evidence and secondary accounts?"

Guy shook his head.

"But this is a long way from that kind of reliability. This is said to come from the *Sibylline Books*, prophetic texts purchased from a supposed witch by the last king of Rome, Tarquinius Superbus. They foretold events to come. Alas, like many of the great Roman texts, these were destroyed. Some say it was Tarquinius himself who destroyed them in his last days, so none could benefit from these secrets. However, they suppose the great Greek writer Phlegon of Tralles copied several passages into his work, *Book of Marvels*."

132

"And this is from that?" Guy asked, bringing the ancient text closer to his face to make out the language.

"Not quite," Margaret said. "These too were lost. But in the time of the Crusades, a Templar Knight, lost upon his journey home, stumbled upon an ancient temple where elders passed down stories from this book orally for generations. The Knight rested there for some days, and this is what remains of his account of what he heard."

Guy studied the page. Much was faded and the sentence construction archaic. Many of the words he couldn't read and others he didn't understand, but when he reached a rudimentary understanding, with his eyes weak after his study by candlelight, he looked up.

"What can you tell me?" Margaret asked. "Why do people throw themselves in front of a witch's horse?"

"Idolatry..." Guy ran his finger across the page. "They will fall before his wagon to show they give all to he who is as their messiah."

Margaret nodded. "What does that tell you?"

"People worship Hastings. If they gave a piece of themselves to him, it shows they are faithful, that they follow him." Guy gazed out at the darkness through the window. "Why worship witches?"

"So, you see what we're up against?" Margaret pointed to the window. "The people out there, they'd tear us limb from limb if they understood what we did. That's why we keep things quiet."

"But this," Guy indicated the paper, "is so old... how can they have known about Sandys, Hastings, and Walsingham back then?"

"My boy, this is a story that plays out time and again. The demons raise their heads, the weak will follow, and it's up to people like us to drive them back into the ground."

"And we can't stop them for good?"

"Well, they say only God himself can forever bring the power of demons to an end..."

"But if he were to do that," Guy interrupted, "he'd give in to wrath... he'd be as bad as they were."

"So it goes," Margaret said.

133

"So it goes," repeated Guy, staring at the page.

"Listen, don't be down. How about a nice bit of pork before I send you on your way?"

As much as Guy usually enjoyed this perk of working for a butcher, he made his way home with the meal sitting heavy in his gut.

The next day, Margaret's theory proved true, for many of those previously absent returned. Still, that dark atmosphere lingered in the corridors. For their first lesson, which Pulleyn would normally lead, an older pupil took the floor, leading them through reciting Latin phrases with vigour. Guy had seen him in training swinging a sword with skill. Today, his sword arm hung limp by his side.

Later, Francis Ingleby was present to lead them through a basic composition exercise. As uninspiring as it was, Guy welcomed the taste of normality.

At the end of the day, the hidden door in the library had been restored to its previous configuration, and pulling the right books in the right order gave access to the subterranean areas once more. The tiny library at the bottom of the stairs was in disorder, with several books missing and those that remained left somewhat haphazard on the shelves, some stacked horizontally, and others with the pages facing outwards.

When Guy and Kit took their seats ready for their book study, Pulleyn emerged from the back of the chamber, his face much changed. Over recent years Pulleyn's hair had begun a slow crawl away from his forehead. The colour had changed from black to grey, but now, white had replaced the grey, and the hair had become thin. The raven-headed walking stick he often held and pointed with was now needed for its original purpose, to support his stance when he stood and to steady his walking.

"From now on," Pulleyn said, "you will train with weapons."

Kit couldn't keep a triumphant yelp from squeaking between his lips.

134

Guy knew he should feel the same, but the mood around the school, and the look of Pulleyn, suggested events elsewhere had necessitated this change. Guy turned towards where the other boys trained. They numbered fewer than they had done at the end of the previous week, and yet fewer weapons remained in the racks.

Kit stood up, but Pulleyn urged him to sit again with a weak wave of the hand.

"Oswald would like to see you before he leaves."

From out of the shadows Oswald hobbled, a crutch under one arm to support his weight. One leg was bandaged, his arm was in a sling, and part of his face, including one eye, was also bandaged. He struggled into a seat.

Guy stared at Oswald. He'd seen him change so much over recent years, becoming stronger, and with it, Guy's admiration had grown. His one visible eye was ringed red with a heavy bag beneath it. Worse was his look of defeat.

"What happened?" Guy asked. He wasn't sure he wanted the answer.

Oswald reached forward. He grabbed one end of the bandage and untwisted the cloth, revealing the horror of his leg. At first, Guy only saw blackened flesh, but that gave way to bulbous pustules alive with pulsating fluid, the skin around these scarlet.

Oswald stared at Guy. "A demon hand wrapped around my leg." His voice was hoarse, and the words didn't come easy. "You know what it wanted?"

"Your soul..?"

"Of course, but that comes later. First, it wanted my confession; it wanted my betrayal. Its voice came directly into my brain, and even though I'd severed the head, the hand still had the power to grasp me, and the head still had the power to communicate."

"But if you sever the head…"

"Not with these demons. Every limb we lopped became another weapon bent on our destruction, but only after we'd betrayed our friends."

135

Pulleyn edged closer. "Do you think you could sever the tongue of a lifelong friend to stop him naming your kin? That's what Oswald had to do."

Guy understood the darkness in Oswald's eyes, the despair on his quivering lips.

"That's why I'm leaving," Oswald said as he bandaged his wound. "I have to know there's more to it than this. I can't keep fighting those things without knowing there's a reason."

"When did it get so bad?" Guy asked.

Pulleyn nodded to Oswald, excusing him. "We did all we could. We used your father's records; we destroyed buildings and closed passages all over the city. Even so, evil escaped. The witches operating in York are allied closely to the underworld."

Pulleyn edged away, opening his body to encourage the boys to head for the weapons. "It's a dark day indeed when we must train two as young as you to take on the horde, but they number many, and we need all the help we can get."

Kit rushed to grab a sword, picking one much like his brother used. He rushed to join Jack while Guy pondered over the weapon rack. When he'd first seen Oswald pull out his sword and bring it to life with that powerful incantation, he'd wanted to do the same, but seeing what it had done to him, how it had sucked the life out of him and left him feeling lost and alone in the world, Guy wasn't sure he could do it. And what had happened when he'd taken hold of Ingleby's blessed weapon? He heard the sound of that blade slicing through his father's neck. He heard the head crash to the floor, but then, he heard a voice.

"The one on the far left would suit you."

Guy turned, expecting to see Pulleyn, but he was resting against a pillar. Instead, hanging in the air in a corner was the floating head of Thomas Percy.

"What if I choose no sword? What if I walk away?"

"Face the demons empty-handed?"

"Why do I have to face them at all?"

"As I told you, we cannot change the path we are on, but the choices we make dictate how long we stay on the road."

"Is it a road worth staying on?"

"You forget, Master Fawkes, that your road crosses others. Should you not reach the junction, others that should cross your path may fall, too."

"So that's it? I can't even stop because doing so means others fail?"

"That's a choice you have to make. It starts by choosing a blade."

Before Guy could continue the discussion, Percy disappeared. It was an awful habit he had, and one Guy didn't think he'd ever have the power to change. Refusing to pick up a weapon wouldn't undo the wrongs of the past. Not doing so could mean he'd not be able to protect others he loved if they encountered witches and demons. That would be worse. Guy glanced at the suggested weapon. While Guy had always imagined himself holding the straight blade of the Romans and the Vikings, and one day upgrading to an enormous broadsword, Percy had suggested a curved blade, a scimitar of Persian origin. He grabbed the hilt, and while he was expecting to find it cold, warmth radiated through him. He lifted the sword; heavy at first, the balance of the weapon meant it swept through the air cleanly. At the end of the hilt, a red gem gave a little decoration absent from other blades. Something about its colour reminded him of fire. Yes, with this he could send legions of demons back into the fiery pits of Hell, but he'd learn the lessons of those that went before. He'd stay on the road and learn from those he met along the way. He'd keep his tongue, and he'd make sure those responsible for the pain and suffering in his city paid for their misdeeds.

Chapter 20

IN WHICH GUY FAWKES SUCCUMBS TO HIS LUST FOR DEMON BLOOD

With his elevation in status at the school, Guy found his circle of friends growing. In combat training, Guy worked with a group of five other boys. While disappointed to be separated from Kit, the challenge of working with those already adept with a blade forced him to learn fast. First to knock him on his arse was Robert Clifton, the son of a York blacksmith and the only person Guy had ever met with hair more ginger than his own. A stout lad named Hugh Potter preferred a shield to a sword. He encouraged Guy to run at him to try to knock him down, but every time Guy ended up on the floor. Ralph White posed a fresh problem. As a left-hander, his blows came from the opposite side, catching Guy out on more than one occasion. Two other residential pupils, James Nevell and Nicholas Fairfax, made up their number.

There were several new trainers for Guy to learn from too, Vicars, Gaunt, and Adamson. Only Adamson and Gaunt had Guy seen around the school previously and they very much lived their role as teachers, barking out orders and expecting absolute obedience. Vicars, though, allowed a little more freedom of expression while training with the weapon. He encouraged Guy to use his weaker hand and to strike when off-balance if the opportunity for a critical strike arose.

Pulleyn busied himself with a new crop of infants, five young-sters plucked from the bottom three years of the school. Either he considered the experiment of bringing Guy and Kit in young an abso-lute success, or he was every bit as desperate as he had sounded on the day Walsingham left York.

The weeks passed, which turned into months and the days grew longer and blossoms decorated the trees. Pulleyn received a letter from Oswald confirming his arrival in Rome. He'd supplied no return ad-dress. Jack ingratiated himself further with the older students, working hard on his swordplay, but still struggling for balance. Guy and Kit spent much of their free time in York. Guy had memorised every ad-dress from his father's notes and had drawn a map, with each location marked. He'd worked out a route around the city that included all addresses, passed the King's Manor, and looped around York Minster. While there were often soldiers around these locations, no building work took place and there was no extraction of the piles of rubble that blocked the entrance to the demon doors. But then, when April came, news of Walsingham's impending return to the city spread, and a fervour gripped those that lurked in the shadows.

Day by day, more soldiers poured into the city, and the work to clear the sites of the demolished buildings began. It was the 11th of April 1581, the day before Guy's eleventh birthday, and as Guy and Kit walked their usual route, troubled by the increase in shady characters gathering on the streets, they stumbled across Hastings and his retinue. His party had swelled once more. While in his first encoun-ters with Hastings, he had a few soldiers with him (plus his familiar), now there were eight. At the corner of Castlegate and Bridge Street, soldiers loaded the remains of a building destroyed in January onto a horse-drawn cart.

Hastings presided over the work, looking more flamboyant than ever, having added a large medallion to his attire, which sat at an odd angle against his ruff, and on his head was a yellow beret with a thick black tassel. His familiar was, for once, off his horse, walking awkwardly on those tiny feet. The clean-up operation must have been ongoing for some hours, as those recovering rubble only had their heads and shoulders visible. If there was a tunnel, and with it a door to the demon dimension, they were hell-bent on finding it.

Hastings barked commands. His voice had the same grating quality as the point of a sword being dragged along a stone floor, and the way he shaped his mouth to sound his vowels made his face look like it was performing complex gymnastics.

"Here it is!" called a voice from within the pit. A pair of arms came into view, holding a rock that bore a slight red glow.

"Careful," Hastings screeched.

Hastings' familiar closed on him, whispering secrets once more.

Hastings reached to offer a hand to the man who had recovered the stone, his voice now softer. "I apologise for my tone, but you have uncovered a precious artefact. Allow me to demonstrate."

Hastings helped the man from the pit. He pointed at the rock, and the man picked it up. The familiar moved behind him and touched the back of the man's neck. In reaction, as if he had ice placed against his spine, he tipped back his head. From the rock, a vapour rose and drifted into the man's nostrils.

Guy recalled the moment of his father's possession, but here, the result was not so immediate. The man stumbled backwards, and Hastings guided him into a sitting position on the cobblestones.

"You have done your country great service today," Hastings said. "You have earned a rest."

With that, Hastings took the rock, placed it in one of his horse's saddlebags, mounted his steed, and urged the rest of his party to do likewise.

"Shall we follow?" Kit asked, one leg already raised, ready to give chase.

"No." Guy's eyes remained on the man sitting upon the cobblestones. "We keep our eyes on him."

Dust covered the man's clothes, his hair too, and his face had a slack and vacant look. In his eyes, Guy perceived the man's truth. Purple laced the whites of his eyes, and the irises were edged with yellow.

Guy whispered to Kit. "They've done something. He's a demon now."

Kit pulled out his knife.

Guy stepped in front of Kit, obscuring the weapon from watching eyes. "Put that away. We can't stab him in the street."

Kit tucked his knife away. "What do we do, then?"

Before Guy could respond, a voice called from within the pit. "Are you coming back to lend us a hand, or are you gonna sit out there on your arse 'til night?"

With that, the cursed man pushed himself up, struggling to his feet and stumbling. Instead of joining his colleagues among the rubble, he had a new purpose. He waddled down the road, scraping his shoulder against the wall to keep himself upright.

"We follow him," Guy said. "Keep the knife sheathed unless there's danger."

While the streets of York weren't the cleanest, the stench coming from the stranger exceeded every worst comparison: a fermented mixture of rotting eggs and raw sewage. He stopped and gave out a belch that ripped through the air. It sounded like something tore inside him. He leant against the wall, vomited and continued on his way.

Guy stopped when Kit grabbed his arm and pointed down at the stranger's mess.

Among the yellow bile and the browning chucks, maggots the size of their little fingers wriggled. The maggots seemed to be aware of their presence, aware of the eyes upon them, and they gave out a low-pitched whine before writhing closer to the wall, hunting for safety. The acidic smell was so strong that a queasy feeling overcame Guy. He reached out and grabbed Kit's arm.

"We can't stop," Kit said. "He's getting away."

Once Kit had dragged him a yard or two from the maggot-ridden vomit, Guy found himself able to move unaccompanied once more. As slow as he moved, the possessed man had put distance between them. He turned down a narrow street, pushing himself around the corner off the wall again.

At the end of the alley was a tavern, and that's where the stranger headed. The streets outside were quiet, but as soon as Guy and Kit approached the entrance, they realised the tavern was packed. Inside, men leant away from the stranger and turned their noses up at his stench.

By the time Guy and Kit had stepped inside, the stranger had reached the bar.

"What can I get you, friend?" asked the publican.

The cursed man moved quicker than his shuffling along the streets suggested he was able and grabbed the publican's hand.

The publican stood with his mouth open; all colour drained from his face as sweat began pouring from his brow.

Guy heard a hiss. His initial assumption, that the sound came from the possessed man, passed when he smelled burning flesh.

The publican's lips trembled, and Guy understood the demon's purpose: to harvest information. Who in the city knew more about shady rendezvous than publicans?

"Now," Guy called, drawing his knife.

Kit did likewise, and the two of them plunged their weapons into the back of the cursed man and drew them down. A cascade of black blood gushed from the wound, covering Guy and Kit from head to toe.

The stranger's form shifted as if he were a vessel containing nothing but that sick, black filth, and as the liquid continued to spray, the top half of the body collapsed into nothing.

Guy blinked blood from his eyes and turned to Kit, who stared at the rapidly deflating body.

Guy misread Kit's movement. He thought he was about to run, so he moved to follow. Alas, Kit did not run, and Guy's movement carried him into his friend, knocking them both on the ground, the deflating skin collapsing, the last of the liquefied insides spilling over them, the floor, and any patrons that lacked the good sense not to cower in the corner.

Guy shuffled one way and Kit the other, untangling limb from limb. Standing was another matter, with the floor slick with blood and undissolved innards. Every time either of them tried to stand, their legs would give out, or one would catch the other, and they'd collapse onto the floor again.

As he struggled to his feet once more, Guy felt a hand on his back. With force, the publican ejected him from the bar and left him with a face full of dirt. He scrambled up before the publican hurled Kit out to join him.

They looked back at the publican, who dusted his hands. He seemed oblivious to the raw wound on his forearm where the cursed man had grabbed him. Those in the tavern remained stationary, too shocked to react.

After running to the city gates, they stopped to catch their breath.

"We did it," said Kit. "We destroyed a demon."

Guy nodded, too out of breath for words. He couldn't share his friend's enthusiasm. This demon had been too easily defeated based on everything he'd learned. The man at the bar had surrendered no names, despite being in severe agony, which aroused his suspicion.

"What now?" asked Kit.

Guy stared at his friend, whose face was dark with blood. "We've got to get cleaned up." The drying blood made his skin sticky and tight, and his hair felt alive. Now and then, a thick drip of blood ran from his hair into his face, which he wiped away before it reached his mouth.

"I can't go back to the school like this," Kit said. Only his eyes were visible through the thickening slurry of blood on his face.

"Uncle Thomas will be okay if you clean up at the farm," said Guy, "and we can rinse it off in the river on the way."

But Uncle Thomas was very much not okay.

Chapter 21

IN WHICH GUY FAWKES PREPARES FOR A DEMON ASSAULT

While it would be accurate to say Uncle Thomas had been a father figure to Guy since the death of his father, he was not a strict disciplinarian. His approach was often to let Guy learn from his mistakes to engender resilience and self-discipline. Guy, however, was soon to see his uncle angry, much angrier than he had been when Guy had wanted to launch a single-handed assault on York Minster.

With the skies dull and darkness looming, Uncle Thomas and Guy and Kit approached the cottage from different directions, Guy and Kit from the city, and Thomas from his fields. Lambing season neared, and his flock needed close attention. It was a limitless duty, for Guy had often heard him moving across the fields in the middle of the night or glimpsed his lantern from the hayloft as he crossed the distant fields in darkness.

As Thomas closed on them, Guy witnessed his uncle's expression shift from pleasure to confusion to concern. After visiting the river, their clothes were still soaked, and yet they hadn't been able to get all the blood and gore off. Uncle Thomas picked up the pace and dashed over to the boys. "What's this?"

Guy checked over his shoulder, always wary of who could hear when he spoke of demons. Recalling the event made his heart grow large and pound in his chest. "Kit and I... we took down a demon in town."

"Is that what's on you? Demon blood?" Uncle Thomas grabbed hold of Guy by the shoulders and peered over him at his back and in his hair. "Quick, take your tops off."

Guy and Kit looked at each other, but the tone of Thomas's voice told them not to tarry.

Kit pulled his top over his head, while Guy struggled with something snagging at the rear.

Thomas grabbed Kit, turned him around, and scanned his back. "You're clean," he said and shoved him to one side.

Guy shuffled his top off, hearing the material tear as he did so. He glanced at Kit. He was far from clean.

Uncle Thomas grabbed Guy and turned him around. "Foolish boy!" he cried.

"What's wrong?" Guy tried to look over his shoulder at his back.

"Don't move," Thomas said. He reached into his pouch and took out a length of twine.

Kit stepped across to stare at Guy's back. He was too far out of Guy's field of vision for Guy to see his reaction, otherwise, he might have panicked more. "What is it?" Kit asked, flat.

"What is what?" Guy moved his hand around to feel his back, but Thomas batted it away.

Thomas worked with the twine. Guy could feel it being wound around something by the brushing of his uncle's hands against his shoulder blades.

As Uncle Thomas wrenched away whatever had troubled him, pain shot up Guy's spine followed by a wave of nausea so extreme it was all he could do to stop himself from turning his stomach inside out. He collapsed onto his knees in a fit of coughing while Uncle Thomas snatched something from the ground.

"You know what this is?" Uncle Thomas thrust something under Guy's eyes. Discombobulated from the pain ransacking his spine, his vision refused to clear.

"You've damned us all, boy, do you hear?" Thomas continued.

Then, as his uncle withdrew it, he saw the thing: a bulbous eye, bloodshot, with an enormous pupil rimmed with the faintest ring of blue. The tissue at its rear became stiff and barbed. A little of Guy's blood remained on the barbs.

Thomas dropped it into the dust and stamped on it with the heel of his foot, leaving only a splatter of goo.

"They'll come for us." Thomas gazed out across his fields, to where the lambs grazed. "We'll have to send your mother and your sisters away."

Guy couldn't take his eyes off the mess on the ground. How could he have been so stupid? Was the whole thing a trap? The publican must have seeded him with the eye… Had Hastings lured him there?

Thomas turned to Kit. "They didn't seed you. You're safe. Hurry back to school."

"But what are you going to do?" Kit asked.

"Our best to survive." Thomas's words lacked conviction as he stared at the ground.

"I want to stay and fight," Kit said.

Thomas shook his head. "I'm not about to sign the death warrant of a child. Besides, I have other business for you." He turned to Guy. "Prepare the cart."

And as Guy moved in one direction, his friend moved in another, leaving Guy to wonder whether he would ever lay eyes on him again.

The last of the sun was visible over the hills as Edith Fawkes helped Elizabeth into the dog cart. Again, Guy found it hard to find his mother's eyes. She had mourned his father for a long time, but in the last year had seemed almost content once more. Now, this.

Anne, however, voiced her protest. "It's not fair to send me off like this."

Guy held her hand. "Go. It's the only way to keep you safe, little sister."

"But who will keep you safe, big brother?"

"And what would you do if you stayed?"

"I'd hurt those men who killed our father."

"But you don't know how to fight."

"Whose fault is that? Every day I've asked you to show me."

"I showed you how to milk a cow."

Anne smiled. "That won't keep us safe, will it?"

"No, but it'll help to keep you fed. Look after your mother and sister. They need you to be strong."

"Really? You think I'm strong?"

"Strongest girl I know."

With that, Anne hopped on board the dog cart to join her sister and her mother and the few possessions they could fit in a chest. Edith pulled at the reins, glancing back only once, her face emotionless as the horse took them into the distance. Their destination was the former home of Guy's grandmother. She had willed the property to her son but ensured that her companion, Helen, had tenancy rights for the rest of her life. While she would not be happy to put up the remainder of the Fawkes family, she would consider it a duty, the last favour for the woman she'd shared a part of her life with.

Once the cart was out of sight, Guy joined his uncle as he sat outside his cottage sharpening sticks. "Tell me again what happened?"

Guy told the short version of the story–spotting Hastings outside one of the known addresses, the glowing rock, the bizarre actions of the cursed one, and the events in the tavern.

Thomas shook his head. "They played you, boy. You've spied too often, too obviously. They knew eyes were on them, and played a simple trick. That tavern must be a hive of demon activity, and you walked right into it. They knew you'd follow. You even let them plant the eye on you."

"What was I supposed to do, wait for someone else to avenge my father?"

"Oh, is that what you were doing? I hadn't realised you'd succeeded in your quest."

Guy shook his head. "I'm sorry! I had to do something."

Thomas grabbed the sharpened stakes and shoved them into the ground in an arc around the front door. "You've been given a lot of privileges because of that nonsense about your destiny as a demon hunter."

Guy swallowed hard. Regret about coming clean to his uncle washed over him.

"You think Thomas Percy is the first person to send his skull seeking saviours after his death? Your father had a visit, too. The floating head of Anne Boleyn told him his destiny was to take on the might of royalty and dethrone the demon scourge. Do you know what he did with that? Nothing."

Guy stood opened mouthed as the shock hit him. But his father *had* taken on the might of royalty with his letter to Walsingham.

"Your grandmother believed too, trained both your dad and me to fight demons even though our father wouldn't allow it."

Guy pictured his grandmother in her bed in her dying days, lacking the strength to do any more than lift her hand. Could she once have wielded a sword?

"You still got that whistle?"

Guy remembered the trinket he'd rescued from his former home and nodded.

"You know what that does?"

"It doesn't work."

"Oh, it does. I've seen it. It's a demon whistle. Blow that in their proximity and you'll soon know who's risen from the underworld. Next time you want to check if someone is a demon, I suggest you give that a blow rather than sticking a knife in them."

Thomas placed the last of the stakes as Guy scanned the area. "What's going to happen?"

"They will come tonight. They will come for you." Thomas leant on a stake and looked up at the emerging stars. "They won't stop until either you are dead, or they are."

"Can we stop them?"

"Maybe for a while. You go to that school, but you don't understand the lengths they've been going to keep the numbers down."

"I saw what they did to the buildings in York. They closed the demon doors."

"That's not half of it."

"Those buildings though... they were the ones father had recorded."

"Aye. His work did more than anyone to reveal the source of the threat." Thomas sighed and turned towards his home. "We wait inside. We barricade the doors and windows. It won't last till daylight, but it might give us a chance."

Before entering the cottage, Guy climbed the ladder to the hayloft that had been his home for the past three years. He grabbed the whistle and put it in his belt pouch. He took the angel and his father's papers down to the ground. With the pitchfork that stuck out of what remained of the hay, he loosened the earth and buried them. That way, they wouldn't fall into the wrong hands.

Inside the cottage, Thomas had a decent supply of wood left even after the long winter. Those who had his knowledge didn't let their supplies get low, always accounting for emergencies, whether they be cold winters or unexpected demon attacks. He'd already brought sufficient wood indoors when he grabbed what he needed for stakes, and he began covering the windows. As soon as that was done, he nailed wood across the door.

"We can't see out now," Guy said.

"We don't need to see. We'll hear."

No sooner had Thomas spoke, than a sound, like the high-pitched click of bats, caused Guy to cover his ears, and a second later it grew into an ear-piercing wail.

"That's one going into a stake," Thomas said.

This awful sound was soon followed by more of the same. Thomas snatched Guy's hands away.

"Don't hide from the sound of the death of your enemy. You need to listen to what's going on out there."

Beyond the demented death wails, there was something else—the sound of horses, and soon, the howls petered out, replaced by thuds on the outside walls.

The room shook, sending dust cascading from the beams above.

"What are they doing?" Guy said.

"Throwing themselves at the walls. Demons like this cannot think."

The thudding continued from every side, a maddening drum-beat of destruction.

"Where do they come from?"

"I'm sure you've been told of the Furies? They called those straight from a Hell-gate."

Soon the sound of thudding ceased, replaced by scrabbling above.

"They're on the roof." Thomas drew his sword.

While Thomas had mentioned his training, Guy gasped when his uncle said the words that imbued his blade with demon-killing power. Guy had always assumed his uncle was a knowledgeable outsider, not one trained as a warrior with the power to embellish weapons.

Thomas's blade was long and straight; at full size, it almost reached the roof. He swung the blade as the first demon head emerged from the chimney. The head fell into the fireplace and disintegrated into a mass of black worms. The rest of the body soon followed. But it was as if they'd uncorked a bottle of evil.

Guy, too, grabbed his sword. He had not the knowledge to imbue it with greater power, but Pulleyn had told him that Gretchen had blessed all weapons in the rack with holy water and would still do a job. An instant later, he confirmed that as he drew the blade across the neck of another demon invader.

"Stay back," cried Thomas. He continued to scythe down enemies that appeared in the wide radius of his blade swing. Such was his death toll, that the entire floor was alive with the writhing residue of death, the black worms.

With his sword, Guy lunged and slashed and sliced at anything that evaded Thomas's attacks, moving in rhythm to avoid getting in the way and making a nuisance of himself.

For how long the flow of demons down the chimney lasted, Guy didn't know, but the level of the worms wriggling away on the floor had grown to ankle height. He didn't want to find out what would happen if one got inside his hose.

The stream of demons slowed, and, after a dozen more were slashed into inexistence, stopped altogether. Once more, Thomas and Guy became dependent upon their ears.

A rustling, shuffling sound told them what was coming. "They're coming through the thatch. They'll drop right on top of us."

"What are we going to do?"

"Grab the axe and start chopping the boards from the door."

Guy glanced at the door and saw it covered in those awful writhing worms that had burst from the creatures. "But the worms…"

"Chop through them, and for the love of all that's good and holy, keep your mouth closed."

Guy gazed up at the source of the sound above. He could see movement in the thatch. He tucked his sword into his belt and grabbed the axe. With the first swing, he understood why he was to keep his mouth closed as worm segments flew into the air, striking his face.

Meanwhile, Thomas took one of the sharpened sticks, wrapped the end in cloth, and then lit it from his lantern. "Ready?"

Guy looked around and then back at the door. There was still significant work to do. "What? No!" He swung the axe again, splintering another barricade free.

Thomas lifted the torch to the dried-out thatch above.

As Guy continued to work the door, the fire spread above. The brightness dazzled Guy as he swung his axe again. The crackling sound once more brought him to its thrall, and as flaming bits of thatch dropped to the floor, he watched it spread. Was he to watch another home ravaged by flames?

Worm bodies exploded as fire touched them, pulling Guy from his trance. He brought the axe crashing down again, splintering the last of the barricades away from the door.

"Stay behind me, and watch my back," Thomas said. He kicked the door open and stepped outside, continuing until he was clear of the porch and standing by the horse post. Guy followed, looking in every direction at the mayhem surrounding the farmstead.

Chapter 22

IN WHICH GUY FAWKES LEARNS THE COST OF HIS ERRORS

At Thomas Fawkes' farm, the monstrous wailing of crazed demons intensified. At the periphery of their view, deformed shapes rose from cracks in the ground, but before them were men on horseback. A dozen of them formed a line, some carrying flaming torches, which revealed the familiar sight of Sandys and Hastings. Their lack of action only troubled Guy more. What were they waiting for? A thud as a beam in the cottage collapsed turned Guy around. The sight reminded him of his duty–to watch his uncle's back.

The night sky was alive with the colour of fire. Figures danced on the rooftop, revelling in their fiery demise with a chaotic flurry of limbs, some disappearing out of view as the flaming thatch beneath their feet could no longer support their weight with one beam having collapsed. One turned towards Guy, only its lower half aflame, the flesh bubbling, and pockets of fat exploding around the fat of the thighs. It lifted an arm to point, and its jaw twisted into a sick grin. "Feast of giblets."

A thud in the wooden horse post drew Guy's attention. He glanced at the newly homed crossbow bolt, and then at the men on horseback. Sandys reloaded his weapon.

Remembering the threat from behind, Guy turned around again.

The flaming demon was no longer on the roof. Among the flames within the building, a shape hit the floor. It stood, wafting smoke away with its arms and emerged through the door. The charred carcases of worms stuck to its lower body from where it had landed upon them, giving its lower half a black and crispy coating.

Guy still held the axe. He let the creature take another step and then swung the weapon, catching the creature in the throat. A bloody slurry plopped out of the front, and the head tipped back, throwing the body off balance, causing it to fall to the ground. But the axe was not blessed or anointed in holy water, and so, the creature lived. The body squirmed as it tried to push itself back up. Guy wedged the axe into the stump, pulled out his sword, and slashed the creature across the chest, stilling it for good.

With that threat expunged, Guy turned back to face the men on horseback. Flaming torches illuminated the crooked smiles and wicked faces of Hastings and Sandys.

"I trust you still have your whistle?" Thomas said, his eyes trained on his enemies and their demonic horde.

Guy plunged his hand into his belt pouch. "I do."

"It's time to find out what it does. Be ready to run for the barn."

Guy clutched the whistle. Surprisingly cold, it felt as if the whistle were constructed from ice rather than bone. He lifted it to his lips and blew.

Despite having turned the whistle over in his hands on numerous nights, putting it to his lips and blowing into it every way imaginable and every time experiencing the same empty silence, on this occasion, Guy expected to hear something. When he didn't, his former misconception came to the fore: the whistle did not work. But as he continued to blow, he looked at the men on horseback. While Hastings and Sandys seemed unaffected, a few of those with them twisted their necks at painful angles and cupped their hands over their ears. Hastings' familiar struggled. His horse had reared up, and he was at a loss whether to grab for the reigns or continue covering his ears.

The demons nearest to them, the ones that had been closing ever since they emerged from the cottage, froze on the spot and shuddered.

Thomas had spread plenty of dried hay on the ground outside the house. He turned to Guy, yelled, "Run," and knocked one of the flaming torches onto it.

Before they were more than five yards from the house, a wall of fire had risen behind them.

"We'll hold up in the barn. We may keep them at bay until…"

When Thomas stopped speaking, it took Guy a few seconds to piece together what had happened. Thomas dropped to his knees, clutching his leg, screaming. As Guy moved to help him up, he realised the cause: a crossbow bolt sticking through his upper leg.

He turned back to the flames, but the wall of fire was too high to see where Sandys was aiming his crossbow. If, however, Guy thought it a lucky shot, the high-pitched squeal from above gave him other ideas. A cloud of bats hung in the sky. No doubt among them were familiars, sending location messages back to their masters.

"Duck," called Thomas, before giving out another cry of pain.

Guy did as he was told and heard the whistle of a crossbow bolt an instant before it parted his hair.

From his crouched position, he turned. Again, he couldn't see the men on horseback, but shapes moved within the flames before emerging from their cover, red-skinned beings with contorted limbs that made their speed slow.

"Come on," called Guy. He bent next to his uncle and tried to put an arm around him to help him move.

They managed a couple more steps before the sound of whistling came again. Guy bowed down as he continued, slowly, determinedly, cautiously, towards the barn, taking as much of his uncle's weight as he could. A few yards nearer, Thomas yelped once more, becoming very heavy as if he'd dropped an anchor.

Guy shifted his grip and found another bolt in his uncle's back.

"Get to the barn," Thomas said through gritted teeth. He shrugged Guy off him and pushed him away.

"No," Guy cried. "We can make it." He turned again. More of the red-skinned hell spawn emerged from the flames. Those that had passed through first were closing, with fewer than twenty yards between them.

Guy blew into the whistle once more. The creatures behind him shuddered, and momentarily, they stopped. As Guy reached for his uncle again, he swung out an arm. "Go!"

"No!" Guy circled to the other side, wrapping his arms around Uncle Thomas's waist, and shuffling him forward. Uncle Thomas worked with him, rocking as he made slow progress towards the barn.

There was another whistle, and a bolt thudded into the ground in the place Thomas had been mere seconds before. Guy turned his head, and the creatures were closer still, almost in spitting distance.

Together, they shuffled forward a couple more yards, but the barn remained distant.

"We have to speed up," Guy said.

Thomas renewed his efforts, crying out in agony with each movement.

Guy felt wetness all over his uncle's body. He didn't know whether it was blood or sweat; nevertheless, he pushed him forward. A rush of air came behind him and a hiss, not a whistle. The creatures were upon them now.

Guy let go of Uncle Thomas.

"Keep going," Guy cried, but without support, Thomas slumped to the ground.

Guy blew the whistle again, stunning the creatures. He unsheathed his sword, and in two quick swings, he'd knocked the hellspawn to the ground. He looked beyond, back to the fire. There were so many. He blew the whistle once more. With each blow, the effect seemed to lessen, as if they became accustomed to its sound. He stepped forward and slashed at a couple more creatures. While he'd practised swinging the sword through the air and had built up some strength, slashing through demon flesh sapped his strength quicker. The sword had become heavy in his hands, and it had so much more work to do.

156

He turned to the barn again, then back to the fire and the creatures emerging from it, trying to calculate the answer to the impossible sum before him. He lashed out again, and another creature fell. But no, they emerged quicker than he could take them down. He had to move.

Guy sheathed his sword and stepped back towards Uncle Thomas. He tried to lift him. His arms were weak, and Thomas wouldn't shift.

"Come on," he cried. "Help me."

As Guy shifted his hands to try again, he realised another bolt had found its home there.

"Go." Thomas's voice was little more than a whisper.

Guy glanced up and saw the creatures coming. The hooves of their masters' horses neared, and he knew his uncle was right.

Guy stepped away.

"Go." A little more strength came to Thomas's voice. "Fight to free York from their repugnant influence."

Another bolt flew, passing in the space between Guy and his uncle.

"Barricade the door."

Even though its effect had weakened, Guy blew the whistle again, hoping the microsecond it gave him would be enough. Moving alone was so much faster, though with every step he carried the weight of guilt. He reached the doors and looked back at Uncle Thomas, who was up on one knee. "Come on!" called Guy, a rush of remorse hitting him so hard it almost knocked him from his feet.

"Barricade the door!" cried Thomas again. He struggled the rest of the way to his feet and turned to face the demon legions and men on horseback.

Guy cried out, but his uncle was deaf to his pleas.

The demon masters had bypassed the wall of flame. Sandys raised the crossbow, aiming it towards Guy, a cruel grin spreading on his face.

Guy slammed the door. A crossbow bolt thudded into it, breaching the wood and poking a couple of inches through. He grabbed the wooden bar and dropped it into place to seal the door and dragged a couple of hay bales across to further brace it. He climbed the ladder to the hayloft. From the window, he could only see across the fields to the rear. To see what was going on at the front of the property, he had no choice but to wriggle out of the window and clamber up onto the roof. He shuffled along the thatch, following the beams to the front of the barn.

With Sandys' sword to his throat, Thomas stood, his awkward stance indicative of the pain that ransacked his crossbow-bolt-pierced body.

Hastings dismounted his horse and gesticulated, drawing shapes with his hands before pointing to the ground and raising his arms. His lips were moving, indicating that he spoke, but from his position atop the barn, Guy heard nothing.

Once the ground shook, it was clear he'd spoken a dark incantation, and as the first limb breached the surface, its effect became apparent. From underground, from the bowels of the earth, a fresh horde of creatures rose, augmenting the forces already surrounding the barn. Humanoid in form, their skin was a dirty red, rather than the livid red of the earlier crew and covered with charred black smears. Yellow eyes burnt in their tiny heads, and their grins revealed rows of sharp teeth, which forked tongues poked between. From the tips of their spines came small, curled tails which ended in cruel barbs.

The creatures stood on the spot on which they had risen and faced the man who had summoned them, awaiting orders.

Hastings spoke: "Boy, I know you spy upon us, and I know you must dread the sight before you. Be in no doubt that these beings which I have imbued with dark life will tear your very limbs from their sockets and the flesh from your bones should I command it. Come out now and we shall spare your life, and that of the man who stood with you."

"No!" cried Thomas.

"You have the count of five," Sandys said. "One."

Guy surveyed the area, racking his brain for some kind of plan.

"Two."

"I'm bleeding badly, Guy," Thomas shouted.

"Three."

Guy raised his head and considered lifting his arm in surrender. He couldn't let his uncle go like this.

"I won't make it," Thomas cried, his voice hoarse and forced.

"Four. Last chance to save yourself."

"He lies. He won't let us go."

"Five."

Sandys drew his sword across Thomas's throat, spilling his life into the soil below. His body slumped forward, but his last act was to raise his hand, to point towards the barn, and it was as if a speck of starlight caught the end of the finger and radiated a beam in Guy's direction.

Hastings stared at Thomas's fallen body and sneered. "And now he lies... on the ground, spilling his blood to feed our forces."

Guy lent over the edge of the barn and cried out in anguish before he felt a jolt in his side.

Sandys pointed. "We'll spill your blood next, my child."

Guy reached for his scabbard and felt heat that had not been present moments earlier. Hearing a call, he glanced down to see Hastings gesturing towards his beasts. Within seconds, they tore towards the barn. Guy shuffled back to the central beam from where he could see any that reached the top. He pulled out his sword and the blue glow told him all he needed to know about his uncle's final action. All the weight went out of the weapon. Wielding it brought new life to his limbs. Gazing at the ethereal light his sword swelled with, he didn't notice the distant torchlight across the fields.

Chapter 23

IN WHICH GUY FAWKES LOPS OFF MANY A LIMB

Guy didn't have time to ponder another tragic loss. His uncle had left him with a chance, and he would not fall without a fight. When the first demonic hand came to rest on the roof, Guy swung his blade, which connected with the flesh with a sizzle as it sliced through, causing the creature to plummet to the ground. It scurried back to its feet, but bereft of a hand, it would struggle to climb the barn again.

Another pair of demons scaled the wall. Guy placed his whistle to his lips and blew. He hoped to see their clawed hands go to their horned heads and for them to tumble to the ground, but they held firm, shrieking curses in annoyance. So, the whistle wouldn't keep him safe, but it would buy him time. Across the other side, a creature had reached the roof. The barn was constructed with three central beams, a shallow gradient between them, with a much steeper slope leading to the side. It's what made the hayloft so spacious. But the stone walls that made the barn warm and strong also made it easy to climb. On top, the thick thatch could take his weight, but perhaps not alongside a dozen demons. He and Uncle Thomas had replaced the thatch the previous summer, and the rafters were closer even than in the cottage. The creature struggled to move its feet on the surface, its claws snagging on the straw and reed. Guy blasted the whistle to distract it, stopping it from evading a slash of his blade that bisected its chest. Both parts tumbled from the barn, the head and upper torso colliding with another climber and sending it cascading to the ground. As Guy gazed down in triumph, a crossbow bolt zipped through the air inches from his face. Sandys had circled the barn to find a better striking angle. Guy backed out of his sight but knew it was only a matter of time before Sandys would find another angle.

Two more creatures had reached the top; they turned to him, gnashing their teeth and flexing their claws.

The sound of hooves below revealed Sandys was behind him. He had to move, but the pair of demons occupied the safest spot. They hissed in tandem and hurried towards him. Guy lunged, impaling one demon's sternum. The familiar sound of metal tearing through the air made Guy lean back, angling his blade to divert the bolt into the second demon's eye.

He remembered Oswald's warning, that dismemberment and death were of no relation, and stepped away from falling, grabbing hands. With a kick, he knocked the bodies off the roof, hoping once more to knock down a few climbers. He kept low and headed for the front, reaching down to slash at any hands closing on the rooftop. Twisting his neck, he saw a pair had climbed up at the rear, and a third soon joined them. He blew on the whistle to cause a moment's distress and then held aloft his blade. He studied the blue flame that ran along its edge. While it still felt light in his hands, he could feel his hair pasted to his face and the cold wind stuck his clothes to his sweaty body.

Guy had no time to slow. He ran, swinging his sword in an arc from down by his side, going into the first creature's ribs and exiting at the neck on the opposite side. He raised his foot to kick it from the building, spun round and lopped the legs off the second creature with a downward arc. The third slashed at him. Guy barely had time to lift the blade to deflect the blow from his face. The creature twisted with the momentum of its swipe and assaulted Guy once more with a lash of its barbed tail. It was too close to slash at, so Guy jumped. But upon landing, his foot became embedded in the thatch. Blood rushed through his veins, his heart working overtime. His foot swelled. A quick tug wouldn't release it. He'd have to fight where he was. The creature hissed and lunged forward once more. Guy was in the wrong position to strike. He tossed his sword into his left hand, and a swing of the blade left the creature headless. He manoeuvred his weapon again to guide the rest of it to the steep edge. A body without legs dragged itself across the thatch towards him. From the other side, two more had reached the top and with his foot stuck, he was a sitting duck for Sandys' crossbow.

The most recent two were of a different breed, sinking onto all fours once they'd reached the top. They bounded towards him like maniacal dogs. He pulled at his leg, but it was stuck in the thatch. If only they hadn't packed it so tight! The first dog closed and leapt into the air. Guy leant back, lifted his sword, and as the creature sailed over, he sliced open the creature's belly, the contents raining down onto him. While trying to straighten himself, he felt his hair snag. The crawling demon had hold of his hair. The warmth of its claws radiated on his scalp. He slashed blindly, first hitting only thatch, but with a second hack, the familiar sound of a sword sinking into demon flesh came, and Guy was free. He stood, only to see the second dog in mid-air, leaping for him. There was no way to move. It was impossible to lift any more than the hilt of the sword. From the corner of his eye, he saw a ball of light, and an instant later, the creature was aflame, its path diverted beyond him. Where it landed, the thatch set light.

Using the sword for leverage, Guy finally worked his foot free. There were creatures on all sides now, at least a dozen. His blade remained hungry for demon flesh, but how could he take on so many when they would come again, and again, and again? At that moment, a creature on his left burst into flames. A second later, he caught sight of a flaming arrow that struck another. Salvation! But where the creatures fell, fire spread. He couldn't leap from the building right into the arms of his enemy.

"Come on!" called a familiar voice as the top of a ladder hit the side of the barn.

Kit jumped onto the thatch, struck a demon with his sword, and then took Guy by the hand.

"Climb down; I'll cover you."

Guy raced for the ladder, slashing at nearby creatures, adding to the mass of lopped-off arms and tails. He rushed down to where an army of familiar faces, all wielding flaming weapons, stood. Robert Clifton, James Nevell, Nicholas Fairfax, Ralph White, and Hugh Potter were all there, the gore on their jackets indicative of the battle they'd been through to reach him. They formed a circle, protecting Guy and striking out at any creature that got too close. Further back were the archers, some still focused on the roof, which Kit had now left, others focusing on thinning the numbers of the undead beasts that sought only bloodshed, misery, and chaos.

"Aye up, chummer," called an archer. Guy recognised the voice, but it wasn't until he pulled down his cowl that he believed it was Jack. He'd never been the most adept with hand-to-hand weapons, but with the bow, he'd found his forte.

"Come!" cried another voice. Guy spun round to see horses before him, their riders a blur. He shrank back, weary of Sandy's crossbow.

"Guy," came a familiar voice. He was not facing a crossbow, but Francis Ingleby. Giving Guy no further time to think, he thrust out a hand and dragged him up, handing him to the hooded rider on the neighbouring horse. A deep voice urged him to hold tight, and off they rode, away from the barn, away from the farm that had been his home, and away from the men that Guy had so desperately wanted to see meet their end.

He'd had a lucky escape, and he knew it. Maybe his friends would remain behind to finish what he could not. His actions the previous day (for the rising sun in the distance told him a new day had dawned) had been foolish, and once more, in trying to do the right thing and getting it so very wrong, he'd made yet another tragic mistake.

The rising sun reminded him of something else. It was his birthday. Guy Fawkes was not sure he wanted any further gifts from the universe.

Chapter 24

IN WHICH GUY FAWKES GOES FARTHER FROM HOME THAN EVER BEFORE

Guy was aware of many parallels with the death of his father. Once more he'd witnessed the awful spectacle, and once more he was sped away from the scene. Worse was the guilt present for both. Blame pummelled his brain with every pound of the horse's hooves. For hours, Guy clung to the rider, assaulting his mind as the distance grew from Uncle Thomas's farm.

Dawn light revealed only glimpses of scenery. The rider remained silent no matter what pleas Guy made until they came to a stop among trees. The rider leapt from the horse and tied it up before helping Guy dismount.

"Where are we?" Guy looked for a familiar landmark, but the early morning sun shone on nothing he knew.

The rider shoved Guy, guiding his direction. Guy stumbled over uneven ground until the rider gripped his shoulder and forced him to the left. The trees grew thicker, and the ground sloped downwards. Before him was a wall of jagged rock. Guy explored the cold rock with his hands until his forceful companion shoved him along the wall to a tunnel with a set of steps carved into the rock and leading downwards.

Near the bottom, the flicker of flames lit a clearing from which a murmur of voices rose. The rock wrapped around three sides of them with thick tree cover on the other side. Dappled light of early morning fell upon the ground.

No sooner had Guy stepped out of the tunnel than he became aware the rider was no longer behind him. He turned back, but no trace of the man remained. With nowhere else to go, he stepped towards the flames, only to feel the point of a sword press against his neck.

"Master Fawkes, you should learn to be lighter on your feet."

Guy held up his hands, and the weapon dropped from his neck, leaving nothing more than the memory of its presence.

Stepping from the shade, the features of a young man became apparent. His almost-white hair shone, and coupled with his fair complexion, gave him a look of someone who wasn't quite there. Many times, Guy had seen faint apparitions, the restless dead wandering the streets, but never had they approached him in this manner.

"Are you a g-g-ghost?" said Guy.

"You can call me Ghost if you like…"

His accent was quite unlike any Guy had heard before. He certainly wasn't from York. Hearing him speak and looking at him more closely revealed that he was indeed of the world and not part of the spirit plane, which eased Guy's troubled mind to some degree.

"Take a seat," Ghost said. It was only then that Guy realised others sat around the fire. Their brown cloaks threaded with dead leaves camouflaged them well. Beyond, a cave mouth called to Guy, summoning him into its darkness.

As Guy sat down, the men around him nodded and mumbled greetings.

"We're careful who we trust around here, especially when we know certain people can't help but get others into trouble," Ghost said.

Again, Guy saw his uncle fall and saw Sandys' wicked grin as he'd drawn the blade across his throat.

"What is this place?" Guy asked.

Some of the men grumbled and turned their backs on Guy.

Ghost sighed. "Seems silly actions that risk thinning our numbers don't endear you much to people around here. And make no mistake, Master Fawkes, people have died because of your actions."

"But they would have got them, right? Sandys and Hastings?"

More grumbles. One man turned around. A full beard hid most of his face. He shoved Guy from the tree stump and stared at him with his one good eye. The other was permanently closed and scarred over with a thick gash. "You don't know what you're dealing with, boy." He spat on the ground. "Can't believe we sent men out on a rescue mission for this runt."

Ghost stepped between them, but the man had already turned his back. Ghost helped Guy to his feet and led him from the circle towards the cave mouth. More than anything, Guy wanted to be swallowed up by the darkness, removed from existence so he could cause no more pain. Ghost lit a lantern, and together they entered the cave.

"Tonight was not about taking down Sandys, Hastings or even Walsingham... though where he is, nobody knows. Ingleby insisted we rescue you, no matter what the cost."

Guy tipped his head back in frustration. "But... we outnumbered them."

"You'd best keep your ill-considered opinions to yourself unless you want those men to show you the full extent of their wrath." Ghost guided Guy down a narrow passage.

"So, why couldn't they get them?"

"What did you see? Did they pull the red-skinned horde from the ground?"

"Yes, and I defeated many of them."

"And then what did they do?"

"What? Nothing."

"The red horde is only the very tip of their power. They're nothing more than the vermin of Hell. Had any of those evil men desired, they could have summoned a beast to swallow you whole."

"Then...?"

"Why didn't they?" Ghost stopped moving as the passageway opened up again. "Their power is granted by the leaders of the underworld. They dare not ask for too much at a time. Had you remained, I don't doubt that Sandys would have summoned a stronger demon."

Guy froze. If that was only a fraction of what he was up against, what hope did any of them have?

Ghost continued. "The men here don't all believe in the idea of Percy's disciples, but they don't want that flame of hope to die, either."

"What's that mean?"

"It means both they're incredibly pissed off at you for nearly getting them and their friends killed, but likewise, a part of them believes you're the best hope they've got."

Guy shook his head. What good was he? He couldn't save his father. He couldn't save his uncle. How was he supposed to save York from the scourge of demons?

Ghost lit the oil lamps in the cave, revealing elaborate wall paintings and a stone altar topped with a skull and bones.

"Sandys and Hastings called the red horde, hoping it would draw us out. They hoped that demon hunters would flock to the area so they could exterminate them."

"And they came for me." Guy stared at the altar.

"You know whose bones they are, right?"

Guy looked at the skull. Now clean of hair and dirt, it wasn't as he'd first seen it; even so, it could be no one else. "Thomas Percy."

"Correct." Ghost pointed at some of the wall paintings. "This is the cave of Saint Robert. Four hundred years ago, he resided here, and he foretold all that was to come, until the death of Thomas Percy."

"And Percy came to me..." Guy gazed at the pictures on the walls, valiant knights with flaming blue swords taking on ferocious many-headed beasts.

"For that reason, we have to believe you're worth fighting for, but by all that is good and holy, you have to be smarter. But don't for a second think that makes you unique. We meet dozens like you every year, their head full of Percy's babble."

Again, Guy heard his uncle's words about the nonsense of prophecy. Again, he saw Uncle Thomas fall. Again, he recalled the sensation of severing his own father's head. "Sleep now, for only when all return can we account for our losses and plan for the time to come."

Ghost led Guy to another chamber and indicated a sack stuffed with straw to serve as a mattress, and soon Guy was left in darkness.

Chapter 25

IN WHICH THOMAS PERCY AND THE SURVIVORS RETURN

Sleep was to remain a stranger for a little longer for Guy that night. Not long after the echoes of Ghost's footsteps ceased, an eerie glow filled the chamber.

"I thought I might see you," Guy said, sitting up and leaning against the cave wall as the head of Thomas Percy floated in.

"I no longer see a child before me," said Percy. "But it's time for you to focus your mind on the hard times to come."

How could the hard times be to come? He'd lost his father and his uncle to men in the thrall of demons. "What more can happen?"

"The demon scourge will decimate this secret sect of which you are now a part over the coming years."

Guy felt like a weight hit him, dropped from high above. "And only I can stop them?"

The skull flashed, filling the room with the brightness of sheet lightning. Its image burned into Guy's retinas, and the light faded.

"You must learn from your mistakes if you are to be everything you can be."

"How do you know? Ghost told me you speak to loads of people, fill their heads with these ideas."

"I never saw you as the jealous type…"

"That's not what I'm saying. You made out it was only me you were depending on."

The brightness flared and Percy's head swung towards Guy. "So, hero complex, is it you have, Fawkes?"

Guy shuffled back. "No. But you told me I was on this path, that it was all inevitable."

Percy backed off. "That remains true. There are inevitabilities for the others I converse with, too."

None the wiser, Guy sighed. "What do I need to do?"

"Watch. Observe. Learn."

"How is that going to stop anyone?" Guy struggled to his feet, certain it was more than exhaustion and exertion that made movement difficult. He felt at the walls as he made for the chamber with the wall paintings.

"One day you will have great power, but you cannot defeat every enemy that comes before you. No one can."

Without the benefit of a lantern, finding what he wanted was an ordeal, until after groping at the air, his hands fell upon the edge of the altar.

Only when he found it did the skull offer more light, glowing as it spoke. "A great darkness will befall us. And yes, you will encounter great enemies. Only if you choose your battles with care will you survive."

Guy fumbled for the bones and lay his hands upon the skull. "How can you be both here and there at the same time? You're not real!"

"I am real, Master Fawkes, and I know what you can become."

"It's impossible. You can't be floating in front of me and dead on this stone!"

"Yesterday you would have told me it was impossible to raise the dead or to bring creatures out of the very earth, and yet you witnessed that."

"I don't want any of this. I want to go back to my mother and my sisters." The remainder of his family flashed into his mind, and he thought of Anne and her persistent annoyance that so endeared her to him.

"Soon you will be able. For now, they will not be under any direct threat, but there may come a time you must leave them behind, too."

"For what, my destiny?" Guy almost spat out that final word.

"No, because of your decisions." With that, the glowing skull of Thomas Percy disappeared, leaving only the single skull in Guy's hands.

As he placed it on the altar, tiredness overcame him, and he stumbled to his bed, where sleep consumed him.

Guy woke to intense brightness and the heat of fire. He sat up so abruptly that Kit barely pulled the flaming torch away in time.

Besides Kit was Jack, leaning against a wall, his shoulder slumped.

"Kit, you're back! Jack, what's wrong?"

Jack shrugged.

"He broke his bow. Demon dog bit right through it." Kit's eyes were wide, and he could not remain still.

"You fought a demon dog?" Guy asked, looking first at Jack and then back at Kit.

"Kind of."

"Ran away from would be more appropriate," Jack said before slumping against the wall again.

Kit's eyes were alive with excitement, but Jack looked drained and despondent, leaning against the cold rock. "Are you both all right?"

"They couldn't catch me. I was too quick." Kit moved from one side of Guy's bed to the other.

Jack, meanwhile, turned his head, and even with only a torch to illuminate it, the split in his ear was clear.

"How'd you do that?"

Jack nodded at his brother. "Kit, 'ere, did it."

"Yeah, saving your arse."

"What happened?" Guy asked, the sluggishness of sleep shaken off.

"Well, Jack was wandering around the barn…"

"I was collecting arrows. I was all out…"

"And this demon jumped him…"

"I had my knife ready. I could have taken him…"

"But I was there, and I stabbed right through the back of his head and out of its eye…"

"And into my bloody ear…"

Kit looked at his brother. "Well, sorry for saving your life."

Jack responded with a sound that was half-sigh half-growl. "I told you, I 'ad my knife."

Kit turned back to Guy. "He didn't."

Guy smiled. He looked over Kit's shoulder at Jack. "It's lucky your eyesight's good then."

"Why's that?" Jack asked, his brow furrowed.

"You'll never be able to wear a pair of glasses now."

Kit fell back, laughing, and Guy joined him.

Jack stood up. "I'm leaving you daft pair of buggers together. I turn up and help save your arse and this is the thanks I get. Piss-taking pair of bastards."

Jack walked away.

Guy called out, "I appreciate it. You were amazing with that bow."

Jack held up a dismissive hand and kept walking.

"Didn't you hear me?" called Guy, and again fell about laughing.

Once they'd finished chuckling, Guy started the interrogation.

"What happened after I left?"

Kit recounted events, acting out certain parts and embellishing the truth where he could, particularly, Guy suspected, regarding his kill count.

In summary, the second Guy was on the horse, and Sandys and Hastings realised he was escaping, they renewed the assault, drawing up another horde of charred creatures, complete with a dozen more of the demon dogs.

"Then," Kit continued, drawing in a few deep breaths to ready himself for the next part, "Sandys did some other sort of summoning. They'd had some of their men round up one of your uncle's lambs, and when he sacrificed that, one of those big demons flew out of the ground—you know, like the one we fought before."

Fought wasn't quite the right word for it, Guy thought, but he didn't want to stop Kit mid-flow.

"And this thing spoke with this booming voice."

"What did it say?"

Kit gazed up, as was his habit when trying to recall something. One hand had gone into the pouch at his belt to fiddle with his stones. "He called us 'sour-souled meat sacks' and said he would 'crush our chicken-scratch bones to putrid paste and feed it to our Lucifer-loving mothers.'"

"How'd you escape?"

"Uncle Francis gave the signal to flee. I saw him take out his bow, but he didn't fire at the demon…"

Guy stared at Kit. "He fired at the familiar."

"That's right."

"Kill it?"

"No, that cat hopped out of the way and escaped with a graze, but the demon swirled back into the earth."

"And is your Uncle Francis okay?"

"Aye, he arrived an hour ago."

"Is everyone else okay?"

Kit shook his head, his enthusiasm dropping for the first time. "I saw one demon take poor Hugh Potter. The colour just went out of his face, the life drained from his eyes. And you know how big he was? He crumpled in on himself to nothing."

Guy shook his head. Not Hugh. He'd only ever treated Guy with kindness, giving him tips on how best to position his legs when holding a shield. How much more blood was on his hands? He hardly dared ask. "Did we lose many?"

"Uncle says up to half a dozen. He hopes they may have fled in the opposite direction, but they didn't make it to the rendezvous."

Guy looked down. If men had died, it was in coming to rescue him. That rescue was only necessary because he'd spied on Hastings. Maybe the floating head of Thomas Percy was right. He had to be more careful.

"So where are we?" Guy said.

"Didn't Spencer fill you in?"

"Who's Spencer?"

"Blonde hair. Pale face. Speaks like a southern softie."

"Oh… Ghost. No, he didn't."

"They call it Saint Robert's Cave."

"He told me that… but… where is it? I rode for hours in the dark and the rider told me nothing."

"We're close to Knaresborough."

"Are we not going back to York?"

"Uncle Francis reckons we might have to stay here for a bit. You okay with that?"

Guy leant back on his bed. Where else did he have to go?

174

Later that afternoon, Ghost summoned Guy to join the others outside the cave. The sun shone through the gaps in the trees in stark contrast to the grim looks of the gathered men. When their eyes fell upon Guy, their faces became sourer still. He took his place among them, standing with Kit and Jack, his head now bandaged.

Ingleby stepped into the group. The others moved to form a semicircle around him. He was wearing a white vestment, adorned with crosses in red and purple thread. Beside him, Ghost stood, leaning on the hilt of a broadsword with the point embedded in the earth.

"Dark days are before us, friends," Ingleby said. The men around him bowed their heads. "But now is not the time to be downcast. Yes, our numbers may dwindle, yes, we are hunted, but that is why we must continue to spread the word, and remain ever vigilant of the threat to all mankind."

Ingleby gave direct orders to several men in the group and general instruction to the others, after which they left the clearing, some returning to the caves, others climbing the steps that led back into the woods, until Guy remained with only Kit and Jack beside him, opposite Ingleby and Ghost.

"Sit." Ingleby pointed to the tree stumps.

Ghost joined Kit, Jack and Guy on the stumps while Ingleby spoke.

"While last night's skirmish was because of your actions," Ingleby nodded at Guy and then his nephew, Kit, "in truth, it has been a long time coming.

"Forces are gathering strength. Our allies in the capital tell us the corruption reaches into the very heart of the nation. While our Queen has yet to fall for the demon corruption, every branch of parliament is rife with this hellish scourge. Queen Elizabeth's master of spies, Walsingham," Ingleby nodded to Guy, "the man your father trusted to report Sandys and Hastings dealings to, is trying to put every centre of power in the country under the command of high-ranking demons from Hell.

"Sandys and Hastings are in league with the foul denizens of Hell, their lips carrying the names of Master Leonard, of Arcan Rex, of Mammon."

The final name sprung a memory from Guy's mind. The very first demon he'd encountered had been called in the name of Mammon, though Mammon it was not. Pulleyn had taught of demons and their legions, with Mammon particularly powerful, capable of corrupting men with the promise of great wealth, a demon so powerful other lesser demons would often answer his call in their desperation to cause corruption on earth.

"Make no mistake," continued Ingleby, "the time has come to stand and fight. Our first stop is to cleanse our city. What I am about to tell you must go no further.

"We have powerful allies. One of our priests has infiltrated the court of Scotland and is an advisor to the boy king, James VI of Scotland. As you know, long have there been plans to bring his mother, Mary, to the throne. Through her, and through her son, we can cleanse our nation at its very core. They will see through the demon scourge in a way that Elizabeth, who is blind to the faults of her trusted courtiers, cannot.

"Trust no one with this information. Trust no one at all. Do you swear it?"

Guy, the Wright brothers, and Ghost all muttered an oath.

"Now Jack, Kit, Guy, walk with me."

They rose and followed Ingleby back into the caves, back to the same chamber where Ghost had taken Guy the previous night. Again, under the light of a lantern, the paintings on the cave walls were illuminated.

"As you were told, this is Saint Robert's Cave. But who was Saint Robert?"

The three boys shrugged.

"The story goes that Saint Robert was once a monk, but seeing the corruption within the church, he gave up that life and moved here as a hermit. Drawn to the cave, the sick and the needy found salvation. The authorities were furious that one outside the church performed what many deemed miracles. They labelled him a witch—one in league with the demons of the underworld. But when they came to put him on trial, they could find not one shred of evidence, and no one person would come forward to accuse him. He remained outside the grip of those that wanted him dead, and this place became a haven.

"Tell me what you know of the Knights Templar?"

Guy had heard stories from both Oswald and Margaret. "They were a military order, around during the great crusades to the Holy Land. But their power corrupted them. King Edward II and King Philip IV of France had them disbanded."

Ingleby shook his head. "And that's how the narrative gets corrupted. Mistruths are passed on the wind. The ignorant know not where they heard it, but they believe it as if it is gospel."

"Then what were they?"

"The first of our kind. For centuries they followed the orders from the head of the church, protecting Christians in the Holy Land, but when those quests took a dark turn, seeking ancient places of demonic power and artefacts used to summon evil from the Under-world, the Knights Templar took a stand. When they tried to report this ill use of their resources, they found the orders had come from the very top. Yes, corruption had reached the peak of the mountain. The church disbanded the Order. King Edward and King Philip consumed their wealth, and the church stepped back from their dark pursuits and focused on eliminating every Templar Knight.

"It was in Saint Robert's Cave that the last of their order hid away. Sir Roberto, to give him his knight's title, took up the guise of a monk. He survived on what he could forage until the forces gave up, considering him and the rest of his order to be dead. From there, this last knight started the process anew. He spread word of the demons that lived among us; it is from him we know how to draw on the power needed to defeat these creatures. Some three hundred years after the reported fall of the Knights Templar, here we remain, protecting the world from the evil that wants to bring it into chaos."

Guy pondered for a moment. "So are all priests, vicars, and reverends corrupt? Do they all seek to turn the world evil?"

"That is far from the case. Those that seek great evil also seek power. There is great power at the upper echelons of the church, and also of the courts, but in the parishes themselves, you find good men, men of God who simply wish to share His word."

"No getting out of going to church, then." Kit gave Guy a playful shove.

"That's the last thing you want to do. They watch. Those that don't go to church, they can turn the community against. No, when you go back to York, and one day you will, you must do all you can to fit in. Only then will you be safe enough to continue our work."

Chapter 26

IN WHICH GUY FAWKES IS REUNITED
WITH HIS FAMILY

Weeks turned to months, and Guy remained at the cave. As Guy waited, he used the time to learn. He practised his swordsmanship. He studied the paintings and bothered Ingleby (when he was there) for more history lessons. Ghost, too, regaled him with tales of days gone by, tales that only made Guy more determined to have his name shared in them one day. Even Kit and Jack had returned to York and back to school, but Ingleby insisted he stay away, for the name Fawkes was synonymous with the events of that dark day. If that name were to be heard in York, once more the forces of evil would resume their hunt for him.

Guy received news from the city through the infrequent visits of Ingleby. Sandys and Hastings were using the schism between the Catholic and Protestant religions as an excuse to put the city under tighter controls. Fines for not attending church were introduced and then swiftly increased, and anyone found practising Catholicism was banished from the city. Of course, this was a ruse to enter people's homes and carry out searches, only pretending to seek priests hiding in hidden alcoves, when they were seeking signs of the fight against demons. Neighbour turned on neighbour, and gossip was rife. With Hastings and Sandys having so many ears so close to the ground, they heard everything, and they always knew where to look.

When Ingleby was not around to answer Guy's many questions, Guy spent his time with Ghost, who was both a fairer sword practice partner and an expert in ancient lore. It was almost like being at school but without reading, writing, and arithmetic. The way Ghost cared for his blade reminded him of Margaret Clitherow and her routines for knife cleaning. Ghost not only kept the blade of his broadsword sharp, he also polished it, and added an intricate decoration to the hilt using red clay and bone to create the insignia of the Knights Templar.

Guy longed for news of his family. Eventually, Ingleby took a diversion on his travels to visit the remaining Fawkes, and with it came the solution to Guy's York exile. Guy would join the family first at the home of his deceased grandmother, and in time they would return to the city, taking on Edith Fawkes' maiden name, Blake; a common name in York, it would arouse little suspicion.

A July morning in 1581, saw Guy reunited with his family. Ingleby told him to pack up his few possessions and climb the steps. At the top, tied to a tree, was a grey mare. Ingleby thrust a map into his hands.

"What's this?"

"You'll need it to find your family."

"And the horse?"

"She's yours."

Guy ran his hand across the creature's mane, and she nickered. "What's her name?"

"She's your horse. You name her."

Guy moved around to the horse's front, looking into her eyes and rubbing the end of her nose, which brought another satisfied whinny. "Any ideas?"

"People often use a horse's appearance to give a name–something like Storm or Silver might suit."

Guy muttered both names while looking at the mare. He didn't like the negative connotations of Storm or the pretentiousness of Silver. "Then I'll call her Pewter."

"Aye, a fine name." Ingleby urged Guy to open the map and indicated the path they'd take before mounting his horse, urging Guy to climb on Pewter for the first time.

Francis let Guy lead the way to the house he'd not visited since his grandmother's death, leaving him to complete the final part of the journey alone. What Guy saw when he arrived was quite the surprise, for in the stable Anne, now nine years of age, stood armed with a bow and arrow aimed at a target that already had three arrows close to the centre.

As Guy rode around, Anne turned her head towards him but kept the arrow pointed at the target. She loosed the arrow; it hit the very edge. She placed the bow down, and, lifting the hem of her dress to stop it from getting dusty, ran toward Guy.

Guy could not stop his smile from spreading. Whatever he had told himself about keeping his family distant, he knew, in reality, it was impossible. He dismounted and tied Pewter up, then held out his arms to welcome Anne into his embrace.

Guy broke the embrace to stare at his sister once more, thinking he'd not seen her for years instead of months, such was her growth. "Anne, it's such a delight to see you!"

"Mother said we might never see you again."

"Well, you did, my sweet, sweet sister."

They hugged once more before Anne took Guy by the hand and led him inside through the door at the back of the house, into the kitchen. She led Guy into the sitting room, where he looked upon the rest of his family for the first time since they set off in the dog cart. His mother stood, looking at him in dismay, but did not approach. His younger sister, Elizabeth, smiled. Her missing teeth at both the top and bottom of her smile alarmed him.

"They say we are to return to York," his mother said.

"That's right, Mother, if that would make you happy."

"My happiness has little to do with this. You are the man of the house now, and we shall follow as you decree."

Edith sat once more, inviting Elizabeth onto her lap. Through the front door came Helen. While everyone else looked to have aged in the interim, this woman looked younger, even though the interval was greater. She barked orders at a young man who followed her in, carrying a basket laden with vegetables. "Excuse me," she said, the coldness still present in her voice, and Guy stepped aside.

Given his welcome, his return to York couldn't come soon enough.

"Guy, let me show you something." Anne dragged Guy back outside, where the feel of the sun was much more welcome than the intense closeness of the cottage. Anne patted Pewter on the nose as she passed and headed to the corner of the stable.

"Look." Anne reached into the straw, taking out his grandmother's golden angel and handing it to him.

"Anne, where did you get this?" Guy knew where he'd buried it, but that only increased his surprise at seeing it before him.

"We travelled back to the farm to see if we could salvage anything."

"And?" Guy's mind took him back to the flames of Uncle Thomas's cottage and the assault on the barn.

Anne shook her head. "All gone. But near one of the burnt beams, this caught the light."

Guy turned the angel over in his hand, once more admiring the intricately carved wings.

"I've been looking after it for you."

"Would you like to keep looking after it?"

Anne smiled. "Really?"

"She was your grandmother, too. You have as much right to it as I do."

"Oh, thank you, Guy. I will take good care of it." She hugged him and then broke away.

"It's only fair that you should have this, too." Guy pulled the bone whistle from his pouch and handed it to her.

Anne placed the whistle to her lips and blew.

"One day, I shall tell you its purpose."

Anne nodded as she curled her fingers around the gift. "There's more."

Anne looked back over her shoulder to make sure no one was watching, and then she brushed more straw away to reveal a wooden box. From it, she took the pile of papers Guy had secreted.

"These were safe too?" Guy turned over a few pages but noticed some were in a hand not his own. "Anne?"

"I watched you spend so many nights copying the words, I thought it must be important."

Anne had no schooling but had expertly copied the writing, nonetheless.

Guy flicked through the pages, calculating the time Anne must have spent on the endeavour. He shoved the papers back into the box and took Anne's hand. "You didn't need to do this."

"I wanted to. Copying your habits made it feel like you were with me."

Perhaps, Guy thought, time back with his family wouldn't be so bad after all. He looked again at the way Anne had changed in the months in which he'd not seen her, and Guy was sure he could see something of his father in the shape of her face where her cheekbones had become more prominent. With this sense of joy at being reunited with his sister came a rising tide of fear, too. As he'd been so rudely reminded, he was the man of the house now. He had not only to make sure that he remained safe, but he also had to make sure the rest of his family didn't suffer the same fate as those that went before.

Chapter 27

IN WHICH GUY FAWKES RETURNS TO YORK

It was only a month before the purchase of a property was arranged, and Edith Blake, alongside her children, Guy, Anne, and Elizabeth, returned to the city, this time residing in Aldwark in the northeast of York. Guy found that every part of what Ingleby had told him about the darkness that had descended upon the city to not only be true, but understated. As they rode through the streets, the volume of beggars was notable, all dressed in dark rags. Guy half expected them to throw themselves under the wheels of their cart, suspecting they were faithful to the dark influence over the city. A bonfire had been lit on the corner of one street with thick smoke obscuring their path, and in every alcove, people whispered secrets. When they passed the commercial areas, the streets were thick with people carrying out their business. But in the shady streets, sinister gangs gathered. And where this threat was absent, men on horseback stood guard, all in the uniform issued by Hastings. No part of the city appeared safe.

Ingleby informed Guy he would not be returning to school. He forbade him from going anywhere near the building–he feared eyes were still on Guy despite his lengthy absence from the city, and he didn't want any risk brought to the operation there. Guy could visit only on rare occasions and at times of great need, but it had to be done with discretion, entering through the secret passages rather than walking through the front door.

At first, Guy avoided The Shambles too, not wanting to visit Clitherow's Butchers until he had a clearer picture of what was going on in the city. Pavement was thick with trade. Gangs of beggars positioned themselves at every entry or exit point in the hope of kindness from a benevolent visitor. Guy did not mind the beggars and made small talk as he passed. But the other groups, dressed similarly in rags, were far more sinister, eyes peering out from covered faces feeding on the constant buzz of whispers. Worse still were the troops that moved thickly through the city like poison running in the blood through the arteries.

Guy picked up work that allowed him to stay close to the King's Manor. As the centre for the Council of the North, they busied themselves with the creation of documents, which were written on parchment made from sheepskin. Guy had ridden out to several sheep farms outside of the city, advertising this need, and one such farm could give supply, already set up to stretch and dry out sheepskins. Guy would collect a supply and, during the week, deliver it to the various places in need. Wearing his cowl meant his tell-tale ginger hair remained hidden. He never pried too far, having learnt his lesson from the past. He used his routine to identify the routes of the troops and to listen to the city's whispers. Hastings had grown bold, and a significant amount more of the city was in his clutches. Aldermen thought out of his reach and successful businessmen with long-standing names held in esteem in the city could no longer hide behind their ancestry, and Hastings leeched donations from them.

Guy continued in this manner for some weeks until he found the days growing short once more and the leaves falling from the trees. As the whispers on the streets grew louder, the frequency of public executions grew, with so-called enemies of the realm regularly swinging from a rope, accused of hideous crimes and plots against the city. Sandys and Hastings were always on hand to watch those executions, Sandys to offer a final prayer and Hastings as the man that signed the execution order, watching to ensure the process was carried out in full accordance with the law. Guy hated to watch the hangings. The sound of the drop and the snap of the neck was bad enough, but the platform was low, and all too often the fall was insufficient for instant death. The condemned soul would swing there, desperately clawing at the rope while the life was choked out of them. The whole time, Hastings and Sandys would look on and grow in stature, as if feeding on the essence of those damned souls.

One late autumn day, after delivering parchment to the King's Manor, Guy overheard a familiar name: Clitherow. He'd been back in York for plenty long enough to know that he could remain inconspicuous among his enemies, so at a distance, he followed the soldiers through the streets. They'd marched down the road with greater purpose than usual. Guy realised this was the scene that in the past would have drawn him in, that he would not have resisted the temptation to follow, but now he remained wary.

Guy didn't follow. Instead, he waited at the end of The Shambles, noticing the craned heads staring toward Clitherow's. Ten minutes later, the men marched back down the road, a third person accompanying them. The first of Hastings' men wiped blood from his gauntlet. As they approached, Guy realised the third man was in manacles. Despite the swelling in his face, he was still recognisable as John Clitherow. Being a man of wealth and a chamberlain, he wasn't the sort Hastings' men would target. If his wealth and status could not protect him from the brutality of those that controlled York, no one's could.

During his time as an apprentice, Guy learned much about how John Clitherow operated. He was beyond cautious in his approach. While not a part of the demon-hunting sect himself, he understood his wife's calling and supported her, but his activities were beyond reproach. Or so Guy had believed. Had he become sloppy in his actions, or had York changed so much that a man like Clitherow was no longer safe?

Guy avoided staring, busying himself looking at wares on a nearby stall. He knew his eyes had to be everywhere, and part of his training had taught him well how to read much from the smallest glance and how to best make use of reflections. He saw Margaret Clitherow long before she reached the end of the street, to where Hasting's men had led her husband.

"Leave him alone!" she cried, her voice thick and slurred. This was not the calm and calculating Margaret Clitherow he recognised.

She hurried towards the men. "He's done nowt wrong. You can't take him!"

She threw her hands open, lacking the deft control she'd taught Guy when training with a knife. So alien were her actions that Guy kept one eye trained on her long enough to spot her giving him the side-eye. Another wild movement of her hand saw her arm fly to her side, then into the air. From her hand, disguised by her actions, came a small projectile, which landed in the gutter near Guy's feet.

Guy took a step and placed a foot on the object, a small piece of bone.

"Madam, I suggest you return to your place of business," said the brute who had earlier cleaned his gauntlet. He lifted his robe away from his side to reveal his truncheon, indicating his willingness to use it.

With this, Margaret turned away, continuing to mutter about the injustice until she was out of sight.

Only when the men were clear of the square did Guy dare reach down.

Carved into the bone in thin letters was a message: *Back of the Black Swan, 7 o'clock.*

Guy left the area with haste. A couple of things were clear to him that caused great unease. Despite his training, despite his extra attention, Margaret had noticed him at the end of the street. If she could recognise him, others could too. Second, she'd passed him the note while in a chaotic state over the arrest of her husband. Perhaps that state was part of the act; the purpose of going into the street must have only been for his benefit. How could she have known he'd be there? So, yes, he would attend the clandestine meeting at the Black Swan, but only after changing his clothes to better disguise himself.

The Black Swan buzzed with revelry, but Guy hobbled by. He carried a stick to take his weight and wore filthy rags to resemble a beggar. He turned down the alley that ran alongside the tavern. He checked the way ahead was clear before turning towards the rear. Empty beer barrels stacked by the rear door would not arouse suspicion, and in the past Guy would not have noticed the subtle differences like the darkened colour of the wood, or the green of the lichen that grew between them. These signs revealed the barrels had long sat in the same place. Given the hustle and bustle inside, they got through a lot of beer. These barrels were decoys.

In the shadows further down the alley, something, or someone, shifted position. He stepped away, back towards the main street, catching sight of a figure observing all.

"You're not so easy to corral into a pen these days," Margaret said.

She stepped towards the beer barrels, checked both ways, and then pulled the front of the barrels towards her, opening a hidden door.

Steps led down and round, into the cellar of The Black Swan, where the tavern stored its genuine barrels of beer and ale. The east wall, however, repeated the trick above, with another door hidden, this one fronted by a cabinet. Through it, a narrow passage led into a chamber where the revelry in the tavern matched that above. In every alcove, huddled figures conversed, and on larger tables in the centre, merrymakers chatted, some breaking into song and clashing tankards. Margaret led Guy to a table in an alcove and urged him to sit.

She poured them both some ale. "When we heard what had become of Thomas Fawkes' farm, we worried for you. It seems our concern was misplaced."

"How did you know I'd be there today?"

"You think that message might only have been for you?"

Guy raised an eyebrow. "It wasn't?"

"I heard rumours of your return."

"Is this place safe?" said Guy, eying the walls, looking for an alternative route out.

"There's a hidden grate that leads down into a tunnel. It takes you through the underground caves to the river."

Guy nodded. Knowing there was a secure route out cleared his mind and let his curiosity in. "What happened to John?"

"They suspect we are harbouring priests and other fugitives."

"But he's…"

"Untouchable? No longer. They've grown bold as their power base rises. And worst of all, they sell it to the people in the name of being holy, of being pious, of being good. They have the gall to call us unchristian."

Guy's brow furrowed. "But they're witches, calling on the power of hideous demons."

"Aye, it's the ultimate ruse of those in power. As long as the words are right, as long as there is a steady procession to the gallows and it looks like someone's paying for society's crimes, the population will believe their leaders are right."

"What can we do?"

"Stand up and be counted and let the people know what we stand against. We do this knowing that our fate is death, but we do it with hope."

Guy thought of all those he'd seen fall. What good had their deaths done? "What hope is there in death?"

"We hope that when life leaves a body, it is not to the cheers of the crowd but to the dawning realisation that there's something wrong with those doing the sentencing."

Guy shook his head. "Is that the only hope we have?"

"It's a whole lot more than none. Now drink up. We can't let good ale go to waste."

While Guy was accustomed to the taste of ale, drinking at speed was not a familiar act, and after finishing only half of his pint, he found his head stirring. Guy gazed at Margaret. Maybe she'd be able to fill in some gaps the whispers had not spoken about. "Have you heard any talk of Saint Peter's School?"

Margaret turned away and beckoned someone from the other side of the room. They had a conversation too quiet to eavesdrop on over the tavern's merriment. Margaret dismissed her friend and looked at Guy once more. "Nothing good, I'm afraid. The headmaster, Pulleyn. The eye has fallen upon him."

Chapter 28

IN WHICH GUY FAWKES MAKES A CLANDESTINE SCHOOL RETURN

The revelation that Pulleyn was a target posed Guy something of a problem. His distance from the school kept the pupils and staff there safe. Not getting involved helped keep his family safe. But how could he not warn Pulleyn? While Guy spent a large part of the night in deliberation, in truth, as soon as Margaret spoke of Pulleyn being watched, he'd made up his mind. Ingleby had told him not to return to the school unless there was a dire need, and to Guy, this seemed dire. He wouldn't do what he would have done in the past. He wouldn't race in through the front door, shouting and screaming, so all and sundry knew his message. No, he'd go about it the right way. Oswald had shown him the secret passage for a reason, and now was the time to use it. In case anyone was tailing him, he started by going about his usual business, delivering the remainder of the parchment. He returned Pewter to her stable, and from there, it was natural to head out of the city through Bootham Bar. It had been a long time since he'd exited the city that way, and the walk was with the ghost of his youthful self, a small boy who had not experienced such loss. Carried on a wind blowing from the past came his father's words again, delivered on that first school day: *"This world consumes fools, and I won't raise you to be a fool."*

As he wiped a tear from his face with the back of his hand, he cursed himself as a fool. Was he any wiser than when he stepped through those school doors so many years ago? His unwise actions had cost his uncle his life. But if he were the same fool, he wouldn't be walking away from the school, would he?

From the road, he slipped into the woods and waited behind the trees in case he had a latent shadow. Several minutes later, he moved on again, pausing to listen for the sound of footsteps. His time at Saint Robert's Cave had taught him the difference between the creatures of a forest and the heavy footsteps of men. So many years had passed since he and Kit followed Oswald through the trees, but his memory of the path returned in an instant.

Many years after his last visit, he was at Gretchen's abode once more. Nature had blessed it with thicker coverage for the roof, and evergreens in the vicinity kept it hidden through the winter. Guy stood at the door, but before he could bring himself to knock, he recalled his last visit, when he, Kit and Jack were oblivious to the full extent of the world's evil.

The door crept open. "Long have you been a stranger," came a voice from inside. "Come in."

Inside was as he remembered. Perhaps the shelves were a little barer, but everything else was identical, including the enormous cauldron bubbling away.

Gretchen, though, had changed. Her skin hung on her face, and her clothes too were looser on a frame that had become frailer. She urged him to sit while she busied herself at the shelves on the wall. A few minutes later, she placed several jars in Guy's lap. "You will need these," she said before sitting opposite him.

She talked through the properties of the different salves and mixtures she'd given him, some to help heal cuts and burns caused by demon blades, others to stave off madness caused by demented wailing. Each would help for some kind of terror or other that Guy was likely to encounter. "But... why do I need these now?" Guy asked.

"The breeze carries my name; it lives on the lips of those that wish to do me harm."

Guy glanced around her abode. "Is this place not well hidden? They'll not find you here."

"They will burn the trees down if they cannot find me."

"Why don't you run?"

"To where, Master Fawkes? Running? It's not for me. No, when the time comes, I shall leave my home and surrender myself to their mercy."

Guy stood. "They have no mercy. They're monsters. You don't have a hope."

"What hope comes when we fall? Let others witness the injustice and seek to put it right for future generations."

Margaret's ideas echoed in Gretchen's words. There had to be a better way than surrendering to death? Could death resonate in any lasting way? Would the people of York remember a sacrifice and celebrate it year on year? Could one act of defiance or one act of surrender echo down the years for generations? For centuries?

"I take it you've decided?" Guy asked.

Gretchen paused. She moved closer to Guy to focus on him with her rheumy eyes. "Yes, there is something different about you, brought on by more than the passage of time, more than the lessons of hardship. Tarry no longer. Go knowing that letting me give you that last gift," she indicated the jars and vials by Guy's side, "has brought me great comfort." She stared into her cauldron. "It may be the last decent act I perform."

Guy opened his mouth but realised no further words were necessary. He placed his gifts in the knapsack, checking the label of each to understand its purpose, simultaneously realising their value and hoping they would never be required. He nodded a goodbye to Gretchen and headed out through the trees to find that rotting oak that hid the access to the school.

Guy made his way down the ladder and struggled through the dark passage, feeling his way with his hands until a flicker of light came into view as he rounded the corner.

After passing two small rooms, both vacant but with additional straw-stuffed sacks acting as beds on the floor, Guy emerged into the main chamber. He'd timed his visit, so training was at its peak. His field of vision grew with each step but first, he saw only ghosts: his younger self running into Hugh Potter and crashing onto his arse, Kit grabbing hold of the nearest weapon on the rack and being unable to release it, Pulleyn standing over three boys introducing them to demon lore for the first time.

Then, in the present, he saw Ralph swinging his sword in his left hand. As he entered the main chamber, more faces came into view, some he recognised, others fresh. James, Robert and Nicholas were among them, and while he smiled to set eyes upon them, his greatest joy came when he saw Kit at the back. Guy moved around the perimeter, a subtle hand gesture indicating those in training should continue.

Even though he could only see his back, Guy knew the shape of Jack Wright. He was in an alcove off to one side, cutting feathers and inserting the flights into a batch of arrows. So focused was Jack on his work, that he didn't turn away, though the tensing of the muscles in his neck made it clear he was ready for an approach.

Guy sat on the low stool opposite Jack and picked up the short-bladed knife.

Jack finished inserting the flight and added the latest arrow to the quiver. He gazed up at Guy and smiled. "Good to see you, Pal."

"While I'm here, I might as well make myself useful. What do I need to do?"

Jack spent several minutes talking Guy through the process, demonstrating each step from the required angle of the feather to the way to cut the base of the arrow to fit the flight.

"Uncle Francis said you'd not much be here no more."

Guy nodded. "Thought it was best if I stayed away."

"You've heard then?"

"Heard what?"

"What we're up to tonight. That's why you thought it necessary."

Guy paused as he was about to cut another feather. "What are you up to tonight?"

Jack paused too. "What do you know?"

Silence hung between them until spoilt by the usual source.

"Guy!" called Kit as he ran over, awkwardly slotting his sword into his scabbard. "So, you're joining us for the assault tonight?"

Guy stood and turned to meet Kit's embrace. He broke free. "What assault?"

Jack gave Kit one of those looks that shut him up. Jack was one of few people with the power to do that.

"Guy, you know we can't blurt out details of what we're planning. Tell us why you're here, and maybe we can tell you what's going on. Perhaps Pulleyn will let us drag you along. We could use all the help we can get."

Guy revealed what Margaret had told him, that the school was in their enemy's sights. Jack shrivelled in his chair. "We're going to have to tell Pulleyn. He won't like it, but we have to tell him."

Jack led the way to where Pulleyn was delivering one of his demonology lectures to the youngest members of their sect. He glanced at Jack, then beyond him to Guy. While it didn't stop his delivery, his pace slowed, and when he reached the end of his point, he urged the youngsters to put their books away and return to the library.

Only when the children were out of sight did he turn to face Guy. "You've grown, Master Fawkes."

Guy could well say the opposite about Pulleyn. No longer the dominating presence that had seemed so fearsome, Pulleyn stooped, his need for a cane evident in every movement. The skin on his cheeks hung loose like his face had lost its elasticity.

"It's good to see you again, Sir."

"I'd say the same, but alas, your presence here fills me only with concern."

Guy saw no need to hold his tongue. "I've heard your school is under suspicion. Hastings is likely drawing up the search warrant as we speak. It will be the usual accusation of hiding Catholic priests, but you know what they seek."

Pulleyn nodded. "It is no surprise. Long have I suspected our days are numbered."

"You can't give up. You've done so much."

"And that, young Fawkes, may be the exact reason *to* give it up. If we disband, our pupils live to fight another day."

"But..." Guy started, but without a follow-up. He understood Pulleyn's point. The fight was not always immediate. Sometimes you had to put it on hold and come back swinging when the time was right.

"I imagine Kit has already revealed something of the plan for tonight's assault... what may be our last."

Guy put his arm around Kit. "You may be surprised, but I know very little."

Pulleyn blinked several times. "Then the school has performed a miracle! If this young man now knows when to hold his tongue, we've done the impossible indeed." A smile spread across Pulleyn's face.

Kit looked from Guy to Pulleyn, his mouth opened as if to speak, but, for once, he was lost for words. Jack reached out and touched Kit's chin, closing his mouth for him.

"Tonight, a sabbat takes place, a meeting of Satanists, at the former Saint William's College building. We have word that Sandys will be in attendance alongside Hastings and some of the city's other powers."

"And what are we going to do? Infiltrate and destroy the lot of them?"

"You've still so much to learn." A half-smile formed on Pulleyn's face. "No, a small group will go on from this place to carry out a ritual of some power. Follow and put a stop to it."

"And I can join you?"

"I wouldn't have told you about it if I didn't want you there." With that, Pulleyn lifted his stick to dismiss them and shuffled towards the stairs.

Guy, Kit and Jack pulled up the chairs on which they'd sat when their demon-hunting journey began.

Guy leant in towards his two oldest friends. "Fill me in on the plan."

Chapter 29

IN WHICH GUY FAWKES WITNESSES A SUMMONING AND BATTLES WHAT'S SUMMONED

Saint William's College was over one hundred years old, but that made it something of an infant compared to other properties around York Minster. Not only that, it was an outcast too, for its original purpose had been to house the priests attached to the chantry chapels. Alas, Henry VIII's dissolution of the monasteries made it redundant, and in the last generation, its new owner had converted it to a house, retaining a large space for gatherings. That owner was Baron William Simnel, a man often seen in the company of Hastings.

Alongside Jack, Kit, and Ralph, Guy waited at Dean's Park near York Minster. From there, they had a clear view of the building's main entrance, so they could see who was coming and going. Many arrived on horseback, leaving servants to attend to their beasts as they entered. Formally dressed, their displays of colour indicated their wealth and enormous ruffs confirmed their status.

While Kit and Ralph watched the house, Jack's duty was to survey the nearby buildings for any sign of other demonic activity, for it was typical for such parties to break into splinter groups where they would carry out a summoning. A pang of jealousy hit Guy as he realised he'd missed out on so much hands-on experience. Other members of the group watched from positions close to Saint William's College. Knowing his eyes were not required in service of the mission, Guy watched York Minster. How he hated that building. He'd looked upon it with such awe as a youngster, but knowing it housed one of such evil, one that had caused him so much loss, meant he could no longer appreciate it as a feat of architecture. Instead, it was like a gateway to Hell, and as he watched, someone emerged from its main exit. It was Sandys, but he was not alone. As usual, guards flanked him, but there was another walking close beside him toward Saint William's College, no doubt as part of the cabal. Guy tugged at his cowl to make sure his hair remained hidden, for taking his eyes from Sandys was not an option. His face seemed thinner, drawn, and his beard greyer, but he strode with purpose. As they were almost level with Guy and his friends, Sandys' companion turned his face in their direction. His hollow cheeks and protruding cheekbones were one notable feature, but more significant was that he had but one eye, tinged with yellow. Guy glanced at this man's hands, but he wore gloves. If not, he was sure he would have seen claws. This had to be Sandys' familiar having shifted from cat to human form. No doubt Sandys needed direct communication with his conduit from the underworld for their planned sinister activity.

They watched Sandys and his familiar enter the building, and a few seconds later came a whistle. Evidently, Jack had moved up in the ranks, for he interpreted the tone and issued orders. "Ralph, head one hundred yards back towards the library. I'll meet you there if anyone exits and heads that way. Kit, Guy, take up a position down College Street observing discreetly. Follow whoever leaves." He waited for Ralph and Kit to signal their understanding, then took off for the building opposite Saint William's College, scaling a wall and taking a position on the roof. He grabbed his bow and adjusted his quiver to make sure he had plenty of arrows in easy reach.

After they'd been in position for half an hour, with no sign of movement, Guy sighed. "Why can't we be where the action is?"

Kit reached into his pouch. His runes still brought him comfort after all this time. "Pulleyn has someone in there. If we're needed, there's a signal."

"If we're needed?" A stiff wind blew down the street and made Guy shudder.

Another whistle came and Kit cupped his ear. "They're done. Eyes open. We follow anyone that comes this way."

In his head, Guy saw Sandys and Hastings. He imagined them walking into an abandoned building, and them being at the mercy of his blade. Mercy would be found wanting.

Alas, when figures emerged and made their way along College Street, they were not those Guy most desired to see, and there were more of them than he'd be able to hold at bay with a sword alone. At a glance, he recognised one man as Baron Simnel, and Kit whispered he was with Lord Aymeric Rowland. Advisors in dark clothing followed alongside a group of five soldiers who bore Hastings' colours.

Guy gazed up to make sure the last of them had passed. "We follow them?"

"Aye, we follow."

"And then?" Guy put a hand to the hilt of his sword.

"We see what unfolds."

Guy and Kit followed at a distance, along Goodramgate and past the cottages of Lady Row, following a couple of turns until they were on The Shambles. With such narrow streets, the party had to thin out. Guy glanced up, wondering if Jack followed on the buildings above, for this was a brilliant spot for an ambush, but they emerged onto the other side of the street unscathed. They continued along Pavement and down Fossgate, coming to a stop outside the Merchant Adventurers Hall, a place that was forever embedded in Guy's mind, a place written on countless documents he'd read repeatedly as he transcribed them from his father's hand to his own.

Here, the party stopped, and the majority entered, leaving a single guard by the door.

"What do you think they're doing?" Guy asked.

Kit glanced over his shoulder. "Summoning."

An orange glow illuminated the basement windows. Guy had seen this building's plans and had memorised every structural feature. "They're in the undercroft."

"Then it must be…"

"A gateway. We have to get inside."

"How?"

"Follow me." Guy strode along the street towards the rear of the building, counting windows as he passed. "Here," he said, coming to a stop where the light was weaker. Guy reached for the window frame.

Kit snatched his hand. "Are you out of your mind? We can't drop into the middle of a demon summoning."

Guy shrugged Kit off. "We won't. There's a storage room below here."

Kit looked at the cobbles leading to the window, the blackened marks indicative of coal being delivered. A door several yards down no doubt led to the steps into the undercroft.

Guy probed at the edge of the window frame until he found the desired spot. With a little wriggling and prying, the window sprung free of the small catch on the other side.

"Hold this," Guy said, and as soon as Kit had hold of the window, he slid through, legs first, on his stomach, onto a pile of coal beneath his feet. He turned and scanned the small storage room. The door at the opposite end was ajar, and through it came the light of the soldiers' lanterns.

"Come on," whispered Guy, and soon Kit was with him.

Together, they approached the door and peered through, Kit with one hand in his pouch, fiddling.

Through the gap, they could see most of the undercroft, except the space hidden by the rows of pillars. The room was bare, except for some barrels in one corner, and a pile of wood against the opposite wall. In the centre, flames rose from a metal brazier. Closest to it stood Baron Simnel and Lord Rowland, Simnel holding an ancient book from which he read in a booming voice. The words were not like any

Guy recognised, and didn't sound like the Latin he had learnt at school either. Pulleyn had warned of these archaic languages with their harsh sounds and spoke of them as the language of the underworld.

Guy grabbed the hilt of his sword. Kit reached out to push it back in.

"We have to stop them," Guy whispered through gritted teeth.

"No, we get help. We can't take them on by ourselves."

Guy glanced through the door again: eight men, four of whom were Hasting's trained soldiers. Another stood outside the door. Yes, Guy's blade knew the taste of demons, but a human opponent trained in combat would be another challenge altogether. He looked back at the window. They could seek help, but where would they find them? Had they not spread in all directions following the witches that left Saint William's College?

"We don't have time. We wait, we watch, and we only act if necessary. How about that?"

"Aye," Kit nodded, and his hand reached for his hilt.

While Simnel read, Rowland tore pages from what looked like a religious text and flung them onto the fire, which flashed brighter, illuminating the frightened faces of the soldiers and the hungry mouths of Simnel's and Rowland's cloaked advisors. While they appeared motionless, Guy could hear them calling out across the spirit plane, singing their song of summoning.

With the final line delivered, and the last page torn from the bible and tossed into the flames, the fire burned blue. Simnel and Rowland tore open their jackets to reveal their chests and their advisors dashed to them, their faces shifting, their mouths protruding to allow them to better suckle from their masters' teats. A few seconds later, Simnel pulled his familiar away from his chest and approached the fire. From his belt, he withdrew a dagger and pulled it across his palm, letting his blood spill into the hungry, blue flame.

First came a croak from deep below, resonating up the pillars and shaking the entire building. Then the flame in the brazier dimmed, and thick smoke poured out, leaving the room illuminated only by the soldiers' lanterns. One of them turned and took off for the stairs at speed, but a tendril of smoke gave chase, wrapped around the soldier's waist and dragged him back to the brazier, lifting him into the air and dropping him. From the smoke, first emerged giant teeth which snapped closed the second the soldier passed between them. Once fed, the smoke took the form of a giant, red-skinned toad, with monstrous teeth and talons at the end of its feet. Another soldier took one look at the creature before dropping his lantern. He broke into a run, but before he reached the stairs, the toad's tongue lashed out and wrapped around the soldier's neck with such force that the soldier's head divorced the body, and shot up to hit the ceiling. The creature pulled the rest of the body into its cavernous mouth with its ulcerated tongue.

Rowland continued to suckle his familiar, his eyes rolling back in his head in ecstasy.

Simnel picked up his book once more. "Great servant of Satan, we thank you for your presence here, and hope you enjoy the offerings…"

Another soldier, understanding the implication of those words, took a step toward the stairs. He knew what would happen if he ran, feared what would happen if he didn't.

Kit and Guy stared at one another. Guy spoke first. "We have to send it back to Hell."

Kit nodded. "Go for the familiars."

"Knock out their link before they complete the contract."

In tandem, Guy and Kit withdrew their weapons and called out the words designed to bless them with the power to tear through demon flesh. They kicked open the doors and stepped into the open area of the undercroft.

The toad's eyes darted to them. It called out in a croaky voice. "Earth-walkers! Scabby minions of the sun! Thy flesh is my nectar, and I feast tonight!"

Its tongue shot out. Guy dived for one pillar. Kit dived for another. The moist appendage flopped to the floor. It drew it back in, an angered croak rumbling in its throat. "Flesh-puppets! Waste of skin! Your sweat makes your inevitable demise smell sweeter."

"Get them!" barked Simnel, turning to his two remaining guards and pointing towards Guy and Kit.

The soldier by the stairs turned and ran, taking the steps two at a time until he was out of sight. The other drew his sword but kept one eye fixed on the eternally hungry, red-skinned, demonic toad.

Simnel took a step towards Rowland and pulled his familiar away from his chest. While in conference, the toad lashed out with its tongue once more. Guy ducked, and a tide of spittle splashed onto him as the tongue wrapped around the pillar. The toad tightened its grip on the pillar, causing a crack to appear. As it applied more pressure, the centre crumbled, and the remainder crashed down, sending brick dust flying around the room.

Guy wafted the dust away from his face so he could see the creature's next move.

"Meat sock! Spindle-stockings! You think I too cannot leap?" The creature shrank back into itself, drawing power into its rear legs. Kit sprinted along one wall. The creature's eyes turned towards him and it leapt, the leg muscles pulsing. Kit slid onto his side. The creature flew over his head, crashing into the barrels against the wall.

Simnel called out in the demon tongue once more before repeating himself in English, "Will you serve us, oh great one!"

As the toad convulsed in the corner, shaking off splintered bits of barrel, Simnel slapped Rowland across the chest. "It's no good. He will not listen while these pests distract him!"

Kit stood and fled back to the pillar behind which Guy hid. "If we vanquish the familiars, they won't be able to control the demon!" he cried.

"I don't think they can control it as it is, either," Guy said, ducking out of sight as the toad scanned the area.

"But they want to. If they do, we'll be in real trouble."

Guy surveyed the room. Simnel and Rowland continued their heated discussion, while their familiars held up their hands in reverence to the demon toad. Shuffling along one wall was the remaining soldier. His sword drawn, he looked far from ready to use it.

"What's the plan?" Guy asked as the toad looked poised to leap once more.

"Rush 'em."

In his younger days, it had often been Kit's first suggestion to run head first into whatever situation arose and deal with the subsequent consequences. For once, it seemed like the best idea. Guy gave a nod and then peered out from behind a pillar. He counted backwards from three. When he got to two, the toad launched forward once more. Guy stepped to the other side of the pillar and called out, "One." The toad smashed through the brick, choking the room with dust, but Guy and Kit were already speeding to the other side. The familiars barely moved. By the time they saw the blades flashing towards them, there was no time to shift form. Both Guy and Kit hacked downwards, thinking that if they tried to shift, they would still hit their target. As it was, the blades pierced the top of each of the familiars' skull and they crumpled to the ground.

"Rotten curs! Ravaging whelps! I'll suck your souls through your skin yet!" croaked the demonic toad.

"Kill them!" called Rowland, pointing to Kit and Guy.

The creature's tongue lashed out once more. With no remaining connection to the underworld. Rowland was its target. He tried to dodge, but the tongue wrapped around his right arm. As it retracted, Rowland tried to stop himself from being pulled along, but the solid floor of the undercroft of Merchant Adventurers' Hall offered no assistance. "Help!" he cried as he reached to pull his dagger from his scabbard.

Bored of his resistance, the toad reared up on its hind legs, speeding Rowland into his jaws, ignoring the growing panic in his screams. Once his upper torso was within its gargantuan mouth, it chomped down, severing him in two. It swallowed without chewing. The tongue lashed out again to collect the rest.

The sound of metal on stone drew not only Guy and Kit's attention but also that of the beast to the soldier who stood, petrified against the pile of wood.

"Rancorous flea! Bug-eyed cretin! I'll jellify your bones!"

204

The soldier turned and ran towards the stairs. There, Simnel crept up, step by slow step, hoping to avoid detection.

The toad flew once more. The soldier dived to one side, and the toad crashed into the underside of the stairs. Without the support of the struts below, the staircase collapsed. Simnel toppled from the falling steps and landed with a thud. The toad oozed around and lashed out its tongue once more, and Guy barely ducked in time, feeling another shower of saliva cover his back. The toad's tongue wrapped around a pillar, and Guy dived at it, sword swinging. As it motioned to retract the tongue, Guy's blade made contact, and as it grew tight, the blade slid through the flesh.

The toad gave a pained croak as the severed section of tongue dropped to the ground, flopping like a landed fish on a riverbank. It retracted the rest of the tongue and tried to speak, but only managed a garbled mess.

"We can cut it," called Guy. "That means we can kill it."

The toad's body pulsed, ready to leap again.

"How do we get close?" Kit called.

"Stay apart. Lure it into jumps and strike from where it can't see us."

The toad leapt, but at neither Guy nor Kit. It landed on the collapsed wood of the stairs, and a scream was the last they heard of Simnel.

"Over here!" called Guy.

The toad wobbled around, then pulsed, ready to leap.

Guy dived out of the way and didn't see Kit move, but he heard his cry, a splash, and something jangling on the ground.

"Kit, you okay?"

"Yeah, I got a toe."

The toad twisted and leapt once more, lacking the vibrancy of its prior leaps. Kit dodged, and Guy ran a few steps before lunging with his sword, embedding it into the creature's back. When Guy tried to withdraw his sword, he found it stuck tight and had to release the hilt as the creature turned.

As Kit tried to edge out of the corner, past the creature, it lifted its back leg, slamming Kit into the wall. Two of its toes were on either side of Kit, pinning him against. The missing central toe saved Kit from a punctured throat.

Without his weapon, Guy didn't know how to fight back.

"Oi! Leave them kids alone!" came a shout. Guy turned to see the last remaining soldier. He'd picked up his sword and wielded it in one hand. His bravery didn't go as far as running in to attack, but that was enough to get the toad's attention. Even though the end of its tongue was missing, there was still enough to fly out and wrap around the soldier's sword arm. He yelled and put all of his strength into that arm, pulling back.

As they continued their struggle, Guy saw his chance. Between him and the creature, shining in the light that glowed from his Hell-spawned body, was its razor-sharp, severed toe. The second he touched it, he felt its heat, felt his skin burning, but still, he wrapped his fingers around the flesh.

The toad's tongue constricted and twisted, pulling the soldier's arm out of its socket and tearing flesh, tendons, sinew, skin and anything else in the way. As the tongue and its cargo travelled back towards the beast, Guy struck, jabbing the creature's severed talon deep into its eye. He felt the eyeball burst, liquid erupting over his hand and down his arm. The creature reeled back, releasing Kit as it did so, but also dropping and opening its mouth into which Guy's momentum would take him.

Kit cried out and lunged downward with his sword, entering the top of the toad's head and travelling through, collapsing the head, pinning the mouth closed. Guy fell into the shrinking mass of the beast as the last of its inner structure collapsed, launching a tide of wetness across the ground. All that remained was its saggy skin and the evaporating goo. Within its mess lay Guy's sword. With his left hand, he picked it up and returned it to his scabbard. The claw he'd held had also disintegrated alongside the rest of the creature, but the pain in his hand remained. With the creature gone, the only light in the room was from a dropped lantern. He turned to look for Kit. After stabbing through the creature, he'd backed away and had crouched down beside the last of Hasting's men.

Guy rushed to join him. Blood gushed out of the gap where the soldier's arm once was, and he muttered deliriously.

Kit turned to Guy. "He said something about Pulleyn!"

Guy touched the man's cheek, tilting his head to make breathing easier. "What did you say?"

The soldier struggled to draw in breath. He stared into Guy's eyes and managed three last words: "Hand of glory."

Chapter 30

IN WHICH GUY FAWKES ENCOUNTERS THE HORROR OF A HAND OF GLORY

A giant demon toad that ripped limbs from their sockets and ate people in no more than two gulps was not to be the worst thing Guy witnessed that night. The second the dying guard had uttered the words, "Hand of glory," Guy suspected further disaster, and he knew he had to act fast. With the staircase collapsed, the quickest way out was the window through which they'd entered. Guy boosted Kit up to speed him through, and then Kit leaned down to pull Guy up.

"What's a hand of glory?" Kit asked as Guy looked along the streets to get his bearings.

"Was there a debrief planned for after tonight's activities?"

"No. We report back the next day... but Guy, what's this about?"

"It's dangerous, the hand of glory... so Pulleyn would head home?"

"Yes, usually."

"Do you know where he lives?"

Kit grabbed Guy's arm, leading the way. "His house is on Little Blake Street. Uncle Francis had me take a letter there once."

As they made their way, Guy explained that he'd learnt about the hand of glory from Ghost. "It's a horrible thing," Guy said. "You take the left hand of a criminal, one executed and having died from hanging, and you dry it out. Next, you use that man's fat to make a candle. You stick the candle in the hand…"

"Wait, like it's holding it, or stick it through the dried flesh and bone…?"

"That's not important. The important thing is the effect. When you breathe in that candle's smoke, it paralyses you."

"So, he's defenceless?"

"Exactly."

With that, Kit picked up the pace. He whistled and continued to do so periodically until a response came. They came to a sudden stop when a roof tile clattered to the ground in front of them. Before Guy had the chance to look up, Jack dropped from the nearby roof.

"Sorry about the tile. Slipped under my foot."

Guy grabbed him and started towards Little Blake Street. "Is Pulleyn at home yet?"

"Should be. He followed Sandys back to York Minster and turned in. Why?"

"Is anyone else close? He's in danger."

"Aye, Uncle Francis is still about."

"Fetch him and bring him to Pulleyn's house. We'll meet you there."

Guy and Kit rushed the rest of the way. They reached the street and slowed, awaiting reinforcements. While waiting, Guy's attention shifted to the throbbing pain in his hand. With every movement came the pain of a hundred needles stabbing at once, over and again. He held it against his jacket, which went some way to easing the pain, but the shape of the toad's dread claw remained on his flesh.

Guy looked at the row of houses. "Which one?"

Kit pointed. "Come on. We've got to get in there and save him."

Guy grabbed Kit's arm. "That's the one thing we can't do. If we go in there, we're at the mercy of the hand of glory too."

"Then what?"

"We stop anyone going in or coming out. A candle can't burn forever, can it?"

"Perhaps if it's made from human fat, it can."

With that grizzly image in their minds, they made their way along the street. Many of the houses were already in darkness, the owners already asleep, but a glimmer of light through the curtains indicated Pulleyn's abode.

"This the one?" said Guy, already sure, but wanting to say something to stop the awful thoughts from taking over inside his head.

Kit nodded. The door was ajar. He moved his head closer to the crack. "I hear voices."

Guy glanced back down the street. Jack and Francis were on their way. Guy sped towards them to explain.

Back outside Pulleyn's house, Francis moved to the window, peering through the edge of the curtain.

"Pulleyn's in there tied to a chair. His servants are down–either dead or unconscious."

"Who else?"

"Uniform suggests they're Hastings' men. They've covered their faces to stop them from breathing in the foul smoke."

"What's the plan?" Kit's hand remained close to the hilt of his blade.

"Jack, get up on the roof and aim at the rear door. If anyone leaves, take them down." Francis helped Jack onto the roof from a couple of doors down so the noise wouldn't be obvious in Pulleyn's house.

"We break the window. I'll knock the candle down with this." Francis bent down and picked up a rock. "I'll give you the signal to enter."

"We're going in?" Kit asked.

"Yes."

Kit pulled out his sword and grinned. He thrust his other hand into his pouch to fiddle with his runes.

Guy tried to withdraw his sword with his right hand, but his swollen fingers wouldn't wrap around the hilt. He had no choice but to take it in his left.

"Kit, I've got your back, but you'll have to take the lead in there."

Kit nodded, but his hand moved inside his pocket with more vigour.

"Okay, on three." Francis began his countdown. When he got to two, he indicated to Kit to approach the window. At one, Kit knocked the glass in with the hilt of his sword and then returned to the door. Francis threw the rock. Light flared inside and panicked voices rose. From his position Guy saw little but heard stamping, and seconds later all light was gone.

"Okay, enter–but hold your breath!"

Kit flew in first, and Guy followed. Guy heard a clash of swords as Kit tussled with one man. In the near darkness, only shapes were visible, but he knew the sound of a swinging sword. He lifted his blade to deflect the blow.

"Back to the manor," came a cry. Guy saw only a shape come for him, followed by a pained yelp as he ran straight into Guy's sword.

Guy felt arms on his shoulder and another shape passed him, followed by Kit. He tried to spy others but the darkness made it impossible.

"Hello!" called Guy, covering his mouth.

"Master Fawkes? Get out. It's not safe."

Guy continued toward Pulleyn's voice, stumbling over a body. "Is there anyone else here with you?"

"They slew my servants, the swines. Get out. Hold your breath."

Knowing Pulleyn was safe, Guy saw the wisdom of his words. He returned to the cool evening air. At the end of the road, Kit and Francis had caught up with the soldier who had fled.

"Jack, you up there?"

"Aye."

"Any action?"

"Aye. One took off out the back. He didn't get far."

"Good job. Could you climb into the garden and open the back door? I'll bring Pulleyn out that way."

Guy took another deep breath and ran in once more. He raced over to Pulleyn and fiddled with the knots that tied him to the chair.

"There's no time for that, boy. Leave me here. We're doomed."

Guy pulled the chair back and thought for a second the weight would be too much for him. But he couldn't let Pulleyn crash to the ground. He gritted his teeth and dragged the chair, Pulleyn still on it, to the rear door.

Once outside, he took his sword to the rope and cut Pulleyn free.

"Run," Pulleyn said as he stood, rubbing at his wrists. "If they find you here, you're dead."

"We got them. They can't tell anyone anything."

"Too late. Hastings was here. That damn smoke froze my bones but not my tongue."

"What do you mean?"

"I confessed. They know about the school. As soon as I said that, Hastings took off. He left those men to get more names from me."

"But we stopped them. Everyone else will be safe, right?"

Pulleyn exhaled loudly and stared at the ground. "I'm done for. My tongue is ever loose because of that poison. They'll arrest me, and they'll get all your names."

"We can't let that happen. You've got to run."

"To where?" Pulleyn took Guy by the hand. "I'm an old man. I've done my part. Maybe my death is the best thing that can come of this."

Guy swallowed hard. "No. We need you."

"I'm a liability."

Guy rubbed at one eye with the back of his hand.

"Guy, listen. I could take my own life, but that would have no meaning. If I fall at the gallows, if others know how much I believe in this cause, then there's worth in my death."

Guy nodded. Jack was at his shoulder, also listening.

"We can't let them use this dark candle against me again. We can't let them draw any more names from me with their magic."

"What can you do?"

"I need one last thing from you, Master Fawkes, Master Wright. One last duty for your headmaster."

"What?"

"I need you both to go into the house, but be swift. Tarry not where the smoke lingers."

"What are we after?"

"Jack, there's a sack in the kitchen. Take it and grab that foul hand. Don't touch it with your fingers. Smash it to bits with a rock, fill the sack with rocks and throw it into the river. Understand?"

"Yes, Sir."

"Off you go."

Jack took a deep breath and headed into the house.

Pulleyn placed his hand on Guy's arm. "Guy, I need you to grab the small vegetable knife from the kitchen and a clean cloth."

"What for?"

"I have my chef sharpen my knives. You never know what you're going to need one for."

"What for?" Guy asked again.

213

"You know better than to ask questions of your headmaster, don't you, boy? It's not too late to visit the birching pony one last time."

Pulleyn's forced sternness did its job. Guy raced through the back door at the same time as Jack went out the front. In the kitchen, he fumbled around for the knife block and took hold of a knife that felt the right size. He grabbed a cloth from the side and hoped it was clean enough for the job. He returned to Pulleyn, wary of the last duty he would have him perform.

Outside, the cold night air bit Guy. The clouds had parted, revealing the moon, shining a silvery light onto Pulleyn that suited the colour of his hair and his eyebrows, which stood out as wild as ever.

"Hand me the cloth." Pulleyn held out his hand.

Guy obeyed, though his hand was shaking so much that he struggled to pass it over.

"The only way for you to protect the lives of every demon hunter I know, of everyone you love and care for, is to cut out my tongue."

Guy dropped the knife. "I won't do it."

"Francis. Kit. Jack." Pulleyn held Guy's gaze for a moment. "See how easily they trip from my tongue? Robert. James, Nicholas. Ralph."

"Okay, okay." Guy reached for the knife.

"These will be my last words, Guy, and they're for you. Do your duty to the best of your ability, and believe in yourself as much as I believe in you." Pulleyn stuck out his tongue.

Guy swiped the tears from his eyes. He took the knife in his right hand, painfully curling his fingers around the hilt. It was only that pain that allowed him to hold it. His concentration was on that, not on what he was about to do. He reached out with his left hand, took hold of the tip of Pulleyn's tongue between finger and thumb and before he could think about it too much, he slid the knife across the tongue. It didn't succumb in the same way as demon flesh did to a sacred blade, or the knife wasn't as sharp as Pulleyn had promised, but he had to apply more pressure, feeling every ounce of resistance as he sliced through the muscle. In truth, the cut took only a couple of seconds, but those seconds lasted a lifetime. Each millimetre of flesh was paid for with anguish that pulsed through his body. And when the last of the elastic tissue gave way and an inch and a half of tongue flopped to the ground, he could hold the contents of his stomach no longer.

Pulleyn rammed the cloth into his mouth, but it failed to muffle his scream.

Guy didn't even see Francis arrive. It was only when he spoke that he realised he and Pulleyn were no longer alone.

"What have you done, Guy? In the name of the Lord, what have you done?"

Chapter 31

IN WHICH GUY FAWKES WITNESSES A DEATHLY SPECTACLE AT YORK TYBURN

There are many stories about the origin of the name Knavesmire, given to the area south of York's city walls. The 'mire' part was obvious to anyone unfortunate enough to visit the marshy landscape, but the first part was up for debate. It had been a spot of execution for a couple of hundred years. Some suggested it was from that it took its name, a place for knaves to meet their end when their unscrupulous acts and their dishonesty culminated in their death at the gallows. Older tales, those told in the clandestine texts, suggested it was named after an Anglo-Saxon ruler by the name of Cenward from a distant age. Why anyone would want to have so unpleasant a spot of land named after them, I don't know. As I'm sure you know, it's much the same today, liable to flood, so no one has ever attempted to develop the land.

In York, there were gallows too at Saint Leonard's Hospital, Saint Mary's Abbey, and York Minster, but the law punished heinous crimes with death outside the city walls in front of the crowd gathered at York Tyburn, a name borrowed from the famous gallows in England's capital.

Several weeks after he had severed Pulleyn's tongue and left the man bleeding into a rag in his back garden, Guy was about to face Pulleyn once more. At York Tyburn, he'd witness the hanging of his former headmaster. Several other enemies of the state were also to be executed. The nature of their crimes made it a public matter that demanded a large crowd. The Council of the North advertised these executions with banners in the streets. The names of those condemned were rarely revealed in advance, and Guy had been expecting to see Pulleyn for some time. On this occasion, the whispers on the street were certain it was the headmaster's turn to swing. While attendance wasn't mandatory, absentees made themselves subjects of the city's whispers. What better way to keep the public under control than by having them witness the punishment for failing to follow the law of the land? As such, Guy and the rest of his family stood on higher ground where the damp was less likely to seep through their boots to watch the executions.

The propaganda machine of the Council of the North had gone into overdrive with reports of the wicked murder of Simnel and Rowland. The promise of a reward encouraged those in poverty to keep a close eye on their neighbours. Whispers at every corner spread the names of suspects. Hastings' growing army thrived on this information and ransacked highlighted properties. Guy kept his head low and his ears open as he continued his business of delivering parchment. Had he known the death warrants for a number of those he cared for were to be written on those same pieces of parchment, he may not have worked so hard. And yet it was on his travels that the most important whispers reached him. Saint Peter's School had a new headmaster, a man often seen in the company of Hastings, resulting in many students terminating their studies. Guy had no word from Kit and Jack or anyone else at the school, and he dared not visit for fear of bringing more trouble to their door.

At Knavesmire, with his mother and his sisters standing close, remaining near the cart so they could travel back into the city after the fatal exhibition, Guy scanned the crowd for familiar faces. Among a group of Shambles butchers was John Clitherow. No sign of Margaret. Guy worried for her. She was no stranger to spending time inside the prisons of York Castle, but those in power were using the threat of incarceration less and less, preferring to make examples of their enemies with a short drop from the three-legged mare—the nickname given to the gallows—and a lengthy death by slow strangulation.

A figure moved through the crowd, his hood covering most of his head, but from the way his left hand hovered close to the hilt of his sword, Guy was sure it was Ralph White.

"Stay here. I shall return," Guy said to his family.

"Aye," said his mother. "And watch this spectacle close for you're likely to end up there, too, if you don't take heed."

Guy said nothing, not looking back as he hurried into the crowd, hoping to catch Ralph. He moved among the masses, hearing anguished cries among those baying for blood. He heard the vendors who had set up stalls shouting out about their wares, and customers bartering for a better deal. With people packed in so close, with so many cloaks in the same shades of grey and brown, it was impossible to follow the figure.

A voice in the crowd caught Guy's attention. "Must we watch?"

Guy turned to see a girl, of a similar age to him, with raven hair emerging from her white bonnet. He continued to move through the crowd with his eyes on this girl when he bumped into someone's shoulder.

"You ought to look where you're going."

Guy whipped his head away from the girl and came face to face with a man in uniform. Hastings' soldiers already had their hands on their swords' hilts.

"I do apologise," Guy said, looking down, hoping they wouldn't press the matter.

"You're lucky we're all out of rope." The soldier nodded towards the gallows. "Or we'd make room for you up there."

Guy swallowed back bilious words. "I should have been looking where I was going."

The soldier spat at Guy's feet. "Depart. If I see you again, I'll run you through."

Head down, Guy let himself be swallowed by the dense crowd, out of sight of the guards. Only then did he place his hand on his hilt. To do so in front of the soldiers would have been suicide, but, when clear of them, he fantasised running *them* through.

Dark thoughts gave way to the memory of the raven-haired girl he'd seen in the crowd. He scanned for her, but with so many people present, it was impossible.

"Guy..." a whisper in his ear.

He turned and the tall figure he'd tracked was walking away from him. It was Ralph, though he dared not call his name. He moved away from the crowds and approached a wagon in the shelter of trees.

Guy stopped several yards away to survey the scene. The figure standing nearest tipped his head back to reveal his face: Francis Ingleby. Guy approached and moved to the rear of the wagon, out of sight.

"You were right to silence Pulleyn the way you did," Ingleby said first.

Guy stood for a second with his mouth open. For weeks he had doubted himself, felt the pain he'd inflicted on Pulleyn had been too much, and Ingleby's initial chastisement had long rung in his ears. But now, with Ingleby before him, it no longer mattered, not when he had so many questions. His mind turned, first, to his closest friends. "Kit and Jack, are they still around?"

"With the one you call Ghost."

"And the school? What happened?"

"Many got away. The new headmaster asked Vicars and Adamson to stay on. They thought it meant they were safe, but I fear they may hang today."

"What do we do now?"

"Guy, I know you won't find this easy but..." Francis gazed at the ground.

"What?"

"I'm leaving. I'm going to Europe to find help. We have allies there."

Guy felt a pain in his gut, abandonment once more hitting home. Oswald had never written again after that first letter. "Will you be gone for long?"

"It could take," Francis shrugged, "years to get the support we need."

"And what are we supposed to do in the meantime?"

Francis placed his hand over his heart. "Survive. Keep your head down and wait."

"And let Sandys and Hastings turn York into a demon's paradise?"

"Go back to Saint Robert's Cave. Speak to Ghost. The folks there will orchestrate what they can to keep them at bay."

"It isn't enough."

"I'll need you when I return. I don't want to come back and discover they brought you here with a sack over your head. I don't want to come back and see your head on the gate."

"I guess this is goodbye, then?"

"Aye, for now."

"For now," said Guy and walked away as the crowd's cheers grew louder. From the distance, horses approached, and behind them, on crude frames, the condemned were dragged towards their deaths.

Guy hurried back to his family, and by the time he arrived, the eight horses had reached their destination. Guy had not thought to count the ropes when he passed the gallows. He'd noted the extended platform, which indicated an increased number of deaths, but eight was more than he expected. He was thankful for Ingleby's warning when the soldiers untied Adamson and Vicars from their frames and dragged them to their place on the platform, with the noose dropped over their necks. Next came a group of three women, all accused of performing gross acts of witchcraft. While Guy did not recognise two of them, he was unsurprised that Gretchen was among their number. The next was a stranger. When the soldier dragged the second to last man to the platform, Guy inhaled. Had he not seen him hundreds of times throughout his childhood, he may not have recognised Pulleyn.

His hair was gone, his face swollen. No doubt he'd suffered incredible torture, but with no tongue, he could cry no names to ease the pain. Yes, it was a tragedy to see eight executions in one day, but had Pulleyn named all the demon hunters he'd trained, it could have been ten times that. Knavesmire would have grown boggier still from all the blood spilt. One spot remained. The last figure was smaller than the rest. They wouldn't execute a child, would they? When they removed the sack, and Guy saw that shock of ginger hair, for a second, he thought he looked into a mirror. A soldier dragged him up the steps, his legs barely touching the wooden frame. He'd only ever known one other person with hair redder than his, Robert Clifton, a boy who he'd wielded a sword against in practice countless times, a boy who had ridden to his aid when he'd had the demon eye planted upon him: a boy who would never become a man.

Guy felt his knees weaken. He wanted to collapse to the ground and shout at the sky. A warm hand curled around his fingers. He turned to Anne. She smiled. He had to be strong. He couldn't afford to bring suspicion upon them. When the executioner gave the signal, when people he loved dropped from the platform and swung from a rope, he didn't buckle. He felt the warmth of his sister's hand and believed it gave him hope. And while the tears welled in his eyes, he did not cry out, for he knew nearby ears would translate the sound into their whispers. And it was through those watery eyes he witnessed a small figure break from the crowd, a girl with raven hair. She ran for the bodies that swung from the ropes. She ran for Pulleyn and grabbed hold of his legs, hoping to bring the kiss of the angel of death that much quicker.

Whether she was successful in her endeavour, Guy never knew. He stayed fixated on her, even when one of Hastings' soldiers broke rank to kick her away, pressing her face into the mud. Instead of watching life slip from those who'd taught him so much, those he fought alongside, he watched the girl, hoping the soldier would remove his foot, hoping she'd rise from the mud. The soldier glanced over his shoulder and then stepped away upon command. Seconds later, the raven-haired girl scrambled to her feet and ran, swallowed up by the crowd once more.

When Guy looked back at the gallows, all life had drained from the bodies and they swung, gently, on the breeze.

Chapter 32

IN WHICH ONCE MORE THE YEARS TICK BY

As I mentioned before, there are a few points in the story when we need to skip through the years. We've reached another of those moments here. 1581 reached its end, and Guy could not have been gladder to see the back of it. So much had happened since he had brought demons to his door and Uncle Thomas had died trying to protect him. He'd learnt so much, but what had it led to? Nothing but more death. And those that didn't die had fled York. Guy plodded on, delivering parchment where it was required and keeping out of trouble.

1582 started in the same manner, every week the same, the darkness of winter never-ending. Had it not been for a freak accident, Guy may have plodded onward in the same way. While Guy had stopped paying attention to time passing, time had not stopped paying attention to him, and a few months before his twelfth birthday came another growth spurt. Guy was so wrapped up in self-pity and misery that he failed to notice his hose growing tight, the jackets that came up a little shorter in the arm. The Yorkshire weather did little to brighten Guy's spirits either, with a lengthy period of snow only passing when torrential rain washed it away. Many of the roads Guy travelled to collect parchment were boggy, making his journeys arduous and lengthy. En route to one farm, and trying to make up time lost on a prior delayed journey, Guy pushed Pewter hard, and when he saw the puddle ahead, he pushed her harder still. She'd jumped larger puddles many times in the past, some even at this very spot. She was one of the few that hadn't let him down.

Alas, the last time Guy had urged Pewter on at this location, he'd been a few inches shorter and unaware of how close he'd come to courting with disaster. On this occasion, the branch that had parted his hair last time came into direct contact with his forehead, sending him spiralling off Pewter's back (she, of course, cleared the puddle with ease). He crashed on his back in the water.

The clouds above doubled. Wetness seeped through every layer of his clothing, but there was no strength left in his body to lift himself from the quagmire into which he'd fallen. He turned his head to a nearby tree. His eyes traced a line up the trunk, then along the branch above. A scratching noise, as if a squirrel was scurrying along the branch, made him search for the source, but it only made his vision of the branch split in two as pain ebbed inside his head.

Something obscured the branch, something large and white floating in front of it. Only when he heard a voice did he recognise the skull of Thomas Percy. For once, Percy had little to say. "Saint Robert's Cave," was all it uttered before it was gone, leaving Guy to struggle out of the mud and back onto Pewter. She made her disdain about having to carry his soaking body more than apparent, with a bumpy ride the rest of the way. Guy completed his parchment collection and returned to the stables. After apologetically giving Pewter an affectionate brush, he made plans to return to Saint Robert's Cave.

When he made his way back through the trees, he struggled to believe that less than a year had passed since his last visit. He followed the rock wall down the hand-carved steps, leading him into the clearing. Winter's gloom had not left this place either, and until he saw the light of the fire in the clearing, he could distinguish little.

Sitting around the fire, however, were familiar faces that once more invigorated the spark inside him. Kit couldn't remain in his seat, rushing over to Guy the second he came into view, almost knocking him off his feet. Sitting in the clearing too were Ralph and Ghost.

Guy scanned the clearing and looked towards the caves. "Where's Jack?" There was plenty of noise coming from inside, suggesting they had a decent sized band.

"Didn't Uncle Francis say?"

A lump formed in Guy's throat. What hadn't he been told? Jack wasn't there on the day of the executions. Guy's mouth dropped. He wanted to ask a question, but he didn't know where to start.

Ghost noticed the colour drain from his face. He guided Guy towards a stump and helped him to sit down.

"Wait," Kit said, reading Guy's reaction and understanding the conclusion he'd come to. "No, he's okay. He went with Uncle Francis to France, that's all."

Guy puffed out his cheeks and shook his head at Kit, but when Kit smiled, he knew he'd not stay angry for long.

"What have you been doing?" Guy asked once he'd composed himself.

"Us?" Ghost said, looking around the camp and smiling. "Collapsing tunnels to the underworld, discovering ancient artefacts, slaying demons. You know, the usual."

The malaise that had gripped Guy so hard loosened; he was among friends again.

For a few years, Guy balanced his time between selling parchment and spending time with his friends. Whether they were sitting around the fire at Saint Robert's Cave, sharing some ancient lore or a joke or a song, or whether they were tracking demonic activity, Guy felt alive. Gaunt had escaped York and took on responsibility for continuing the education of those not familiar with all aspects of demonology. The boys kept their swordsmanship skills up with regular practice. In this manner, 1582 passed into 1583, into 1584, into 1585, and into 1586. Guy was fast approaching the age of sixteen. Gaunt continued in his training role, taking a band to Leeds where the pressure was off. He took Nicholas Fairfax with him and a few of the younger lads who didn't have homes they'd be welcomed back at. James Nevell grew tired of the life and started working as an apprentice blacksmith, taking on the very job earmarked for the blacksmith's son Robert Clifton, who Guy could still picture swinging from the rope with his ginger hair waving in the wind. Ralph and Ghost were the last residents of the caves. Ghost has continued to help Guy tune out the voices of the unquiet dead, training him to listen only when those in league with demons cried out in the spiritual realm. Kit was often present at the cave, for it was a mere two-hour horse ride from home. Guy had perhaps the longest journey, taking four hours on horseback, meaning it was only workable to visit at weekends, so all activity fell around then.

For four years he lived this life, remaining anonymous in the city, and doing what he could outside of it to stop the swell of witches and those with dark intentions from finding their way into York. Despite all their efforts, the city had, without doubt, become a worse place to live. Disease ran rife, with corpses cleared from the streets daily. Most of the city was in the thrall of Sandys and Hastings, doing the work of the church or of the Council of the North on rates of pay barely sufficient to keep rooves over their heads and food in their bellies. Beggars were controlled with licensing, and the cost of a license was to fall into line with the rest of the city's whisperers. Guy stayed away from Clitherow's Butchers and only visited The Shambles when he had business to attend to or meat to purchase. He did, however, frequent The Black Swan to share his exploits with Margaret and to hear of the latest underground goings-on in the city, sometimes joining her party on an assault on the evil that threatened to consume the city, doing enough to keep their heads above water.

While Guy grew taller and stronger, there was something from 1581 he couldn't leave behind: the memory of that raven-haired girl clinging onto Pulleyn's legs, trying to bring him a swifter death. Sometimes, in his head, it had a horrific twist: when the soldier removed his foot, when she rose, her eyes had that ring of orange as witnessed in all seeded by demons. Given the prophetic nature of his encounters with the floating skull of Thomas Percy, he felt it had to mean something, but he had no idea of who this girl was. Pulleyn, aside from his servants, lived alone as a bachelor, his whole life dedicated to the school and its underground activities. She resided in the back of his mind, and whenever Guy was among crowds in the city, he kept an eye out for her, but it was in vain. Perhaps, he pondered, she was an angel of death, sent on that day to speed Pulleyn to the grave as thanks for his years of faithful service.

Guy's sisters had grown, too. Elizabeth at ten years old was the shadow of her mother: no longer under her feet, but mimicking her in her needlework, and in every other daily activity. At almost fourteen Anne worked in James William Wilson's Bakery six mornings a week, but still spent much of her time following Guy when he was home. His need to protect his family had remained at the forefront of his mind, and given that Anne was going to mimic him regardless of what he did, he felt it only right that he should teach her the basics. Alas, Anne's eagerness to learn had meant the basics were not enough. As soon as she learned of a world of demons, she wanted to know more. While Guy had only wanted her to be wary of the threat and how to spot the tell-tale signs of a witch, Anne wanted to know how best to stop them. He wanted her to know about familiars, and how they were the link between the witch and the demon. Soon it reached the point where Guy had given Anne a blessed blade (a dagger she could conceal on her person) and taught her how to wield it. She'd attacked with fury, gnashing her teeth and lunging at him with a reach that surprised him. Knowing she could look after herself brought him comfort. But he didn't want her to follow him down the same road, for Thomas Percy had made it clear where that road ended.

Alas, on one of those dark winter evenings when Guy made his way to The Black Swan, after checking no one was loitering in the street, Guy saw someone slip from the shadows at the very instant he'd unlocked the hidden door.

"Guy…" said Anne as she came into view.

Guy grabbed her arm and dragged her through the secret entrance and down into the hidden basement.

"Why did you follow me here?" Guy asked.

"I wanted to see where you go at night. I wanted to take on a demon with you."

Guy raised his hand at some familiar faces who were beckoning him over to a table, Margaret Clitherow among them. "I will never put you in danger that way."

"Then why teach me how to fight?"

"So, you can look after yourself."

Guy was aware of movement and the changes in the shadows that indicated someone was closing on him.

"Who's this?" Margaret leant on his shoulder.

Anne held out her hand. "Anne Fawkes."

Margaret shook it firmly. "I take it your brother didn't want you to follow him this evening."

Guy sighed.

"You would be right there, ma'am."

"Away with your ma'am, I'm not the queen. Call me Margaret."

"Okay, I will, Margaret."

She turned towards Guy. "Why have you been hiding this one from us? Sturdy lass like this will bolster our numbers."

"She's not here for that."

"Why not?"

"She's not meant for fighting demons."

"No? Well, she did a pretty good job of following you here to-night. That's stealth we can use."

"Do you think so?" Anne cut in.

"Without a doubt."

"I won't let you, Anne. I forbid it."

Margaret made her eyes large. She looked from Guy back to Anne. "Oh! You forbid it, do you?"

Guy gritted his teeth. "I'm the man of the house, Anne. You should do what I say."

"But you're not the man of this house, are you, Guy?" Margaret took Anne by the hand and led her towards her table.

Guy gazed around the room, noted the eyes on him. He looked down and followed Margaret and his sister.

Margaret turned to Guy before he sat down. "Go fetch us all some ale, and we'll have a nice chat about the situation. What do you say?"

Knowing it wasn't a question, Guy headed for the bar.

When he returned with a brimming pitcher and a collection of tankards, Anne and Margaret were deep in conversation. He served their drinks.

Margaret nodded at Anne as Guy took a seat.

"We've decided," Anne said.

Guy looked at Margaret with a scowl.

"I don't want to do anything that's going to upset you, but Margaret thinks I should come to her from time to time. You know, to learn a little more. A bit more of the history, how to use my dagger better..."

It was like she'd plunged that dagger into his heart. "Have my lessons not been adequate?"

Margaret reached across and pinched his cheek. "Poor, hurt, little fowl."

"You never wanted to teach me, anyway," Anne said.

She rammed the dagger in deeper still. These were the only moments when he felt he still had a family connection, one worth savouring. "No... I..."

"I still want to practise with you, Guy. If you'll let me."

A bandage over his wounded heart. "Can I stop you?" Guy smiled.

"Besides, Margaret says in the baker's, I'm in a great position to hear things. I can pass information on to her."

"So, no demon raids?" Guy stared into Margaret's eyes, trying to spot a hint of deception.

Margaret shook her head. "Training in exchange for information. And while we're talking information, do you wanna know who I heard is making his way back to these shores?"

"Do tell," Guy said, taking a sip of his drink.

"Your young training buddy, Jack Wright."

Guy nodded, taking in the knowledge, while Margaret started recounting the story of when she corralled Guy, Kit and Jack into her pigpen. Guy tried to work out the implication of this information. If Jack was coming back, did that mean Francis was too? And if so, was it finally time to rid York of demons once and for all?

Chapter 33

IN WHICH GUY FAWKES AND JACK WRIGHT ARE REUNITED

When Guy travelled to Saint Robert's Cave the next day, Kit confirmed the news. His parents had received a letter some days prior stating Jack's intention to return. Given the information in the letter, it was likely Jack was already making his way through France and would seek passage back to England as soon as possible. But days turned to weeks, and soon Guy felt the old malaise gripping hold once more so much so, that on that early February morning, he almost chose not to go to Saint Robert's Cave, not when there was plenty of ale waiting at The Black Swan. A sense of duty drew him back, or perhaps a last morsel of hope. He arrived in the clearing to find Ralph, alone. Ralph told him Ghost was checking the traps for rabbits, and Kit had not shown up the previous evening.

Guy considered leaving but instead drew closer to the fire, watching the flames flicker and rise ever higher. So hypnotised was he by the flames that Guy didn't hear the approaching footsteps. Ralph stood and drew his sword while Guy remained captivated by flame. Rushing into the clearing came a well-built young man, a healthy beard covering most of his face. He wore a long, dark tunic and gloves reaching beyond his wrist. If it weren't for Kit trailing him, Guy may have struggled to recognise Jack.

Guy raced over, and the two embraced. Jack had bulked out, his arms thick with muscle. His face held a touch of colour, making it clear he'd been away from England for some time.

"Is Francis returning?" Guy asked.

"You've not seen me in years and your first question is about my uncle?" Even his voice had changed, his pronunciation softer.

"I'm sorry, my friend. I expected the two of you would have travelled together. How are you?"

"Never better. Getting away from here makes you realise how much more there is to the world."

Guy spied the scabbard attached to his belt. "You've got yourself a new sword, I see?"

"Aye, and the skill to use it. Wanna see?" Jack withdrew his rapier, a sword far more delicate and precise than those he'd practised with in his youth.

Guy stood and drew his sword. Jack had always been so easy to knock off his feet. He telegraphed his moves so they could be avoided with very little thought, but from the second Jack drew his sword, Guy knew he'd changed. His stance was wider, giving him better balance. His eyes were more alert. Guy stood before him, leaning one way, then the other, waiting for Jack to make the first move. Before, he would have swung wildly by now. Guy leapt into action instead, and Jack raised his sword to deflect the blow. Yes, he had improved. Guy stepped back, ready to come again, but Jack feigned to strike. Guy took evasive action and when Jack twisted his body the other way and stuck out his leg, Guy fell.

Guy stood and dusted himself off. "You have improved."

As Jack returned his sword to his sheath, the sleeve of his tunic rode up, revealing a long scar on his lower arm in the gap between the cloth and his glove.

"What's that?" Guy nodded towards the wound as Jack sat on a stump.

"Is this the part where young soldiers gather round and compare war wounds?"

Guy smiled. "Is that what we are now? Soldiers?"

Jack nodded at Kit, who had already taken a seat. "That's what Kit here tells me."

No doubt Kit's account of their exploits had been thoroughly exaggerated, but they'd ransacked a few infested farmhouses. They'd sent several minor demons back to Hell, their familiars following close behind. The cabal of witches they'd vanquished near the River Nidd had been their biggest endeavour.

Guy had only a few minor scars, and Kit only one of significance. Ghost had a long, thin slash across his chest, and Ralph a puncture wound in his shoulder.

"This is no doubt the worst injury." Jack pulled off his right glove first, and then the left.

Guy had to blink several times before he could believe what he saw, for the ring finger and the little finger were almost entirely absent, stubs only remaining. "A hellhound bit right through them." He held out his hand to show the gathered party. The missing fingers weren't the only part, for on the back of his hand was a swirl of burnt skin and the right-hand side of the middle finger was worn almost to the bone.

"That's why you practised your swordsmanship..." Guy stated, still staring at the hand until Jack pulled the glove back on.

"Aye. It's tough to hold a bow steady when you've not got the right number of digits. Anyway, I didn't come here today to talk about injuries."

Jack leaned in closer. "I am glad you have kept yourselves active and haven't suffered the losses I have. Even abroad, word of Hastings' misdeeds spreads, but we have an opportunity to pluck a powerful artefact from his grasp."

Those around the fire closed in too, their focus on Jack.

"We intercepted a communication meant for the Council of the North. It directed Hastings to delve deep into the bowels of Selby Abbey, for something hidden there by one of our ancient order. With it, they can summon beings of tremendous strength. They can call upon the aerial powers to ravage the lands once more."

"We need to tell someone," Guy said, peering into the caves he knew were empty. "We need to gather a party."

Jack nodded. "Why do you think I'm here?"

"Us?" Guy said, turning to look at Kit and Ralph, and Ghost, who had arrived with a brace of rabbits not five minutes earlier.

"Aye," said Jack. "I can't think of anyone better."

After preparing their weapons and stocking up on provisions, they saddled their horses. Selby Abbey was twenty miles from Saint Robert's Cave, and it was already late morning.

The journey passed with tales of Jack's fighting in the Pyrenean Peninsula. After the fall of the Portuguese royal family, a sect practising the dark arts had tried to bring a demon king to the throne, sending ripples all over Western Europe. Jack claimed his role was speeding from one part of Europe to another, putting out fires, and at times, it was as if the entire map was aflame.

When Jack spoke of Spain, his face lit up. Spain, he claimed, was as pure as any country he'd ever visited, with any scent of demonic activity snuffed out. It was clear Jack was an admirer of their ways and their climate. But he'd returned to England with a purpose. They had to stop their enemies from getting that artefact, no matter how much blood, demon or human, had to be spilt.

That started at Selby Abbey.

Chapter 34

IN WHICH GUY FAWKES AND FRIENDS ASSAULT SELBY ABBEY

Darkness had fallen by the time Selby Abbey came into view, illuminated by the full moon. After their long journey, the five companions stopped to survey the scene. Ghost had mentioned that the building was over 500 years old during their journey. In the moonlight, the building looked every one of those years old and made York Minster look like a palace of modernity.

A single soldier guarded a dozen horses outside the main entrance, his uniform that of Hastings' men.

"A second messenger must have got through with the news of the artefact," Jack said.

"What do we do, retreat?" Guy asked. He was done making mistakes that cost lives.

Jack shook his head. "This is a powerful weapon. I saw one like it used on the beach of Bilbao. They turned the sand against us with it. The sand formed giant fists and tried to crush us. We had to flee. We can't let them take it."

"I say we charge in, send the horses into panic and use the chaos to our advantage," Kit said.

"You never change," Jack gave his brother a playful shove, "but I'm after a more subtle plan."

Ghost cleared his throat. "For a long time, the monks based here produced ale, then shipped it along the River Ouse. There must be a way in close to the river."

"Any chance there will still be ale?" Ralph asked.

"Save talk of ale for after victory." Jack strode forward and then indicted to Ghost. "Lead the way."

Leaving their horses a safe distance away, the party took a route to the river alongside a hedgerow, staying low. When they reached the abbey, they saw how the monks had shipped the barrels. A slope led from the river to a half-sized door at the back of the cathedral.

"We get in there." Ghost pointed at the entrance.

A chill wind blew off the river. The slope descended to what was once a dock, but only crumbled stone remained. They clambered round to it, unable to avoid getting their feet wet, and moved along the slope at the perimeter of the abbey. The door was smaller than it had appeared from a distance, only coming up to Jack's waist, who was the tallest of them. A rusted metal brace held the door shut.

"What now?" asked Ralph, looking back down the slope.

Jack grabbed hold of the metal and tugged at it. "It will give with the right leverage. Kit, give me your sword."

Kit reached down by his side, but to protect his weapon, not to use it. "No way. Use your own."

"The blade on mine is razor-sharp, yet thin. It will not stand for this kind of treatment. Yours is a much sturdier weapon, lad."

Kit sighed and surrendered his weapon. Jack slid it against the metal, put one boot against the wall, and simultaneously pulled one way with the sword while pushing his weight the other.

The grate groaned until a snap came, and Jack tumbled back. Ralph and Guy moved in tandem to support him. Before them the tiny doors hung open, the metal brace snapped in two and lying on either side of the slope.

"My sword?" Kit reached out his hand.

Jack returned the weapon, now significantly shorter with a jagged point at the end. "Sorry, little brother."

Kit shook his head and sheathed what remained of his weapon, hoping he wouldn't need to use it.

Through the doors, the slope continued upwards. On hands and knees on the damp and long disused passage, the five of them crawled, with Ghost leading the way. "Quiet now," he said in a loud whisper. "There's another door ahead." He reached the door and pressed his head to the wood.

Guy gave Ghost a moment to listen. "Anything?"

"It's quiet."

"What's on the other side?"

"Should be the former kitchen. I don't know what it's used for now."

Ghost edged the door open, peered through, then crawled out into the darkness. He helped the rest to their feet once they emerged into the chamber. Guy shook the stiffness out of his arms and legs, thankful for the room to stretch his limbs.

Ghost put his head to a wall. "I can hear scraping. Maybe digging. Where did it say this artefact was?"

Jack pondered for a moment as if visualising the words on the scroll. "Subterranean passages that lead west of the crypt. Hang on..." Jack reached for his belt and took out a Y-shaped stick, about a foot and a half long.

Kit reached out to touch it. "What's that?"

Jack held the twin branches of the Y-stick, one in each hand. "It's a mosaical rod."

"What's a..."

Jack lurched forward as the branch shot towards the floor. "It's drawn to magical energy. It's somewhere beneath us."

"Then it'll be in the crypt." Ghost said. "There will be stairs beneath the tower. The spiral staircases of places like this stretch up to the heavens and delve into the earth where those worthy enough were buried."

Kit glanced up and traced the ceiling. "Tower's that way," he said, pulling Guy by one arm and Jack by the other.

"How can you tell?" Guy asked.

Kit looked at Guy with his brow furrowed, as if the answer was obvious. As he spoke, he trailed the route with his fingers. "We entered from the rear, followed the slope around like this... so the tower must be there." He jabbed at the air with his finger.

Guy felt lost in space and could not so much as indicate which way the front was after the twists of the slope, but Kit had tracked every turn.

At each door, they stopped and listened until they reached the spiral staircase, which, as Ghost had suggested, led both up and down. From here, the sound of activity below was clearer, the clang of metal against stone and the drag of shovel through rubble.

"Let's go!" cried Kit, already on the first step leading downward before Jack hooked him back.

"You saw how many horses they had. There are at least twice of them to us."

"So, we let them grab the artefact and turn the wind against us? That's much worse!"

Jack gazed along the dark passages of the abbey. "No, but they must return this way. We set up an ambush. From the darkness, we could take out half of them, even up the numbers."

Kit nodded and scanned the area for places to hide.

"Ghost, Ralph, you're lightest on your feet and quickest should you need to flee. Head down to assess the situation and get us a head-count."

They hurried down the stairs and were soon out of sight, their footsteps a distant memory.

Guy moved closer to Jack. "You weren't only fighting alongside others in Europe, were you?"

"What do you mean?"

"They gave you responsibility, let you lead."

"Aye, a time or two they did after I lost these." He held up his gloved left hand. "They figured maybe I'd take more responsibility if there were lives at stake other than my own."

Jack had changed so much in his years away, while all Guy had done was stagnate. He wanted to prove his worth. "Should we take out the one guarding the horses? It might save us another scrap when it's time to leave."

"Aye. I'll stay here. You and Kit deal with him."

Upon hearing his name, Kit stood tall, eyes alert.

"We're taking out the guard at the front."

"And letting the horses run wild?"

"No, we'll leave them. We don't want them drawing any attention."

"Okay, this way," indicated Kit.

One turn later, they were in the nave, opposite the main entrance. The large stained-glass windows let in the moonlight, illuminating it better than other parts of the abbey. A cold wind howled through the braced-open doors. Guy and Kit kept to the perimeter, creeping lower each time they passed a window, not wanting to cast a tell-tale shadow across the floor. Not that the guard seemed observant. He stuffed tobacco into his pipe while leaning against a horse. When it lifted its tail and dropped a pile of steaming dung, the guard struck its head with the back of his hand. "Filthy beast," he muttered before lifting his pipe to his mouth and trying to light it with a taper.

Kit took off before Guy could call him back. He stood in front of the guard, drawing his sword, before remembering his blade had broken.

The guard bared his teeth, the pipe clenched between them.

Guy moved, staying in the shadows, the sound of the disturbed horses disguising his footsteps.

"What you gonna do with that thing, puny boy?" the guard asked. He dropped the taper and drew his sword. Orange rimmed his eyes, indicative of the demon that controlled his soul.

"It's still got an edge, ain't it?" Kit held the sword towards the guard. "That's enough to skin you."

The guard swung down, slashing at what remained of Kit's sword, hoping to knock it from his hand, but Kit had a grip like a vice, and sometimes couldn't let go of things, even if he wanted to.

Guy slipped into position, and as the guard stood upright, lifting his sword to strike again, Guy struck. The guard slumped to the ground, and the surrounding horses whinnied, one rearing up, then crashing down again.

"There's a whole sword there if you need it." Guy indicated the fallen guard's weapon.

"I kinda like my short blade." He returned his broken weapon to its scabbard and picked up the guard's sword, for, without the reach of a full-length sword, his was as good as useless.

Guy and Kit shifted the body away from immediate view and pulled the doors closed. Once they'd barred the door, they returned to Jack, confirming that they'd dispatched the guard and sealed the exit.

A few moments later, Ralph returned.

"Where's Ghost?" asked Jack.

"Still observing. They've broken through to the chamber."

"Can we stop them?"

Ralph shook his head. "No, our best bet is to ambush them when they try to leave. There's no other way out, but there's more."

"What?"

"Hastings is here. He intends to wield the treasure."

Guy felt sudden anguish grip his stomach. Hastings was a name synonymous with all the loss he'd suffered. But having killed the guard moments earlier, Guy was ready to kill again.

Jack, too, understood the importance of the moment as he reissued commands. "No one leaves this building. Ralph, summon Ghost back. We'll all confront them together. We wait until they emerge from the stairs, and then we strike. Make your first blow a fatal one, and then they'll barely outnumber us."

Ralph disappeared from view only to return seconds later, Ghost panting behind him.

"There's a dark door down there," Ghost said, pausing for a moment to draw breath. "They mean to draw a legion out tonight."

Jack paused. "We can't let them draw anything out. Ghost, with me."

Jack and Ghost hurried down the stairs, leaving Guy, Kit and Ralph waiting above. Guy listened for the sound of movement. The scraping of metal on stone had long since ceased, the silence more unnerving than any activity.

Then came a howl, starting at a pitch almost inaudible, but growing louder and clearer. From the staircase first came a wind carrying odours of long-dead flesh tinged with the sweetness of decay. After the stench, came a shape. Guy, Kit and Ralph stood with their swords by their sides as it flew from the depths of the abbey, a skull-face formed from dust, a trail of spectral light following it, illuminating the chamber and the shocked white faces of Guy, Kit and Ralph. It flew around the corner and into the nave.

Guy moved to follow, but from the staircase came further cries and the clash of steel against steel.

"Kit!" came a shout from below, Jack's voice blurting out between the sound of swordplay.

Once more, Kit had to be held back as Jack called again. "We're coming up. Be ready. There are so many."

Guy looked from Ralph to Kit. The faces of both had fallen, once more resembling boys, not the men they fooled themselves into believing they were. Guy couldn't let them fall, couldn't let this opportunity to vanquish Hastings pass, no matter what ills he'd pulled from the bowels of the earth. "Kit, fall back with your brother and Ghost when they return. They may be hurt. Ralph, stand with me by the staircase. Once Jack and Ghost are free, we block this staircase with the bodies of whoever tries to escape."

Kit and Ralph took their positions. The sound of panicked gasps, of sword on sword, grew louder, then Ghost reached the top. He cradled one arm, his sword limp in his hand. Kit rushed to him, as the back of Jack's head came into view.

"Turn and run!" called Guy. "We've got this."

Jack spun around and leapt up the last couple of steps, his frame almost filling the entire doorway. A skeletal arm reached for his boot, but Ralph came down with a slash that splintered it to bits. Another creature followed, and Guy slashed, crumbling its rib cage. All that slept in the crypt of Selby Abbey had been awoken and invigorated with dark purpose.

Ralph slashed again, bringing a skull to dust. So much for the plan to block the staircase with the bodies of their enemies! They crumbled as more and more continued to rush through, some carrying swords and spears, others with shields as brittle as their bones.

Soon Jack joined Guy and Ralph, taking his turn to slash at whatever emerged.

Then, from the depths, came a single cry, the unmistakable language of the underworld, and from within the staircase, a green light ebbed.

With a whoosh, the spectral creature, the skull formed of dust, swept back into the chamber. Jack slashed at it, but his sword passed through it with no effect. Unlike those of ancient bone, there was no solid mass to strike, the cloud of dust particles dispersing as the blade swooped through. The phantom rushed past him and into the staircase.

The flow of skeletal soldiers ceased, and there was silence once more.

"Block them in," Kit cried, rushing to topple a statue that stood in the centre of the chamber.

Guy, Jack and Ralph rushed over and shuffled it towards the staircase, but again came the whoosh, and the spectral light returned, no longer as a skull, but as a giant fist. It collided with the statue and broke it into a hundred pieces. From out of the staircase flooded more of the skeletal creatures alongside what remained of Hastings' men, those not sacrificed to lure the dead back to life. Jack lunged at one soldier, avoiding his block and planting his blade into his stomach. Kit held another man at bay, brandishing both his broken sword and that he'd taken from the felled soldier. Guy and Ralph, too, had swords drawn and slashed at the creatures to thin their numbers while monitoring the more dangerous foes, the soldiers with the demons controlling their souls, and the aerial power that weaponised the dust of the abbey. After felling another, Jack retreated to Ghost. He'd shifted his sword to his weaker left arm while the right hung limp at his side, blood dripping from a hidden wound down his arm and off his fingers.

The spectral creature, with the power of the air, still in the shape of a fist, departed once more, heading back to the nave.

"It means to open the door," Ghost cried. "He'll let them all out."

No sooner had he finished than the sound of splintering wood exploded from the main body of the abbey.

With his escape path clear, Hastings emerged from the staircase, a green gem glowing in his hand, and his familiar, weak after the summoning, clinging to his arm for support.

The soldiers pressed once more. Guy deflected one, then another, but was always mindful of the other threat, that of the skeletal creatures, for dismemberment did not stop them. He glanced down, wary of hands attached to shattered arms dragging themselves along the ground towards him. In his training, he'd learned that balance was key and having to shift position to crumble a skeletal hand was doing little for his stability. After deflecting a couple more blows and jumping onto another demon claw, he pondered using them to his advantage. He sidestepped, and instead of stepping on the hand, he kicked it at his adversary. It crumpled against the leg, but when his enemy glanced down, Guy lunged forward and planted his blade into his neck.

Guy looked up. Hastings was out of sight. A horn sounded. The remaining men rained down their final blows and turned to flee for the horses. The skeletal warriors parted to allow them through and then strode for Guy, Kit, Jack, Ralph and Ghost.

"A pew!" Kit cried.

Yes! That would do the trick. Guy ran for one end of a pew as Kit reached the other. Ralph and Jack moved to the middle, and Ghost staggered behind. They lifted the pew to chest height and stomped towards the entrance, the wooden barrier knocking any adversary to the ground. Once they'd felled the last of them, they dropped the pew, clambered over it, and made their way to the exit.

More horns sounded.

In the distance, the lights of a dozen torches shone, a small army approaching from the south.

"It's Francis!" Jack called. "It's Uncle Francis, he made it!"

Archers felled some of Hastings' men and split their pack. Those that remained turned back towards Selby Abbey for cover.

"Ralph, take Ghost to safety. Go around to the east of the building and flag down one of Francis's men," Jack said.

Ralph nodded and helped Ghost to stumble away.

"We only need to hold them until Uncle Francis arrives," Jack said. "Don't take any risks."

"Kit," whispered Guy, "hide behind that gravestone. Leapt out and take them down if you get the chance."

Jack shook his head.

"Jack, we have to act. We can't let them escape."

"You know what happens if we act rashly, Guy. We have to wait for Francis."

"I'm hiding," Kit said. "Guy's right. We acted too slow before, and Pulleyn died. So did Robert, and Vicars, and Adamson..."

"Kit's with me. Are you?"

"When you tried to strike out last time, they burnt your uncle's farmstead to the ground. He lost his life to protect you."

243

"Jack, I've grown since then. We need to do this."

Kit ducked out of view as three men on horseback returned to Selby Abbey. Hastings still held the green jewel that radiated light. Beside him was his ever-present familiar and one other soldier.

"Surrender," said Jack, holding out his sword.

"To you, worthless peon?" Hastings spat at the ground. The creature he'd summoned from the ill air of the crypt formed once more before him and rushed for Jack, lifting him from his feet and smashing him into the walls of Selby Abbey.

Kit saw his opportunity and rose from behind the gravestone, his splintered sword in his hand, alive with the light of the demon hunter. He slashed at the man closest, Hastings' ever-present familiar, sinking the broken blade into his gut.

The familiar gnashed his teeth together and hissed; first, saliva sprayed from his mouth, and then bilious foam, and finally blood. As it splashed onto Kit's arm, he withdrew the blade and tossed it to the ground.

"Guy, it burns!" Kit called, as he brushed the frothing blood from his arm.

"You have to wash it off. Quick."

Kit looked from Jack, crumpled against the wall, to Guy, to Hastings.

"I've got this. Go now, or lose your arm."

Wailing in agony, Kit turned and fled for the river.

An arrow whistled through the night and burst through the chest of Hastings' last soldier, who fell from his horse. The steed turned and ran.

Hastings's familiar slid off his horse and collapsed in a heap on the ground.

"He's gone," Guy cried, pointing his sword at Hastings. "Your link to the demon world is severed. Dismount and let us finish this."

Hastings dismounted. "Foolish boy. You think I need a familiar when I have this?" He held out the gem, and his eyes flashed green.

244

The spirit that had hurled Jack to the wall rushed back to Hastings, entering his body. Hastings swelled, a green hue radiating from his body. He pulled a sabre from his side.

Aided by the aerial power, he dashed at Guy at an inhuman speed. Guy barely had time to leap out of the way.

Hastings turned and stretched his arms, every joint cracking as he did so. "I'll decorate the Abbey with your brains, whoreson! Feeble fool!" He pulled a knife from his belt and threw it.

Guy lifted his blade, deflecting the knife from its path, causing the hilt to bounce off his head. He'd have a lump, but that was better than a gash. Another knife came with all the fury of a gale, but again his blade met it, deflecting it onto a nearby gravestone.

Hastings ran at him again. Guy held firm, positioning his blade to block the telegraphed blow. He may have had the strength of the wind, but his swordsmanship was nothing to admire. And while Guy blocked the blow, the force knocked him from his feet and threw his sword from his hand.

Hastings stood over him, ready to plunge his sabre into Guy's chest.

A whistle of an arrow pierced the air, but Hastings moved his head ever so slightly. Guy watched the arrow as the wind changed its course, and it thudded into the ground some distance away.

Guy kept his eyes on Hastings. With the gravestone beside him, there was only one way to roll when the blow came. Even the most ill-trained swordsman would prepare for that. He reached out, failing to find his sword. Instead, his hand fell upon something with a smaller hilt–one of Hastings' knives.

Hastings smirked. Only the need to divert another arrow had stopped him from finishing Guy's life.

"Fate's jester, be home to my blade." Hastings raised his sword into the air.

Guy wrapped his fingers around the knife's hilt and flung it towards Hastings. He had to believe the stone held all of Hastings' power, that his action would be strong enough to stop him from plunging that sword deep into his heart. He watched the knife fly, Hastings oblivious. It struck the gemstone in Hastings' left hand, splitting it in two.

As if shoved in mid-air, Hastings spun round and fell onto his back.

Before Hastings could so much as cry out in frustration, Guy was upon him, grabbing his sword from the ground and jabbing the point into Hastings' neck.

"Stop!" Hastings lifted his hands in surrender as far as he dared. "You have saved me from that evil demon curse!"

Guy pushed the tip of his blade harder, breaking the skin.

Hastings suppressed a yelp. "Think about what you're doing, boy. I can give you riches. I can give you power!"

"Can you bring back my father? Can you bring back my uncle? What about my friends?"

Hastings opened his mouth, but no words came.

"Guy!" came a cry, and the sound of hooves closed on him. He didn't need to look up to know who it was.

He plunged his sword into Hastings' neck before Ingleby could talk him out of it.

Chapter 35

IN WHICH THE FALLOUT FROM HASTINGS' DEATH HITS HOME

When we look back upon a noble life, there are often points of no return, irrevocable actions, unavoidable consequences. This was such a point for Guy Fawkes. But there was no great swell of relief when Guy saw the life disappear from Hastings' eyes. There was no chastisement from Ingleby, either. Guy had expected another tongue-lashing, but instead, Ingleby helped him to his feet.

Next, they attended to Jack, who, other than having had the wind knocked out of him, was unhurt. There would be bruises, large ones, but he'd broken no bones. Kit was likely to have a more lasting stain on his body from the familiar's acid blood, but his quick visit to the river meant there would be only a scar. It had not eaten beyond the skin at surface level. Guy applied some of the lotion that Gretchen had given him, immediately cooling Kit's wounded skin.

When they reunited with Ghost, they found Ralph had sewn up the gash on his upper arm rather competently. While Ghost looked whiter than ever, Ingleby stated there was no reason he shouldn't make a full recovery.

Ingleby's men set up a camp close to the village of Wistow, close to a tributary of the River Ouse. Once there, Ghost was given a comfortable bed (or as comfortable as a hastily made campbed could be) and Ralph remained by his side. Once Ingleby had delivered his orders, including setting up sentries and patrols, he settled around the campfire, alongside his nephews, and Guy, among others.

"We cannot tarry here. Before sunrise, I plan to ride for York. Word of Hastings' demise is likely to spread swiftly, and the consequences will be dire."

"I'm coming too," Guy said. The thought of not being with his family if they came for them was too horrific.

"Me too," chimed Kit and Jack together.

"Then you'd best turn in. A few hours' sleep will make the ride all the easier."

Kit and Jack shuffled off to find somewhere to get their heads down, but Guy remained by the fire, staring at the flames, watching them dance to the rhythm of the crackling logs on which they feasted.

"You're not tired?" Ingleby asked.

Guy shook his head. Sleep wouldn't come, for when he had closed his eyes, he had seen the spectral demon riding on the wind. "Jack said he'd seen demons like that before–aerial powers, he called them."

Ingleby snapped a branch into smaller pieces and lay them on the fire. "In Spain, we saw many things. They have great power, yes."

"It's worse over there?"

Ingleby shook his head. "In Spain, there is hope. Those with power oppose the demons. Their royalty joins the fight against witchcraft. They don't support devilry. Their government coordinates the fight. They don't draw on dark powers to control their people."

"So, why are you back?"

"The hope we found in Spain: we need it here."

"How do we bring it here?"

"Have you heard of the Low Country across the sea?"

Guy shook his head.

"King Philip II of Spain rules that land known as The Netherlands. His father had united the seventeen provinces decades earlier. It is, by rights, Spanish territory. But England interfered. Last year, Elizabeth sent troops to this area. Spain and England are as good as at war."

"Why?"

"Conquest is in our English nature, but for King Philip, there is more. He was king, here, on our shores, long before you were born through his marriage to Queen Mary. He knew of the demon scourge even then and wanted to rid our lands of the plague... but when Mary died, he lost his title and any power he had here. Of course, he proposed to Elizabeth, but she rejected marriage, leaving Philip powerless against our demon sickness."

"And now?"

"He has grown tired of diplomacy. He sees Elizabeth's actions in the Low Countries as an act of war, and he will retaliate. Whether through invasion, or whether he succeeds in his plot to bring Mary Queen of Scots to her rightful position on the throne, he intends to take this land back under his control. Then we can fight demons together."

"So, you came back to help him? To prepare for his arrival? To overthrow the Queen?"

Ingleby placed another broken branch on the fire.

"That's treason..." Guy said.

"Aye, but for the best of reasons. We can't live under a monarchy and a government under the thrall of demons! People have tried to persuade Elizabeth how far this infestation has spread through the country, but she's deaf to it. If we wait for her to wise up, we'll be overrun. The rest of Europe will call us Demon Isle."

Guy continued to stare at the flickering flames.

"That's why we must race for York. The Council of the North will react to the death of one of their own. There may be an opportunity to further open up that wound, to sever the head of this beast once and for all."

It was all Guy had desired for so long: to bring down Hastings and Sandys. His father's ambition had been to rid York of corruption. Did he realise how deep the seam ran? Did he understand the effort required to dig it all out? If so, would he have kept his investigations going? Did he believe it was a cause worth dying for? If there was a chance to excavate every nugget of evil from York, they had to try. It could serve as a catalyst for salvation for the rest of the land, too.

"I'm going to get my head down for a while, and I suggest you do the same." Ingleby stood and moved away from the fire.

When he returned, Guy was still in the same place.

The distance between Wistow and York was less than that from Saint Robert's Cave to Selby Abbey, and breakfasting before sunrise meant they had reached the walls by midday. Guy had told Ingleby of his intention to speed home and to remain alert, monitoring any activity within the city.

Ingleby was to find accommodation for him, Kit, and Jack as they planned their next strike. More than anything, they needed information. They needed to track down other key members of the Council of the North. Ingleby believed Walsingham was key. If they could take him down, if the council had no control, a northern rebellion could work by taking strategically placed cities that would draw a great military response from London. Then, Spain could strike.

But Guy's mind kept turning back to Sandys and the way he'd drawn the knife across Uncle Thomas's throat. Would ridding York of the evil influence of the church be a better starting point? Securing one city and spread salvation to others?

Guy still felt unsure about aiding a foreign invasion, but if Ingleby believed in it so wholeheartedly, there had to be good in the plan, however wrong it seemed. Anyway, he had to deescalate his concerns from an international level to his own home. Even if he planned to bring Sandys down, protecting the remaining Fawkes was the priority.

They approached York's southern entrance, Micklegate Bar. The heads on the spikes had not been renewed for at least a week, and those above were in a state of decomposition that the ravens found particularly appealing.

The ravens cawed, and as the group slowed to pass through the gate in single file, a chunk of flesh fell from the beak of a bird. It landed on the ground in front of Guy, as one had all those years ago when his father took him to school for the first time. The guards at the gate were no more meticulous than usual in their activities, asking what brought the party to York and from where they were travelling. Ingleby answered on behalf of himself and his nephews, and Guy stated his address, which sufficed to allow him to progress into the city.

On the other side of the gate, he bid his companions goodbye and rode for the stables. Pewter whinnied her frustration at being ridden so hard for two consecutive days, making Guy feel guilty about only giving her a cursory brush down and a small treat. He dared not stay away from home for long. He hurried from the stables through the city's streets, keeping his eyes open for any unusual activity. York, however, seemed as normal as ever. The whisperers on street corners remained in place, but they lacked the fervour one would expect if something was imminent. And while there were no warning signs, no obvious need to be wary, the closer Guy got to home, the more concerned he became. Those with evil intent in the city had to know. Pulleyn had always said that demonic deception came because of their ability to travel at the speed of light. After witnessing a spectacle in one location, they'd whisper of it at another almost instantaneously, thus feigning foresight, for news travelling on horseback was so much slower. The dark forces at King's Manor and York Minster had to know their ally had fallen. So why was the city acting as if nothing was amiss?

Even when Guy pushed open his front door, everything seemed typical. His mother and Elizabeth sat close to the fire, both armed with sewing needles.

"Mother!" Guy looked around the room. "Is everything okay?"

Edith gave her son only a cursory glance. "Why would it not be?"

"Where is Anne?"

"Yet to return from work."

All the baking was done early morning, and the preparation for the following day did not take Anne long. As it was not her duty to run the shop, she was often home by this hour. That could only mean that she'd gone elsewhere, a place she liked to visit in secret. He pulled his hood over his head as he moved through the streets, taking the quickest route possible to The Shambles, where normality had abandoned the city. On the streets nearby, Guy noticed the paucity of beggars and the absent groups of bedraggled whisperers. They knew something was coming, something even they did not wish to witness.

When Guy reached the southern end of The Shambles, he paused, looking down at the last of the blood from the morning's slaughter as it trickled down the gulley in the street. While the premises on The Shambles were rarely quiet, on this day, few wandered down the cobbled street, and none paused outside shop windows to ponder their purchases. Clitherow's Butchers was halfway down The Shambles. Neighbouring shops were shut when trade was typically busy. The door to Clitherow's was locked, despite a display of freshly butchered pork in the window. Guy peered in, but there was no sign of movement. Hearing footsteps behind him, he turned and watched a gentleman rush past. Then came a sniffle. The small door through which he'd hidden after fleeing his first home was ajar. He crouched till the sniffle became a sob, a cry he'd heard so many times before: Anne. He grabbed the door, pulled it open, and as she gasped, he called her name. "It's okay, Anne. It's me."

With that, she shuffled out. Her hands covered her face as if shielding from the light, though the street was as gloomy as ever.

Guy guided Anne's hands away, revealing a black eye and swollen face. His chest tightened as he spoke: "What happened? Who did this to you?"

"I let her down, Guy. I let her down." Anne wept again.

Conscious of the danger of rogue ears, Guy decided it wasn't time to press. He didn't want to take her home, for their mother's concern about seeing her daughter in such a state would make questioning Anne impossible.

"Do you want to go to the stables? Do you want to check on Pewter with me?"

Anne nodded.

Guy looked both ways across The Shambles. Guy elected to return from the same way he'd approached. Whenever Anne made to speak, he shushed her or changed the subject, not wanting any ears to hear them or eyes to fall on them and follow.

When they made it to the stables, Pewter did not look pleased to see him. No doubt she feared he planned to take her out again, and Pewter was of the mind that she'd earned a rest. When Guy reached to stroke her mane, she tilted her head away. Anne, however, was free to stroke as much as she liked.

Guy watched a smile spread on Anne's face, followed by a wince when it reignited the pain. "Now tell me who did that."

"They took Margaret."

"Who?"

"It's all my fault." Anne leant into Pewter.

"Anne, start from the beginning. You finished work at the baker's and you made your way to Clitherow's…" Guy encouraged.

Anne sniffled, moving away from Pewter, who gave a satisfied nicker for the attention.

"I helped her with the display. She went upstairs, only for a moment." Anne gazed down. "That's when the soldiers came."

"What did they do?"

Anne swallowed hard. "There were three of them. They closed the door and forced me into the back room, demanding to see Margaret and John. John was at the market, and…" Anne sighed. "I must have looked to the staircase because one of them ran upstairs. Another of them came close…"

"Was he the one that struck you?"

Anne nodded. "But not right away. He asked a question first, whether any enemies of the state were on the premises. I didn't understand what he meant. He said it again, same words, and when I shrugged, he struck me."

Guy reached down and balled up some hay in his hands before letting it go.

"Then he asked, 'Is anyone else hiding here?' I didn't want to give anything away, but I glanced at the corner."

"What's in the corner?"

"A trap door."

Guy remembered no trap door in his time working in Clitherow's, but he knew also that Margaret had increased her activity since his apprenticeship. "What was down there?"

"Nothing. But its existence proved justification enough."

"Enough for what?"

"To take Margaret. I didn't see what happened. That one soldier stayed with me. Cuffed me again, dropped me to the floor and kicked me while I was down." Anne folded her arms over her belly and grimaced with the memory of the pain. "From upstairs I heard a right carry-on, lumping and banging and things smashing. They dragged Margaret down the stairs on her front, legs first. When they pulled her to her feet, her face was red with blood."

Bilious anger stirred in Guy's gut. "Then what?"

"They took her. I locked the door, and I hid in the pigpen until you came along. What are they going to do?"

"I don't know," Guy said.

"It's all my fault." Anne wept once more.

"No," said Guy, moving over to comfort her, "It's not your fault." And he said it with authority. Coming for Margaret was a direct response to Hastings' death. How many other premises in the city would they strike?

Chapter 36

IN WHICH GUY FAWKES SEEKS MARGARET CLITHEROW

People always worry about the consequences of their actions, and Guy felt guilty about Margaret's plight. Less often do we consider the consequences of our inaction. What chaos would Hastings have brought upon the people of York if he had control of so strong an aerial power? Over the following days, Guy learned that soldiers had stormed dozens of properties and taken many to York Castle for questioning. Torturers flayed flesh from bones and branded skin with hot irons to give the powers of the city their desired confessions. York Tyburn was to become very busy indeed throughout March, with confessed enemies of the state to be hanged for many reasons, primarily treason, but some for the crime of witchcraft. The Council of the North knew they had to maintain the pretence of opposition to this form of evil and hide their true purpose. Every execution weighed on Guy's conscience regardless of the worse events he'd circumvented.

In discreet meetings with Ingleby and with Kit and Jack (never all together, though), Guy learned Walsingham had been in York when news of Hastings' death arrived. From there, he gave orders to investigate one hundred separate premises. Before the first of these orders was actioned, he and his retinue left York, bound for Durham under the pretence of readying for an invasion by the Scots. Francis's spies told him he had remained with the Prince Bishop, secure in Durham Castle, allying with the powerful Dudley family.

Of Margaret, there was no word. Banners around the city boasted of the confessions of all who had admitted their misdeeds (or confessed to that which they were innocent to spare themselves further torture). Reading the names of so many he knew and had stood alongside sickened Guy. Many of the patrons of the secret tavern beneath The Black Swan were there, good men and women who didn't deserve to swing from a rope. Guy had visited John Clitherow, who attempted to keep his shop open despite the considerable strain. Had it not been too much of a risk to spend time there, Guy would have offered to wield the butchery knives once more, but he kept his visits short, simultaneously comforted and traumatised by the words that slipped from John's agonised face. "She'll not be broken," became his mantra.

Each day, more soldiers arrived in the city under the pretence of heading north to stave off the threat of a Scottish invasion. And yet, once housed at York barracks, they did not need to travel any further, spending their time on the streets of York, as if the noose could tighten around the entire city, not only those at Tyburn. Soldiers flooded the streets. During executions, they spread among the crowds, their eyes trained to spot signs of distress: if anyone wept at the hanging of a witch or an enemy of the state, they too were arrested for corruption. As quickly as the dungeons were being emptied by the gallows, the cells filled. And still, no news of Margaret Clitherow broke, not until spring emerged and March's days neared their end.

Guy spotted the latest banner posted at Pavement. The news shocked him. He put his hand out to steady himself against the wall. It advertised not a hanging, but a pressing, and not at York Tyburn, but at the Toll Booth on Ouse Bridge, on Good Friday. Guy had avoided witnessing a pressing in the past, but he had heard about the barbaric act. The suspect lay on top of a sharp stone with the door to their house placed on top of them. Executioners added weight until the suspect either confessed or died as result of the weight upon them. Margaret's fate meant only one thing: she'd given nothing away. By refusing to put in a plea, she'd avoided a trial. This would have involved questioning John and her children about what went on in the Clitherow household. Avoiding bringing her children under suspicion was no doubt her goal. If her children spoke, they were at risk of falling foul of the law themselves. If they mentioned a secret place, or a person hidden within their house, they too could be sentenced for abetting enemies of the state. The last thing she wanted was her children swinging from a rope.

Guy read the banner on Wednesday afternoon. That didn't give him long. First, he called on the guesthouse in which Ingleby was staying. Alas, Ingleby had departed that morning. Guy headed back onto the street and stood outside, pondering his next move. The hoot of a bird alien to the city came from the vicinity of the narrow alley. Guy followed the sound to where he found Kit and Jack, both in cloaks and cowls, loitering in the shadows.

"What's going on? Where's your uncle?"

"Away to Durham," Jack said.

Durham? Then he was after Walsingham. "Alone?"

Kit stared at the ground and played with the pouch on his belt, feeling the shape of the stones inside.

Jack shook his head. "He took a group. He didn't want us with him." The hurt in Jack's voice was palpable.

"It's for the best we're here, anyway," Guy said.

Jack's eyes grew large. "Uncle Francis is going after one of your biggest enemies and you're not fussed? What's going on in that head of yours, Guy?"

"Friends come first. You can deal with your enemies another day, but sometimes your friends need urgent help."

"Who?" Kit asked.

"They're pressing Margaret on Friday."

"Is that where they...?" Kit gestured placing rocks on the body with his hands.

Jack brushed Kit's hands away so they couldn't evoke such disgust. "What can we do?"

"I don't know. We can't let that happen. It's not right."

"Then we go see her. Convince her to say something so they spare her life," Jack suggested.

Kit looked at him, and then at Guy, and when Guy didn't speak, he did, gesturing elaborately once more. "You know she's in York Castle? They'll have her in Clifford's Tower, with the moat, and all the guards watching it. How are we going to get in there to convince her of anything?"

Guy looked from side to side, checking for eavesdroppers. "You know my father's records of York?"

"Aye," said Jack, and Kit nodded.

"York Castle isn't the bastion of fortification and security it once was. We've got a chap called Robert Redhead to thank for that."

"Who's that?"

"He's the gaoler… and he likes to make a bit of money on the inside where he can. He's been selling off the fallen stone from the walls for lime-burning for years. If he won't sneak us into the castle for a few quid, then he might let slip where the weaknesses are."

Kit stepped away. "Let's go then…"

"We can't approach him at the castle. If we so much as loiter nearby we'll be slung in a cell, but Father's records listed his address. We'll catch him there on his way home."

They patrolled the city to pass the hours, soon falling back into following their old route, passing various buildings Edward Fawkes had recorded. As they walked, they reminisced, sharing memories of time spent at Clitherow's Butchers and the lessons learned from Margaret.

When darkness fell, they knew the gaoler's shift would be near completion. They returned to the vicinity of his house and positioned themselves at the entrance to the ginnel that led from Little Coney Street towards the river. Along this dark passage was a single door–the home of the gaoler, Robert Redhead. If they were going by name alone, they never would have accosted the strange fellow who turned down the alley, but Guy had set eyes upon him before when he made it his business to know about all the addresses in his father's documents and of all those named within them. Redhead did not live up to his name. Upon his head, he wore a Paris beau. Straggles of long, grey hair escaped the perimeter and hung by his face.

"Robert Redhead," called Guy, following down the ginnel.

Redhead turned. His lips curled back, revealing black and twisted teeth. "What do you want?"

"May we come inside?" Guy asked.

"Get lost." Redhead put his key in the door and unlocked it.

"I guess we'll have to speak to someone else about the stone missing from the castle." Guy turned away.

"Maybe I was being hasty." Redhead reached out and touched Guy's shoulder. "Come in and we'll have a bit of a chat."

"My friends and I wouldn't want to inconvenience you." Guy raised his voice. "After all, the security of the castle isn't solely your business."

Redhead grabbed Guy by the arm and dragged him toward his door. "Come, come. The streets are not a place for such loose lips."

Redhead's damp home reeked of wet ash. He urged Guy, Kit and Jack to sit on the seat against the wall, though there was barely sufficient room for the three of them to squeeze on. He lit a candle to tackle the gloom, placed it on the table, and sat opposite.

"What is it you young men need?" Redhead removed his hat and placed it on the seat next to him. He brushed the thin strands of hair from one side of his head to the other in a futile attempt to cover his blotchy scalp. "You after some quality stone? Are you looking to get into the business?"

Guy leant forward. "We need access to the gaol."

Redhead shook his head. "Oh, no. I can't give anyone access. I'm responsible for the keys. My head would be on a spike the second the cell door cracked open."

"Can you take us inside?"

Redhead grimaced. "I'd swing from a rope if they found out."

"And if they found out about the missing stone?"

Redhead shuddered. "It'll cost you your silence."

"You have our word."

"It'll be quiet Friday afternoon. I can take you in then."

"That'll be too late."

"I take it, it's 'er you want to see then."

Guy nodded. "Aye, it is."

"You'll not like what you see. She's made up her mind."

"We thought we might persuade her to loosen her lips."

"You'll not have much chance."

"A chance is all I ask for."

Redhead sighed. "Okay, tomorrow morning I start at six. I can take one of you in as my assistant. You can help with my delivery." Robert smiled, showing those black teeth again. "You'll be gone before the clock strikes eight."

Guy looked at Kit and Jack, then nodded. "Okay, I'm in."

"Then I have your word you'll say no more about my business?"

"You have my word."

Long before sunrise, Guy positioned himself on Little Coney Street and awaited Redhead. Soon, the bedraggled gaoler exited his house, locked the door, and hurried from his home. His eyes fell on Guy. "Didn't change yer mind then?"

"I have to do this."

"And don't ye forget what ye have to do fer me. I take you to the woman, but then you complete my shipment. Scrub my name from yer list and we're square."

"Understood."

Guy followed Redhead through the dark and solemn streets to York Castle and into Clifford's Tower without so much as being questioned once.

"They respect a gaoler, see?" Redhead said once they were alone inside the guard's room. When the night gaoler returned from his last patrol, Redhead dismissed him and sat beside the chair. He sniffed at the jug on the table and, unperturbed by the smell, drunk the dregs of ale left by his predecessor.

"We'll start with 'er so you can get my business done and be gone."

Guy followed Redhead down three sets of stairs to the lowest dungeons, far beneath the ground, lower even than the level of the water which dripped in through cracks. Moisture hung in the air, and the lanterns didn't burn bright enough to illuminate much of the gloom.

Together, they approached the cell.

"Leave me," came a call, weak, but unmistakably Margaret.

"It's me," Guy said.

From the darkness in the corner, Margaret emerged, shuffling on her knees. "Guy... they got you, too?"

"No, I'm..." he gazed at Redhead.

"You've used your charms on this one, I see." Margaret came to the bars, clinging to them for support. On her right hand, three of the fingernails had been torn off, and she had lost her little finger altogether.

"You can't let them press you," Guy said.

"I can't?" Despite the obvious ruin of torture, defiance remained in her voice.

"Give them a name. Say you're in league with Guy Fawkes for all I care! That name's dead in this city. Watch them run in rings trying to track it down. It'll buy you time."

"If I stand trial, they'll ruin John. They'll question my children. Your sister, too, will get called in."

"But you can't let them pile all that weight on top of you."

261

"Did I teach you nothing?"

"What?"

"The thing about good people, the thing about living a good life, is that there's always weight on your shoulders."

"That's not the same."

"And whatever the pressure, those that are good and true can always take more weight."

Guy swallowed hard, couldn't stop a tear from escaping and fleeing down his cheek. "They'll crush you."

"If the only way they can break me is with barbarism, they lose. The people won't take it. Their good will rise. You know I'm right. You know it's true."

Guy shook his head, but he had no words with which to counter.

"Come on. Time to hold up your end of the bargain," said Redhead, turning away from the cell with the lantern in his hand, plunging Margaret back into the darkness.

"Guy," Margaret said.

"Yes?"

"I appreciate you coming. If yours is the last friendly face I see, I can go to my maker, happy that those left behind have strength and courage."

"Come on," called Redhead.

Guy reached to touch Margaret's hand on the bars, but she'd already let go.

Chapter 37

IN WHICH GUY FAWKES TRUSTS IN HOPE

As much as Guy's shoulders ached when he woke on Friday morning, it was nothing compared to the pain that ate away at his insides. Was there no way to stop Margaret's death? Would the barbarous act awaken the dormant good in York's citizens? Part of him thought attending this horror show would be a betrayal, but likewise, he knew the eyes of the city would watch those that did not show up. Under the name of Blake, they had come under little scrutiny in York, but if anyone pointed a finger at Anne and said they'd seen her at Clitherow's Butchers, that could change.

Once dressed, Guy waited downstairs for the rest of his family.

His mother and Elizabeth made their appearance first, dressed in dark colours, but not black, for they did not wish to appear in mourning and arouse the negative attention of the city's soldiers.

Before the exhibition, given that it was Good Friday, everyone was expected to attend a morning church service, and already the clangour of bells called worshippers to attention.

"Hurry, Anne. We'll not want to be late," called Edith Fawkes.

Anne called back from upstairs. "I'm not going."

"We must or we'll have every alderman in the city speaking our name."

"Let them speak it."

Edith huffed and pointed at Guy. "You speak to her. It's your fault she's so headstrong."

"It's in her blood, mother." Guy started up the stairs. "It's as much from you as it is from Father."

Guy heard his mother huff again before he went into the small bedroom Anne and Elizabeth shared.

"Come on, Anne. You know how anxious Mother gets when we're late to church."

"I can't make it through this without tears. You've told me our tears make us targets."

"Listen," Guy sat on the bed. "You can't tell anyone else this, but I saw Margaret yesterday."

"You did? How?"

"I don't have time to explain… but she's ready for this. She has hope, and she'll want you to share that hope."

"What hope?"

"Margaret knows how awful this is going to be. When the people see how cruel their masters are, she hopes it will turn those with a shred of good in them against the control of the church and the Council of the North."

Anne nodded and took a deep breath. When she left the room, he did likewise.

The church service passed with the usual lack of urgency, ironically delivering the Easter message of rebirth, of life from death, of sacrifice for sin, and as the church bells resounded once more, the whole procession made their way to the river, following it along to the Ouse Bridge.

At the Toll House, the murder party waited. Guy knew the faces of the executioners well after so many trips to Tyburn. The administrator, too, was familiar, a regular among the meetings of the Council of the North, though he held no formal title, known only by his surname, Dunbar. Somewhere behind the congregation, the guards held Margaret. Guy could see the outline of the hurdle on which they'd dragged her from York Castle to the Toll House, no doubt to the cheers of the masses who had gathered first–those belonging to the nearest church or those bold enough not to be in attendance on a day when the city was sure to take notice.

Guy kept his eyes peeled for John Clitherow and the children, but he hoped they'd stayed away. In the crowd, first, he spied Ralph, for his height made him an easy sight. In the same vicinity were Kit and Jack. As much as Guy wanted the support of his friends to get through the forthcoming exhibition of cruelty, he needed to support his family more.

A soldier stepped forward and issued a blast on the bugle to draw the crowd's attention. A low platform of wood had been erected on which to perform the murder. The administrator, Dunbar, approached first. To one side was a pile of enormous rocks, some crude and jagged, others block-like. Perhaps some had fallen from York Castle before Redhead could squirrel them away to sell later. Dunbar reached out and took a rock from the top of the pile. He held it aloft for as long as his arms could take the weight. It was at least a foot across, with two jagged peaks at either end. He lay it in the middle of the platform. Soldiers dragged Margaret to stand beside it. She wore rags that were typical prisoners' attire and had a sack over her head. When the soldier tore away the sack, she blinked. The dirt smeared across her face did not hide her bruises. Bare patches on her scalp showed where her torturers in the castle had snatched out clumps of hair.

Flanked by half a dozen soldiers and with his ever-present familiar by his side (as a human, not as a cat), Sandys strode to the platform.

As he spoke, he held aloft a sceptre. "Margaret Clitherow, you are accused of crimes against your Queen, harbouring her enemies

265

and lending them your support. As your queen is appointed by God himself, it is against God that you are accused of making a stand. Your failure to enter a plea and seek fair judgement under God's eyes in His court of law means you are hereby cast from His Kingdom. A trial by pressing has been deemed lawful by the Council of the North and shall continue until you enter a plea or share the names of your co-conspirators. Do you understand?"

"Aye," Margaret said with a heavy breath.

Sandys retreated with his guards to watch from a nearby seat.

Dunbar stepped forward once more. "Now you understand the process, deemed lawful by the powers that be. Do you wish to enter a plea?"

"I do," Margaret said, drawing another heavy breath, "not."

"Do you wish to name any of your co-conspirators against Her majesty Queen Elizabeth?"

"Nay."

"Gentlemen, position the prisoner."

Dunbar stepped back, and the two executioners stepped forward. The first tied a blindfold around Margaret's eyes, while the second grabbed at her rags, drew his sword and cut them away, leaving her standing naked before the eyes of York, her punishment clear to see in the welts on her skin, the burn marks, the cuts, and the bruises. Guy scanned the crowd, noting that as many heads turned away as strained to see better.

The two executioners grabbed Margaret's arms and dragged her to the centre of the platform, posing her, facing the bridge, the rock behind her. One of the executioners kicked her in the back of the legs, causing her to collapse onto her knees. The second grabbed her shoulders and pulled her backwards, the centre of her spine across that vicious rock. She yelped, then swallowed the pain, not wanting to give her executioners or the baying crowd the satisfaction of feeling it with her.

"The door," called Dunbar.

Together, the executioners picked something up from beside the platform. As they held it up, Guy recognised it as the door to Clitherow's Butcher's, wrenched from its hinges for this very purpose. They placed the door on top of Margaret and shoved it down, causing her to exhale.

"Are you ready to enter a plea?" Dunbar asked, bending down beside her.

"Nay." The door jiggled as Margaret shook her head.

"Then, gentleman, apply the first stone."

One executioner looked at the other. He nodded his head towards the rocks. The other did likewise. They both took a step towards the pile.

"Gentlemen, do your duty," Dunbar called.

One executioner lifted the top stone from the pile. He turned with it, looked down at the door, and placed it back on the pile.

Boos resounded from parts of the crowd while others looked on in silence.

One executioner shook his head, tore away the brassard that bore the city's coat of arms, dropped it and walked away, heading into the crowd gathered on the bridge.

The remaining executioner glanced from the rocks to Margaret's position under the door.

"Do your duty!" cried Dunbar.

Guy felt Anne's hand go to his, felt her squeeze hard as the second executioner imitated the first.

"Arrest those men!" cried Sandys, standing and pointing at the fleeing executioners. His soldiers left their position to march across the bridge, but the crowd had swallowed the executioners and held a solid line when Sandys' soldiers tried to break through.

Sandys moved to the centre of the platform. He placed one foot on the door and applied pressure. "Who here in the city will step up to perform the function of the law?"

Silence.

Anne squeezed Guy's hand once more, and he gazed down at her, seeing a smile on her lips for the first time in weeks.

Sandys reached into his jacket. "There must be men among you who could use a little gold." Sandys held a pouch out. He turned it over, letting coins drop into his hand.

"And there must be some among you who would appreciate being in the Council of the North's favour?"

As Sandys looked up, the ring of orange in his eyes was unmistakable. Some would claim it was the reflection of the spring sunshine, but Guy knew better; he knew the evil that resided in him and the power over others he commanded.

From the crowd, four men moved forward, three of them in the rags of beggars, but one was a man of wealth, signified by the yellow of his doublet. It was clear power had lured him.

"No," Anne cried. "No, they can't."

Guy shook his hand free of his sister's and shushed her. "Anne, you can't make a scene. It's not over yet. Have hope!"

The first of the beggars approached the stone pile. He looked to Sandys, who shook his bag of gold.

The man in rags reached for a rock, every muscle in his body straining, but it wouldn't move. A second beggar stepped across to help him, and together, groaning with every strained muscle, they lifted the rock and shuffled to where Margaret lay under her door. They placed the rock down, dropping it the last few inches, causing another groan from Margaret, which she suppressed.

The well-dressed gentleman moved to the rock pile and waited for the last beggar to join him. Together they hefted another rock onto the door, placing it next to the other, balancing the weight across the door and onto Margaret. Her body shook beneath the weight.

Dunbar stepped forward. "Have you a plea to enter? A name to surrender?"

Margaret reached out her hand.

Dunbar crouched beside her.

"Annie…"

"Annie, Annie who? Speak and you shall have your salvation."

Anne tugged on Guy's arm, the colour drained from her face.

"Annie Moore…" Margaret smiled.

Dunbar scrawled the name on a piece of parchment. "Anyone else?"

"Annie Moore…"

"Yes, you've given us that name. Who else?"

Anne now looked at Guy in confusion.

"It's okay," Guy muttered. "She won't give you up."

Margaret grunted. "Annie Moore… Any more… weight?"

Dunbar's face twisted in anger. He turned to the volunteers. "Keep going."

The volunteer executioners placed another rock. This time Margaret could not stifle her cry. The next brought another howl, and her hand reached out once more.

"There's still time to save yourself. There's still time to win favour in the eyes of God and be welcomed back into the Kingdom of heaven." Dunbar held aloft his hands, a show of power for the crowd.

Margaret took in several rasping breaths before she spoke. "Moe…"

Dunbar crouched by Margaret's head once more. "Moe who?"

"Moe… stones…" Margaret twisted her hand into a fist and raised her thumb.

From somewhere in the crowd came a cheer, followed by the first peal of laughter.

"Continue," called Dunbar.

Someone in the crowd booed, which was echoed by a second, then a third party. When the first pair of volunteers struggled with the weight of the next rock, the crowd jeered.

They struggled with the rock and dropped it on the door. A crack followed. Margaret, no longer capable of drawing sufficient air into her lungs, managed only a whimper.

As the next pair of volunteers moved back to the rock pile, she spoke once more, at a level almost too low to be heard. "Wait." She tried to twist her hand to hold up the palm and muttered it again. "Wait."

Dunbar opened his mouth, but a wall of noise from the crowd drowned his voice out. He shouted, "Will you cease this foolish word-play and enter your plea?"

The crowd paused, awaiting Margaret's response. "Wait..." she said once more. She lifted her hand as far as she could and again raised her thumb: "More weight!"

Laughs and cheers rang out from the crowd once more. Angry, Dunbar gestured at the volunteers. One beggar held up his hands and moved to walk away. Sandys gestured to his soldiers. A particular large man, his face scrunched into a permanent scowl hurried behind the beggar and rammed his sword through his back. As the volunteer executioner collapsed to the ground, the crowd silenced. A few people at the periphery walked away. Others watched them leave, wishing they too could make a show of defiance. Less than half the crowd watched the remaining three volunteers lug the heaviest of the rocks towards the door. They held it for a second above and dropped it.

With a sickening crunch, the last of Margaret's resistance caved.

Boos rang out from the crowd. Dunbar stood to deliver his final message, no doubt a warning to the people of York, a demand for compliance, but a song of disdain left him forever unheard. Sandys too gestured at soldiers as the crowd dispersed.

"Come on," called Guy, placing his hand on the small of his mother's back and urging her to move. "We must not tarry here."

Guy led them towards home. Soldiers moved through the crowds with swords drawn, looking for any excuse to swing them. Guy urged his mother to turn down a ginnel which brought them onto a quieter street, where the anger of authority had yet to reach. They continued at pace until they reached home, and once inside, Guy locked the door.

Edith stood at the hearth, resting her hands on the brick of the fireplace. "That was a disgrace in the eyes of God. I'm sorry you had to witness such a barbarous display."

Elizabeth rushed to her, and as soon as she was close, her tears fell.

Guy went to the window and looked out to see others returning to their homes. He could almost hear doors being barred for security.

Anne sat at the table. When Guy turned to face her, it was almost as if she had been waiting for him. "Was that… was that what Margaret wanted?"

"Don't be ridiculous, child!" Edith called out, before turning her attention to the weeping Elizabeth once more.

Guy sat next to Anne. "She said there was goodness in York that could beat evil, that could rise against corruption. That's what we saw today. We saw the absolute worst in people, and we saw others wouldn't tolerate it."

"What next?"

"There will be a reaction; don't doubt that, but momentum is on our side. We're close to salvation."

Guy reached out and took Anne's hand. She squeezed in response.

Chapter 38

IN WHICH GUY FAWKES IS COMPLICIT IN THE RECOVERY OF MARGARET'S BODY

Only once darkness fell did Guy dare to venture onto the streets of York. Aldwark had been quiet. During his vigil at the window, Guy had seen only one patrol. It was a quiet part of town where people knew better than to step out of line.

A couple of streets over, the carnage of the day was clear. The sound of the cart that collected bodies clattered over the cobblestones, regularly stopping to load another corpse. Few people wandered the streets. Some, like Guy, had emerged to witness the aftermath of the afternoon's events. Soldiers patrolled the streets, their bloodlust sated, their remit now to act only as a deterrent through their presence, hoping the show of force had taught people a lesson. But the looks on the faces of those who walked alongside Guy suggested the bloodshed that followed the horror of Margaret's murder had not quelled public unease but stirred the revolutionary spirit. Margaret was right: these people would stand against vicious tyrants. Where once the sound of whispers and the fear of listening ears kept people quiet, too scared to speak in case they fell afoul of suspicion, now conversations contained hope that rendered the whispers powerless. This was a York Guy had never experienced before, a York with the power to overcome evil.

Walking without purpose, Guy found himself drawn back to the Toll House at the Ouse Bridge. Had he expected to find Margaret's body still in place, the rocks that crushed her, still pinning her corpse to the wooden platform? But there it was. Perhaps the Council of the North intended to leave it as another warning, like those heads on spikes at the city's gates. Guy, however, did not expect to find countless spring flowers placed in the gaps between rocks. Violet crocuses, powder-blue irises and yellow daffodils brought beauty to the horror. The vibrancy of the flowers represented the life that would continue even in view of such a hideous death. This was the Easter spirit brought to life.

Guy watched as people checked for soldiers, before hurrying to the platform to add yet more colour. One visitor lay daffodils on the platform and made the sign of the cross, and when she removed her hood, Guy gasped. That raven hair! It could only be the same girl who had been at Pulleyn's execution. Here she was again at the death of someone so significant to him. Surely, she had to be some kind of angel of death? She'd resided long in his dreams, and despite the years that had passed, she had grown up as he'd imagined her.

As she walked away, pulling her hood up once more, Guy followed. She turned down the street out of his view.

"Guy!" A whisper.

He followed a few more steps, reached the turning and watched the girl take a narrow passageway between two houses.

"Guy!" louder this time. He turned to see a figure in a hooded cloak. He'd known Kit long enough to see through any disguise.

Guy looked back to the pathway down which the girl had disappeared and knew he'd lost the chance to continue his pursuit. Instead, he waited for Kit to reach him, and pulled him into his embrace.

"How are you, friend?" Kit asked. His face bore the strain of the day, eyes still ringed red.

"It has been quite the day." He looked around at the people in the streets once more. "The city is alive with opportunity."

"We have heard they plan to break this spirit. They're coming to remove the body."

Guy returned with Kit to a position where they could see the Toll House. A group of a dozen guards arrived, following behind a horse-drawn wagon. Four of them turned away any approaching pedestrians. Their hands moved to the hilts of their swords to show violence was the preferred method of dealing with confrontation. The other guards moved over to Margaret's body, dismantling the monument, flinging flowers into the river or onto the ground and crushing them underfoot. They lifted the rocks from the door, one at a time, working in pairs, stacking them by the side of the Toll House. The door had splintered in two. One soldier hurled half of it into the river, and the other he rested beside the pile of rocks. Only Margaret's broken body remained on the platform. Two soldiers moved to her body, one grabbing the legs, the other picking her up under the arms. The way her body hung showed her level of suffering at the end, but this only augmented Guy's feeling of victory, for as broken as her body was, her spirit remained true. The soldiers flung her body into the back of the wagon. Four climbed in alongside it, and the rest of the soldiers dispersed in pairs, urging any loiterers to move along.

Guy moved without words, heading towards the bridge, towards the Toll House to follow the wagon. Kit fell into step beside him.

As soldiers approached, they grimaced. "Where are you going? What's your business here?"

Kit pointed to the streets on the other side of the bridge. "We live on that side of the river."

"Then hurry home. We have little patience for vagabonds causing trouble on the streets tonight."

Guy and Kit lowered their heads and continued on their way, reaching the vicinity of the Toll House where crushed flower heads littered the ground. Guy looked down. The flowers disguised the edge of the blood shadow on the platform.

Guy and Kit followed the wagon from a safe distance as it headed south. They stopped before Micklegate Bar, not wanting to face the challenge of the gatekeepers so soon after the wagon had passed. Instead, they waited for the next group to approach, a rowdy bunch of older men singing slurred songs. Guy and Kit fell in behind them, leaning against each other as if they needed support.

274

"What is your business?" asked the gatekeeper.

The men at the front of the group broke into song once more.

"Do you live outside the city walls?"

The response combined cheers of agreement and continued song.

"Go on," called the gatekeeper. "Away to your beds before my sword guides you to an eternal resting place."

Laughter and cheers came in response, and the pack, with Guy and Kit part of it, shuffled out of the city. Guy and Kit continued to follow until an opportunity arose to slip out of sight behind a single pear tree. The wagon headed for the area close to Tyburn. The boggy ground of Knavesmire was more than appropriate for their purpose.

"We should be able to close upon them to watch where they bury the body." Guy moved away from the path onto the softer ground.

Kit remained by the tree.

"Come, we need to see where they bury her."

Kit shook his head. "We alone cannot retrieve the body. What would we do, march her back through Micklebar? No, you follow, note the location. I shall liaise with Jack and we will talk it through."

"Will you return?"

"Aye, before the clock strikes one, I'll be back with a plan."

"You'll not go back through Micklebar?"

Kit huffed. "Please? You know me better than that."

"Aye, I know you for a fool."

Kit smiled. "Only for being your friend."

"Then I shall see you before the clock strikes one, friend."

Kit took off, heading back for the wall. He knew more places where one could slip into the city than anyone, and he had no qualms about wading through water up to his neck if necessary. Maybe, Guy pondered as he sunk into a puddle that near swallowed his whole boot, Kit would have been better suited to wandering in the dark through Knavesmire with a single, distant light for guidance. But soon, his eyes became accustomed to the darkness, and the moon served as his ally, shining slithers of light on the firmer patches of ground where grass grew. Guy closed on the wagon. The soldiers appeared close to finishing their endeavour, not more than fifty yards from where he stood. In the dark, he tried to eye other landmarks which would help him locate the spot when Kit returned. Guy realised the futility of his actions: one o'clock would carry only greater darkness. Instead, Guy marked several trees with arrows, the point at which they'd converge being close to the burial site.

He remained hidden while the soldiers returned their tools to the wagon, hopped aboard, and left the unmarked grave. In the distance, he heard church bells signal ten o'clock. He had significant time to wait for Kit's return.

He made his way back across Knavesmire, marking trees as he went to make the route back to the body easier, even in absolute darkness. He came to a stop by the pear tree and sat at its base, resting his eyes for just a moment…

From the branches of the tree, Thomas Percy's skull floated down. "York is ripe for cleansing, but dark days are ahead."

Guy sighed. "Aren't they always?"

"You're at a crossroads. Both roads are weighted equal, success on one hand, failure on the other."

"Is there any other path?"

"Many, but they all lead to the same choices."

Guy pondered. Perhaps he could use Percy's foresight for good. "Does a girl lie on one of these paths?"

Percy closed on Guy, eyes flaming. "The girl with the raven hair?"

Guy pictured her again. "Yes."

"Indeed, she does."

"Which path?"

"I'm afraid your premature death is the only way to stop you from meeting her again."

"You're afraid?"

"For you, yes."

"What do I need to do?"

"Worry not about her. Whatever choice you make, you must stand and fight. Evil is a beast with many heads, and while you sever one, it may feast on a friend with the other."

"So, what do I do?"

"Your best."

"Guy!" a shout shook Guy from his sleep. Thomas Percy's head disappeared, leaving Guy lost in time and space.

When he stood, he realised Kit had woken him, and he was not alone. Ralph was there too, alongside some folk he did not know, one in the attire of a religious man.

"This is Father Mush. He was a friend to Margaret in life, and will see right by her in death."

Guy nodded and shook the man's hand.

Kit came between them. "Take us to the burial place, then our duty is done. These good folk are travelling away from here, into Lancashire. They know of a sacred place in which she can rest."

Guy took a moment to get his bearings before moving from tree to tree, feeling for the marks that would tell him where to go next.

After a slow journey through the marsh, he returned to the spot where he had marked the converging arrows. Even in the moonlight, the signs of digging were clear. The party moved to the spot and began digging.

"Do you wish to stay to make sure we have the right spot?" Kit asked.

"No, I am quite finished with this endeavour. It's time I turned in, for tomorrow is another day."

Thomas Percy's warning came to Guy once more.

"And I fear it is another day that will bring great hardship."

"No, friend. Tomorrow is another day that will see us march towards bringing York freedom from this demon curse."

Guy placed a hand on Kit's shoulder. "Aye, I hope you are right."

But he was left to wonder at what cost that freedom would come.

Chapter 39

IN WHICH TWO LETTERS CAUSE DIVISION

The city of York hung as if on a knife's edge with a plummet to destruction on one side and glory days on the other. Every moment the city remained on the blade, it dug in a little further, threatening to slice all agents in two before it toppled in either decisive direction.

News spreads slowly when not raced around on the tongues of demons, and in this case, news travelled in from different directions, from both north and south. While news from the south had further to travel, it was being delivered with greater haste. Into the city raced a horseman, carrying the banner of Her Majesty Queen Elizabeth. He sped first to Pavement, where he sounded his bugle, before posting his message and then made for York Minster.

Guy was not among the first to see the message but heard it spoken of as soon as he ventured out among the crowds. Sentiment in the streets was strong, for Queen Elizabeth had heard about the pressing of Margaret Clitherow and had condemned the act.

Guy found a considerable crowd around the banner at Pavement. Soldiers of the Council of the North were in attendance, and however critical the note was of those that held power in York, they dared not remove the words of their Queen. When Guy reached the front of the queue and read the banner, he could not believe the depth of anger. Queen Elizabeth described the pressing as 'deplorable', 'brutal', and 'ungodly'. She wrote that the pressing was not done in her name. Her outrage was clear, and someone needed to take the blame.

Following the path of the messenger, Guy found himself at the workplace of an old friend. He entered the workshop of Clifton Blacksmiths, where James Nevell hammered out a horseshoe at the anvil.

After a brief exchange, reminiscing about school days as if they'd never been part of a secret society of demon hunters, Guy turned the conversation to the information he sought.

"Is Queen Elizabeth's messenger among your customers? I imagine his steed will require re-shoeing before they make their arduous journey home."

"He is, aye."

"Did he tell you where he was going?"

While York had become a safer place to share information, James still looked over his shoulder before speaking.

"Aye. He had a message for the attention of Edwin Sandys at York Minster, and another to go to King's Manor."

Guy bid his old friend thanks, leaving him with a coin for his troubles. Was this the opportunity to strike that Thomas Percy had suggested would come? Should he follow up on Sandys' royal reprimand with an attack to rid York of his evil influence?

He could rouse Kit and Jack into action. They could take Sandys down alongside whatever support he summoned from the underworld.

Guy raced to the inn where Jack and Kit had relocated after Francis left York.

Guy expected to find the pair in buoyant mood but instead found them in the bar of The Starre staring into the bottom of their ales.

"What troubles you, friends? Have you not seen the proclamation of our Queen?"

"Aye, we have seen it," Jack said, his voice as sour as his face.

"Then what brings you such trouble?"

Jack pushed a sheet of parchment across the table. Guy scanned the page and his face dropped to match Kit's and Jack's. It was from one of Ingleby's men in Durham. Francis was missing, feared captured. They were calling for assistance.

"As I was explaining to Kit, we can't very well ride on Durham and wrench him from gaol."

"But why not?" Kit threw his hands up. "The tide is on our side. We can hail a storm of blows upon that city and save him for sure."

Jack sucked air between his teeth. "Did you not see the volumes of troops that stopped here on the way north? It was thrice as many as remained in the city. Besides, according to this, Walsingham is not only ingratiating himself to the Dudleys, but he also has the Lancaster and the Worthill families toadying up to him."

"Then Guy can help us come up with a better plan." Kit turned to look at Guy.

Guy felt the pain of a division. Desire tore him one way, duty to his friends another. Could he let this opportunity to strike down Sandys pass? Was this not the very man his father had fingered as the monster responsible for all the city's ills? "I came to seek your assistance in an assault of my own."

"Join us as we head for Durham first, then we'll stand with you," Kit said.

"It's Sandys, isn't it?" Jack said.

Guy nodded. This was the crossroad Thomas Percy had told him fate would bring him to. Percy had not, however, warned him that his friends would face a different direction. Was the loss Percy had warned him about the loss of his friends? And yet, he knew he could not let the death of his father pass unavenged for so much as a second longer than necessary.

"Friends, this is where we must part for now. I can only hope fate will bring us together again in success soon. I will join you in Durham. That must be your priority, I understand, but I will only make my way there when my business in York is done."

Jack reached across to place one hand on his shoulder. "We wish you every success in your endeavour. As always, your enemies are our enemies, and we shall pray for their fall."

"No!" Kit thumped the table, causing their tankards to jump. "Have you forgotten what you said only a few days ago, Guy?"

"Kit, I'm sorry, but…"

"'Friends come first,' you said."

Guilt churned within Guy's gut. He opened his mouth, but Kit cut him off.

"No! Francis rode for you when they came to your uncle's farm. Now you're abandoning him?"

Guy stood up. "It's not like that. I will join you, but there's something I have to do first."

"What if it's too late by then?"

"Please understand, Kit. I must do this… my father."

Anger drew Kit's eyebrows closer and his jaw tensed. "Then go. We know what friendship means to Guy Fawkes. Go on, go your own selfish way. We don't need you."

"Kit…"

Kit gritted his teeth. Guy turned to Jack, who shook his head, indicating that it was pointless to continue the argument.

Guy looked at the floor. "I wish you both the very best. I will join you soon."

Neither of the Wright brothers replied. Guy sped through the bar and out into the late afternoon air. As he stood on the street, the bells of the Holy Trinity church rang out. Why they were ringing, Guy had no idea, for no service was scheduled. He remembered his first meeting with Francis Ingleby and guilt hit him once more. But Ingleby had told him the bells carried strange whispers. Guy didn't need to listen to understand that knell told him time was up for Sandys.

Chapter 40

IN WHICH GUY FAWKES CONFRONTS EDWIN SANDYS

Guy's first journey was home rather than to York Minster. While armed with his sword, he needed to collect his salves and potions in case they were required. In truth, he wanted to spend a few quiet moments in the company of his mother and his sisters before he took on the man who had torn a significant part of their family from them.

Once back in Aldwick, Guy found his mother and Elizabeth in the garden. So often they huddled together in the living room, so to find them enjoying the spring sunshine was a welcome change.

"Look, Guy," called Elizabeth.

In the soil, he saw the green of some plants.

"It's my herb garden," Elizabeth said.

Edith pushed down the soil at the base of a plant. "Your brother won't much care for that, I'm sure." She didn't turn to face her son.

"I'm very proud of you, Elizabeth." Guy mussed her hair. "To be green-fingered is a gift indeed."

With Guy's hope came pain. His mother would never consider him part of the family again; that he knew. It had been true when he exiled himself to the hayloft at Uncle Thomas's, but worse in the time after Saint Robert's Cave at Helen's abode, and for all he'd done in his role of man of the house, he was as good as an outcast there too in his mother's eyes. Perhaps dispensing with the other man who his father had sought to bring down would repair that rift.

"Where is Anne?" Guy asked.

Still, Edith's focus remained on the soil. "She is in her bedroom reading from one of those books your father was always so fond of."

"I have more business to attend to. I may not be back until well after dark."

"Suit yourself."

"Well, good day." Guy rushed into the house and grabbed what he needed. Anne's door was open a crack. He peered in to see her at the desk with the book in her hand. Yes, she too would be okay.

He left the house, which had never felt like a home, and made his way to York Minster, all the time wondering if he was doing the right thing. Kit's words had hurt. He'd follow to Durham soon. He couldn't let this opportunity pass. If he saved York but lost his friends, what was the point? Was he doing it for a family that didn't care for him? He thought of Anne sitting in her room reading his father's books. No, that's who he was doing it for. With Hastings already dead, bringing Sandys down would complete his father's work. He may not be free from his fate as a demon hunter, but Anne's vendetta, the one he'd pulled her into by whispering those words to her, would end. She'd be free. Yes, there was Walsingham to contend with, yes, he'd betrayed their father too, but he was outside of York, and all Edward Fawkes had wanted was to rid York of its corruption.

As Guy closed on York Minster, he realised he didn't have any kind of plan. The only reason he believed Sandys would be at York Minster was either fate or faith. He wasn't sure he could distinguish one from the other anymore. Guy knew he wouldn't be able to walk in through the main entrance to the east, stroll down the nave, and strike Sandys dead in the pulpit. Instead, he headed for the less grand entrance that led into the south transept. While a patrol of guards moved around the building, no one waited by the doors, and as they turned the corner, Guy approached and tried the door. It was unlocked. He slipped in and hurried through to the nave. It had been a long time since he'd been inside. The scale of the building and its elaborate decoration made him draw in a deep breath. He scanned the pulpit, but no one was there. He made his way to the right of the central tower, where a flicker of light suggested someone might be loitering. Yes, from the steps that led down, the light offered a clue to someone's presence. Of course, Sandys would be in the crypt.

From behind, he heard the door of the southern entrance close. He darted into an alcove and watched. A figure, well-practised at remaining in shadow, moved around the perimeter of the building, a figure he'd recognise anywhere. He waited until she was close, then whispered her name. "Anne!"

Her head darted to his, and she joined him in the alcove.

"What are you doing?" Guy asked.

"I followed you."

"You can't be here."

"I know what you're doing. I've read all of Father's papers. He abhorred Sandys."

"But do you know what he is?"

"I saw his eyes. Margaret taught me enough about the corruption alive in the hearts of the powers of York."

"It's dangerous."

"Less dangerous with two."

She was right. Guy had sought Kit and Jack because he didn't want to do this alone. Now, he didn't have to. Anne had lost her father, too. She, too, deserved a chance to gain revenge. "Okay, but stay back. Keep yourself safe. Only act on my signal."

Anne nodded.

"Follow me."

They hurried down the steps. The crypt was a series of separate chambers, but Guy headed towards the only one that was lit, an oil lamp revealing stone memorials and sarcophagi.

Alas, Sandys was not present.

Anne jumped.

"What?"

"Nothing. A cat, that's all."

"A cat?"

The creature moved into the light, its one yellow eye staring at Guy. From above, the door to the entrance to the crypt slammed closed.

Guy drew his sword and lunged at the cat, but it reeled onto its back legs and hissed. It shifted form into a bat and it flew back into the nave through a vent carved into the stone.

Through the same window came the voice of Sandys speaking the dark tongue.

Guy grabbed Anne by the shoulder. "Did you bring a blade?"

Anne reached down to pull out a butcher's knife from her boot.

Guy held it and muttered the words to imbue it with life. It grew in size only slightly, but the blade ran blue.

"Get your back to a wall and slash at anything that comes your way." He thrust the knife back into her hand.

From beneath him came a hiss. Guy blessed his weapon. The glow of his sword illuminated the darting tongues of a dozen snakes, writhing through the tarry substance the floor had become.

"Stomp your feet, Anne. Slash at their heads. Don't let them bite."

Guy slashed towards the ground, slicing one creature in two.

The grating of stone on stone stopped him from continuing his assault. He turned to where the lid slid from the sarcophagus. A skeleton sat bolt upright. Guy dashed forward and lunged, the blade knocking out the top of the spine, causing the head to crash to the floor. As the floor writhed with serpents, the lids of other sarcophagi crashed off.

"Get on the steps, and watch for snakes," Guy called.

They were everywhere. From distant chambers, more scrapping stone echoed. The dead were rising throughout the crypt. Closer, skeletal feet clattered on the stone ground.

And ran to the top of the steps and pulled on the door. "Is there another way out?" Anne called as the door remained firmly wedged into the stone.

Secret tunnels led from York Minster in all directions, but whether he could find his way through to any of them was a different matter. How he wished Kit was there.

"Stay as high as you can."

Guy kept off the floor, leaping from one sarcophagus to the next, dispensing with a risen corpse whenever necessary, kicking a head away here, slashing through a grasping skeletal hand there. He reached down and grabbed the handle of the oil lamp. The light revealed the undead masses shuffling from their coffins from the chambers around the corner. Behind him, the undead had emerged from another chamber he'd not known about.

"I'm going to throw the lamp at the door. It's the only way out."

Anne leapt to the base of a pillar that held up the crypt's roof.

Guy flung the lamp at the crypt's door. It shattered as it hit the top step, oil splashing against the wooden door and igniting. Soon the door would lose its strength. Soon he'd be able to kick through it and escape back to the nave. First, he had to survive. Skeletal creatures approached from all sides, feet scraping along the ground, arms out. He swung his blade in a huge arc, cutting off limbs that reached from every angle. Still, they continued to push forward. It was no good. He couldn't fight them off alone.

But he didn't have to.

"Anne," he called. "I need you."

"To do what?" Her voice, too, was strained, and he heard her swipe with her weapon.

"I'll come to you, and we'll stand back-to-back. That way, we can see them coming."

"Okay!"

Guy turned and leapt, pushing through a bunch of corpses with his shoulder. As he struggled back to his feet, Anne lunged with her knife, spiking the creatures that reached for him. Together, they slashed away at snakes and skeletons until the floor was thick with the remains of both.

Guy turned toward the door. It remained aflame. The door would be weak enough to crash through, though. It had to be. Corpses continued to rise and flood forward. Reaching the door was an impossibility.

"We have to try the door. It's now or never," Guy cried.

Anne tugged at something around her neck. "Should I use this?"

In the darkness, Guy couldn't see what Anne held. "What is it?"

"The whistle, grandmother's whistle."

Guy saw his grandmother's face, saw his father's face, and his chest swelled. "Yes, and be ready to run."

Anne put the whistle to her lips and blew, and before the creatures began their frenzied wails, before they raised their skeletal hands to non-existent ears, Guy took off for the stairs, pulling Anne along behind him.

Too distressed by the pitch of the demon whistle, they didn't so much as reach out with a bony finger. Flames still licked at the door, but Guy flew at it, nonetheless. It gave way, leaving him collapsed against its flaming planks. He dropped his sword as fire leapt from the door to his clothes. The heat wrapped around his body, and smoke filled his lungs. He rolled around, trying to extinguish the flames. Anne grabbed his hand, dragged him to his feet, and picked up his sword.

He patted his arms to put the fire out, but he could feel it on his back, too. "Help me get it off," he cried.

Anne snatched at the sleeve of his doublet, and he yanked out his hand, then twisted the rest of the way out of it.

Anne grabbed his arm, and he glanced up to where she led him: towards the font. No sooner had they reached it than a booming laugh rang out. Sandys stepped from the shadows to the front of the pulpit, in his hands a tattered book, the thick pages a sick yellow under the light of the lantern he used to read. Beside him, his familiar stood, human once more.

Sandys' voice was deep and powerful, his dark words rooting Guy and Anne to the ground. As he read the last word and slammed the book closed, the very walls of York Minster shook.

"Your sacrifice will herald the beginning of a new dark age!"

"Give me my sword." Guy reached his hand for the weapon, but in doing so, pain erupted in his arms, the burnt skin refusing such strained movement. He gritted his teeth and closed his hand around the hilt.

A roar came from above, and then, as if having emerged from thin air a few yards up, a figure crashed to the ground in the centre of the nave. He was humanoid, but with the legs of a goat, and three horns protruding from his head. Coarse hair covered the lower part of his body and charred red skin covered his torso and arms. In one hand he held a flaming blade, in the other a whip. Guy's mind cast back to the days at Saint Peter's, reading encyclopaedia entries about the denizens of hell. He's heard the rumours that Sandys was in league with particularly powerful demons from hell. This creature, known as Master Leonard, was the grand-master of nocturnal orgies of demons, a creature known to shift forms.

"Feast, and do my bidding!" Sandys called.

The familiar reached across Sandys' chest, desperate for the teat on which he could suckle as reward for summoning a champion from Hell.

"Master Leonard answers to Mammon himself! After he's feasted on you, he will give us access to the superpowers of the under-world!" Sandys grinned.

The demon opened its mouth to show its teeth, running a forked tongue along the top row and down to the tip of a pointed incisor. "I'll lick clean your bones and suck out the marrow, boy. I'll take such delight in your flavour."

Guy took a vial from his belt. He shoved it into Anne's hand. "Draw a large circle, large enough so his blade won't reach you. Stay inside it."

Anne rushed for one of the shadowy parts of York Minster while Master Leonard strode across the nave, his eyes fixed upon Guy.

"Offer yourself to me willingly, and I shall make your death quick." It licked the incisor on the other side. "You may even taste pleasure at the moment of your demise."

"Never!"

"Then feel pain with every bite." Leonard lashed his whip at the ground, sending a shockwave through the floor, pinning Guy to the spot. Only when he took another step was Guy free to move. He'd never taken on something of this size and never confronted a creature of this nature alone. His blade didn't have the reach of the creature's weapon and the burn on his arms made movement painful. Heat radiated through his exhausted body.

"I sense your weakness." The creature smiled. "Give in to me. It is inevitable." Now close, Leonard flicked the whip. Guy spun away and raised his sword to deflect the blow of the creature's blade that followed. Guy leapt back to avoid a follow-up strike. Leonard's sword struck the floor, cracking the stone. The creature laughed once more. He leaned back, cracking every bone in his spine. Two additional arms burst out of his sides. Its face contorted, cheekbones jutting out as the mouth widened. Leonard smiled, revealing elongated teeth. He transferred the weapons to his lower limbs and came again. Guy once more dodged the whip, and then held off the sword, but he could do nothing about the fist swinging from the other side, catching him in the cheek. Blood exploded inside Guy's mouth as the flesh tore against his teeth. Another blow from the other fist clattered into the other side of his head, and he dropped to the floor. All around him spun. He rolled, scrambled to his feet, and backed away. His vision doubled and eight angry arms raged before him. He took a deep breath and blinked, restoring correct vision.

Master Leonard came again, first with the whip, then with the sword, which Guy avoided as before. Expecting the fist, he ducked, but instead of following up with a fist, he kicked, smashing Guy's nose with a cloven hoof. The blow turned him around as blood exploded from his face. Before him, though, was sanctuary. A door that he'd not seen before. Open, and leading into darkness. He stumbled toward it, reaching for the doorframe when a voice came to him, words of advice from many years earlier. *"When you see the blackest void, run the other way."*

Guy stopped. The darkness before him inhaled, pulling him toward the door. He placed his hands against the doorframe to hold himself away from it.

"Surrender, worthless peon." Master Leonard lashed out with his whip, catching Guy's fingers, pulling the hand away from the door frame. He felt himself slide towards the void.

Gretchen had armed him with potions against every eventuality. He'd checked each label, and brought one of each with him. The one marked *light* he'd had no idea of its purpose, but there was no better time to find out. He dug his feet into the ground to slow the pull into the void, grabbed the vial, and hurled it through the door. Blinding light radiated out, and whatever force drew him in ceased as Leonard's whip caught Guy's other hand. He let go of the door frame, but it had lost its pull.

Guy turned back to face Leonard, the light behind him renewing his strength.

Master Leonard raised its unarmed hands to the sky. A crack of thunder boomed above and the squeal of rats came from every corner.

"Every minion from Hell will share a taste of your flesh, you defiant cretin!" The rats ran to the beast, and he launched them through the air. Guy slashed with his sword. Each creature burst as if it were a bag of fluid, the blood splashing over Guy, stinging where it splashed onto exposed flesh. The demonic general continued to hurl vermin, and Guy slashed them as they flew through the air. Guy wiped the raining blood from his eyes between slashes, but soon, the hilt of his sword became sticky with blood.

"Now you look worthy of a place in hell itself!" Master Leonard strode forward.

Guy glanced down and saw every inch of himself bathed in blood. As the demon slashed with the blade, Guy raised his own to deflect it, but with the hilt slick, he couldn't hold his grip and it clattered to the floor.

The whip lashed, wrapping around Guy's forearm and growing ever tighter. With his upper arm on the opposite side, Leonard reached out and grabbed Guy's other arm.

"I could end this quickly and bite your head right off!"

A smash from behind him and a sickening cry made the demon turn.

Over its colossal shoulder, Guy saw Sandys' familiar cowering behind its arm, liquid running from his head, drawing the flesh from the scalp as it sunk into it. Guy didn't understand what was going on, but as the whip around his arm loosened, he was glad of the intervention. Guy jerked free. He glanced up, hoping to catch sight of Anne, but she'd not followed his advice. She'd not drawn the circle. She'd not put herself in safety.

Guy twisted his body around and sank his teeth into the demon's forearm, causing it to release its hold on his arm.

Guy grabbed his sword. The red gem in the hilt glowed. He looked up again and spotted Anne. On the pulpit, she continued her assault, grabbing a golden candlestick and ramming it through the familiar's eye.

As he crumpled to the ground, the demon huffed.

"No!" cried Sandys. He reached out and slapped Anne with the back of his hand, causing her to stumble from the pulpit.

"Continue to do my bidding, oh dark one!" Sandys cried.

The creature turned to face him.

Sandys flicked through the book, scanning the first words on each page before moving on.

Guy saw the opportunity. He fell into a forward roll, bounced up from his feet, and cracked the demon on top of the head with the gem at the base of the hilt of his sword. Leonard arched its back, cried out in agony, and exploded, the ejectamenta splashing onto pews and embedding itself into the walls. The creature's blood splattered onto Guy. He roared as its acidity burned into his skin.

Guy collapsed onto the floor, writhing in pain.

Anne dashed to him.

"Don't touch me," he cried. He grabbed a bottle from a pouch and smashed it on the ground. He reached in for the fluid, rubbing it onto the exposed parts of his hands first, which had taken the brunt of the demon blood wash, before spreading the rest on his face.

From across the room, they heard frail footsteps. Sandys leant against a pew, one hand gripping his chest.

Guy struggled into a sitting position, but each attempt to draw breath was agony. "We've got to stop him," he muttered.

Anne looked up as Sandys crashed to the floor. He reached for the pew but lacked the strength to pull himself up.

"Get him…"

"There's no need," Anne said. "Time's got him."

Guy tried to crane his neck to better see his enemy. "What do you mean?"

"Something Margaret told me about those that rely on demons. Some do it for power, but others do it to cling to life. With him, it was likely both. He was rotten through and through. Without his familiar, that poison reached his core."

Sandys' hand lost its grip on the pew and slumped to the floor.

Guy needed to be certain. "Check he's dead."

Anne sighed. She grabbed the butcher's knife from the ground, just in case, and then approached the body. She turned him over to look at the whites of his eyes.

"He's gone."

Guy tried to push himself up once more.

"Where are you going?" Anne hurried back to Guy's side.

"I have to go…"

"Where? It's over. I read Father's papers. It was Sandys and Hastings that corrupted the city. It was them he wanted rid of. You've done that. You can rest easy now."

"But Walsingham… Durham…"

"There will always be another name, Guy. You need to know when to give up the fight."

"My friends…"

"They'll be waiting when you're ready. You can't stand. You're cut to bits. Half of your body is burned, and God only knows what poison you've swallowed."

Guy tried to pull himself up once more.

"I'll help you home, but then you're to stay in bed."

"But…"

"Guy, you won. Everything our father wanted came to pass because of you. Don't you get that? You're free of whatever obligation you had."

What about the man who pulled Sandys's and Hastings's strings? What about his friends in Durham? The words wouldn't come. The strength wasn't there. Maybe that was someone else's fight. He had come face-to-face with a lord of the underworld and come out the other side. What more could he do? Anne helped him to his feet. He could feel something ill pulsing through his veins, and every inch of his skin was on fire. Maybe he needed a little bed rest. He could set off for Durham tomorrow.

He remembered little of the struggle home, knew that Anne took much of the burden. When he collapsed through the door, he was aware of his mother's concern, but it was Anne who helped him up the stairs to his bedroom. People came and went, but only one face stuck in his mind. Hovering in the corner through it all was the skull of Thomas Percy.

When he was alone, Guy called out to him. "Is Anne right? Is it over? Am I free?"

Thomas Percy laughed.

Epilogue

Sidney takes a few deep breaths. "That's why York should consider Guy a hero."

Jamie shifts in the hospital chair, his legs asleep after so long on the uncomfortable plastic.

"That's why we shouldn't burn Guy in effigy." Sidney looks at the bandages on his hands.

Jamie leans forward and rubs his legs, then he turns to the old man. "But there's so much more... the Houses of Parliament... the Gunpowder Plot?"

"You asked why we shouldn't burn Guy here in York. I told you why he's a hero."

"But what he did at the end, that surely negates his good in York?"

"Aye, but you don't know why he did that, neither."

Jamie sits up straighter in the chair. "You could tell me."

"I could, but I won't."

"Why not?"

Sidney turned away. "You don't believe me. I won't tell another tale for you to laugh at me."

"No, please. I'm interested. Honest."

"You need to do something first. Prove this is more than a diversion."

A smile forms on Jamie's lips, the investigative journalist in him coming alive. "Go on."

"Leave here and come back when you can tell me something about Maria Fawkes."

"Who's Maria Fawkes?"

"That's what I want you to tell me. Interested?"

Jamie pushes himself up from the chair, feeling the protest in his legs. "I'll return with the information on Maria Fawkes. Then will you tell me how it ends?"

Sidney laughs. "We have a long way to go before we reach the end. Believe me, we've hardly got started."

ACKNOWLEDGMENTS

'All this happened, more or less.' These are the words that open Kurt Vonnegut's Slaughterhouse Five and they were words I kept in mind when writing this novel (and indeed, the whole trilogy.) It's one of the reasons I dedicated this story to historians, too, because a lot of this did happen. Of course, a lot of it didn't happen too. But I have the dedication of historians to thank for bringing the 1500s to life in a way that gave me insight into Guy Fawkes' young life, and Tudor England, in particular York, over 450 years ago. Many of the characters in this story are people that existed in York in Guy's younger days. We know Guy Fawkes attended Saint Peter's school with Kit and Jack Wright. We know Oswald Tesimond was an older pupil at the same school. John Pulleyn was also headmaster at that school. Was he running a secret training facility for young demon hunters? I'll leave you to decide. By far the most shocking event in that period of time was the death of Margaret Clitherow, a truly horrendous. Yes, she was pressed to death on Good Friday at the Toll House in York. You can visit the site of her butchers on The Shambles in York. It's a shrine to her now. So, while I've used the knowledge that historians present to us so clearly, remember, that this is a work of fiction. I've borrowed characters, that really existed, and used them for the purpose of fiction. I take full responsibility for this presentation. My intention is not to present them as they would have been, but for the purpose of my story. Where the history is inaccurate, that's on me, despite my attempts to make it authentic. I do have to mention Nick Holland's wonderful biography, The Real Guy Fawkes. This book helped me find the truth from which I formed the fiction.

My thanks also go to the team at Shadow Spark Publishing. Thank you for believing in this project. The editing process made this a stronger work. Your eyes and your expertise picked up parts that needed a polish, historical errors, and parts that didn't quite add up. It's a stronger story thanks to you.

Thank you also to my family, and my friends (both in real life and online) for your support and encouragement.

BENJAMIN LANGLEY

Benjamin Langley lives, writes, & teaches in Cambridgeshire, UK. He studied at Anglia Ruskin University, completing his MA in Creative Writing in 2015. His first novel, Dead Branches was released in 2019. Is She Dead in Your Dreams? is his second novel, released march 2020.

Benjamin has had over a dozen pieces of short fiction published, & has written Sherlock Holmes adventures featured in Adventures in the Realm of H.G. Wells, Adventures Beyond the Canon, & Adventures in the Realm of Steampunk.

He can be found on twitter @B_J_Langley

Printed in Great Britain
by Amazon